Daughter of Aphrodite

Rome in the first century AD is a turbulent, glittering city where fortunes are easily made and lost, where death can strike even as the victor reaches for the palm. With Emperor Tiberius remote and ageing on the throne, his heirs jockey perilously for advantage. The glamorous, cut-throat *demi-monde* of Rome, with its courtesans, dancers and charioteers, watches them with cynical fascination while itself scrambling for jewels and fame.

The lovely Greek courtesan Danaë has fought her way upward from the stinking slums of the Subura, and has brothers and a sister to support: she hungers for wealth and security. So she cannot afford to care for Marsyas, the dark, reckless charioteer racing for fame in the deadly mêlée of the arena. He is too like herself for comfort, with the spectre of a terrible death ever at his elbow.

The rich and powerful lovers drawn to Danaë by her beauty and her dancing bring her more than just wealth. Prince Drusus, Tiberius's son, opens her eyes to honour and nobility; but Sejanus, ambitious captain of the Praetorian Guard, deep in intrigue and playing for the highest stakes, involves her (and her clever, amoral, young brother Paris) in his terrifying plans, till the enemies that surround him, threaten her too ...

In this rich and enthralling historical love-story, Brenda Jagger brings to the reader a vivid awareness of everyday life in Rome as well as the bizarre and bloody complexities of the politics of the time.

Also by Brenda Jagger

Antonia
The clouded hills
Days of Grace
Flint and Roses
Sleeping Sword
Winter's Child
A Song Twice Over

Brenda Jagger

Daughter of Aphrodite

Constable · London

3809321

First published in Great Britain 1981
by Constable & Company Limited
10 Orange Street London WC2H 7EG
Copyright © 1981 Brenda Jagger
Reprinted 1986
ISBN 0 09 463840 3
Printed in Great Britain by
St Edmundsbury Press
Bury St Edmunds, Suffolk

For Mike, with thanks

1

I had never known a heartache that a visit to a good jeweller couldn't cure, and so when my friend Aemilius Scaurus went off to govern Cilicia, taking his wife and children with him, I charged to his account an amethyst and a pearl or two, and removed myself to the holiday town of Baiae in Campania, feeling that I had earned a rest. And there, on the first mellow, gold-flecked evening, wearing a new silk robe, with Scaurus' pearls in my ears, I called to pay my respects to a woman who advertised herself as the most fascinating creature in the world, and may even have been right.

Three years ago, when I'd been a hungry young dancer with little to distinguish me from a hundred others, except that perhaps my appetite was a little keener, a shade more determined, I'd spent hours of every day hanging around this woman's house in Rome, laughing at her jokes, praising her clothes, dancing at her dinner-parties for no other fee than the chance of being noticed by her guests. But since Aemilius Scaurus had singled me out, and one or two others showed signs of following his lead, I had promoted myself, whether the dazzling Erato liked it or not, from the position of humble client to that of colleague and friend.

She was no beauty. She had the skinny, jaunty body of a monkey, a pert face that was never still, tight African curls, and a flat-tipped, impossible nose, but if one looked at her long enough she made conventional beauty seem dull, elegance tame, and for more years than she may have cared to remember she had played emotional and financial havoc with a good proportion of Rome's most famous names. And although I couldn't always admire her style, I had to admit that there was nothing about her now to suggest the girl she'd once been, the young tigress who had clawed her way from a waterfront brothel at Ostia to become this jewelled idol, worshipped by men who, really, should have had more sense.

She had investments in the city that always seemed to pay, cash and jewels, property in Rome, her villa by the sea, and although she was careful in small ways – mean, sometimes, with her dinner guests, since she judged everyone's appetite as tiny as her own – she lived with a casual grandeur I intended not only to copy but to surpass. Yet, as I entered her garden that night and saw her perching on the edge of a divan, a wisp of gold cloth across one shoulder, a rainbow swirl of jewels scattered all over her thin chest, my own pearls felt suddenly very small, my amethyst ring shed a great part of its sparkle, and I was forced to admit, if only to myself, that although I would succeed in the end I still had a long way to go.

'Ah,' she called out, gesturing enthusiastically with her peacock-feather fan, her arms in the lamplight garlanded with bands of green and blue flame. 'Here comes my little friend – really – my dear friend, Danaë,' and although neither of us could afford to be any woman's friend, we touched hands and smiled; and as we did so her mind whispered to me, 'Arrogant, half-baked little slut,' and mine answered, 'Gaudy old tart'.

The garden was hushed, fern-screened, tree-shaded, planted with women more exotic than the flowers, and as I made my careful greetings – acknowledging myself as the newcomer among them, a girl newly risen from the chorus line who might, or might not, last another season – I perfectly understood their veiled hostility, our common anxiety in a world so full of ambitious women, lovelier, and younger, as the years went by. And although I was only just nineteen I knew, as clearly as the rest of them, that time was not on my side.

'How wonderful to see you,' I murmured to my rival, my enemy Chloe, elegant and silver-pale, a cithara-player and singer of mournful songs she professed to compose herself, although they all sounded much alike to me, and who had started life in a butcher's shop in Corinth.

And then, 'My dear – how are you?' to Xanthe, a charioteer's daughter, an acrobat once, who had worked every sea-port on the Aegean until some sprig of a military tribune had brought her back to Rome with him, smoothed out her Latin and her table-manners, and converted her from a cheerful young harlot to a star courtesan.

Finally, with the respect one pays to anything which, in this frail world, has found the way to endure, I made something not quite an obeisance to the imperious, eternal Cynthia, sitting a little apart, a tawny, green-eyed woman of Erato's age whose past was so overlaid now by the sheen of her fabulous success that not even Erato could uncover her common origins.

Counting myself among them, we were five women who, in the course of our working lives, would cheat each other as much as we had to, yet who in this off-season could come together almost in friendship, rivalry submerged by the weight of our problems and our expenses. Xanthe, I knew, had two children to support, a pair of plain, swarthy little girls left over from her acrobatic days, who would need a hefty dowry apiece to settle them anywhere in life. Chloe, almost as frail as she looked, was haunted by the passing of every hour, while Erato and Cynthia, far richer than any of us, had both grown addicted in recent years to the costly game of falling in love with decorative young men – actors, charioteers, musicians and the like. While in my own view I was the most overburdened of all, for not only had I a young brother and sister to take care of, but an elder brother, two years my senior but just as likely to get into trouble, who made a precarious living driving racing-chariots for the 'Blues', and who was Erato's current passion and despair.

She was waiting for him tonight, furious with me for not bringing him, furious with her own undignified jealousy – for charioteers are ten a penny and not one of them could hope to last as long as she had – and although once, before Aemilius Scaurus had recognized my talents as a dancer and a woman, I would have hastened to tell her all the reassuring lies her vanity required, I had no need of that now.

'I haven't seen him for days,' I murmured, and, knowing quite well he was on the beach a mile away, with the downy young wife of his faction director, I smiled straight into her eyes, sipped her wine, and settled down on the couch at her side.

I was the youngest of them all, for even the athletic Xanthe wouldn't see twenty-two again. Chloe was easily twenty-five, Erato and Cynthia much older. But youth itself did not impress me and I'd never seen much in it but its market value. I'd been earning my living at thirteen, ever since the day my mother, who had been a dancer too, had gone off to an engagement and forgotten to come back; and with my brothers and sister to think about, and my father, who had disappeared soon afterwards to escape his creditors, there'd been no time to feel young. I'd danced for pennies in wine-shops, dragging my exhausted bones from one cut-price supper club to the next, selling myself cheap until the chance came to sell myself dear, and if now I had a smart little flat in the Street of the Yoke-makers in Rome, with a woman to dress my hair, and my own dancing-master and musicians in tow, no one was going to tell me it was less than I deserved. I'd learned how to drink my wine from a jewelled cup with poise and style, learned how to conceal my poor Latin with the husky enticing accent of a Greek, although all that was really Greek about me was my name and my father, who had been a Greek of sorts. But for all my hints of a childhood spent among flowery, foreign islands, the truth was that I had been born in the Subura, the meanest of all Roman slums, and the stink of those tenements, those littered, shameful alleys, was never far away. And nothing – absolutely nothing – was ever going to take me back there.

Aemilius Scaurus had helped, but his pearls alone wouldn't suffice me when my looks ran out, wouldn't give me the income to educate my clever young brother, or to get my sister decently married. I had allowed myself ten years, but I could break a leg tomorrow, or lose a tooth, or my splendid brother Dion could be crippled the next time he went out to race – and what would Erato want with him then? As always I was haunted by the spectre of time.

There was a governor due back from the East this summer with the spoils of his province to share, a general who had been a long time with the armies of the Rhine and who would need to cut a dash when he came home, and, in addition to all the rich men and the ambitious men with whom this holiday coast abounded, I had heard a rumour that the Emperor, our crusty sour-faced old Tiberius, having eliminated a sufficient number of those who thought he had no right to be emperor at all, had at last given permission for his son to return to Italy. Since I could only suppose that this imperial prince, this Drusus, who had been sent to the legions in Pannonia for safe-keeping during our recent troubles, was a man like any other, his homecoming was of the greatest interest to me. Scaurus had given me jewels, and since his departure for Cilicia I had received offers that flattered and tempted me, but this son of Tiberius had the revenues of nations at his disposal, and the woman who caught his eye would have the means to put us all in the shade.

'What are you dreaming about, Danaë?' Erato asked, flicking

me with her fan, meaning, 'What schemes are you hatching? And where is your brother?' Shrugging with a dancer's professional nonchalance on purpose to annoy her, I said, 'Oh, just simple things like men and money. They tell me Governor Paulinus landed yesterday.' And instantly every one of those languid, dainty ladies sat up and sniffed the air, as alert as so many old war-horses at the scent of battle.

Erato smiled, hiding her face in her richly carved wine-cup, and then, speaking to the sweet, golden liquid, she whispered, 'Ah yes – Paulinus – well, he's a generous man, as I have good reason to know. But we've all had our provincial governors before, haven't we? Perhaps we could do a little better this year – at least, one of us could.'

I saw Xanthe's eyes open wide, Chloe's pale, elegant head droop forward to hide the flash of excitement in her face, but Cynthia, who made a speciality of political liaisons, gave Erato a level stare, letting it be known by the arrogant curve of her lips that her sources of information were vastly superior.

'You mean Drusus, I suppose,' she said, speaking of the imperial prince with the air of one who was, at the very least, in daily contact with his closest friends, and in receipt of the most positive assurances that she would soon be sharing his supper-couch and his bed. And choking back my annoyance, for Cynthia was a woman of enormous cunning and experience, and had very likely bribed some officer of the Pannonian Legions to tell Drusus all about her famous green gaze and her ankle-length red hair, I said, too sharply, 'Is it certain then? Is he coming home?'

She smiled, lazy and secret as a cat, her green eyes touching lightly on the new pearls in my ears, reminding me how little an Aemilius Scaurus could mean to her.

'But my dear, was it ever in doubt? He may even be here already, spending a few quiet days with the Emperor – his father.'

'Are you sure about that?' Xanthe exploded unwisely, while Chloe, her pale eyes gleaming, said at the same moment, 'They have a villa at Tarracina, haven't they – the imperial family?' And for a moment it looked as if the two of them were about to go and scour the district then and there.

But Erato, disliking Cynthia's air of state secrets and unfair advantage – and ready to dislike Cynthia herself most viciously if it turned out to be true – said tartly, 'Why not? What is there now to keep him away? One could see the point to it last year, when all our aristocratic friends were longing for Tiberius to die so they could make his nephew, Germanicus, emperor in his place. Don't you remember how they kept on telling each other how old Tiberius was looking, and how he shivered in the Senate, and was so hoarse they could barely hear him speak? And if he had obliged them by dying just then, they'd have proclaimed Germanicus emperor and Drusus would probably have had a nasty accident, somehow or other, to make it that much easier. Well, naturally, the poor old gentleman didn't want anything like that to happen to his only son and it was no more than common sense to keep him out of the country. And then, when it was Germanicus who died instead and they were all saying Tiberius had poisoned him, and were doing their best to prove it – well, *that* wasn't the moment for the new heir to show his face. Things looked nasty last year: there was going to be revolution and a return to republican government and we were all going to lose a lot of money. But that's all settled now, and if Drusus doesn't come home soon they'll start saying he's got something to hide. It won't take long before somebody remembers how he took fits as a child, or turned strange at the full moon. And Tiberius won't stand for that. He may be old, but he's still staggering down to the Senate every day, isn't he? And however hoarse he may be, he makes sure they hear him and do as they're told. Yes, we shall have Drusus with us before we're much older, making himself pleasant, hoping we'll all forget how much we loved his cousin Germanicus – and I expect we shall forget, because, when all's said and done, a dead hero is no competition for a live prince.'

'Ah –' Cynthia began, implying that she knew what she knew, and that if an imperial freedman should arrive at any moment to summon her to Drusus' side it would be no surprise to her. But just then the sounds Erato had been longing for were heard at last, and, waving Cynthia to silence, she turned to greet the men who were coming towards us across the garden: my brother Dion, his faction director Bassus, and a stranger, someone who looked familiar although I felt quite certain I had never seen him before, strolling all three together, arm in arm, Bassus laughing as if he hadn't a care in the world, and no suspicions at all about the conduct of his new young wife.

My brother and I were not alike. I was dark, ivory-skinned,

brown-eyed like my Roman mother, and he was tawny gold, beautiful, with my father's light Athenian eyes and chestnut curls, and although he was feckless and self-indulgent – as my father had been – I had always adored him and was not in the least surprised when other women adored him too.

Nor was he surprised about it himself. As a small boy in the Subura, the tenement women, not noted for their gentleness, had rushed to clean up his cuts and bruises, the fruit-seller had allowed him to steal her apples, the cook-shop woman had fed him sausages and pies when the rest of us had been glad of a bowl of gruel. And when, later, unable to decide which girl he wanted, he'd make up his mind to sample them all, no one had resisted, no one had blamed him. He'd seemed to them like a prize, so rare and special that they could see no humiliation in sharing him. And watching him now, as he stood before Erato, a little unsteady on his feet, smelling strongly of wine and perfume, knowing he was in disgrace and not caring a fig for it, I doubted if she had more power over him, for all her vast experience, than anyone else.

'Here I am,' he said, telling her plainly that if she wanted him he would stay, but if not he was just as ready to go away again.

'Yes, here you are.'

And immediately there was a great stirring and bustling to accommodate him, servants running in all directions to bring a stronger wine and a larger cup and the spiced meat pies of his tenement days, served now on silver dishes, garnished with twists of lemon and sprigs of parsley.

'Just move over,' he said, helping himself to Erato's cushions, shoving me to one side so that, perched on the edge of the divan, I had a perfect view of Bassus – my brother's employer – looking at him with malice and calculation; and of the stranger, the man I knew yet couldn't know because I would have been unlikely to forget him, who, answering the call of Cynthia's outstretched hand, was sitting close beside her, their heads touching.

'Who's that?' I asked and Dion shrugged.

'Oh, him – don't you know? That's Marsyas, Bassus' new boy, the one Bassus is grooming to put in my place.'

'Did he tell you that?' I said, shocked, aggressive, ready to do battle with Bassus and a dozen like him if my brother's career was at stake; but Dion himself was totally, maddeningly, unconcerned.

'He didn't have to tell me. He just told everybody else. So what of it? There's always a new boy, and it's no secret Bassus doesn't like me. I expect he has his reasons.'

And, as his lazy mischievous smile told me exactly what those reasons were – for the whole world knew how Bassus valued his wife, a girl of good family, who had brought him prestige as well as a dowry – I got up and, walking across the garden, gave Bassus the greeting of a dear friend, determined to defend my brother's cause with the best weapons I had. And as I moved I was painfully aware that the stranger, lounging by Cynthia's side, lifted his head and looked at me.

I had known Bassus ever since the days of Dion's apprenticeship with the 'Blues', a stocky, middle-class Italian, a power to be reckoned with in the sporting world. Although Dion had been winning for three seasons now and earning vast sums of money which seemed to enrich no one but the wine-merchants and the jewellers and the gambling-houses in the Subura, I knew what Bassus could do to him if he had a mind. Dion was good, but not so good that the fans would put up a serious fight if Bassus dismissed him from the team, not so good that the other factions would fall over themselves to employ him – particularly if Bassus put it about that he was unsound – and I had no intention of letting them send my brother to provincial arenas, to race broken-down chariots and ill-matched horses for pennies and the fair chance of an uncomfortable end.

'Bassus,' I said, 'you're looking so well – an absolute temptation.'

But he knew I didn't trust him, and he knew why, and when he had paid me a few standard compliments he patted my hand and said, in the tone most men use when they are talking of horses or litter-bearers, 'What do you think of him, then?' And although I knew he meant the other man, the stranger who was still looking at me over Cynthia's shoulder – talking to her, stroking her arms, putting his mouth against her hair, and looking at me – I answered quickly, 'Dion? He's very fit.'

'Oh yes – Dion. Well, he's always fit for one thing or another – we know all about Dion. But I'm talking about this new lad of mine, Marsyas. He'll give you all a thrill in the September Games, you can rely on it. If he keeps himself straight you may even see him next year as well.'

And I understood, with an additional tremor of distaste, that this was as much as any of them meant to him, just hungry lads from nowhere with nothing to lose, who would wear his colours for a month or two, a year or two, and then disappear, swallowed up by a wrecked chariot or burned out in the blaze of their own glory. I had heard of a charioteer – once – who had reached thirty and retired honourably, sensibly, on his investments, but watching my brother reach out an indolent arm while Erato refilled his wine-cup, I knew, with the stab of panic that lived on the fringes of my mind, that, left to himself, he'd never get so far. And since only money could save him, my desire for the imperial Drusus and his millions became not so much a matter of ambition and self-esteem as of stark necessity. The ten years I'd allowed myself to make my fortune were too long, because Dion couldn't last ten years. I had to do something now. I had to have Drusus now, while there was still time, and I didn't care what I had to do to get him.

'Yes, he's looking fit, our Dion – a real charioteer,' Bassus said, his shrewd eyes flickering over my brother's luxurious, pampered body which should have been harder, leaner, picking out the jewellery and the silk tunic and the perfumed curls, the honey-gold skin gleaming with rich oil instead of the raw good health that comes from training and self-discipline. And I knew it was useless to tell him that it had all happened too fast, useless to ask him how a boy from the Subura, who had gone barefoot most of his life, could be expected to cope with such rapid fame and fortune, with the men who offered him gold every time he risked his life and the women who offered him their bodies. Bassus would accept no excuse, and so, understanding the necessity for it, I forced myself to look coolly at this new man – this Marsyas – who, through all the tawny magnificence of Cynthia, continued to stare at me.

He was a year or two over twenty, old for a man with his way still to make, and if at first I'd thought I knew him, it could only have been because there were so many like him, a multitude of hungry, shady men, night-prowlers, living by their wits and their needs, with small hope and no pity. He was handsome, if one could afford to care for such things, deep-set black eyes, a thin, hard mouth that smiled to order, not for amusement, black hair curling low on his forehead and well below his ears, screening what I took to be the dark face of an Oriental Greek; a body that was as taut and lean and menacing as a whip-lash. His hands, hovering now over the coils of Cynthia's hair, were lean too, ringless, predatory, and as he changed position slightly, adjusting the robe of fine white lawn Bassus had surely given him, I saw, by the new, impossibly smooth, skin around his ankles, and the fringe of scars above them, that once, and perhaps not too long ago, he had been in chains.

'And just where did you get that one?' I enquired, wanting Bassus to know how little I was impressed. 'Was it before, or after, they took the shackles off him?'

But he knew I was worried and that I had good cause, and he merely smiled. 'Ah well, these boys, you know – if they weren't the kind who get into trouble they wouldn't be much use to me. He's no beginner. He's been racing a year or two out East, but I wouldn't care to ask the why and the wherefore of it. By his name he should be a Greek, but there again – well – how many of us here tonight are using the name we were born with? It's his performance in the arena that concerns me, and that much I can vouch for. Come, Danaë, you could like him if you put your mind to it. He needs to be seen in town with people who know how to get themselves noticed. And I'd make it worth your while.'

'I hardly think so,' I told him, cool, offended, alarmed because we both knew he had the means to force me. 'My life is full to the brim just now, and anyway Cynthia seems to be taking care of all that for you.'

'Ah yes – Cynthia,' he said, patting my hand again and beaming, recognizing my fury at the ease with which men of his sort could manipulate women of mine. 'Cynthia's all very well, but she has a possessive nature – tends to swallow her men alive, and he's not ready for that. Perhaps in a year or two, when he's tired – like your brother, eh? – he'll need someone to mother him. I'd be grateful to you, Danaë, if you'd oblige me in this, and just a shade disappointed – upset – if you turned me down. It's a good bit of business I'm putting your way, and friends should help each other, isn't that so? I'm only asking you to make a show in public. What you do in private is up to you. If he can't find the means to persuade you then neither can I – because I'm not a procurer. I'm a businessman and it's only the publicity I'm after. And if you take against him they'll only say it's because you're afraid of the competition – for Dion.'

'Then they'd be talking nonsense.'

'I quite agree. I'm definitely on your side. But people will talk, and if it got around that you had so little confidence in your own brother – well, that wouldn't inspire anybody else to back him, would it? And if people stop backing him then he'd have to stop racing, it's as simple as that. Terribly unjust, but what can one do? It's a business, after all, a racing faction, not a charity.' And he had no need to add, 'And if I stop him racing before you can afford to take him in hand, what will he do then? How long will it be before he drinks himself to death, or they find him in an alley with a jealous husband's dagger in his back? Mine, maybe.'

And before he had finished speaking I was on my feet.

Dion, I knew, would never ask me to make this sacrifice, would throw back his curly head and roar with laughter at the mere idea of it, but Dion had always needed me to explain what was good for him. So, whispering a few words to Bassus which may have looked like love-secrets but which actually were, 'How much and for how long?' I strolled across the garden – hoping that if I started now I could have it over and done with before Drusus came home – and paused by Cynthia's side.

2

Perhaps she expected me to fight her for Governor Paulinus, certainly for Drusus. I had already fought her for Aemilius Scaurus, and won. But my interest in this wayfarer was so unlooked for that for a moment she didn't understand what I was doing, standing there at the foot of her couch, looking at him. And when she did she merely put her long, imperious hand on his arm, every one of her fingers bearing an emerald that would have financed six months of my brother's retirement, and gave me a smile that said, 'Run along, little girl. Don't bother me.'

'I just came to say good-night,' I told her, looking not directly at him but vaguely in his direction, gripped suddenly with the superstitious dread that if I scrutinized him too closely I'd see, beneath his dark face, the face of someone else, someone I knew.

'Good-night,' Cynthia said, making the word into a snap of the fingers, a dismissal, and, smiling at the warm night air beyond his shoulders, I walked away. As I went, stopping to say good-bye to Erato and Dion, spending a moment with Xanthe who wasn't a bad sort and didn't believe in ghosts, I could feel his eyes on my back.

I didn't know if he would follow me, for Cynthia was beautiful and exciting and willing, sometimes, to be generous, but Bassus must have rehearsed him well, for my bearers had scarcely fetched my litter when there he was, appearing at my side as silently and suddenly as if he had risen from the ground.

'Well, you're a brave man at any rate,' I said, startled into flippancy, seriously annoyed by the stupid jangling of my nerves. 'You'll have to watch your back now, because Cynthia won't forgive you for walking out on her.'

'She can suit herself,' he said and his words, the first I had heard him speak, shocked me, for I had thought him some kind of mongrel Greek and it was profoundly, ridiculously, disturbing to hear on his tongue the coarse speech of the Roman Subura which Dion had never lost and which I had worked so hard to obliterate.

'I'll walk home with you,' he said, reaching out for my hand, and wrenching myself free of his hard, insolent fingers, I wheeled round to face him, meeting the black glitter of his eyes – because I had to look at him sometime – and announced crisply, 'Yes, I'll send my litter bearers ahead and then everyone can see us together. But, before we take another step, let me make one thing very clear. Bassus is paying me for this, as you must know, paying me to make a show in public – and that's as much as you'll get. I expect Bassus explained it to you, but I'll go through it again because I don't suppose you're used to this sort of thing and I'm in no mood for misunderstandings. I've agreed – for money – to be seen with you for the rest of the month, and that's as far as it goes. At the end of the month, when my agreement runs out, so do you. He's a great showman, Bassus. I hope you're grateful to him, because I'm expensive and he's doing you proud.'

He twisted his fingers through mine again, hurting me slightly – deliberately I thought – and, raising my hand, instead of kissing it as Aemilius Scaurus or any other man would have done, he looked at it for a moment, his thin mouth smiling as if, at last, it had found some cause for amusement in the contrast between my pampered white skin, my elegantly tapering nails, and his own.

'You're very good at it,' he said, 'very good. You're almost real.'

And although I didn't know what he was implying, I knew it was an attack and that when it became clear to me I wouldn't like it.

'Just what is that supposed to mean?'

'What I say. You're very good at it – very stylish. It's just the foreign accent that makes me wonder.'

So there it was, a blow in the gut, delivered, as we always delivered them in the Subura, foully, viciously; for in the Subura it had always been necessary to make one's point by force. But I was years away from that now and surely he had made no more than a lucky shot in the dark? How could he possibly know the embarrassment I suffered at being forced to use this affected Greek accent, when even the best elocution teachers had failed to give me the cool, precise tone of an upper-class Roman? Yet it seemed to me that he knew, and I hated him. And realizing that none of this foolishness was important enough for hate, I hated him even more.

'I speak the way I was brought up to speak,' I said coldly,

carefully, turning to dignity as my best defence.

'You're a Greek then, after all?' he asked, somehow quite certain that I wasn't, the black glitter in his eyes a taunt I couldn't mistake. 'You dance, too, don't you?'

'And what do you know about dancers? You'll have only seen them in the wine-shops, swinging their bellies and stamping their feet and hoping for the best – and that's got nothing to do with me at all. I'm a highly-trained professional entertainer. If you had the slightest idea of the fees I can command, you'd be smiling on the other side of your face.'

'All right,' he said, 'I'm impressed.' But he wasn't, and, my temper flaring, I almost shouted at him, 'Oh, for heaven's sake, get a move on and let's get home. It's a pity Bassus forgot to buy you some decent perfume when he got your sandals and your robe, because that cheap stuff you've soaked yourself in is giving me a headache.'

He laughed, a sound that accorded well with the thin, sneering line of his mouth, and shook his head.

'Bassus has nothing to do with it. Bassus gives and I take – why not? He's not doing it for free. I left that old tart just now because I wanted to, and if I'd been in the mood to stay then I'd have stayed. If I feel like going back to her tomorrow and telling her you weren't anywhere near as good as I thought you'd be, then I'll do that too.'

'You'll do no such thing,' I yelled, dignity deserting me as I felt myself torn between amazement at being spoken to in this way by him – by anyone – and fury at the thought of being whispered about, giggled about, shamed. If he embarrassed me, I'd hurt him – or get someone else to do it – and I'd hurt Bassus too, for putting me in this atrocious position.

'Don't threaten me,' I warned him, 'Don't play clever games, because this is Baiae – and Rome – not some flea-bitten little hole in the provinces. By God, I expected you to be vulgar and a damned nuisance, but I didn't think you were raving mad.'

'You expected me to be grateful,' he said, the glitter dimming for just an instant, leaving his eyes dull, murky, somehow very dangerous.

And because I refused to be afraid of him, I snapped, 'It wouldn't hurt you. You should be grateful. And you should give a thought to Bassus. If I break our agreement because you're impossible to work with, he'll still have to pay me. And if you get on the wrong side of him you'll have cause to regret it. My God, look at you, limping along on your scabby ankles. It takes more than a flashy smile and a bottle of cheap scent to make a star charioteer.'

We had come to a halt by the sea-wall, my bearers a long way ahead of us, and suddenly, fiercely, he pushed me back against the rough, cold stone, holding me with one hand and thrusting his other hand a bare inch from my face.

'Have a look at that, girl,' he said, turning it palm upwards to show me the callouses where the reins had bitten into him, then back again so I could see the split knuckles, the agility of the wrist; and then holding it quite steady, transforming his living flesh to a motionless claw of iron, as I knew Dion could no longer do.

'What do you know about racing? Just because your brother ponces about in a silk tunic and has his hair curled every day? Well – I'll tell you. There's a place in the desert where they mark the track with knives and if you lose, and your patron thinks you didn't try hard enough, you get one of them in your gut and no questions asked. And there must be a hundred small towns between Carthage and Antioch where your horses can drop dead on you – from old age – just as you start turning in close to the posts. When you're injured – which is about half the time – you either grin and bear it, or you starve, because there's no faction doctor, no faction barracks with a classy mess-hall like the "Blues", no Bassus to pay your salary and hold on to your prize-money. And when you've outlasted your welcome in one arena – which doesn't take long – you raise the money any way you can to get to the next. You keep a set of decent clothes, and you smile at old women, and old men if you have to – and not for pearls either, for bread and dates and a blanket – or you hire yourself out to some local villain who knows how bad you need the money and won't expect you to be fussy about how you earn it. And when you've made your travelling expenses you move on. That's when you've got your training. That's when you can call yourself a charioteer.'

'Why do it? What is there in four horses and a platform on two wheels to make it worth all that?'

'Stupid bitch,' he said. 'You know why!'

And he was right, for I too had strained every nerve and muscle, had punished my body and still punished it to attain excellence as a dancer, not for the dance alone, but because it was the only thing I had that made me special, that lifted me from the faceless, filthy begging of my childhood, to my present heights of begging on silk cushions in scented dining-halls. Recognizing in him my own refusal to be buried alive, hearing, somewhere in his head, my own voice clamouring to escape the trap of my birth, my anger melted away. For I had escaped and he had not -- and he was older than me. The least I could do was to be kind.

'We're almost there,' I said quietly. 'You'd better come. There's no sense in standing here like this – I'm cold.' And nodding, he walked with me silently, sullenly I thought, down the stony little path to my rented seaside home.

Last summer I'd been obliged to share a house with a singer from Syracuse and her hawk-eyed, spiteful mother, but Aemilius Scaurus had found this place for me, small but daintily appointed, with a colonnaded courtyard looking over the sea, and a garden just big enough for a fountain, a flowering tree, and the marble statue of Terpsichore, the Goddess of the Dance, which Scaurus had ordered as a parting gesture and which I was determined, one way or another, to take back to Rome with me. And as always, on entering any property which, however loosely, I could call mine, a vein of deep, solid satisfaction awoke inside me, lightening my mood, and making everything easier to bear.

'You may as well have a drink,' I offered, leading the way into the garden, for in an establishment such as mine, where visitors can be expected at all times of the day and night, there is always wine set out on a table under a tree, always a couch and a stool placed close together, a lamp left burning. 'Moody creature,' I thought. 'First he's up, then he's down. Like Dion, I suppose.' But he wasn't really like Dion at all, for he seemed to have no capacity to enjoy life as Dion did, to swallow it down in great, golden mouthfuls and hold out his cup for more. He was too scarred by life to take pleasure in it, and although I couldn't know enough about him to make that judgement, I did know it. And once again I couldn't look at him, afraid that if I did I would see myself, as I might have been if I too had failed.

He sat down on the rim of the fountain, one foot on the stone bench that encircled it, making no effort to conceal the shameful scars on his ankles – that sign of what? of slavery, of imprisonment, of private vengeance? I couldn't tell – and as the plain, sensible serving-woman who had been hired with the house gave him his cup and melted discreetly away, I saw that although his hand was still admirably steady, there was something about him that spoke of sickness and strain, of long days on the road without food and shelter, of dust in his lungs, and men, half a day behind him, who didn't wish him well. There were hollows, in the lamplight, beneath his cheekbones, poverty-lines deep scored from nose to chin, and in his lean, tanned body I could tell that something ached, something was raw and had failed to heal.

'I mean what I say about Bassus,' I warned him, fighting off the sympathy I couldn't afford to feel. 'He never stops smiling, but unless you want to finish up back in the desert you'd do well to keep on the right side of him.'

He eased his position, stretching himself, preening almost, enjoying the fine spray of the fountain on his back, and although there was no flesh on him, no real substance, that glimpse of frailty, quite abruptly, was gone, so that he looked tough and insolent, altogether refreshed, as if all he'd needed to do was locate some source of nervous energy inside himself and release it.

'I'll only need Bassus until September. He keeps telling me I'm good, and he's right – I'm bloody good. All I want from him is the chance to prove it. It suits me right now to let him feed me and dress me and get me back into shape, and if you'd seen me a month or two back you'd understand why. He wants his profit out of me, that's all; the same as everybody else, and I'm not going to be grateful for that. He may control the "Blues" but that's not the only faction in Rome – there's "Green" and "Red" and "White". If I can give the crowd what they want then Bassus will have to worry about keeping on the right side of me. It's the fans that matter and they're not all rich men with their whims and fancies, they're just lads from the tenements like me, and I know where I am with them. If I can keep on packing them in then I'll race for the faction that pays me best, and Bassus can run after me like everybody else, with his money in his hand.'

And because once again I could see myself in him, because I too had strutted and preened and boasted just as he was doing now – and because I knew how badly he wanted it all to happen that way and I didn't think he had a chance – I said coldly, 'How old are you? Twenty-one? Twenty-two? My brother's age?'

'I suppose so – something like that.'

'Then haven't you left it late? Dion got his apprenticeship with the "Blues" at thirteen, his place in the team at seventeen. If you're so good, what took you so long?'

He scowled, the brooding, menacing look on him again. 'I'll have all that too, don't worry about it,' he muttered, 'I got my apprenticeship at thirteen as well, but other things got in the way.' And then, his sullenness vanishing, he looked up and smiled quite disarmingly, a boy again.

'Are you really a Greek?' he said, wanting to know this time, and my mind still back in the alleys my tongue betrayed me and gave him an honest answer.

'My father was from Athens, or so he said. But my mother was just a tenement woman like yours, I expect, doing the best she could.'

'And your father?'

'He was an actor.'

'A good one?'

'Oh yes – far too good for the trash they put on nowadays, so most of the time he lived on my mother's earnings and pretended he didn't, so he wouldn't have to call himself a pimp.'

And abruptly the trap closed over me again, and I knew I had been fooling myself, knew I'd never lose those foul odours of the past, never shake myself free from the dread of sinking into that cess-pit again, of being dragged back there by accident or by a man like this. I looked down at my manicured hands, my silk robe, as if they were a talisman to ward off evil. I touched the pearls in my ears, inhaled my own perfume. But none of it was enough, none of it could form a barrier between me and the woman I might have been – should have been – who would be old now, at nineteen, whining and sickly and used up by a man with Marsyas' hard hands. 'Go away from me,' I thought. 'I look at you and I see my own fears, my own nightmares, and I hate you. They've damaged you too much. And when you fail I don't want to see it. I don't want to care. I can't carry us both.'

But a mood of emotion had been created. I had said much more than I had intended to say, was drifting now, dangerously, towards him. And I had no idea if he knew it, if he had planned it, or if he was drifting too.

'I could sleep now,' he said. 'If that's all right. Can I stay here, in the garden?'

'But you'll be cold. I'll get something to cover you.'

And then, as I hesitated, furious with myself, for no woman in my position should be willing to fetch and carry for a man in his, he spoke my name, just that, for the first time.

'Danaë.'

'Yes.'

'Don't go just yet.'

And there was pain in his voice and in the whole anguished movement of his body as he sank back against the cushions and put one unsteady hand to his head.

'You're in pain? What can I do?'

'Nothing.'

I sat down beside him and let him take my hand, my eyes drawn to a scar that sliced its way the length of his forehead; baffled and intrigued by the way his energy came and went.

'There's something wrong with you, isn't there? Does Bassus know?'

'No. And he won't get to know. You won't tell him?'

'Not I. But he'll get to know all right, if it happens in the arena when you're doing one of your clever tight turns – except that you won't be alive to care.'

And with the part of my mind that had always feared for Dion, I saw it, the sunshine and the flying sand, that crowd of tenement lads come to cheer him on, the triumph he'd dreamed of all his meagre, savage life, and then the splintering wood and screaming horses, that terrible, mangled ending. And it wasn't fair. It was pitiful, appalling, and it wounded me.

'It happened six months back,' he said. 'I overturned a chariot and the man behind ran over me. Split my head open and now it hurts, which I can live with – but I go dizzy too, now and again, and Bassus wouldn't take a chance on me if he knew that. But, I thought it over, and I ask you, just what have I got to lose?' And because it was true I didn't move away when he touched my cheek and my neck and shoulders, and put his mouth enquiringly and then ravenously on mine.

'He's had nothing in his life,' I thought, 'and now it's nearly over. What can it cost me to give him this?' And returning his kiss, tracing the outline of that dreadful scar with my mouth, I think there were tears in my eyes.

'Oh you're marvellous,' he sighed, 'just marvellous. If only I'd met you sooner,' and, taking his face in my hands, kissing him again, I missed the warning signs, failed to notice that the black glitter was there, once again, in his eyes, the sneer around his mouth, until, shockingly, he threw back his head and crowed with laughter.

'Well, there's always a way to get to a woman,' he said. 'Sometimes it's one thing and sometimes another. With you it's pity. I got this crack on my head five years ago, in a wine-shop in Syracuse, and I've never had a headache since the day it happened. But don't let that stop you.'

I threw the wine-cup at him and myself after it, murder clawing inside me, and when I saw I couldn't hurt him, I yelled at him – choking on the inadequacy of it and the uncomfortable feeling that he had heard it many times before. 'Get out of here! And keep out of my way. Don't ever let me see you again!'

'I'll go when I'm ready,' he said, and when I started to tell him I'd call the bearers and the dogs, he raised his arms in a gesture of insolent surrender.

'Why? What's changed? You thought I was going to get killed in the arena, and maybe I am. I told you a lie all right, but you don't know which is the lie and which is the truth. I may have hurt myself in a brawl in a wine-shop, or I may have done it in a chariot crash. You can't be sure. Maybe I just didn't want your pity. Maybe I wanted you to know I could have you with or without Bassus.'

And taking my arm in a grip I seemed unable to resist, he drew me very slowly towards him.

'No,' I told him, 'you can't have me at all – ever.' But it was only the surface of my mind that spoke the words, only the outer layer of my skin, the veneer of these few pampered years, that resisted him. For the tenement girl inside me had already lifted her face to meet the harsh bite of his kiss, had taken the weight of his hard, dry body on hers, finding nothing to surprise her in his hunger and his haste, since a tenement man has no thought for love's niceties and, if there is pleasure to be had, is intent merely on making sure it will belong to him.

And when it was over and I had turned my bruised body, my shattered self-esteem away from him, he got up and, without speaking a word to me, went away.

3

I waited, the next morning, for him to come back, longing for the pleasure of throwing him out. But it was Bassus who came instead, very much annoyed, to ask me what I'd done with Marsyas, since he wasn't at his lodgings, no one had seen him and he'd left no word. I spent days, then, searching for his face in the crowds, despising myself, so that when I finally saw him, very late one night, waiting at my door, I was as scathing as I knew how to be. But in the end I let him in and although I warned him, 'We'll go back to our agreement, with no extras,' that wasn't the way of it for long. To stave off that treacherous emotion, the ridiculous feeling of belonging, we quarrelled, watched each other warily like adversaries more than lovers, the noise of our combat covering the things neither of us could afford to feel. But one day silence fell between us, and, walking together through the blue and gold shimmer of the afternoon, my hand slid into his and I could hear his mind talking to me, could insert myself inside his head and his skin, could take the whole of him into the whole of me. And I knew that had I not been terrified I would have been blissfully, stupidly happy. I had arranged to meet him that night at a party but I didn't go. I stayed at home and told my doorkeeper he was not to be admitted. But he didn't come; and I learned the next day from Erato that he had gone back to Cynthia.

'How galling for you,' Erato murmured, savouring the moment; but although I was scorched, although I hurt, I was thankful too, for now I had no choice but to come to my senses and take up my hectic, anxious life once more. I became dazzling again and calculating, smiled at Cynthia, sharpened my ears to catch the faintest whisper of Drusus' imperial name. I became, in fact, my own creation, the woman I chose to be. It was a relief when the summer dragged itself to a close and we could all go back to town.

The racing season opened early in September with the Great Roman Games, which, sprung from the seeds of an ancient wine festival, now spanned a full sixteen days of sudden death and easy money, an appetizer to whet the public taste for more. And there was more to come. Golden October would begin with a new festival, eight days of thrills and idleness instituted by our late master the Emperor Augustus, who had always known the value of keeping his people entertained; and it would end with an old one, the six-day celebration of Sulla's long-passed victories, remembered annually now by the money that changed hands in the circus colonnade. A halt then, of three days, for men to mourn their losses or spend their winnings, to beg and borrow where they could, and the Plebeian Games would be upon us, another ancient vine cult, now a monster spectacle of fourteen days with gambling-fever raging like the plague, carrying us through to the Saturnalia in December, the Festival of Fools, when even the most serious-minded of men – even the Prince Drusus – would be unable to hold aloof from the dinners and parties, and the entertainers who came gliding in between the courses to sell their talents and themselves.

I returned to my flat in the Street of the Yoke-makers to spend a few days of lush self-satisfaction vetting my advance bookings for the season, discarding a few, since it has never paid to seem too eager. And, having rearranged my furniture and walked a little on Mars Field to remind the fashionable loiterers of my existence, I went to the Circus Maximus on the first day of the Games, arriving late as a successful woman should, in proof of my ability to hire men to come here at dawn and keep good seats for me.

It was a fine, saffron-tinted morning, the sky a thin, fragile blue above the crowded tiers of the arena, and although it was my business to look serene and radiant, the clamour and the odour of so much tight-packed humanity, the heat of their collective excitement, struck me between the eyes, warning me that it would be a long, aching day. I had been sleeping badly since Baiae, relying too heavily on the medicines I bought from an old Egyptian behind the Temple of Diana, so that it took time in the morning to clear my head; and perhaps today the presence of my sister Marpessa was an extra burden.

She was thirteen – marriageable, marketable – but a child still in a way I could never remember being, and although she was tall and well-grown, and people thought her very like me in appearance, I could never bring myself to credit her with much good sense. She was a fidget, a nuisance, an attention-seeker, liable to feel thirsty or sick at inconvenient times; and since the Circus, for me, was not so much a place of entertainment as of business – a place where I could be looked at and remembered – Marpessa, who wanted to be looked at too, was unwelcome.

'Just make sure you keep an eye on her,' I'd warned Chrysothemis, an old friend who lived with me because she had nowhere else to go; and although she'd agreed and smiled – being in a position to do no other – I knew that when it came to it she'd be busy trying to draw attention to herself, and would leave Marpessa to me.

Chrysothemis and I had started out together seven years ago as a double-act, working the wine-shops and the supper clubs and cheap bachelor dinners, scraping a living. We'd shared the same dancing-master – Agathon, at one time the greatest mime in Corinth – who'd agreed to teach us because he owed my father a favour. And even Agathon, who hated youth because he was old, and hated talent because his own had withered away, had been forced to admit that Chrysothemis had the makings of a brilliant artiste. I would do nothing, he said. Once my first bloom was gone I'd turn hard and bold and end my days in a common whorehouse. But Chrysothemis, who was made of moonlight and may-blossom, would endure in men's minds forever.

She was a gifted classical dancer, a superb actress – I'd never doubted it – and the day she told me she was going solo because I was holding her back I'd turned sick with panic. Yet here she was, living in my house, unable, with all her splendid artistry, to make a living; while I – every bit as hard and bold as Agathon had predicted – had more work than I could take. And there was Agathon himself, who'd expected to end his days basking in Chrysothemis' glory, now sleeping every afternoon like an old lizard in my courtyard, waking only to be fed, and shuffling home now and then to the room I paid for and the hefty slave-woman I'd bought to look after him.

Naturally it wasn't fair – I knew it and Chrysothemis knew it – but it suited me to make use of her taste and skills, suited her to know where her next meal was coming from, and we would have got along well enough if she hadn't taken it into her head, lately, to spend too much time with my young brother Paris, a clever lad of seventeen who was as handsome as my actor father and just as feckless.

They had chosen good seats for us near the Imperial Box, with a clear view of that famous hair-pin bend where the drivers, conscious of the imperial eye, perform their most suicidal tricks, making those elegant, lethal manoeuvres that either send them thundering off amidst roars of applause or leave them lying in a mangled obscenity of horse-flesh and man-flesh and shattered wood – the shipwrecks that, for Dion's sake, I'd learned to dread. I had seen men killed here many a time, dragged to pieces by their own maddened teams or ploughed into the sand by the team behind. But, because Dion was racing that day, it was bad luck and bad sense to think about dying, and, pressing my fingers against a certain amulet I wore hidden away among the more respectable jewels at my throat, I banished it from my mind. I had already consulted astrologers and magicians on his behalf, breaking Tiberius' laws with the horoscopes and the lucky charms I bought, the formulas I repeated over and over again at certain phases of the moon. And, to leave no stone unturned, there wasn't a temple in the city I hadn't visited at one time or another, from the splendid gold and marble palaces of Rome's own official gods, to the smoky dens beyond the city gates where the prayers and the priests were fiercer but they took my money just the same. And so there was nothing for it now but to settle down to my own concerns and leave it – as one is forced to leave most things in the end – to chance.

Erato was sitting not far away, her tiny frame crackling with vitality, and, waving a hand that flashed ruby fire in the sunlight, dazzling a row of honest citizens with her pert, mischievous smile, she obliged them all to move along so I could join her.

'What fun,' she said, ignoring Chrysothemis who was too insipid, and Marpessa who was too young, to give her trouble. 'The senatorial benches are all full. And isn't that an improvement on last year when they were all plotting their revolution and daren't show themselves in case Tiberius could read their minds? They've all come out of hiding, bless them, I knew they would. And what about this new lot, eh? Don't they look fit, with their Syrian sun-tans and all that parade-ground swagger? Look, over there –'

And, among the familiar figures of the politicians and financiers we all knew, she indicated a group of youngish, soldierly men, staff-officers of the dead hero Germanicus, who last year had all come back to Rome convinced that his death in Syria had been no accident, and determined to bring someone – the Emperor Tiberius if possible – to justice for it.

Throughout the winter they had been men with a mission, spending their time in grim consultation with Germanicus' widow, but now that the fuss was over and Tiberius had managed to reduce their talk of vengeance to the level of common grumbling, I supposed they would be as ready to enjoy themselves as anybody else. So I smiled at them, for if the affair of Germanicus ever blew up again and Tiberius and his son Drusus should be lifted off the Palatine by its blast, I might need to get out of the city in a hurry. And in that case it would be as well to know the man on duty at the gate.

The Imperial Box was full too and, straining my eyes towards it, I saw the long, spare figure of Tiberius himself, his shoulders hunched forward as he scrutinized not the race in progress but a bundle of official documents held up to the light for him by a kneeling slave. He was prepared to pay for the games, it seemed, just as he was ready to maintain the bulk of the city population on the dole – for even I knew that men who are bored and hungry are dangerous, and could appreciate the sound, political sense of keeping them entertained and fed – but, unlike his predecessor Augustus, that true Father of the State, Tiberius was not a man who could stoop to share his people's pleasures. He would sit all day in the dust and heat, suffer the din, but he found nothing in the whole fearfully costly scene to merit his attention. And even in the close confines of the Imperial Box, hemmed in by the cream of his nobility and the deference of visiting potentates, there was a certain solitude about him, some unseen barrier, uncomfortable and cold, that he seemed able to erect at will to shield him from any real contact with other men.

If the people wanted pomp and magnificence, a stadium that could seat 200,000 citizens, with the captured obelisk of an Egyptian pharaoh in its centre, and solid bronze dolphins to mark off the laps; if they wanted gilded statues and a big parade, a shower of lottery tickets that could win them a racehorse or a farm or a bag of gold, and a public banquet to finish off the day; if they wanted horses from the best studs of Africa and Spain, their harness scattered with gem-stones, and the wildest, bravest men in the world to drive them – if they wanted blood on the sand – then all that could be arranged. But as for himself, he had work to do and wished merely not to be disturbed.

A woman sat on either side of him, his son Drusus' wife, the Lady Livilla, who had also been sister to the murdered Germanicus, and Germanicus' widow Agrippina, who in Germanicus' lifetime had been first lady in Rome. And it struck me that her presence here today was a sure indication of a lost cause, for when Germanicus had died so strangely in Antioch, and she had brought his ashes back to Rome, no one had doubted her intention of laying the crime at her uncle Tiberius' door. She was a woman of the very highest nobility, the grand-daughter of Augustus himself, and although her mother had been a notorious adulteress Agrippina had always been a model wife, had loved her husband with a rare devotion and, in a world where few women would care to risk themselves in pregnancy more than once, if at all, had given him nine children.

Augustus had made no secret of his intentions where she and Germanicus were concerned. Having no sons of his own, and discarding the middle-aged Tiberius, his wife's son by her first marriage, he had looked to the younger generation of Caesars for his heir. He had selected the golden Germanicus, had married him to his favourite grand-daughter, appointed him to magistracies he was legally too young to hold, put the showiest of military opportunities his way. He had allowed him to earn the title of 'Germanicus' for his victories against the tribesmen of Germany, had encouraged the whole world to love him. But Augustus had died before Germanicus was ready, and Tiberius, waiting in the shadows, had walked disdainfully on to the imperial stage, a man already soured by a lifetime of hard work in Augustus' service for which he well knew Augustus had never intended to reward him. All Augustus had been able to do for Germanicus at the end was to oblige Tiberius to adopt him as his son, and express the hope that, setting aside his own son Drusus, Tiberius would make Germanicus his heir.

It had seemed at first that Tiberius had little choice, for Germanicus' popularity with nobles and people alike was immense. Germanicus was the rising sun, Drusus a pale star, easily eclipsed, Tiberius a peevish old man who would oblige everybody by lying down to die. But then, suddenly it was

Germanicus – lately appointed to the Supreme Command of the Eastern Provinces – who had died instead, and his wife Agrippina, after first exhibiting his body in the main square at Antioch to prove he had been poisoned, was coming home, his ashes in her arms, accusation and vengeance in her eyes.

Aristocratic Rome had rallied to Agrippina's side, some from genuine concern, others because an imperial widow of marriageable age is a prize worth the taking. Since it was clearly impossible to bring a direct accusation of murder against a ruling emperor, a scapegoat had been found, old Gnaeus Piso, the Governor of Syria, the man they believed Tiberius had sent out East to do the foul deed for him. And they put him on trial, hoping he would incriminate his master.

'Tiberius can't get out of this one,' at least a hundred people had told me. 'If he stops the trial and lets Piso go, he'll be admitting his own guilt. And if he allows Piso to be condemned then Piso will talk, to save his life.'

But Tiberius, inscrutable as always behind his barriers of silence, had done neither of those things. He had allowed Piso to stand trial, but somehow the evidence which had seemed so overwhelming in the hot Syrian air, cooled under Tiberius' infinitely weary gaze, and it wasn't long before those ambitious, hard-headed nobles began to reflect uneasily on the known vindictiveness of their ageing Caesar, and to wonder if it was really worth the risk of their lives. And so, when the proceedings were adjourned and Piso obligingly went home and fell on his own sword, it may have been a relief to them all. No verdict had been reached, and there were few people left with the courage to enquire too loudly whether the sword in Piso's gut had really been his own or whether, in fact, it had belonged to some trusted member of the Praetorian Guard. No one, now, could ever know for sure if Tiberius would have tried to save his henchman or not – nor even if murder had actually been done at all, since the East is full of fevers, and the opinion of a doting wife is not always reliable. There had been nothing to do but bury the dead and learn to applaud the living. And today it seemed that even the Lady Agrippina, who had vowed never to look on Tiberius' face again, had remembered how much she needed his imperial favour to establish her sons and marry her daughters, and had come to win it.

'But where's Drusus?' I murmured, trying to locate him among the immaculate, purple-bordered togas and the high-ranking uniforms around the Emperor. Erato shrugged.

'Yes, where indeed? One supposes he's gone to the amphitheatre to see the gladiators. I hear he likes to see the blood flow. I made it in my way to meet one of his staff-officers from Pannonia – a dear boy – and he tells me Drusus is quite well known for it. Always inspects the weapons himself before the show begins, to make sure they're lethal enough – refuses to be fobbed off with a bit of fancy sword-play and a surface wound or two and then back to the barracks, all mates together. He absolutely insists on a fight to the death every time, which upsets the organizers because they get a discount on how many men they send back alive, and when Drusus is presiding it's never more than half.'

It wasn't a pleasant trait, this enthusiasm for blood and guts in company with the rowdiest elements of the city mob, and perhaps I would have preferred to think of him in the restrained atmosphere of the theatre, enjoying a Greek drama, or here – under my eye – a keen racing-man. But it was Erato's sly reference to that staff-officer from Pannonia which really held my attention, that 'dear boy' who by now would be firmly committed to her interests. She had been willing to share with me the snippet of information about Drusus' questionable enthusiasm for sword-fights, but what else did she know? What else had the bemused young soldier whispered in her ear? What promises had been made? And what did Cynthia know, sitting a good few rows nearer to the Imperial Box than I was, in a dazzle of green silk, her day-time emeralds crowning her sensational red hair? She had been laying out money, I knew, bribing palace servants to find out Drusus' tastes in food and wine, promising her future influence as an imperial mistress to any enterprising politician who might help her, now, to attract the imperial eye. And, having done all these things myself, I wouldn't take it kindly if her information, or Erato's, proved better than my own.

I had spent a fortune – the equivalent of my fee for ten performances – wining and dining one of Drusus' freedmen, had served him red mullet on silver dishes and old Falernian wine in a jewelled cup I'd allowed him to take away with him, in exchange for his assurances that he would engage me as a dancer when

Drusus started to entertain. And even now, in the clamour of this painful place, I was waiting for a man who had promised me an introduction to someone much closer to the Prince than Erato's staff-officer was ever likely to be. Peering through the crowds to locate him I was as heedless of the spectacle going on before me as Tiberius himself, until Erato, drawing my attention to the line-up for the next race, murmured wickedly, 'So now we are to see Bassus' new star, it seems. This Marsyas we've all heard so much about. Wasn't he a summer whim of yours, Danaë – for an hour or two at Baiae?'

And my friend Chrysothemis – light as air, cool as water, sharp-eyed as an eagle – who had been eating my bread for the past year and should have been kinder, put her pale, narrow hand on my arm and said sweetly, 'Never mind, dear. The feeling is that he won't last the season.'

I thought there was every chance of it and, glancing at the stall where Marsyas stood in his blue racing-tunic, perfectly still as charioteers always are before a race, I felt again that terrible blending of hostility and compassion, that dreadful feeling of involvement. My self-esteem had ordered me to forget him, and I'd obeyed. Yet ever since Baiae, lulled into artificial sleep by my Egyptian drops, I had been plagued, night after night, by a dream in which I was bearing his child. I knew I wasn't pregnant, by him or anyone else, but the dream kept on coming, his child growing inside me like a disease, murdering me, and no soothsayer had been able to help.

He had drawn an unfavourable position on the outside near the stands, and, being up against skilled competition, men who knew every grain of sand on the track, I doubted he would do great things today. To win his first race would be a tremendous boost to his career, and I knew Bassus was not above bribing the other drivers to hold back when he wanted to launch a star; but I'd heard Marsyas' relationship with Bassus was already turning sour, that he'd failed to show proper gratitude, and Bassus was not the man to throw good money after bad. 'No,' I thought, 'he's on his own. All they really want him to do for them is die.' And it distressed me, frightened me, to have this certain, mysterious knowledge of his aloneness.

Silence fell, the hush before delirium, and then the President's white napkin fluttered through the air and descended slowly to the ground, a dainty signal releasing the fury and clatter of sixteen horses and four frail chariots tearing down the straight. And with them the heady spice of danger – other men's danger – that flicked at the crowd with a sensuous hand, setting them writhing and shouting as if they too were strapped in there with the reins bound tight around their waists and a knife to cut themselves free, if they could, when death beckoned. Whips were idle for the moment, the drivers leaning slightly backwards, holding in their teams, for it was no great advantage at this point to be out in front. Position was what counted in this early stage and the 'White' charioteer, who had drawn the best place in the inside lane, next to the central Spina, would be lucky to keep it. I knew him slightly, a man already in his late twenties, close to retirement, and I doubted if he would risk his neck. 'Red' was pressing hard behind, manoeuvring dangerously, and as he came up, lashing his horses into the back of the leading chariot, 'White' lost his nerve and started to give way. The crowd – who had nothing to lose but their money – howled abuse and I doubt if anyone but me even looked at Marsyas.

'Green' had made a bad start, his trace horse shying as the trumpet sounded, and for eight laps Marsyas ran third, gaining only little by little on 'White' who, certain of second place, seemed to have forgotten about him. He was driving well, turning in close to the posts in a spectacular manner, but it was exhibition work – the kind of thing one sees on Mars Field – until suddenly, about the tenth lap, he leaned forward, giving his horses their heads and, thundering up the straight, shaved the turning post with nothing to spare and brought himself neck and neck with 'White'. They came up the straight again, wheel perilously close to wheel, and there was a yell of pure, animal glee as it was realized that Marsyas was about to drive into the other chariot and overturn it. But 'White' gave ground again – thinking about the job they'd offered him as a trainer if he lasted the season – and this time all eyes were on Marsyas, for he had a long way to go to catch 'Red' and not even the most fanatic of the 'Blues' supporters thought he'd do it.

But it was very clear that he intended to try, no matter what it cost him – no matter the cost to anyone else – and men who had never set foot in a chariot, never stirred themselves to do more than collect their dole, shrieked advice to him, rode the hurricane with him as he turned so sickeningly close to the posts that it had to be chance, not judgement, that kept him from disaster. And when he finally caught up with 'Red', 200,000 men and women rose to their feet, screaming, as that dreadful business of racing wheel to wheel began again, their clamour telling him, if he could hear it, that in this place where thrills were plentiful and life cheap, and they themselves had seen it all before, he had succeeded in creating a rare emotion, something they wouldn't forget for a day or two, and would want to see again if he lived that long.

Both drivers were crouched forward now, whipping their teams and, in all the flying sand and dust, probably whipping each other as well. And I knew – everybody knew – that if they were still neck and neck when they reached the turning posts again, one of them would very likely die. It was bound to be Marsyas. It had to be him. And then he made a sudden lunge sideways and forward and there he was, making the turn alone, as the 'Red' chariot disintegrated behind him, its axle broken, its horses pawing the air, struggling disjointedly on the sand. The stricken driver cut his reins and jumped clear, but few people noticed that. They were all watching as Marsyas slowed down, wanting to catch a glimpse of his face as he drove to the Imperial Box to collect his palm branch. 'By God,' I heard someone mutter, 'he's a maniac.' 'He's beautiful,' someone else replied and there could be no doubt that this sensual combination of beauty and madness would be enough to make him a rich man tomorrow, a pampered, strutting, peacock-preening man like my brother Dion: a man I would be unable to avoid.

All around me women were shedding hysterical tears, promising, on the strength of this one performance, to love him forever; and among them was my sister Marpessa, bouncing up and down in her seat, breathless and disarranged, gasping out to complete strangers, 'Oh, what's his name – his name? He's magnificent – I've never seen anything like him. Danaë, you can get to know him, can't you? Dion must know him – invite him –'

'He's good,' Erato said. 'Totally insane, of course, but very good.' And leaning forward, my fingers itching to slap her, I snarled a few harsh words at my sister, warning her of a terrible retribution if she didn't sit still at once, and behave.

'I feel sick,' she said, looking it; and waiting only until Dion had won a palm branch of his own – arousing considerably less fervour in the crowd because they had seen him do it before – I got to my feet, feeling more than slightly unwell myself, and took her home.

And there, in my own house, was the message I had been waiting for all day, telling me that the man I wanted to meet would be at a party that night in a certain garden, and that I was expected.

4

I spent an hour in the bath, hoping to ease the day out of my skin, but the perfumed steam and my serving-woman's clever, massaging fingers did little to relax me. My head ached, my stomach was sour, and even my habitual pleasure in the rose-pink shading of the marble, the flacons of expensive oil, the luxury of bathing alone instead of in a gaping, gossiping crowd, had lost its savour.

I had lived in this flat barely a year, graduating from a series of rented rooms where my brother Paris, like his father before him, had turned up his nose at the neighbours and Marpessa had run wild in the streets. And now, slipping a loose Greek chiton over my head, I wandered restlessly for a moment, feeling a great need to remind myself of my present comfort, not to be compared with Erato's or Cynthia's, of course, but more than I'd once dreamed of.

I had a tiny hall, marbled in purple and blue, where I could receive my morning-calls, a room of my own and a room for my sister, well away from mine; a place for my brother to study, a couch for Chrysothemis in a screened alcove, a yard at the back, converted into a garden by the generosity of Aemilius Scaurus and graced now by the statue of Terpsichore I'd carted back from Baiae. There was a dining-room big enough for my purposes, adequate quarters for my maids, my litter-bearers, my cithara-player and flute-player, a quiet corner in which my old dancing-master could take his ease. And although it wasn't enough, and next year or the year after I would have something bigger and better, it gave me immense satisfaction to know that I could feed all these mouths every day, could pay for Paris' books and Marpessa's fancies, could bribe an imperial freedman and still have something to spare.

But there were times when satisfaction frayed around its edges and, padding barefoot into the garden, the sight of my brother sitting adoringly at Chrysothemis' feet, and the sound of my sister's voice still singing Marsyas' praises, did nothing to lighten my mood. Although it was natural enough for my brother to fall in love with a sophisticated older woman, and my sister with a charioteer, it suddenly seemed as if they were doing it on purpose to annoy me.

'If you go to the faction banquet tonight you could meet him,' Marpessa told me. 'And if you wanted to, you could take me with you. I'm old enough – I'm thirteen – and I'm big enough.' And, dancing up to me, black hair cascading to her supple waist, she tried to measure herself against me, jostling me in a way that was too much for the present sorry state of my nerves.

'You've been helping yourself to my perfume again.'

'What of it? You can get some more. And I don't see why you shouldn't take me to the faction club. Roman girls get married at my age, and you've always done just as you pleased. Father was still with us when you were thirteen, wasn't he, and he never made *you* stay at home at night.'

'No. He sent me to work. And you won't find a husband at a faction banquet, if that's what you're after – somebody else's husband, maybe.'

'What do I care,' she said, dancing away from me, just out of reach in case she overstepped the mark. 'It wouldn't hurt you to take me – Dion would take me. And if you don't, well then, one of these nights I'll just go anyway, and slip back into the house, and you'd never know. Because if you think Paris and Chrysothemis keep an eye on me then you're mistaken. All they ever do is moon about all over each other – making me feel sick.'

'What a vivid imagination the child has,' Chrysothemis said sweetly, raising her pointed, pensive face into the light; but my fastidious, clever brother saw no reason to conceal his disgust.

'You should do something about that little pest, Danaë,' he advised me loftily.' I've been meaning to tell you so for some time. She's rude and noisy and she makes Chrysothemis' life a misery. She treats her just like a servant, and I don't feel I can tolerate it much longer.'

'Oh can't you indeed,' I said, furious with him, with Marpessa, with Chrysothemis, not knowing which one to attack first. But Chrysothemis, who knew the value of a good dinner even if my brother didn't, came gliding between us, smoothing the ruffles away.

'She's young,' she murmured. 'And I don't mind. I'm happy to do anything I can, Danaë, you know that. You have enough to contend with, dear. Don't get upset now, if you have a big night ahead.'

'How good you are,' Paris muttered, earning her misty smile, and although I could have told him a thing or two about her goodness, I bit my tongue, for I had no time to spare just then and I knew he wouldn't have believed me in any case.

'No, no,' she cooed, 'not good, just sensible. Poor Danaë works so hard – one must never forget it.'

'I'll bet you never forget it,' Marpessa cut in, young and cruel and possibly unaware of the true value of Chrysothemis' wasted talents. 'I expect you'd be glad just to work at all.'

'Bitch,' Paris said, pinching her arm with fingers that had forgotten to be sophisticated and refined. As she began to howl – and nobody could howl louder than Marpessa when she put her mind to it – Chrysothemis came once more to the rescue.

'Really,' she lectured Paris gently, 'you shouldn't do that to your sister. She's very young, and it's a painful time of life. And you should know better than to bother Danaë like this before a party. Come Danaë, I'll do your hair. That maid of yours has two left hands.'

Yet for all her pretty show of anger, she paused in the doorway and told him, by a subtle movement of her fine features, that later when the house was quiet she would reward him most rapturously for his support.

I wasn't sure how far things had gone between them, for although he was in a romantic frame of mind, she was clever enough to know that what he got too soon wouldn't content him for long. But he was ripe to fall in love with somebody, and better Chrysothemis, I thought, here, where I could keep an eye on them, than someone like Cynthia who would soon show him how easily a handsome and not-over-industrious lad like himself could make a living. When it was over he wasn't kind-hearted enough to let Chrysothemis' presence in the house trouble him, and she was too sensible to make a fuss. But Marpessa's threat to slip out of the house one night alarmed me, for I knew she was capable of it, and, having shielded her from the harsher side of life, I didn't for one moment imagine that she could cope. She looked like me, sounded like me sometimes, but she was, indeed, very spoiled; and although I had been the one to spoil her – just as I spoiled Paris and Dion too, when I could catch him – I resented the problem she presented and knew that, sooner or later, I would have to sit down and think it over.

I painted my own face, for it was too important a task to leave to anyone else, but I allowed Chrysothemis to wind the long coils of my hair and fasten each one with a pearl-tipped pin, to drape my white silk robe and my elegantly contrasting palla of black, embroidered with silver threads and tiny seed-pearls worked into the shapes of stars and flowers. Pearls in my ears, a collar of silver filigree, pearls at my throat, a white feather fan held on ivory sticks – and the unpleasant memories of the morning were, for an instant, erased. These were my working clothes, my full dress uniform and the medals of a dozen campaigns. And, so attired, what could it matter to me that a lad from the Subura was being carried shoulder-high by a pack of racing-fans who'd drop him soon enough when the wind changed?

I was met at the gate of that discreet garden across the Tiber by a young nobleman who took pleasure and money from intrigues of this sort; and, following him to a shadowy little summerhouse surrounded by high box-hedges, well away from the drinking-party that was in progress, I sat down to await the pleasure of the Commander of the Praetorian Guard. Although I had schemed for this interview and spent time and money to obtain it, I was nervous, for if he had consented to see me at all – and he could yet change his mind – it could only mean he had reasons which might well have nothing to do with mine.

His name was Aelius Sejanus, an opportunist from the middle-classes, of whom, until Tiberius came to power seven years ago, no one had heard very much. He had been a soldier of moderate distinction, a loiterer on the fringes of imperial favour, a noted seducer of influential women, a useful man, perhaps, in a tight corner; but his particular brand of shrewdness and toughness had not appealed to our late Emperor Augustus, who, having done his share of scheming and seducing in his youth, had become very virtuous in old age. But Tiberius, that secret, sinister man, shunning the noblemen who considered it their right to advise him, had been quick to appreciate Sejanus' lack of scruple and had soon put him to work.

Sejanus, it was said, thought only of the reward, caring little for what he had to do to earn it, and certainly his performance as Commander of the Guard had been impressive. Under his orders the dandified Praetorians, formerly good for little else but to decorate a parade, had become a disciplined fighting force, and, since they were the only troops in the city and the threat of them had done much to quell Senatorial ardour after Germanicus died, their leader could no longer be ignored.

Patrician Rome might not love him but, as things were just then, patrician Rome was in no position to complain. Too many noble families had backed Germanicus too heavily, and lost. Too many of them had rushed to greet his Agrippina on her return, and pledged her their support. Too many had talked too loudly of jealousy and murder and had sat in the Senate House at Piso's trial hoping to see Tiberius lose his nerve and, if possible, his life. Too many of them had raked up the past, remembering the unconcealed dislike between Augustus and Tiberius, and whispering that there must have been good reason for it – that Tiberius was not only crafty and cruel but had nasty personal habits besides. So there was no cause to be surprised when, offended and possibly embarrassed, Tiberius had turned his back on them.

Since Germanicus' death the Emperor had become more secretive and suspicious than ever, more difficult of access, yet still the rumours about his private life – his murderous inclinations, his unnatural lusts – persisted. And I had heard that Sejanus, now, was not only the Commander of the City garrison but the imperial spymaster as well, tracking down the source of these rumours, noting who whispered and who laughed, and storing the knowledge away in sealed files that could one day be used to imperial advantage.

I had seen him countless times in the distance, had danced at parties where he had been a guest and, once or twice, had appeared at his own house, engaged by his plain, efficient wife. But although his reputation with women was notorious, his affairs had always been for profit rather than pleasure, his tastes running to noble ladies who could do him some good in the world, and he had never looked my way. Yet he had been with Drusus in Pannonia for a while, must see the Prince daily at the palace, and if I could convince him somehow – anyhow – that I could be of use to him, then Erato's staff-officer and Cynthia's imperial butler would be wasting their time.

I hadn't, at first, expected him to see me, and even now, as I heard a brisk step on the gravel, there was a moment of alarm when my throat dried in a premonition of danger. But I didn't believe my interest in Drusus could be called treason, and so I stood up, offering instant proof of my skill by stepping slowly into a shaft of moonlight, letting its pale beam rise from my daintily manicured feet to my pearl-decked head, revealing myself to him by inches.

'Yes,' he said. 'I like that. Danaë, isn't it, late of the Subura, then Pomegranate Street, and the Via Nova, and now the loveliest resident of the Street of the Yoke-makers? Friend of my friend Aemilius Scaurus, who certainly didn't deserve you. Why have we never met before?' And, as a servant hurried in with wine and fruit and dates, I knew I was in the presence of the most attractive man I had ever seen.

He was in his late thirties, no handsomer than a hundred others, a weathered, humorous face, a strong, rather lopsided, mouth quizzically smiling, a deep cleft in his chin, grey eyes, hair of no particular colour, but with something in him so vivid and alive, something so compelling, that I found myself gazing with sheer, honest delight, assessing him with vast appreciation, immense curiosity.

His impact was in no way similar to the complex, deep-rooted sensations Marsyas had aroused in me. Marsyas was shadow, the dark side of myself, but this man's appeal was all of the outdoors, fresh air and smiling cornlands, raw good health and granite-hard endurance, and, above it, like a polished surface on wood, a layer of easy, carefree charm that told me he was well acquainted with his own fascinations and knew how to use them.

'So,' he said, 'what is it I can do for you?' And understanding him to be well aware of my motives and the methods I was ready to employ, the flowery phrases I'd prepared seemed inadequate, unwise, and I said, 'I would like to meet Drusus.'

'Would you indeed? And are you always so direct?'

'No. But your time is valuable, and I think it would irritate you if I tried to be coy.'

'Ah yes,' he said, his mouth curving in a lopsided grin that sent excited little tremors down my spine, 'Drusus – of course – and why shouldn't you meet him? I suppose anyone may meet him –

since every good prince knows it is part of his job to be affable, and to let his people love him. And although Drusus isn't sociable by nature, I expect he'll force himself to follow in Germanicus' footsteps. A tragedy, wasn't it, the loss of that young man?' And the twinkle in his grey eyes told me that for him the death of Germanicus had been no tragedy at all.

'Yes,' I said quickly, feeling thin ice beneath my tongue, 'tragic for anyone to die so young. But these things happen, and everything is all right again now.'

'I'm glad you think so. But doesn't your heart bleed for Agrippina? Poor woman, brought up all her life to think of herself as an empress, and now where is she? Giving precedence to Drusus' wife, and left to bring up all those children, with no man to help her.'

'Well,' I told him briskly, knowing that no show of ignorance, no commonplace declaration of loyalty to Tiberius would suffice, 'in her place I'd take them all into the country and make sure they got plenty of fresh air, because I saw them the other day and they looked positively out of sorts.'

He laughed, a sound rich with enjoyment, knowing perfectly well that had I been talking to a supporter of Germanicus – to Aemilius Scaurus for instance – I would have answered differently. And sitting down he patted the empty space beside him.

'Indeed,' he said, his whole face alive with mischief. 'May I take it, then, that you don't think much to Agrippina?'

'I don't know that I think of her at all. She's not likely to engage me as an entertainer, since she doesn't entertain – and in general women don't arouse my curiosity.'

'You mean you can see no profit in them?' he said, taking my hand, his slow, uneven smile a challenge, an enchantment. 'But you're wrong, Danaë, quite wrong. You should look very carefully at women because they can tell you a great deal about their men. Aemilius Scaurus' wife, for instance, is pious and very sweet, a superb housekeeper, and perhaps that was why it pleased him, sometimes, that you could be tart and not pious at all. And it applies at the very highest level. Our late Emperor Augustus was married to one of the shrewdest and most forceful women the world has ever seen, but, between ourselves, his private tastes were very simple slave-girls who couldn't answer back. Germanicus had eyes for no one but Agrippina, because I don't think he had much choice. She was so popular with the common people, you see – still is, I'm afraid – that they'd never have forgiven him for making her cry. So he was a model husband. And if he was bored to distraction he managed not to show it.'

And I understood that, like so many other influential men, he was enjoying the freedom of gossiping with a woman whose business it was to be totally discreet.

'So,' he said, favouring me once again with his lopsided smile. 'What do you know about Drusus' wife? Not much, I'll wager, except that her jewels are very fine and you think they'd look better on you. Well – I'll tell you. Livilla is regal and rather beautiful, and although her father was only Tiberius' brother, and her mother was the daughter of Mark Antony – Augustus' arch enemy – while Agrippina's mother was Augustus' own daughter, I imagine she's always felt herself a cut above Agrippina. She's Drusus' cousin as well as his wife, and although they've done their duty by each other – for they have a daughter and those little twin boys born the year Germanicus died – one has the feeling that it was no more than that. So, if you do happen to meet him and you turn out to be his style, he has only himself to please. And since you are bound to meet him eventually when he throws himself into the social whirl, and since I happen to know you are already negotiating with his freedman about bookings at his parties – I really don't know how I can serve you.'

And there was my difficulty, for how could I remind him outright of the rumour that Drusus' return had weakened his own influence with Tiberius? Just what that influence was, it was hard to say. He might be no more than an imperial tool to be employed whenever there was dirty work – no more than the man who had held that sword for Piso, the man who guarded Tiberius' privacy like a glorified doorkeeper – but he gave himself airs about it, took liberties with other men's dignity and with their wives. And it was no secret that those haughty aristocrats – like my own Aemilius Scaurus – who considered the political game to be their birthright, were determined to get rid of him, and would cause friction between him and Drusus in any way they could. A woman who was close to Drusus would know, at least, who else was close to him; and such information would be worth its price.

'Oh well,' I said carefully, 'it's true, of course – Drusus will see me somewhere or other. But he'll see so many people – so many women – some of them, perhaps, who wouldn't be very good for him –?'

And again I was delighted by the uncomplicated, audacious peal of his laughter.

'You mean some of them wouldn't be very good for me – say it, my dear, say it, because you're absolutely right. Noble ladies with husbands and brothers to recommend to his notice, daughters of great families who think they have every bit as much right to an empire as the Caesars. Yes, they'll all be swarming around him like greedy little bees because, having failed to turn Tiberius against me, Drusus is their only hope. They'll let him know all about my ambition and my arrogance and they'll try to make him jealous – they'll tell him I have too much influence with his father, that I'm trying to steal the old man's affections, and persuading him to confide in me when he ought to be confiding in his son. Naturally they've started already – these immaculate, stainless gentlemen – and if they can put a woman in his bed to reinforce their opinions, one of their own wives or daughters, then they'd be well pleased. Do you imagine I don't know that?'

'I'm perfectly sure you do.'

'Good,' he said, giving my hand a companionable squeeze, 'you've given me the right answers so far, which is only what I expected, since they told me you were clever. I like you, Danaë. I like you very much. And you like me too, don't you?'

'Oh yes – yes, I do.'

'Well, that never hurts. And you're not sentimental – and I can't tell you what a relief that is. Sentiment bothers me. That's one of the things I admire in Tiberius. That's why he's survived. Germanicus was sentimental, and Agrippina, and their sons show every indication of being the same. You don't govern nations on sentiment. To meet an unsentimental woman is a rare pleasure – a joy.'

'And Drusus? Is he sentimental?'

'Oh, my dear, hardly that. You won't like him, you know. Does that matter?'

'No. All that matters is that he may not like me.'

'Quite so.' He got up, still holding my hand, pulling me to my feet, and although no other part of his body touched mine, I was as aware of him, of the breath in his perfect lungs, the rippling of muscle and energy beneath his tanned skin, the bone and sinew and the good red blood of him, as if I had been a dozen times already in his arms. And it was a holiday, an adventure. It was fun.

'We'll see then,' he said, 'just what we can do. Continue your negotiations with his freedman, and certainly you'll dance at his parties – and mine. And one evening, when you're looking particularly enticing, he may ask me to present you to him. If I do my work well and you do the same ... but I won't insult you by stressing the extent of your obligation to me. You didn't make that hazardous journey from the Subura to the Street of the Yoke-makers without learning that nothing comes free of charge in this life. You understand your commitment, I'm sure of it.'

'I'll be so grateful,' I breathed, 'so grateful –'

'Yes, yes, I know it and I expect it. I think I may even take a little something in advance now – yes? Nothing you can't spare.'

And, as his mouth covered mine, tasting, savouring with a sensualist's leisurely appraisal, I was so spellbound, so intrigued, that I quite forgot he had just recruited me as a spy.

5

I went home on a wave of bliss, sleek and smug and, so far as it was in my nature, almost happy, for although Sejanus couldn't deliver me Drusus and his millions on a silver platter, his quizzical eyes had smiled approval, his cool brain had found a place for me in his delicate, dangerous scheming, and, convinced by now that he was a genius, a magician, I felt myself half-way there.

'I'm at home to no one,' I told Chrysothemis the next morning, for I had no time now for the idle chatterers who gathered every day in my hall. They would still be there when my chance with Drusus had come and gone, and now I planned to devote myself entirely to my face and my clothes and the production of some new dance-routine that would dazzle the city, something erotic without being vulgar, something to suggest there was more to me that breasts and legs and long black hair. And if I succeeded – if he liked me and turned out to be generous – I'd be so kind to them all. I'd send Paris abroad on a grand tour of study and pleasure like a real gentleman, which, in his heart, was what he considered himself to be. I'd find out what Chrysothemis and my old dancing-master Agathon wanted most and see that they got it – a dancing-school of their own, perhaps, where Chrysothemis could be the star, at last, and pay me just a small percentage of the profits in recognition of my goodwill. And I'd have time, then, when I was no longer harassed and hard-pressed, to concentrate on Marpessa. Perhaps I'd take her abroad too, when the great affair was over, to show her the sights, find a man, somewhere, with money of his own, who wouldn't be ashamed to marry the sister of a rich whore, the daughter of a bankrupt actor.

I worked it all out, feeling tender and sentimental in the very way Sejanus despised, regretting all the times I'd been angry or sarcastic or hadn't bothered to listen. But my summons to the palace didn't come that day, or the next, and soon Marpessa was on my nerves again, making too much noise, doing anything she could to catch a glimpse of Marsyas; while Paris, torn between his ambition to be a poet or a philosopher and his natural inclination to do nothing at all, seemed determined to provoke me at every opportunity with his useless, unproductive ideals, making it clear that only Chrysothemis had the intelligence to understand him. And then there was Dion, strutting into my house to borrow my money and turn the heads of my silly maids, spilling wine on my best damask divan-covers and involving me in his quarrels with Erato and Bassus when they came looking for him – Erato to get him back into her bed, and Bassus to get him back into training after a binge in the Subura.

'I'm sick of the lot of you,' I yelled at them, dosing myself with my Egyptian drops. 'One of these nights I'll take too much of this stuff and never wake again.'

And when Paris, raising an eyebrow at Chrysothemis, indicated that he'd heard it all before, I flew at him like a spitting cat.

'You may not miss me, but you'd miss your allowance that I seem to pay out twice every month …'

'I'll leave,' he said. 'Right now.' But it was a threat he made every other day and, disregarding it, I went off in search of other crimes and found Marpessa, sitting in her room with a wooden medallion on a leather thong in her hands, Marsyas' picture painted garishly on both sides of it.

'What's that?' I shrieked, as appalled as if I'd found her nursing a dead rat. 'Get rid of it!' And although my wildness must have taken her aback – for charioteers' pictures are on sale at every boutique under the circus colonnade, and there isn't a girl in Rome who, at one time or other, hasn't slept with one under her pillow – she squared up to me, fists clenched around her treasure, with no intention at all of letting go.

'What's the matter with you? Why shouldn't I have his picture? Everybody has them.'

'I don't care what everybody else has. I won't have trash in my house and that's what it is – that's what he is. If that's all you can think of to buy with the money I give you, then I give you too much and I'll put a stop to it.'

'It's mine,' she screamed, 'because I didn't use your rotten money – I didn't buy it.'

'How did you get it then? Steal it? I wouldn't be surprised.'

'I did not. He sent it to me – yes he did – he did!' And then realizing she had said too much, she hung her head and shuffled her feet, mulish but by no means overcome.

'What are you saying?' I hissed at her, my stomach lurching. 'What have you been up to? I'll shake it out of you, I warn you.'

And, as I advanced towards her, ready to do just that, her sullen eyes shot wide open and she said, quite viciously, 'I haven't been up to anything. It's what you've been up to that's more to the point, because he was here, looking for you, the night of his first race. You were out, of course, like you always are, and Chrysothemis said not to say anything about it, that she'd wait for a good moment to tell you herself. So, since she always knows what's going on and I never do, I thought I'd best keep out of it. Go and ask her, if you don't believe me. He left something with her – I don't know what, because she'd shooed me away by then, just like she always does, and like you always do. But I got a chance to tell him how marvellous he is and he promised to send me a picture. I didn't think he'd remember, because he was drunk – oh, and you should have heard the racket they made. His fans were all over the street and the neighbours didn't like it a bit. Chrysothemis had to go and apologize the next morning. Anyway, he remembered about the picture. A faction servant brought it to the door. And if you make me give it up I'll just go and ask him for another. You make out you don't know him, Danaë, but it sounded to me as if he knew you all right. I'll bet he was the reason you sent me back from Baiae a month early –'

'What else goes on in this house,' I said, 'that I don't know about?' But it was only a way of bringing things to an end, of getting away from her pitiless adolescent eyes; and going out into the passage I leaned against the wall for a moment, breathing hard, and then shouted into thin air, knowing she wouldn't be far away, 'Chrysothemis!'

'Oh dear,' she said, 'I see the child's been talking – well, darling, I'm sorry, but there really hasn't been a moment since it happened when I've cared to burden you with it. You've been so busy, and so tense waiting for this big booking to come up; and although I don't want to get things out of proportion, I just didn't think it fair to give you something else to worry about. That naughty girl, really, she's old enough now to know better. I expect she intended telling you all along, hoping to cause trouble.'

'What did he want?' I asked. 'And what did he say?'

'Oh, my dear, he wanted you, he made that clear enough, and

he didn't say much else to the point. But I shouldn't worry about it. He was quite drunk and crowing like a barnyard cock, very pleased with himself. And all those dreadful people with him. I thought your brother's fans were bad enough but Marsyas seems to bring out the worst in everybody. The disturbance in the street was horrific, and that kind of thing can't do your reputation any good. I'd have thrown him out straight away, if only to stop Marpessa making such a fool of herself, but then I remembered that time in Baiae, and I really didn't know what to do for the best.'

'He's getting at me,' I thought. 'Getting into my life, through the chinks in my walls, through my sister and this woman who knows too much. I'm not safe.' But I merely said, 'He left something for me?'

'Yes – so he did.'

And, talking all the time about the hard job she'd had pacifying the neighbours, letting me know the things they'd said about me and my disorderly life – that one of them had gone so far as to suggest I should be registered with the aediles as a common prostitute – she led the way to her own treasure-chest and put into my hands a single palm branch.

'His first trophy,' she murmured, her face speaking volumes, and as I took it from her it burned my fingers, and then froze them.

It was tattered, now, at the edges from being paraded around the city on that drunken spree, the familiar charioteer's odour of wine and perfume embedded into its fibres, a senseless, vulgar thing – not the first to come my way – and all I had to do was smile, and tell her to throw it out. Yet no effort of will could make me speak the words, standing there, with that pathetic emblem of courage and desperation in my hands.

And, worst of all, I knew exactly why he had come. When he'd done his preening and his crowing, when he'd got it all in his hands, I knew, as surely as if I'd been inside his skin, how hollow he'd been with it. He was equipped for struggling and for losing, for the fight but not for the victory. And, once again, fear of him flooded my mind, for if I had been here that night – instead of with Sejanus – I might not have turned him away.

'Why don't you give the nasty thing to Marpessa,' Chrysothemis suggested sweetly. 'She seems to have made up her mind to worship him – quite natural at her age, I must say – and she can sleep with it under her pillow like all the other silly little girls do.'

And because that was what I should have done – what I badly wanted to do and couldn't – I was ashamed to meet her eyes.

'Well, never mind,' she said. 'But do put it down somewhere, dear, because what I came to tell you is that Drusus' freedman is waiting in the hall.'

And, in that sorry state of self-doubt, I learned that a change of plans had given the Prince an unexpected evening of leisure and that an entertainer was required.

I was taken on a familiar journey to an imposing villa across the Tiber, standing luxurious and aloof in an acre of landscaped garden, for Drusus could hardly amuse himself with entertainers in his father's house on the Palatine; and there the freedman Lygdus, who had eaten my red mullet and taken my money, led me to a dressing-room with the air of a man who had never seen me before.

'You'll have a long wait,' he told me huffily, as if I was to blame. 'They've only just started eating and it's a complicated menu.' And although, in normal circumstances, I would have made sure that whoever was keeping me waiting paid through the nose for it, I was happy now to use the time in finding out the names of the other guests. I would not have been pleased to discover that Erato or Cynthia were out there, queening it on silk couches while I was jittering with nerves; would have been mortified to learn it was an intimate little dinner for Drusus and one of his senator's wives, or even his own. But my maid, who had been on foraging expeditions many a time before, reassured me instantly.

'The Commander of the Praetorian Guard,' she said, and as she began to identify the others, fashionable men I could count on for applause, I knew how eager I was to see Sejanus again.

I had decided to dance 'Leda and the Swan', leaving the swan to their imaginations, an enormous feather fan, and my skill as a mime, giving them, in fact, no more than the portrait of a woman who allows herself to be seduced, wishes she hadn't, and then realizes it might not be such a bad thing after all. Not Leda, really, but Danaë taking no chances, playing the careful housewife who, with important guests to dinner, prepares the dishes she has served many times before and knows how to handle.

Chrysothemis, of course, would have created a true

mythological experience correct in all its nuances, and had, in fact, shaken her head that afternoon at my last-minute rehearsal, and given my brother a glance that had said, 'Really, these great artistes, they have tantrums instead of talent.' But she was sitting at home now, brooding, and I was here, with something in me that could make these people smile when I asked them to, or shed a tear, something easy and colourful to please the senses and make few demands on the intellect; worthless, perhaps, as Paris often implied, but which earned us all our daily bread. And when it was over, 'What an amazing woman,' someone said, and someone else, 'Superb. She never lets us down,' and although they said much the same about their racehorses and their pet monkeys, I had long since come to terms with that.

My only thought was, 'Will he present me? Will he do it now?' But I was back in the dressing-room, in my street clothes and none too pleased about it, before one of Sejanus' servants brought me a request to join his master in the little rose arbour at the bottom of the garden. And then, perversely, I wanted to go home, for Drusus had looked disturbingly like his father in the candlelight, and remembering those tales about the gladiators I was ill at ease.

The garden was dark and full of fragrance, the river just out of sight beyond the wide sweep of lawn and rose-beds, and finding Sejanus already waiting for me, I snaked an arm around his neck and pressed my whole body against his in greeting.

'Don't do that,' he said, laughing, his hand on the small of my back, holding me closer; and dizzy with him all over again, bubbling suddenly with laughter, I said indiscreetly, and perhaps prophetically, 'You should be an emperor. Before I even knew what an emperor was, I thought he'd look like you.'

'Yes,' he said calmly, 'so did I. But that's not why we're here tonight. There's a man you want to meet – someone who looks imperial enough in his own way. And if it should happen that he takes a fancy to you, then let me remind you of this – when those bribes start rolling in from men who want you to whisper something in his ear, by all means take their money, but whisper to me first just who they are and what they want done, however trivial. Yes? Do we have a bargain?'

And the pressure of his iron-hard body told me that if I failed him he'd know about it, and I'd be sorry.

'Of course we have a bargain. You know we do.'

'Yes, yes, I know that very well, and I know how much you need the money, and why you need it. And at this moment I trust you, Danaë, because I know you can see no profit in going against me. In the few months you'll be likely to hold Drusus' interest, I doubt you'll change. Don't think too much about it – just feather your nest, like the exotic little bird you are, and if you should ever feel the temptation to wonder why certain things are important to me and others not, resist it. And then, when it's over, we can still be friends. I'd like that, Danaë. And you'd like it too.'

'Are you going to present me now?'

'Yes, let's see how it goes. If we walk this way we're bound to meet him. He took an after-dinner stroll down to the river – something about a new boat, but the truth is he can't stand a stuffy atmosphere, and he needed the air.'

And for all his loyalty to Drusus' cause, he didn't try to conceal his contempt for a man so fussy and invalidish – so odd – as to be upset by the steams and vapours of an ordinary supper-room.

The garden seemed empty, the house a casket of light and laughter made small by distance, and then quite suddenly four men appeared, walking among the golden autumn trees, identical in the twilight, and I had my first indication of Sejanus' increasing authority when Drusus' companions – each one a man of senatorial rank – fell back a little, in case Drusus should wish to speak to Sejanus alone.

He was tall and dark, a Roman patrician with the high-bridged nose of his class and a long, finely-moulded mouth that smiled automatically, a shade wearily, as he saw us approach. His hair was fashionably cut, his evening robe expensive but very plain, the best quality fabric with no adornment but his own arrogance to proclaim his exalted status; and as he turned his narrow head, his eyes were exactly like his father's, hooded and secretive and unutterably bored.

'Good evening, sir. Is everything all right down there?' Sejanus said briskly, very much the Commander of the Guard who would know exactly what to do if it wasn't, and the imperial mouth moved once again into a smile, not grudgingly, since it was imperial policy just then to be affable, but a shade disdainfully, as if he found all this smiling most unnecessary.

'Perfectly all right,' he said, and glancing at me he raised an enquiring eyebrow, the gesture of a man who invariably has a slave at his elbow to remind him of names and faces. And then, his nomenclator being unavailable, he made the effort himself.

'Ah yes. The entertainer. A beautiful performance – quite unique – my compliments.' And his eyes flickered over me in the way men look at objects which are for sale, when they themselves have no particular wish to buy.

I murmured a word of thanks, made a graceful gesture, making myself light and warm because I remembered he had a regal, cold-hearted wife, but if I had a talent at all it was my ability to read an audience, and I felt I was wasting my time. It was very clear to me that dancing-girls were not at all to this man's high-bred taste, and as he moved on, even though he paused a moment in response to a whispered word from one of his companions and glanced back, first at Sejanus and then at me, I couldn't believe there was a glimmer of hope. And for just an instant my faith in Sejanus' judgement wavered.

He turned the corner, disappeared, and Sejanus glanced down at me, his eyes wicked with glee.

'I told you you wouldn't like him.'

'Well, he doesn't like me, which is more to the point – so there's an end to it, I suppose.'

'My dear girl,' he said, laughing, 'don't be too sure. He doesn't like anybody. He takes after his father. They don't like people. They don't see the necessity for it, or even understand what it means. The strongest emotion he has is curiosity. He may not remember your face, but he'll want to know why I seem to like it so much. He's heard a rumour, you see, that at last I've met my match – didn't you notice Aulus Plautius whispering to him just now, saying, "Have a good look, sir. That's the one"? A girl who can make a man of my reputation suffer a little must have something special about her, wouldn't you think? And the fact that I allowed him to catch me making an assignation with you in the garden when I should really have been in the house paying court to those very wealthy, very useful ladies – that must really have set him wondering. Yes, Danaë, for a moment there you began to doubt me. I'm surprised at you. Did you think I'd leave a thing like this – or anything else, for that matter – to chance?'

'I'll never doubt you again.'

'Please don't. Of course there's more to it than just curiosity. We get along well enough, Drusus and I, but sometimes – well, he'd never stoop to jealousy, but there's something about a self-made man like me that upsets even the best of these high-toned gentlemen – starts them wondering if they could really have made it on their own without their ancestral millions behind them. And although Drusus may not realize it himself, I think he'd be well pleased to take something away from me that I cared about. He'll certainly want to know just what there is in you to fascinate me, and since I won't tell him, he may just come and ask you. So go on home now and think of something clever to say if he does.'

And he went blithely off about his own affairs, leaving me with the uneasy feeling that it was all going to be far more difficult than I'd thought, for truly, I didn't like Tiberius' heir. He was dangerous, I was sure of it, and because I had always thought of danger as something hot and fierce – Marsyas – the chill of Drusus, the impersonal, bloodless quality of him, seemed doubly terrible. I danced for him again several times during that fine, saffron October, watched him moving inside his circle of distance, immaculate and severe, older than his years, saying to everyone what it was right and proper to say, unfailingly courteous yet completely unnerving since no one knew the meaning behind his words. His presence, for all that it was so empty and passionless, imposed such a strain that no hostess could be truly sorry when he left her table halfway through a meal or, as often happened, failed to come at all. I saw hardened socialites twittering with nerves they hadn't believed they possessed when he entered a room, cringing under the lash of his scrupulously correct conversation. I saw self-opinionated politicians stumbling over their words, stopping short like amateurs with no idea what to say next; and beautiful women suddenly aware, under his cool appraisal, of what it must feel like to be plain. And one day when he was presiding over the races, I saw his eyes watching, with clinical concentration, as a man was ploughed into the sand beneath the Imperial Box. And I shuddered, and went home soon after.

But, just the same, when Lygdus, the imperial freedman, called some days later with a more personal invitation, I recognized it as an imperial command which, considering the depth of my commitment to Sejanus, I did not know how to refuse.

6

He was not a man I greatly cared for, Lygdus, this rich man's servant with his honey-gold curls and polished white teeth, his great air of condescension towards poor, freeborn creatures like myself who were forced to live in cramped city flats instead of the gold and marble palaces to which his servitude had accustomed him. But he had been useful to me and now, following him apprehensively into the street, resisting the temptation to tell Chrysothemis what to do with my jewels should I not return, he seemed the only friend I had.

He took me not to the grand villa of the gala receptions, but to a smaller one, an hour's drive from the city gates, and there was no comfort at all in being so far away from home. It was approached by a narrow cart-track, winding away forever through darkness and silence, no lights, no neighbouring houses, no help; yet, although panic touched me briefly, it was a risk I took almost every night of my life, and there was nothing I could do about it now.

'He's just a man, you know,' Lygdus said easily. 'You'd better relax. After all, what can happen to you that hasn't happened already?' And, taking his hand, I got down from the carriage, knowing he was right and that, one way or another, I'd see it through.

There was a guard at the gate but the house was shrouded and dim, an empty shell for an empty man, one grey room leading to another, until a door suddenly snapped open and I was in a circular apartment, blinded by the light of what seemed a hundred lamps, flame leaping on silver and the stark contrast of black and white marble, the chill of the night wind sweeping in from a broad terrace completely open to the weather. And it seemed to me that the entire room, built out on a kind of shelf above the river at a point where the land fell steeply away, was suspended in space between fresh air and deep, slow-moving water.

'The lady, sir,' Lygdus murmured, and the imperial Prince, coming down the few, shallow steps from the terrace, blinded me all over again, for, instead of the correct, plain, evening synthesis I'd expected, he was wrapped in the Oriental robe of some Persian king, gleaming with gold and purple embroideries, stiff with seed-pearls and amethysts. An extravagant garment for any man – any woman – but on a highborn Roman for whom even the wearing of silk was considered decadent and, occasionally, illegal, it was quite shocking; marking him, surely, as a secret sensualist, the worst kind, whose appetites would disgust and amaze me. And then I saw that his face, above those gorgeous folds, was unchanged, guarded and remote and severe as always, marking him as a man who would know how to be cruel.

'How kind of you to come,' he said in faultless Greek, the kind my father spoke on his good days, and when I replied correctly – for, although my Latin was uncertain, this pure Attic was the only decent gift my father had ever made me – I saw a flicker of surprise in him and knew he had expected my accent to be common.

Lygdus disappeared, dismissed by a gesture I barely saw, and, as those hooded eyes looked me over again – cynical, bored, with nothing in them I could recognize as desire – the dry chill of him withered my professionalism away, leaving me with no defence.

'You were recommended to me very highly,' he said, not troubling to conceal the yawn in his voice. 'So highly, in fact, and so persistently, that it became a matter of courtesy for me to see for myself.'

And as his voice trailed away into thin air, finding nothing more it wished to say to me, I understood that Sejanus had not really deceived him – as perhaps a warm man can never entirely deceive a cold one – and that I was here quite simply because there are times when it is less annoying to say yes, and get it over with, than to say no.

'May I look at the river?' I said stupidly, as if I'd never seen it before, and, barely waiting for his languid consent, I went tripping up the steps to the terrace, to find the way blocked by a bed, in itself unusual in that chilly, windy place, but such a bed as I had never seen before, the couch of an ancient pharaoh, framed in carved ivory, covered with a shimmering fabric of gold, embroidered all over with purple flowers and the illegal magic symbols of the East. And, sitting in state upon it, a large cat, blinking at me with its yellow eyes, a jewelled collar around its elegant black throat.

It got up slowly, velvet body stretching, claws heedlessly flexing themselves in that gorgeous material, staring at me with a disdain equal to its master's, and once again I was thrown into confusion, for he was not at all the man for that fantastic robe, this priceless bed, and it worried me. 'He's odd,' I thought, 'odd and dangerous like his father, and perhaps all the things they say about them are true. This is going to be painful, and difficult. It's going to be bad.'

But all at once a more present danger faced me as I saw there was no railing of any kind around the terrace. It hung in mid-air, a frail platform jutting out into the night, while below it the river promised, if not certain death, at least a perilous landing.

'But that's dangerous,' I said, the hair rising on my neck as I became aware of this strange man close behind me; and, smiling faintly, he walked past me to the very edge and stood looking down.

'Very dangerous. But that has an appeal all its own. Don't you feel it?'

'I do not. What kind of a fool – I mean, no, not at all.'

'Come here.'

He held out a hand and, because I had spent my childhood trying to keep pace with Dion, and because this man's authority was irresistible in any case, I let him draw me close beside him on his precarious perch, gritting my teeth and vowing that if he pushed me over I'd take him with me.

'You're afraid,' he told me, observing my fear as clinically as he had observed his sword-fighters' agonies, and, closing my eyes, I shook my head.

'I'm not afraid,' I thought in an effort to keep my crumbling nerve. 'Why should I care about heights? I've chased my pig of a sister along the tenement rooftops often enough, and belted her when I caught her. And I can swim.'

And it wasn't until I heard the dry, vaguely unpleasant sound of his laughter that I realized I had spoken the words out loud.

'Really? What entertaining things one learns, at the oddest moments, about the humbler sections of one's compatriots. But you're afraid, my dear, whether you like it or not. Well, it's an emotion that's easily aroused, and since emotion is supposed to play a part in what we have in mind tonight, then fear will do well enough. I really wouldn't know what else to suggest. My dear girl, I'm not going to push you over – not yet, at any rate – afterwards perhaps?'

I stepped back hastily and, quite mechanically, he drew me towards him, his hands cold on my skin, the temperature and odour of his body so faint, so distant, that I felt confused and clumsy, a beginner, out of my class. I felt like a tart, and it gave me pain.

'Well,' he said, his smile gone, 'I don't require you to be heroic, just obliging. I must tell you – I make a point of telling everyone on these occasions – that I always find the first sexual contact with a new partner somewhat unsatisfactory. Shall we get it over with? We may even enjoy it the second time – if we get that far.'

And there was no answer to that. I took off my clothes, sacrificing allure to speed, and got into that scandalous bed with my eyes tight shut, shrinking for the first time in years from a stranger's hands, a stranger's breath, behaving like an amateur and damning myself for a fool; and there was an ugly moment when I knew that if he didn't kiss me, if he simply took me like a street-walker or a slave-girl and turned away, my nerve would snap and I'd do something stupid like bursting into tears, or something fatal like slapping his face. But, after a certain hesitation, his mouth came expertly if not amorously on mine and I settled my body beneath his, closing my mind to the impersonal chill of him – to the astonishing, shaming suspicion that he didn't much want me either – and thought about Cynthia and Erato, and Sejanus, and what I'd say to them tomorrow. I expected some peculiar demand, something bizarre and embarrassing I wouldn't want to think about afterwards, but instead – and perhaps this was the greatest shock of all – his love-making was straightforward, not affectionate, not particularly considerate, but (although the word only occurred to me later) wholesome. And even when it was over and he turned away from me with his face in the pillow, I was not alarmed, for he wasn't the first man I'd known to be disgusted with himself, to feel sweaty and soiled in those vulnerable moments after physical pleasure. And with the knowledge of another person that intimacy brings, I was amazed yet again, for I believed he had revealed himself as a man who needed – whether he liked it or not – rather more than I had given; a man, perhaps, who found it convenient, safer, to buy love and had taught himself to live with its imperfect satisfactions.

I waited, like the good working mistress I was, for him to relax and then, when he finally turned towards me, because he looked younger and kinder than before, and because awkward situations always loosen my tongue, I said, 'That wasn't really so unsatisfactory.'

'I'm delighted to hear it. Perhaps next time you'll be less afraid.'

'I'm not afraid.'

'Yes, you do keep on telling me that, and of course it can't be true. My dear girl, I must inspire you with terror, and if not, then I'd like to know why. A man of my authority and my reputation – I assume you can read? Then you must have seen the elegant little obscenities they write about me, scrawled all over the city walls. The last thing I heard was that I have gladiators butchered at my supper table and do odd things with the remains. They say my father rapes ten-year-old girls three at a time – and, even considering his rather advanced years, you can't be sure he doesn't. Oh yes, you were afraid. I expect it. I judge people by the way they carry it off. And you handled it well. In fact you gave me two surprises – you have courage, and your grammar is quite exceptional. May I know who taught you to speak Greek like that?'

'My father.'

'Indeed.'

'Yes – he was an actor.'

I saw disdain, disappointment, in his face, for, in spite of his Persian robe and the silk cushions, he was a Roman who couldn't believe the stage to be a fit place for any freeborn man. And then, making the best of it, he said, 'Well, so much for your Greek, but I can't deny your beauty. I'd heard so much about you that I'd prepared myself for a disappointment. And perhaps, for reasons of my own, I wanted to be disappointed. But you're beautiful – perfectly lovely, and with a hint of something else in you that may not really be there at all, but which one could spend a pleasant hour searching for. If you wish to sleep please don't hesitate. I may need you again before morning.'

And, turning his back, his face towards the cold night, the sharp-scented whip of October, he disappeared inside himself, leaving me quite alone.

I woke, an age later, abruptly, as one does in strange places, disturbed by the breeze coming in from the river, and by something else, something worse. I was chilled to the bone, but the man beside me – who had been so cool, so neutral to my touch – was drenched with sweat, heat rising from his body like steam. And as I peered forward to look at him, the odd, wheezing sound that was his breath erupted into a cough, and with the jerky, unco-ordinated movement of pain he was on his feet, gripped by the most fearful convulsion I had ever seen. He was choking, his chest torn apart by the violence of the spasms, an attack so absolute that there was nothing I could really do but wait until it was over, and wonder what would happen to me in the morning if they found him dead.

'Get out,' he gasped when he could speak. 'Leave me – at once.'

But I didn't know where to go, and it has never been in my nature to walk away from human distress. He may have been an imperial Caesar but in that moment, so far as I was concerned, he was a man who could hurt and bleed like any other – a man who had just made love to me, pleasantly enough. And in any case, in times of crisis I have always felt that I know best.

He fell back on to the bed again, his chest heaving, hurting, and I said, 'No. Sit up. You mustn't lie flat.'

As I put out a hand to touch him he knocked it aside and began coughing again, coughing and cursing and struggling, with no more sense and no more idea how to help himself than my young brother, so that at last, kneeling beside him – afraid no longer – I slipped an arm around his shoulders and forced him, with the gritty strength beneath my dancer's grace, to be steady.

'Sit up and let me prop the cushions behind your back. Do stop thrashing about. You'll use up too much air. I do know what I'm talking about. I know about breathing. I'm a dancer, remember. So do sit up. You'll feel much better.'

'Go away,' he said, but he was drowning in sweat, his face grey with pain and his desperate effort to deny pain, to cancel it out by the force of his will, and there was nothing he could do but close his eyes, cancelling me out too, since he lacked the strength to dispose of me in any other way. And, immovable – as any woman worth her salt should be at such times – I arranged his cushions, talking all the time and saying nothing, making my voice into a lullaby, a reminder that someone, however lowly, was there, until gradually the rasping of his breath began to ease and his body's tight, ferocious protest relaxed into simple exhaustion.

He lay then, resting, composing himself, refreshing his lungs with the raw, October breeze, aching inwardly, I knew, from the mauling of that dreadful cough, taming it with the brutal concentration of a man dominating a wild tiger. Then, when it had gone snarling and sullen back to its lair, his eyes opened and he said coldly, 'Thank you. You may leave now. I am perfectly well.'

'Yes, of course.'

'You were most efficient – one wonders, is there no end to your uses?'

'Oh, it's not the first time I've seen a thing like that. My young brother coughs every winter, and never fails to get into a state about it. Silly boy, all he needs to do is relax and breathe deeply. I'm always telling him so.'

'Indeed. So you have a brother, have you, as well as a sister and a father? How diverting. One thinks of people like you as coming singly, one fails to credit you with the concept of family – yet I suppose you must come from somewhere, and be related to somebody. But your domestic affairs, child, hardly arouse my enthusiasm...'

He got up slowly, his face haggard, a hundred years older than it had been an hour ago; and, understanding what it cost him to hold himself erect like that without coughing, I wondered why he thought it worth the trouble. 'I must warn you,' he began, 'that I would be displeased – seriously so – if one word of what you have seen tonight should ever be made public. I would not be kind to you, and I can think of no one who could offer you protection against me. And that would be a pity, since you are a nice little thing...'

But there are moments in my life of supreme recklessness when, like my brother Dion, I care nothing for the consequences, and, raising my hand, I told him with one perfect, professional gesture, knowing quite well it could be my last, to be silent.

'Please – there's no need at all to threaten me. I know perfectly well you could have me murdered on the way home, and the fear of that is quite enough to make me silent. But it's not necessary, because there are some things one just doesn't talk about. You have your code of conduct, and you must allow me to have mine. All I've seen is that you have a cough – well, my brother got his from sleeping on damp mattresses in a tenement attic, but most people we knew coughed their guts up all winter anyway, and we didn't think anything of it. If you were impotent, I wouldn't advertise it to the world and I could understand why you wouldn't want people to know about that. I don't really understand why it matters to you about your cough. But I see it does, and that's enough. I understand that it's personal, and although I may enjoy telling everybody how much you paid me for tonight – whatever it's going to be – personal details aren't for sale. I'm an actor's daughter, and perhaps to a Roman one can't get lower than that. But the odd thing is that I don't feel low. I don't think I ever have. If that surprises you – well – you're a clever man and I imagine you can recognize the truth.'

He stood for a while looking at me, his eyes unreadable, his face, in the shadows, so like his father's that I was afraid of him again. Then he lay down wearily, carefully, as if he was glad to be back in bed again.

'You could pour me some wine,' he said.

And as I ran to fetch the cup and put my hand over his to steady him as he drank, I understood that there are times when even a prince doesn't care to be alone.

'Don't – fuss – me,' he said through his teeth, and then, 'You're cold. Get back into bed, and put another pillow behind my back. Not there – lower down, you're supposed to be an expert. And now talk to me. I won't sleep again tonight, so why should you? Tell me about that tenement, and the family you surely haven't got – and tell me why I should believe a word you say. You're a woman, and a Greek of sorts – a sensible man can have no faith in either.'

7

The next day, or the day after, when the news leaked out, I would be the sensation of the city. I knew it, part of me gloried in it, for even if he never asked to see me again, I'd been the first and my value would rise accordingly. But, just the same, I came home that smoky October morning as restless as a sick cat, cold and weary and not knowing what ailed me. I had gone to Drusus expecting to find a monster, a pervert, and instead I had seen immense courage and self-control, a wry, clear-sighted humour, a living man beneath the ice. All through that day I was burdened by the notion that he deserved far more than a greedy girl from the Subura. And since I was not accustomed to feeling humble, it troubled me.

I had an engagement to dance that night at a noble house on the Esquiline, and afterwards, unwilling to go home and face Chrysothemis' enquiring eyes, I remembered an invitation from Erato and had myself carried to her door. Her house behind the Temple of Diana showed an unpretentious face to the world, its discreet entrance squeezed between two shops, her narrow vestibule giving no hint of the opulence to come. But once past the bare, marbled hall, one had the impression of walking inside a treasure-chest, each room a jewel in itself, and Erato the most costly of all.

She came running to meet me, winged sandals on her quick, excited feet, feathers at the hem of her robe, feathers in her hair held in place by sapphire pins, her smile so dazzling that I knew she'd heard a whisper about Drusus and had decided to swallow her mortification, choosing, if she couldn't get close to him herself, to be the very dearest friend of the woman who could.

'I've been waiting for you, darling. And Dion is here – he wants to see you too.'

But, as I followed her down a flower-filled passage to the cosy room she reserved for her friends, my brother gave me no more than a passing glance, his mind being fully occupied with the girls on either side of him, a pair of the young hopefuls Erato always had around her.

'They amuse him,' she said, her arm still through mine. 'And that's the great thing – keeping him amused. It's boredom that makes him so naughty – I've often noticed it. And, because he's lazy too, if he can have his fun here, in my house, he's not likely to stir himself and go looking elsewhere. That may sound like defeat, dear, but actually it's called wisdom.'

And, tripping into the centre of the room, she called out 'Here's Danaë' and abandoned me to my own devices.

Silver-haired Chloe, her cithara at her side as an indication that she too had just come from an engagement, nodded to me vaguely, one or two others raised a hand or a smile and, to avoid Cynthia and the man with her – who was certainly Marsyas – I went quickly to Xanthe, cheerful and uncomplicated, who in her leisure hours had few interests beyond her children and her horses.

'I suppose you've heard,' she told me at once, 'that Valerius Messalla has given me his new mare – that lovely chestnut he was showing off on Mars Field and vowing he'd never part with?' and as she began to supply details of how she'd wheedled the animal out of him and how torn she was now between the pleasure of showing it off on Mars Field herself, and the sound common sense of sending it to her stud farm in Etruria, I forced my eyes to look at Cynthia.

She was sitting in a shadowy corner, a lamp just above her head crowning the abundant richness of her hair, searching out the fire at the heart of her emeralds. Marsyas lay with his head on her lap, in a black silk tunic with a gold border, gold bracelets on his arms, gold chains and medallions and lucky charms around his neck and, among them, a single emerald that was certainly Cynthia's. He looked everything he'd said he'd be, a star charioteer, wild and beautiful and dangerous, his thick hair expertly curled, his body rich with scented oil, pampered by an expensive woman who would give him free use of her fortune and of herself for as long as her passion endured. He had everything now that Dion had. He was the substance of every tenement lad's dream, yet his face, above all his flamboyant splendour, looked altogether spent, as if he'd reached a point of exhaustion – of staleness – where sleep was no longer of any use to him. And feeling again that treacherous, inward opening of my body towards his, I shuddered and turned away.

'What I need now is a good stallion,' Xanthe said, startling me back to attention, 'and then, with my Spanish mare and this new chestnut of Messalla's, I really think I could make a fortune.'

'Oh yes,' I said. 'Absolutely –', but her words touched no more than the surface of my mind and I knew I couldn't stay in this room for long, sipping Erato's sickly-sweet wine, with Marsyas lying there while Cynthia coiled her golden tentacles around him, couldn't stay and admit that although I was afraid to take him myself, I didn't want anyone else to have him. And, struggling with my own folly, it completely slipped my mind that I had spent last night with a prince.

'You'll come and see me in Etruria, won't you, Danaë?' Xanthe chattered on. 'You'd love it there. The outdoor life – there's nothing to beat it. I just ride all day with the children and fall into bed, worn out and alone, every night – and it's sheer luxury. Come next summer.'

As I agreed that I would, a hand fell on her shoulder, dark fingers with an emerald ring on one of them, and Marsyas – awake now, his eyes glittering – was kneeling on the couch behind her.

'What's that about a stallion?' he said, and he began to nibble her neck and her ripe, bare shoulders, as horses do.

'Now just stop that,' she said placidly, 'or we'll have Cynthia scratching my eyes out – not that it would bother you. You'd have a good laugh, wouldn't you?'

Cynthia – not in the least worried about me, since he'd had me already and would have paid for his emerald ring and his pendant by telling her he didn't want me again – got up, her eyes green daggers in Xanthe's breast, and put her hand on Marsyas' arm in a way that could not be misunderstood.

'I'm going now,' she said, bending towards him. 'I have an appointment I can't put off, but I won't be long. So you'll go home, and wait –'

'Will I?'

'Yes, you will.' And bending nearer she pressed her open mouth against his and then, flexing her long, pointed nails like a cat, sank every one of them into his bare arm.

His fingers clamped themselves around her wrist, twisting her hand away, his mouth, for a moment, quite ugly as he saw she'd drawn blood. But Cynthia was bold and brave and wouldn't have minded a public fight, and, laughing, he got to his feet, flung an arm around her and drew her head slowly towards his, so that I saw his tongue tasting her mouth, her teeth clamp themselves briefly on his lower lip, before they locked themselves together in an embrace that deserved a round of applause.

'Yes, perhaps I'll go home and wait.'

'I rather thought you would.'

And it was a scene I'd witnessed a thousand times before, the professional beauty playing at love with her tame lover; a younger man getting what he could, considering a few scratches, a few tantrums, a small price to pay.

But he could have done no more than see her to her litter, for Xanthe had scarcely returned to her description of the good grazing in Etruria before he was back, pushing himself between us, asking Xanthe why she didn't go and talk to Chloe. And when she did he said to me, as if he was merely continuing a conversation that had been going on for days, 'I told you I was good, didn't I?'

'Yes, you told me.'

'And you saw my debut?'

'Yes, as it happens. My brother was racing that day.'

'So he was. And I seem to remember coming to your house afterwards and leaving you my palm-branch. I left it somewhere, anyway.'

'People are always bringing me things.'

'Yes – but a first trophy, that's like virginity. You should have acknowledged it.'

'You can have it back. I didn't ask you for it.'

'You kept it, then?'

'Did I? Oh – possibly – I don't know. I can ask my maids.'

'Or your sister. She'll know all about it. She wouldn't throw my virginity away. Her own, maybe –'

'Well, she won't be throwing it in your direction, that much I am sure of. And having said that, I don't think there's much else I care to say.'

'Why?' he said, abominably pleased with himself, a typical taunting, bragging charioteer now that his fatigue was gone. 'Because I ditched you and went back to Cynthia? Well, you were going to ditch me, weren't you? And Cynthia's what I'm used to. She knows about alley-cats. She feeds me and keeps me warm. She even loves me.'

'Yes, so I imagine – until the next one comes along.'

'And what's wrong with that? It's good enough for me. But she loves me now, all right – look what she's given me to prove it.' And he tapped the emerald, swinging against his chest.

'She's given you nothing. She's just lent you a few jewels that's all, to put her mark on you, and she'll have them back soon enough when she starts to fancy somebody else.'

'Oh yes,' he agreed, 'I quite see that – it's common practice – but I know, and you know, and she ought to know, that I'll have sold them long before that happens.'

'She'll have you beaten up, then, or get somebody to put a knife in your back. So you'd better watch out.'

But since men had been coming after him with knives for most of his life, he brushed my warning aside as a matter of small concern. Watching him playing the peacock, preening and crowing like the rest of his kind, I found it easier to meet him at this superficial level; and if I hadn't been so ridiculously shaken I would have been grateful.

I got up, arranged my draperies, gave him a dazzling, disinterested smile, said my good-byes to Erato and Dion and to anyone else who noticed I was leaving; but when I went outside he was waiting by my litter and, telling myself it was merely to avoid a scene in the street, I let him walk beside me. I would have to endure him, I thought, like illness, until it was done. One way or another I would have to share this city with him, and learn not to care. And if I couldn't kill this great stirring and softening inside me, this feeling of terrible empathy, then I would have to control it.

I didn't ask him into my house, didn't even look at him as I got down from my litter, but I didn't tell my bearers to chase him away and bar the door, and he was still behind me as I entered the hall.

My maid took my palla and disappeared, my bearers went to their rest, my doorkeeper went back to his dogs and his warm corner, leaving us alone; yet, as he shrugged his cloak from his shoulders, letting it fall to the floor in the gesture of display one artiste recognizes in another, and stood there, peacock-vain in his silk and gold and Cynthia's jewels, I knew that someone else was there too, a presence in the shadows behind me, unseen, but watching, listening. Chrysothemis, I thought, prying as usual, or someone else, sent by Sejanus, to make certain I wasn't wasting his master's time. But if Marsyas had any sense of being observed he paid no heed to it.

'So,' he said, holding his arms wide, 'the first time I came to a house of yours I was in borrowed clothes and you were complaining about cheap scent. Have I done better tonight?'

And walking towards me he stood quite still, not touching me, but something in him penetrating the pores of my skin, an invasion and a gradual conquering, although I was fighting still, fighting hard.

'Make it real for me, Danaë,' he said. 'Don't let me down,' and his bought mouth and my bought mouth came together almost clumsily, like the uncertain experimenting of children. And not even the remembrance of that hidden watcher stopped me from raising a loving, fearful hand and touching his face.

'That's right,' he murmured. 'Yes, that's right –' and once again the lines of my body blurred, a painful, irresistible metamorphosis of part of myself into part of him, part of him into part of me, so that the sudden tumult in the street, the loud knocking at my door, was a little thing, and very far away.

'All right, all right,' I heard my doorkeeper grumbling, calling up his dogs, and before I had time to warn him that no one could be admitted the room was invaded by flickering torches and the noisy arrogance of rich men's servants, with Lygdus, the imperial freedman, in the midst of it, draped in a robe that was almost, but not quite, a royal shade of purple.

'Well, well,' he said. 'Here I am. And if you're surprised then you're not the only one, because I never thought he'd want to see you again so soon – if at all. But don't let it go to your head – he's not been well and he's peevish – my word, he's peevish.'

And then, glancing at Marsyas, 'Not a good moment for you, dear? Well, I'm sorry about that, but what's to be done? You could say you were indisposed, or I could say you were not at home. He wouldn't be pleased, and he might not believe it, but I don't know that he'd actually do anything about it. It's up to you.'

But was it? I didn't look at Marsyas, could in no way cope with him at that moment, but behind me, in the shadows, I knew someone was still there. And although it was probably Chrysothemis, whose interest was only personal and spiteful, it could be a maid of mine with a handful of Sejanus' gold in her purse, or a litter-bearer in a hurry to buy his freedom. And if Sejanus learned I had refused an imperial invitation which he'd taken trouble to procure, I knew I would be called to account for it.

'I'll come – naturally,' I murmured, and Lygdus nodded and smiled.

'Naturally – not much of a choice, really.' But I knew that for the rest of my life I would never be certain of the answer I might have given had it not been for that listener behind me, that unseen presence holding me to a commitment that now was both a burden and an escape.

'Well then, shall we proceed?' Lygdus said brightly. 'A little tidying up, perhaps, won't go amiss.' And then, his glance sliding to Marsyas again, 'My dear fellow, it comes to me now just where I've seen you before. My word, I'm not a racing man myself – the noise and the glare, not my kind of thing at all – but that last win of yours – absolutely sensational! I shall certainly come and see you again.'

'Yes – you do that,' Marsyas said, a deliberate coarseness in his tone, once more the swaggering, rough-grained charioteer giving the customer what he wanted; and, seeing the flash of excitement in Lygdus' face, one of his black eyes closed in a wink that promised, 'Any time. You'll know where to find me.' And I turned cold and sick.

'Yes,' Lygdus said, flustered, and rather pleased about it, 'indeed I will – I'll treat myself to that. We could have dinner perhaps, afterwards – at your faction club?'

'Why not?'

And, taking up his attitude of peacock-preening, letting us both see what we were missing, Marsyas stood for an instant in the doorway, smiling, glittering – not speaking a word to me – and was gone.

'The dear boy has left his cloak behind,' Lygdus murmured, already exploring the possibilities of picking it up and returning it, but I reached it first and, holding the heavy, empty thing in my arms, Marsyas' scent once again inside my head, I had a feeling almost of bereavement.

'Milesian wool,' Lygdus said, fingering a corner of the cloth. 'The very best quality. Heaven knows what it must have cost, and I wouldn't like to hazard even a guess about who paid for it. So put it away carefully, dear, until he comes back for it. Yes, I know, you don't have to tell me – these affairs of the heart ... I do understand about feelings, because my own are rarely less than boiling-point – very rarely – so I sympathize. That's one thing these rich men will never allow us to have, our feelings. I don't just mean Drusus, because they're all the same. Come on, dear, tidy up those curls a little. A splash of rose-water on the hands and face – nothing like it. And the cloak, dear, do put it down. You can't sleep with it under your pillow tonight –'

'No,' I said, suddenly very brisk and bright. 'Not tonight, and not ever,' and walking forward, I called 'Chrysothemis' into the shadows. But no one answered, and, going into my room with the cloak still in my arms, I folded it carefully and put it away, uncertain of what I meant to do with it. I didn't think he would come back to claim it. I couldn't imagine myself sending for him or going to find him, and to leave it with Cynthia, whose property it probably was, seemed quite impossible. I would just keep it a while, give myself time to think it over. But when I came home the next morning the cloak was gone, and many years were to pass before I learned who had taken it.

8

'I'm afraid it's out of the question,' I heard Chrysothemis say coolly to the man of senatorial family who had been waiting for some time in my hall. 'She's leaving for the country almost at once, and hasn't a moment to spare. I'm sure she'd like to see you, but we can't always do just as we'd like, can we?'

And then, coming into my room, feather-light and serene in white muslin, wearing the pearls I'd given her for consolation when I sent Paris to Athens in the spring, she smiled and shook her head indulgently.

'Really, the man simply won't go away. But don't worry about it, dear. I'll deal with him.'

And I was in no doubt at all that she found my success – which enabled her to 'deal' with these men of rank and fashion – immensely satisfying.

In the old days before Drusus, when I had gone shopping in the Via Nova or on Mars Field, Chrysothemis had always guided me to the boutiques where she could be sure of drawing a small commission for her trouble, but now the jewellers and the merchants of Oriental silks and embroideries, the sandal-makers and the dealers in perfumes and cosmetics, came to me; and since it was Chrysothemis who first inspected their wares and decided what would be of interest and what would not, I could only conclude she was doing very well.

There were many others who wished to ingratiate themselves. Men who had once dismissed my skill as a dancer as mere froth and frivolity – much preferring Chloe's mournful cithara – had discovered now, during these eight months of imperial favour, that I possessed a rare talent, something without which none of their dinners and receptions could hope to succeed; and I was so much in demand, there was such a quantity of dealing and scheming with Chrysothemis in my hallway, so many freedmen bearing invitations and gifts, that my house was in chaos, my staff on the verge of collapse, and Paris had been glad to take his leave.

'Aulus Plautius sent his freedman six times,' Chrysothemis would tell me, 'then he sent flowers and fruit and a bearded mullet on a silver dish – very good silver too, very heavy – and then he came himself. I imagine he wants something doing for that son of his – the one who didn't get the command in Germany. Well, I hinted to him that you never meddle, but he's very well off and if he enjoys giving things away then I really can't see the harm –'

And so Plautius' silver dish was put with all the others, its value carefully checked and noted down by Chrysothemis, while I – having mentioned the matter to Sejanus if he happened to ask and if I happened to remember the man's name – forgot it entirely.

'They amaze me,' I told Sejanus more than once. 'They keep on hinting at things they'd like me to do, and they're so terribly discreet about it that half the time I don't even know just what they mean – so I couldn't do it even if I wanted to. You'd think they'd know, by now, wouldn't you, that they're wasting their money? And what worries me is that when this is all over and I'm just a dancer again, somebody is going to remember just how much he paid out for nothing, and ask for it back.'

But Sejanus only laughed, telling me, 'Keep on as you are. You're doing fine.' And so, this hyacinth-blue June morning I was content to leave my house and my sister in Chrysothemis' tender care and set off for a day, or possibly two, in the country.

The villa was at Laurentum, fifteen miles from the city, an easy journey for a man like Drusus who needed the escape of fresh air and uncluttered rooms, and the luxury of being able to cough out loud – who needed, in the tumult of his public life, an oasis, a Persian robe, a pedigree cat, an expensive woman, to make him feel different from his official self.

There was a sandy road, dwindling away to nothing, an empty landscape until one met a fringe of tall trees, a high, ivy-clad wall, thick hedges, and the house, open as all his houses were, to the weather. There was very little inside it, a couch here and there, white silk cushions on a framework of silver, an alabaster bowl of white flowers, a fragile table inlaid with mother-of-pearl, bearing one exquisite piece of carved ivory, a view, wherever one looked, of sky and water, calm lily-ponds and the feathery jets of fountains jewelled with sunlight: and now, on this lovely day, the new season's roses, white and cream and the palest, most delicate, of pinks.

As the carriage entered the gates and Lygdus came out to meet me, I felt again the uneasy blending of apprehension and excitement Drusus always aroused in me. I was no closer to him now than I had been eight months ago, when I had come to him still bruised by Marsyas. He was a body, a face, a closed smile, refinement and good taste, arrogance, an occasional show of ill-temper, a needle-sharp wit that wasn't always kind; easily bored, very apt to withdraw quite suddenly into a silence that was like a solid wall set with bitter spikes. He was all these things and, threaded though them, a rare moment of humanity, amazing me every time it appeared, because when it receded I never expected it to come back again.

Other men had told me in vulnerable moments about their childhood miseries and fears, had admitted to loving parents or children – or hating them – had exposed the needs of the heart as well as the body, and shown themselves better or worse than their face value: but Drusus told me nothing. 'Talk,' he would say on the nights when his new responsibilities as consul and his social obligations had strained his nerves beyond any hope of rest. 'Tell me about those non-existent brothers of yours, and that abominable little sister. Amuse me.' And so, on the many nights when he couldn't sleep, I'd walked with him in his garden across the Tiber, entertaining him with my family's escapades and philosophies, inventing more when truth ran out. And contrary to even my own expectations, I had survived the winter and won through to this glorious June.

'Oh, so it's you again,' Lygdus said, helping me down from the carriage rather gingerly, liking me to know he didn't care to handle this kind of merchandise. 'I keep thinking we've got over you, but I suppose we've been too busy lately, with an empire to govern, to bother making changes. Well, and how long are you staying this time, or didn't he tell you?'

'No. But I expect he told you, so do stop fussing. You know you have a soft spot for me, Lygdus, so you may as well admit it.'

'Don't you be too sure, my girl,' he said, although it was quite true. 'I don't allow myself to get too fond of my master's fancies, because they come and go and you'll be no different from the rest. He's easily bored, always has been, and he's curious, and that doesn't make a faithful man. He spent a long time, the other day, talking to that new wife of Valerius Messalla, and a fetching little thing she is too. I could see he was impressed. Anyway, who's he bringing with him today? Or didn't he tell you that either?'

I shook my head, not caring.

'Well, three couches in the small dining-room – that's what I've been told, so he's bringing somebody. I suppose you know he had dinner with his wife last night?'

But wives were none of my concern and, kissing Lygdus lightly on the cheek because I knew he didn't like it, I went into the house to bathe, to adorn myself, and to wait.

He was late, having been detained by some meeting of the Senate, and when he finally appeared, Sejanus was with him – Sejanus, carrying the spicy scents of outdoors in the folds of his cloak, tanned and tough with the gritty endurance of sun-baked rock, and Drusus, impersonal and faintly weary, conveying nothing, so that I had no idea whether he was pleased to see me, whether he wanted me – no idea at all.

'Danaë,' Sejanus said, his warm hands instantly clasping mine, 'I won't trespass long on your time. Just a little unfinished business – and since I was riding this way in any case. Shall we get it over with, sir, and then you can have your dinner in peace?'

'Oh, my dear fellow, I think not.' Drusus sounded listless, indolent, the languid aristocrat careless of anyone else's convenience. 'Your energy does you credit. Believe me, one finds oneself exhausted sometimes just watching you. But I think not. I really must bathe and change, and dine too, I'm afraid, before I can give my mind to anything else.'

He smiled, almost yawned, and Sejanus smiled too – having no choice in the matter – but I felt the snap of impatience in him, heard his mind say, 'Is that how he means to govern his empire – after a bath and a good dinner?' And I thought it, in some ways, a pity that he had no way of knowing, as I had, that the dust of the road was still in Drusus' chest, and that after a day in the Senate, talking, smiling, issuing those crisp, impeccably phrased commands, dispensing the cool justice that brought him small popularity even with those who admitted he was invariably right, he needed that hour in the bath, and another in his doctor's hands, to be fit for anything at all. And, as always, I closed my mind to the thought – the certain knowledge – that this recurring ailment of Drusus' would be of interest to Sejanus and that he would be displeased with me should he ever find out I had kept it from him. For I had told him everything else, supplied him with the names of every man who had offered me gifts, repeated to him the loyal words they had paid me to whisper to Drusus. And I could see a distinct pattern emerging.

I knew that Sejanus, who would have been instantly dismissed from any court ruled by the strait-laced Germanicus, was becoming painfully aware of Tiberius' advancing years and failing health, and that since Germanicus' widow Agrippina – every bit as strait-laced as her husband – was Drusus' cousin, it was essential to keep them, and the men who surrounded Agrippina, apart. Sejanus had no intention, on Tiberius' death, of sinking back into obscurity, of finding himself open to the vengeance of the men he had insulted in the Emperor's lifetime, and it was vital for him to know whether or not Drusus was inclined to listen to the tales Agrippina's party were now spreading against him. And suddenly, sitting in the summer garden, I realized my position and felt my stomach lurch into panic. It had been a game, the only coin I had been able to think of which would purchase Sejanus' help, nothing to be taken seriously. Yet now – when I couldn't withdraw – I was left stupidly to wonder, 'Have I harmed anyone? Is anyone going to harm me?' And as I concluded that it was very likely, Sejanus himself came to join me on the garden seat.

'Well, well,' he said, far less respectful now that Drusus was not there to see. 'You're doing very well, aren't you? Better than we had any right to expect. Eight months and no signs of flagging. Clever girl. And I believe you actually like him.'

'I believe I do. Does that – matter?'

'To me? Not at all. Why should it?'

'Well, liking is sentimental, isn't it? And you don't like sentimental women.'

'Ah yes, but that's only when they get sentimental over me – which is a sheer waste of time on everybody's part. But in this case I don't mind a bit. I think it's charming, and useful – it could even hold him to you a little longer, if he's noticed it, that is.'

'Yes – well – for as long as it lasts, then.'

He gave me a brief military salute. 'Indeed – for as long as it lasts. Now then, we haven't much time, because he'll be along presently, and there's a little something you can do for me – if you will – and if the opportunity arises. You've been very good so far, dropping names and telling me more with your chatter than you probably realize. You chatter to him quite a lot too, don't you? Do you think, one of these nights – but I'll allow you to choose your moment – you could casually mention the subject of betrothals?'

'Betrothals?' And I was so taken aback that he laughed and took my hand.

' Yes – and why not? Such a lovely season, this early summer. Is it any wonder that betrothals – and marriages – are in the air?'

'Not in the air I breathe.'

'No, I suppose not. I wonder if you appreciate your good fortune? Tricky things, marriages. One can win, or lose, a great deal and not just money either, even though money is the reason one commits the folly in the first place. My own wife – believe me – is exceptional. Dear Apicata, I can't praise her highly enough – rich, loyal, well-connected, silent, never puts herself forward, no male relatives to complain to even if she had any complaints, practical, devoted, economical, fertile ... shall I go on? You know, of course, that they are talking of marrying Drusus' daughter to Agrippina's son? A very sound, very obvious piece of political thinking. Agrippina must be highly delighted, for if Drusus were to be *suddenly* taken from us, we'd have no choice but to give Agrippina's precious son the throne she insists was promised to his father? But with Drusus and his own two little boys to follow him, I don't think we have to concern ourselves with that.'

And although I had no idea why, it was suddenly an immense relief to me that it was in Sejanus' best interests to keep Drusus alive and well.

'However,' he said, 'I have a daughter of my own. And Drusus' cousin, Claudius, has a son of a suitable age – well, not entirely suitable because he's ten or twelve and my girl's not quite four – but near enough, don't you agree?'

I stopped in my tracks, surprised but rather proud of him just the same for he was aiming high. I could see no possibility of the ailing Claudius ever becoming emperor, but he was Tiberius' nephew, the brother of Germanicus and Drusus' wife, Livilla, so a marriage alliance with him would bring Sejanus into the imperial family itself. And when Tiberius died, whether Drusus dismissed Sejanus from his service or not, he would be in honour bound to protect a kinsman.

I gave a low whistle, a common, street-urchin's whistle I would not have liked Drusus to hear, and Sejanus grinned down at me, his face shrewd and self-assured, his eyes twinkling with a gleeful, wicked delight.

'What can I do?' I asked hastily. 'I have no influence?'

'Of course you haven't, and you never will have, either. Drusus isn't the kind to be manipulated by women, I told you that at the start. But I'd like to know something of Drusus' own opinion before anyone else gets to him. He won't like it. In his view one doesn't marry the daughter of the Commander of the Guard, I'm well aware of that. But he may find it convenient. He may see the advantages to it. And although his consent is not required at this stage – since Tiberius is the one to dictate his family's matrimonial policy – yet the children are very young, and Tiberius is very old, and Drusus could well be in a position to cancel the contract before they've had time to consummate. So you see what I mean about marriages? Tricky things. May I rely on you?'

And since it wasn't a question, and Lygdus was beckoning to us from the house, I bowed my head, and went in to dine.

The meal was ample, well-served, uninspiring, for Drusus was not greatly interested in food and no chef of his ever needed much imagination; and afterwards, while they transacted their business, I went once more into the garden and sat listlessly, ill-at-ease, in the rose-scented twilight, unwilling to face the cause of my malaise. It was true that I liked Drusus, true that with him, once the challenge and the triumph had worn away, I had found something new and strange for which now, sitting quietly among his roses, I found a name. With Drusus I felt safe – that was it exactly – safe and free from the hauntings of my past. There were no tenement smells in his garden, his walls were too high for Marsyas to climb. I trusted him completely. And, trusting him, it followed that I wanted him to trust me, and it grieved me deeply that he couldn't.

Sejanus came, all affability, to say good-bye, as fresh now at the end of the day as he'd been on waking, finding the prospect of a long night ride no problem at all. And when he had gone, and Drusus at last looked my way, his face was completely closed to me, the face of his public appearances that had unnerved stouter hearts than mine.

'What a busy creature he is,' he said, his hooded glance going through me, his eyes indolent, half-closed, and then suddenly they opened wide, holding me like a fly in syrup.

'Tell me,' he said, his voice quite toneless, the voice he used to servants and strangers and with which, in a moment, he would surely dismiss me, 'yes, I think you had better tell me now, since I must know sooner or later. Sejanus was whispering to you before dinner. I saw you from the terrace, my dear, and it wasn't small talk, and I don't think it was sex either.'

'Oh heavens – no, it wasn't.'

'I thought not. He uses sex, I imagine, to purchase the goodwill of my senators' wives, but with you money would suffice – and he doesn't waste himself. I must conclude he was campaigning?'

And wanting it over and done with, knowing, with fresh panic, that my store of easy lies, easy charm, were useless to me – that for the first time in my life I was unwilling to deceive – I whispered, 'Yes.'

'So – shouldn't you tell me about it? Or at least the bits he wanted you to tell me, so I can fill in the others?'

'I'm sorry,' I said and he shrugged wearily, a mere sketch of a movement, telling me how little my emotions concerned him.

'I dare say. Most people are sorry, I find, when one catches them out. Poor child, what a dilemma you are facing – trapped between the two of us. I ask myself, can there possibly be a way out? Unless, of course, Danaë, you wish to change sides.'

'*Sides?*' I looked up and then away again, hurt by his face. 'But I – surely – you and Sejanus are on the same side? I didn't believe – and I did think about it – that he meant to harm you.'

'He doesn't,' he said, but his voice was still cold, offering me no pardon. 'Harming me is definitely not to his advantage – my goodness, where would he be without me? No, no, he wishes to be as close to me as he is to my father – I perfectly understand that. You may have been useful to him there – one must hope so, for your sake.'

And, incredibly, he was smiling.

'Please,' I said desperately, 'I don't know what harm I've done, and I don't ask for pardon. To begin with all I thought about was the prestige and the money, and then – oh, I've never had any loyalties, never cared about how I was governed or who was governing. And I don't think I care now. But I do care about – about – your good opinion, and losing it means far more to me than losing money, which is positively amazing, knowing me – truly – because I thought I could do anything for money. Oh, you can't possibly know what I mean.'

'You will oblige me', he said 'by not bursting into tears. I know exactly what you mean. You are declaring your loyalty to me as your future Emperor – in your odd way – which is very kind of you. And I have no intention of refusing it. So tell me what it was my father's minister was after this time?'

'He wanted to know what you think of his daughter's engagement.'

'To Claudius' boy? Yes, it would be on his mind. What shall we tell him?'

'Whatever – whatever you decide. I'll do anything you say.'

'Yes, I know. Well then, you may tell him that I yawned and made some remark about middle-class upstarts, and what a state the world is in when one feels obliged to marry them, but that it can't be helped. And, indeed, the man is so useful that one has to give him something. Tell him that. And, really, what are we actually giving him but a ten-year wait with a promise at the end of it? The girl is very young – such a long time before they can consummate. Who knows, we may none of us survive it. Naturally, you will not tell him that.'

'How do you know?' I said, my teeth chattering. 'I could tell him. How do you know I won't.'

'Yes. How indeed?' And once again there was that incredible smile, the brief, tantalizing glimpse of his humanity, moving me so intensely that I could have gone down on my knees then and there and pledged him my lifelong service. It hurt me that there were so many fools in the world who still dreamed of Germanicus.

'Because', he said quietly, 'you told me that you had a code of conduct, and, although it has it limitations, you haven't betrayed it. I have an ailment, have I not? Not serious in itself, but a nuisance to me, something I choose not to speak of, since I see no reason to give the lampoonists the chance to call me a diseased brute instead of merely a brute, no reason to raise false hopes in certain relatives of mine who would find it convenient to think of me as an invalid. Whatever else you may have told Sejanus, you haven't told him that. Sejanus has an agent in every household – even mine, even my father's, I imagine – and so long as I know it's you, I don't have to worry about the woman who massages my back, or the boy who pours my wine – or poor old Lygdus who would fall in love, so indiscreetly, with any handsome lad Sejanus put in his way. So I think we'll stay as we are, Danaë, for the time being. You're upset, aren't you? How interesting. Do come and stand under the light: one so rarely has a chance to observe – what is it? – shame and a touch of indignation, I suspect, at being put in such a false position. And, just at the moment, a certain eagerness to behave better in future. Now I do think I've made you angry. That should stop the tears, at any rate.'

'It won't,' I said, far beyond caution. 'I think you'd better let me go inside, because I don't cry very often and when I do it comes in floods. You won't want to see it.'

'But I will. I'm an observer – surely you know that? – of life in all its aspects, and death too. Although death, of course, is quite different, because I have no choice there. I shall have to die, one day, like everybody else, whereas I can keep my distance from life – nothing obliges me to participate, and it's far safer, you know, to be a spectator – infinitely more dignified. But never mind that. Where are these tears you promised me?'

'Here,' I told him, but, as he reached out a cool arm and held me close all that mattered to me was that he wouldn't send me away. 'He may want to make love to other women,' I thought, 'but there are other things besides that. I'll be his spy, or his confidante, or his nurse, anything, if I can only stay with him.' And I amazed myself.

9

I went to Baiae again that year to escape the heat of the August city, and although Drusus was to spend the first part of the month with his wife at their sumptuous villa at Tarracina, entertaining the local notables, and the second half visiting the great city families in their summer retreats, I knew how burdensome he found it. And he had arranged to meet me at Laurentum when it was over.

I refused all bookings for the season, having some idealistic notion of spending time with my family, but it was soon abundantly clear that Paris, recently returned from Athens, tolerated my overtures merely from good manners and because he was short of cash, while Marpessa would have much preferred me to go away again.

'She's at a difficult age,' Chrysothemis soothed me. 'She's got nothing in her head just now but racing and spending money and eating too much. And her language, Danaë! You should ask Dion to be careful, because I can't think where else she hears it.'

But Dion, who had never known a moment's caution in his life, was not approachable just then, for, having injured his back at the Apollinarian Games in July, and then injured it again by getting up too soon, he was spending his time on a couch in my garden, never more than half sober, bickering with Paris and pestering me to write letters for him to a Roman girl of respectable family with whom he'd taken it into his head to fall in love.

'She's beautiful,' he told me, sentimental with wine. 'Just a little thing – a little kitten. And she's a good girl too – it took some believing, I can tell you, but she is. Wouldn't surprise me if she was a virgin. And you must admit, Danaë, that's about the only thing left that I've never had. You couldn't get her to come here, and then clear out, the lot of you? She'd want to look after me, you see, and I'd make sure she did. That's something I learned from Marsyas – the clever bastard. He's left Bassus, did I tell you? Signed up with the "Greens" two days before those extra games we had in July. By God, Bassus was livid – went into his "after-all-I've-done-for-you" routine, and Marsyas laughed in his face. Poor old sod, I think he'd have killed him if he could have afforded it.

'Anyway, Marsyas is wearing green this year – maybe it reminds him of Cynthia. And *there's* one woman who'll never be the same again. Not that I blame her for putting a knife into him when he sold those jewels of hers – especially now he's earning enough to stake himself to anything he fancies – but then she has to go and make an idiot of herself, weeping and screaming for help because she thinks he's bleeding to death. Mind you, he didn't look any too healthy. I was in the house when it happened and she'd carved up his back a bit – I couldn't make out at first whether he was crying or laughing, but he wasn't dying, that's for sure. We had to get the doctor to Cynthia in the end. Look, do you think Paris could write me a poem or two for this girl of mine? She'd go for that sort of thing.'

But Paris when applied to was so scornful that Dion, who didn't care to be reminded that with all his huge earnings and his adoring fans he had never managed to learn to read or write, tried to heave himself to his feet and, stumbling, fell back on the couch snarling that he'd been crippled for life. And when Paris retaliated by another unwise reference to Dion's illiteracy, the air between them became so black with obscenities that Chrysothemis covered her ears, Marpessa opened hers wide, and I prayed earnestly for the summer to end.

And then, miraculously, late one afternoon Lygdus appeared, a little African boy running behind him holding a vivid green parasol.

'Not my time of year at all,' he said, as if I'd been expecting him. 'These delicate skins, peach-bloom in the shade – but there's always a price to pay, and the sun's my enemy. Well, come on with you, he's got a day or two to spare, although I don't envy you because he's tired out. Chaos, that's what it's been – parties every night, wine on the beach to watch the sun come up, chitter-chatter every afternoon – it's all gone to Livilla's head. Somebody ought to tell her she's not Empress yet. The woman never stops. Believe me, I won't be sorry when she goes back to her apartment on the Palatine and he goes back to his. Agrippina was so damned popular, you see, when she used to travel around with Germanicus, everybody cheering her and throwing flowers for her to walk on; and Livilla wants the same. Now then, dear, it's nearly an hour's drive, and it's been a long day.'

The house, on a stretch of the coast I'd never suspected before, was small but one of the loveliest I had ever seen, perching on the cliffside in a nest of wild flowers, each bare room open to the blue air and the tang of salt water; and he was waiting for me on a terrace just large enough for the gold divan and the inevitable ill-tempered cat. He looked tired, as I'd expected, his eyes deep shadowed, his face set in the lines of strain and ennui that too much contact with his fellow-men always produced in him. But I was glad to see him, ridiculously glad, and I didn't care if he knew it.

'Well then, and have I interrupted your sparkling little life?'

'No. You've saved me from watching one of my brothers kill the other – and me from murdering my sister.'

'Are all families so, I wonder?' he said, putting a hand on the cat's black silk neck and smiling when the animal rebuffed him. 'Well, my life, at least, has been excessively gay – painfully gay. My wife, it seems, is determined to make a fashionable man of me. But never mind that. What do you think of this house?'

'It's beautiful – the most beautiful in Campania, I should think.' And, his cool hand at the nape of my neck, we stood in a silence that was almost companionable, watching the luminous blue and gold day quieten into evening.

'It was my father's house once,' he said, 'in the days when he was married to my mother. They used to shut themselves up here for months – one can hardly imagine why.'

'Perhaps they were fond of each other,' I suggested unwisely, for he had never mentioned his family to me before; but instead of the raised eyebrow and the fastidious curl of the lip that would advise me to remember my place, he shook his head, rather carefully, as if it ached, and smiled.

'I know nothing about it. They were divorced when I was a child, so my father could marry Agrippina's mother. And after that the house was shut up until I discovered it some time ago. My Aunt Julia – Agrippina's mother – had no taste for privacy, you see. And no taste for my father, either.'

I looked up in astonishment, but his eyes were fixed on the distant blending of sky and water, and perhaps he wasn't speaking to me at all, merely remembering the women who had stood here before me, his own mother and his father's second wife – Agrippina's mother, the Emperor Augustus' only daughter, the greatest matrimonial prize in the world, given to Tiberius not so much a wife as a trophy, a splendid reward for his services to the empire – a vivacious and beautiful creature who had shamed him with her infidelities and had died for it. And suddenly feeling the cold, I wondered if it was true that Tiberius had ordered her to be starved to death in her place of exile, and this had formed the basis of his hatred for her daughter Agrippina, and for Germanicus?

'Yes,' Drusus murmured, still examining the misty shades of twilight and the gentle night-rocking of the sea, 'it occurs to me – I can't think why – that my relationship to Agrippina must be unique. Just think of it: my mother and Agrippina were half-sisters, both daughters of Augustus' general, Marcus Agrippa, by his various marriages, and so Agrippina is my aunt and I her nephew, although I am a year or two the elder. Her mother then married my father, which makes us brother and sister. She herself then married my cousin Germanicus, and I his sister Livilla, which makes us cousins twice over and brother and sister-in-law. And when my father adopted Germanicus as a son and he became my brother, she became my sister all over again. Such a weight of relationship, there seems nothing left but to be lovers or friends – and I can't think which is the more unlikely. And now, of course, this marriage between my daughter and Agrippina's son unites us yet again.'

'Are you pleased with him?' I asked hesitantly, for I had never seen him so mellow; and letting his hand slide down my back he held me close.

'Nero? I've just come from his house – or rather, his mother's house – and yes, he's well enough. Very much like Germanicus – except that no one could ever be like Germanicus in Agrippina's eyes, and it must be hard for the boy to live up to.'

And then he laughed. 'Poor lad. He's been brought up to consider me as one of his father's murderers – and certainly I was the one to profit most by it. The prospect now of calling me "father" in Germanicus' place was a little too much for him. But he's young. He'll acquire a little more guile with the years – or, at least, one must hope so, for his own sake. It was hard for him to understand how his mother can hate me and at the same time urge him to be a good son to me. Perhaps I liked that.'

He lay down on the bed, brushing the unwilling cat aside, and as I moved instinctively to arrange his cushions, he said, 'You find that difficult to understand too, don't you?'

'I don't try to understand – it just disturbs me that anyone should hate you.' He laughed again, tolerant, not displeased.

'There's no need to be disturbed. I was born to certain privileges that other men find attractive and so I am hated for possessing things which may not necessarily be attractive to me. One learns to disregard it. Tell me – since I've never had the time to hate anyone, and perhaps I lack the emotional equipment in any case – is it such a terrible thing?'

But, glancing at his carefully passionless face, sensing the fatigue behind it, it was not hatred that seemed so terrible to me – not the stark possibility that he might well have condoned his cousin's murder – but his isolation. And, trembling inwardly, because I had never made a physical advance to him before, had merely given him the response he required when he required it, I took his lean, sardonic face between my hands and kissed him on the mouth.

'My word,' he said. 'One could almost believe you had missed me – unless there is a scarcity of young men on the coast this year? But I think I may disappoint you tonight. I'm tired, Danaë. I thought I'd gone beyond sleep – although I was aching for it – but I think I could sleep now, perhaps, an hour or two. And then we'll go down to the beach before the sun gets up. It's delicious then. Yes, I know you don't like the early morning and you feel the cold, but you'll put up with it, for my sake, like you always do.'

And then, his eyelids growing heavy, his mind already half asleep, he murmured, 'Poor Agrippina – she wants her son to be Emperor. She wants to condemn him to working eighteen hours of every twenty-four, every day of the year – hatred and ridicule and a knife in the back if he doesn't watch out. And she says she loves him. At least my father never pretended to do that.'

I lay awake for most of the night, my shoulder a pillow for his head, bearing his weight happily and wanting nothing more than to go on bearing it, to be there, at his side, when he needed – as all men do at some time in their lives – a woman's arms around him in the dark, and a woman's voice to tell him he was going to be all right. And I – knowing that morally and intellectually and in every other way he was my superior – was overwhelmed by the need to give him something, just a glimpse, perhaps, of the multitude of human experiences he had missed.

I went back to Rome in a state of vague unease, prone to fits of gaiety and sudden bursts of ill-temper, not knowing what ailed me, until one September night in Drusus' villa at Laurentum I lifted a bowl of roses from a little table and found a woman's earring concealed behind it, a cluster of pearls in an unusual setting that I had seen before. And instead of putting the jewel down, as I should have done, I kept it in my hand, tossed it in my palm once or twice, telling myself that this had been bound to happen, and that I was ready for it. I'd had my triumph, for I'd been the first. I'd made my name and I could live comfortably now in the after-glow. There'd be a rush of fashionable, famous men eager to take Drusus' place, and my main concern must be to make sure that he gave me some stupendous parting present to increase my value. Emeralds, I thought, finer than Cynthia's, and pearls that would put this paltry thing to shame. But instead of that costly parure, all I could really see was his face as he'd slept in my arms that August night, and all I could feel was the intense sadness of loss.

'Does that jewel have any particular significance?' he said, raising an enquiring eyebrow, an observer again, ready to be amused by my unruly, untidy humanity.

'No. It's not the kind of thing I care for.'

'It's not yours then?' And meeting his cool eyes I understood that it had been left out deliberately for me to see, and that I had nothing, now, to lose.

'No. It wouldn't suit me. It belongs to a woman called Chloe – a cithara-player – she's a friend of mine. A dainty little thing – very soulful. You'd never guess she was an assistant, once, in a butcher's shop, although how she ever held a meat-cleaver in those frail hands I can't imagine. Except that she was younger then.'

'My word,' he said. 'Is this jealousy? How diverting.' And, walking past me, he went out into the garden.

But later, when I was past hope and had schooled myself to settle for the meagre consolation of self-esteem, he said abruptly, as if perhaps he hadn't meant to say it at all: 'Is it possible that you expect your lovers to be faithful to you, when we are not faithful to our wives?'

'Of course not – and I doubt if your wives expect it either. Some of them may not even want it.'

His eyes narrowed, warning me to take care, and then, recognizing the truth behind my words – for his own wife, they said, was a jewelled doll who thought of nothing but her hair and her clothes and her dignity – he clicked his tongue in mock reproach.

'Danaë, Danaë – how you women torment yourselves from pride. And why not? I perfectly understand why you don't want to lose me. There's nothing more glamorous than rank and fortune, and who can compete with me for either? Come now, since we may not meet again, tell me the truth for once – take all that away from me and I'm just a man with a bad chest and a bad temper. I'm not lovable at all, am I?'

'No – you're not.'

'Well then, why all this fuss about an earring? I had forgotten the woman's name until you mentioned it – if that consoles you. But, since the matter has arisen – yes, I think it is time. I'm leaving for Nola tomorrow to spend some days in private with my father, and afterwards affairs of State must take precedence over affairs of another kind. I prefer to tell you this myself instead of leaving it to others because – well, perhaps it pleases me sometimes to be kind. I know the idea of making a scene has never entered your head. I feel I can rely on that?'

'Yes, you certainly can.'

'Good. Now, what shall I give you for a keepsake? Pearls, I suppose, may seem inappropriate. Sapphires then? Or shall I surprise you?'

'Emeralds,' I told him, crisp, businesslike, brittle, for I was an actress after all and if I couldn't convince myself, then I'd convince him and everybody else besides.

'So be it. Emeralds. Lygdus will see to it.'

And so our parting was curt, abrasive, predictable, and, so far as I could tell, completely final.

I spent ten days in pain, knowing that I would heal – furious with myself for not healing sooner, for this idiotic, unprofessional lapse which made healing necessary at all. Yet no one else knew I was grieving, and even when Lygdus called, unbearably smug, his smile saying 'I told you so,' I held out a gracious hand for my emeralds, ready to complain if they were one degree less than my expectations. But he had nothing for me but some muttered comments about the vagaries of the Caesars, and an hour later I found myself once again in Drusus' house across the Tiber, a bare room full of the raw November wind, and a man whose face was no kinder.

He was draped in the formal toga he wore for the Senate and, raising his head but keeping his eyes on the document in his hand, he said, 'Your emeralds, madam,' and with the absent-minded gesture of master to servant, he indicated the small table where they lay in a bower of apple-green silk.

It was the most magnificent parure I had ever seen, enormous square stones set in antique gold, rings and bracelets and earrings, a necklace of cobweb filigree scattered with green stars, a single, breath-taking jewel on a slender chain, treasures beyond price that would proclaim me an empress among my own kind and send Cynthia to an early grave. But their dazzle hurt my eyes, went through me like slivers of green glass – for what were they but that? And I realized, with horror, that my cheeks were wet.

'Thank you,' I said steadily, for I was an actress by choice, a whore only from necessity, and I wouldn't let myself down. 'You are very generous.' But, although the tone of my voice was quite satisfactory, I knew I wouldn't be able to keep it up for long, that I'd have to get out of there soon.

'Yes, I'm inclined to agree with you,' he said, barely interrupting his reading. 'You're satisfied, then – it's enough?'

And unable to hold out any longer, I turned swiftly and fled to the terrace, standing with my back to him, looking out over the dead garden.

'I asked you a question,' he said quietly. 'And I'm not often kept waiting for an answer. Is it enough? Or are you too overcome with joy to tell me?'

'It's more than enough.'

'And your gratitude is boundless?'

'Absolutely.'

'And you'll wear them the next time you invite your improbable friends to dinner – flaunt them?'

'I'll do that all right.'

'And you are leaving my house with everything you came for?'

'Oh yes – and more besides.'

And then, startling me, because I hadn't heard him approach, he put his hand on the nape of my neck and stood close beside me, perfectly still. There was a lamp flickering at the end of the terrace, a quiet sky releasing the red winter sun, the dark blue silence of approaching evening, and I knew I would never lose the memory of myself, standing there, my chest tight with tears I was determined not to cry; would always know how it had felt, holding them back.

'Danaë, what does all this mean? Are you deluding yourself – or trying to delude me – that you care? Because it would be a delusion. Is there one among us who cares for anyone but himself? And there are some of us who don't even do that. So take my jewels and be happy with them. They'll do you far more good than any man alive.'

But his hand remained on my neck, we remained together, and he showed no signs of moving away.

'I have no more faith in you, Danaë,' he said softly, 'than in any other member of my species, for, whatever you feel now, a moment will come when your interests and mine are not the same and you will choose your own gain to my loss – as I would do. Can you deny it?'

'Yes, I do deny it.'

'Then you are younger than I thought.'

But here, at least, I was on familiar ground. 'No, I'm not young. The young are weak and have to be protected. There has to be someone to care if a child gets enough to eat, or comes home safe every night. If there's no one to do that, then there's no sense in being a child. I was never a child.'

'Neither was I,' he said and, going back into the room he stood for a moment, looking down at the array of jewels, smiling.

'You present me with a problem, Danaë. I thought I had seen the last of you. All I had to do was send Lygdus with my emeralds and my compliments. Yet here you are. Are you going to stay?'

'If I can. Do you want me to?'

'One must suppose so – although I make no promises as to how long. But the Saturnalia is almost with us again – the season that some call festive – and it occurs to me that last year you helped me to endure the tedium of it all. Since this year promises to be much gayer – much worse – do you think you could help me again?'

And as I began to move towards him he raised a hand, the gesture of a consul of the Roman people, endowed with perfect authority that brought me to a halt.

'Think carefully, Danaë. Give me a rational answer, because I'm asking more of you now than before. I'm consul-elect again this year, consul the year after in partnership with my father. And all he means to contribute to the partnership is his prestige. He has no intention, at his age, of attending the Senate every day and shifting that mountain of detail they call government – no intention of putting himself on display every waking hour. He'll leave it all to me, the diplomacy, the games, the donkey-work. In fact he may not even stay in the city. He may take himself off to Capri, build himself another villa and close his door. And if there should be an insurrection on one of our frontiers that requires an imperial presence, he has no one but me to send. All the rest of my generation are dead, except my cousin Claudius, who doesn't count; and none of Agrippina's boys are old enough yet to be of any use to him even if he cared to employ them. My own sons are even younger. My father is tired, Danaë, and since there are times when I'm tired too, I need an oasis – a quiet room with a few beautiful things inside it, and a woman who thinks she cares for me. But give me a rational answer, for if you allow it I'll monopolize your time and wear you out – and I have not said I care for you. Think it over and let me know.'

'Yes,' I said, 'I'll tell you in the morning.'

And after that there was peace between us.

10

Laurentum again, another early June, new roses like clouds of white and ivory and apricot, covering the garden: and Sejanus, a little more careful than he used to be, his eyes following Drusus as he walked back towards the house, and saying suddenly – for him almost indiscreetly – 'It's true then? He's not well.'

'Not well? Now where on earth have you heard that?'

'Not from you, my darling girl – certainly not from you,' he said, his lopsided smile tilting the corners of his mouth, his eyes filled with their wicked, merry sparkle.

But I knew he wasn't merry, that his affairs, in fact, had reached a crisis point. And because lying to him, even here in Drusus' garden, was an awesome experience, I shrugged perhaps too casually, to cover not only my fear of him but the ache in my own heart.

'If there had been anything to tell ... He's tired, and why anyone should be surprised at that I can't imagine – his second consulship coming so soon after his first, and all those parties his wife makes him go to. Do you know, I never realized being a Caesar was such hard work. He puts in more hours than a galley-slave, and if that's power – well, I often wonder why anyone wants it at all.'

'You wonder that, do you?' he said, still smiling, his fingers closing around my wrist in a grip that was not amorous. 'Tell me, Danaë – after all this time, are you still so politically unaware? Do you really see so little, or do you just find it convenient not to notice?'

'Oh,' I said, flippant again, as light and insubstantial as the season, 'I expect you mean am I very clever or very stupid? Neither, really. I'm just what I seem, which may not be much, but I enjoy it. I'm not meddlesome, Sejanus, which you must admit suits you very well. I do as you ask me, don't I? I'd never dream of letting you down, but left to myself, well – I just get up every morning and think, "What a lovely day". No complications – I just take life in through the pores of my skin, colour and perfume and sensation – lovely things.'

'Giddy girl,' he murmured, his fingers sliding from my wrist to my elbow, 'I'll give you a sensation, one of these days.'

But, as he walked on through the soft scatter of rose-petals and the tantalizing scents of the summer day, I knew I had not deceived him. And, indeed, I did not altogether want to deceive him, for Drusus' growing listlessness, his enormous, devouring fatigue, formed the substance of my nightmares and I knew of no one better equipped than Sejanus to ease his burden. I had only to say, 'It's too much for him. He can't cope alone. He can't eat, can't sleep, and now and again he coughs until it breaks my heart.' And then, if it was true that Tiberius was going to Capri this summer, never to return, perhaps he wouldn't take Sejanus with him. I had only to speak to spare Drusus pain and earn Sejanus' heartfelt gratitude. But his trust in me was the most precious thing in my life, and when I opened my mouth to betray him – to save him – my tongue produced nothing but banalities about the flowers and the fineness of the season.

I perfectly understood Sejanus' present dilemma. He had worked for years to make himself indispensable to Tiberius, earning himself implacable enemies in the process, and now that the Emperor was at last in sight of his cherished dream of retirement – having a son of proven abilities to govern his empire for him – Sejanus was to share that retirement. The Emperor could not do without his favourite servant. He would need someone on Capri to guard his person, someone to convey his messages to the city, to organize the efficient transport of gourmet foods and rare books and such elderly friends as he might choose to entertain. He would need someone to ensure he was not troubled by deputations from Rome, by appeals for justice or mercy or promotion. And while Sejanus wasted his powerful energies on these things, it would leave the field wide open for his enemies to approach Drusus; for one of them to make himself as valuable to the son as Sejanus was to the father.

I perfectly understood that for Sejanus it would be death to go to Capri. As a simple matter of self-preservation he would have to find some means of getting back to the city, and I knew that already, behind the laughter and the easy charm, his brain was leaping with possibilities and tortuous calculations. And because I too had fought for survival without the help of inherited wealth and prestige, I admired him for it, and didn't want to see him fail.

'You'll make it,' I said suddenly, betrayed by the rapport that had always existed between us; and, laughing, he lifted me off my feet and swung me round to face him.

'So – that's your considered opinion, is it, my butterfly child? Yes, I'll make it. There's always a way when your back's to the wall, you know that as well as I do. And what a lovely back it is, Danaë – exquisite.' As his hands explored the curve of it, sending a remembered tremor down my spine, his will reached out for me, forceful and urgent, and I knew he was really saying, 'Hurry up, girl, before I shake it out of you. Let's see what you know – come on, and I'll take it from there.'

'If he's not well,' he said, 'and believe me, there has been a whisper – then something should be done for him. He's valuable to all of us, and we can't let his father work him to death, can we? Old men are selfish, Danaë, and if they've never had any fun themselves they don't like to see other people having a good time. Now tell me, what ails him?'

And, once again, the temptation to speak was almost irresistible. Drusus would see it as the foulest of betrayals but in the end he'd be glad. He didn't want power. He wasn't ambitious. It was duty alone that bound him hand and foot, and I had the means to ease the cords, not to free him entirely but to give him room to breathe. Sejanus – who was not my enemy – would keep faith with me. Drusus would never know. But I would know; and shrugging, smiling, I said, 'He caught a chill in the winter, and he coughs sometimes at night. But doesn't everyone? Heavens, when I remember Aemilius Scaurus – he used to keep me awake for hours. Between ourselves, I think it's all a great to-do about nothing.'

'You mean he pampers himself?'

'Well – quite honestly, yes I do. If *you* cough once or twice on a hot night, when there's not much air and a lot of candle-smoke, what do you do about it? Do you even notice?'

'No,' he said, 'No – no.'

And although I wasn't sure whether I had convinced him, I understood that in his mind a whole series of loose threads had been drawn together, presenting him with not one but a dozen different possibilities. He had something to work on, something to sniff out – Drusus the hypochondriac, Drusus the neurotic, Drusus the invalid – and my usefulness, for the present, was done.

'So he thinks I'm dying, does he?' Drusus said later that evening. 'Well, let him think so. It may cheer him up during those long evenings on Capri when he has to sit and listen to my father re-fighting his German campaigns. One could almost feel sorry for him, except that he did so want to be the Emperor's right hand, and it's illogical to pity a man for getting exactly what he was after.'

'Do you dislike him?' I asked, and he looked at me with mild surprise.

'No, I don't dislike him. Why should I have any feelings about him? He's useful to my father, and he may be useful to me. He's clever, he doesn't care about getting his hands dirty, and, regrettably, one needs a man like that from time to time. His exile may not be so permanent as he fears. I could very well recall him, in fact I shall probably do just that quite soon, although you'll oblige me by not telling him so. It will do him no harm to fret a little.'

'He would hate you,' I said abruptly, 'if he knew how little you care about him. Everybody else cares, one way or another. Your senators all hate him and hate themselves for putting up with him, and I think their wives hate him too, even if they do queue up to get in his bed. And some women love him so much that it ruins them for anything else. But your indifference would crucify him.'

'Indifference has that effect,' he said calmly. 'Should I pretend to be jealous of him, as people say I am? Do stop worrying about Sejanus. He's not altogether friendless. I understand he's attached himself to my wife lately: perhaps she can find the means to persuade my father to set him free.'

And when my mouth opened in astonishment, and then closed again, because I lacked the audacity to speak, he laughed and leaned towards me, offering me one of the tantalizing moments of closeness that meant far more to me than emeralds.

'Why does it never fail to astonish you that I know what goes on around me? Do you think Sejanus is the only one to have his spies? My dear, I've known, probably longer than you and Lygdus, that my wife spends as much time with Sejanus as she dares. She may not actually be his mistress because she has a lot to lose, but she must want to be his mistress, which amounts to the same thing. And why should I mind? If I wanted more children it would be another matter, since it is essential to be very precise in matters of paternity, and no man cares to take the risk of a cuckoo in his nest. Fortunately, in my case, the matter does not arise.'

He doesn't sleep with her, I thought, burning suddenly with a fierce delight, for I'd never been sure: and to conceal it, I said hastily, 'And does she know you suspect her?'

'Of course not. And I imagine she's very frightened of being caught out. She knows the penalty for adultery and she would expect me to enforce it.'

'And wouldn't you? I mean if she was really his mistress?'

'Ah well, she would have to be very discreet. I cannot allow myself to be made a fool of in public. But with Livilla there is no fear of that. She's wanted to be Empress all her life – believe me, I was brought up with her and I know. If she pays me the compliment of being careful, I wonder if I have any real right to complain? Unfortunately my father wouldn't see it that way, so perhaps it's just as well he's going to Capri. He doesn't like adultery. He'd make me send them both into exile at the very least, and probably worse than that, whatever I had to say about it. And that wouldn't suit me at all. It would oblige me to marry again, you see, and since the only possible bride for me would be one of Agrippina's daughters – well, I don't think I have the stamina for a high-spirited fourteen-year-old any more. Unless, of course, I married Agrippina herself? That would probably be best. We're about the same age and one can't deny she'd be an excellent empress – a very popular choice.

'Why does it surprise you that I can be so calm about the idea of Sejanus sleeping with my wife? Perhaps I'd be less understanding if I thought he was sleeping with you.'

And although he had by no means said he loved me, I knew it was the most I'd ever get, and it sufficed.

But just the same I was uneasy, and after dinner I slipped out into the garden to look for Lygdus, feeling the need to give him a word of warning and to ask him what he knew about Livilla.

'Of course she fancies Sejanus,' he said, stirring the gravel with an elegantly manicured foot. 'Don't we all? It's the fashion, and that's one thing my lady Livilla knows about – fashion. Not that she'll do anything about it because she wouldn't want him to disarrange her hair or smear her make-up. No, he's on to a good thing there. All he has to do is tell her he wants to worship at her feet and she'll believe him, because that's how she sees herself – untouchable – holy. Drusus knows that very well. He's not worried, because if Sejanus laid a hand on her she'd call the guard.'

'And you?' I said carefully, not wanting to hurt him. 'If Sejanus laid a hand on you?'

He stirred the gravel again, not looking up, and then, making an unusually clumsy gesture with his plump, jewelled hands, he burst out, 'What do you know about anything? You think you've had a bad time, but you're whole and free, and you're young. You may have sold yourself, but nobody else ever sold you – nobody ever put you up for auction and castrated you first so you'd appeal to the luxury market. I was ten years old – and for a long time it didn't matter, because for a long time I was young. I was a household pet and I knew I'd never have to work in the fields or get my hands dirty. I never much liked women anyway. And it wouldn't matter now, if Drusus would trust me occasionally, if he'd see I was fit for something other than fetching his women and looking after his damned cats. Yes, Sejanus does ask me things sometimes. What can I tell him? That he likes Chian wine better than Falernian? As for his cough, Livilla can tell him all about that, because she's spent more nights with him than you have. So don't worry that I'll betray him – I've got nothing to betray him with. And do you think knowing what Sejanus or anyone else wants of me makes any difference to what I want? Does it stop you wanting something because you know you can't get it?'

I moved nearer to him on the bench and, very carefully again, slipped my hand into his and squeezed it, my rings making a clinking sound against his own.

'There's friendship, Lygdus. There's liking?' And, flinging himself away from me, flustered and moved in spite of himself, he was about to say something cutting to cover his emotion, when a shadow fell across us and Drusus' doctor Eudemus stood there, his hands folded quietly into the long sleeves of his robe.

He was a man I detested, an Oriental Greek, secret and superior, soft-spoken, soft-footed, so that one rarely heard his approach; and perhaps because he had been Livilla's servant before Drusus had taken him over, I often felt that he watched me and, possibly, made his report.

'Oh, there you are,' Lygdus said. 'I thought you were never coming,' and although they both looked at me pointedly, making it clear that they had arranged to meet here, on this particular bench and that I was the intruder, I was freeborn and they were not, and I had no intention of giving way.

I watched them as they walked off side by side, Lygdus muttering something about whores who needed to be cut down to size, Eudemus a gliding feline, his narrow body blending with the shadows; and although there was nothing strange about it – for why shouldn't they take an evening stroll together and grumble about their superiors – their friendship added itself to the total of my vague fears.

Yet what did I fear? Sejanus would extricate himself from trouble somehow or other, as he always had, with or without the help of Drusus, and it was no surprise, really, that he had chosen to ingratiate himself with Drusus' wife. She wanted his admiration, he wanted her influence with her husband and her father-in-law, and it was all too obvious, too much in character, to have anything sinister about it.

Nor was there anything in my own life to distress me, for my own position with Drusus was more secure than I'd once dreamed possible. He would keep me with him as long as he could – forever if I could contrive it – and I had learned not to question the devotion I felt for him. It existed. He knew it and accepted it, enjoyed it even, and I had no intention of wasting time by picking it apart. So far as his chest was concerned, although it got no better, it seemed to get no worse. He had bouts of illness when he coughed all night and was feverish and foul-tempered all day, but none of this alarmed him nor even surprised him. It had always been so. He had learned to live with it. He understood it and, most of the time, could rise above it. There was nothing to fear.

Yet afterwards, it seemed to me that from that night he was never well again.

11

I consulted every doctor, every charlatan who came peddling his wares in Rome, although Drusus would see no one but Eudemus. I acquired a store of medical knowledge and rank superstition, I prayed at temples and shrines of gods I'd never heard of, pouring money into the hands of indifferent priests. I broke the law and went to astrologers and magicians, and on the advice of one of these, I went to a Thessalian witch who, in the murk of her hiding place, with primitive clay images of some ancient Earth Mother around her walls, convinced me that she could blend Drusus' life-force with mine, exchanging my life for his. And since I was crazed with distress and didn't think I could live without him anyway, I agreed. I paid a great deal of money for my own destruction, and on my way home, my chest scraped raw by incense, my stomach heaving, I thought it had worked and I was going to die in his place. 'He'll be well now,' I thought, but when I got to the villa I knew by Lygdus' face that he was worse.

He was feverish and fretful and at such times, when his chest bled inside and his head pounded, he could be cruel.

'Where were you? I sent them to find you. Why do you still have to go on the prowl like this? What was so urgent?'

'Oh, just some shopping.'

'Shopping. Shopping. Is that all you can think of when I'm so ill – when I'm dying?' And I fell across him, sobbing, for he had never said the word before and – as he spoke it – I knew that once again I'd been cheated. The witch had lied to me: there was no way to give him my strength. Yet in my despair, I heard myself telling him what I'd done, clinging to my superstitions with the panic of a child alone in the dark.

'My poor little one,' he said, and the arms he put around me were like hot, dry sticks. 'Would you really make such a sacrifice for me? Who knows – if it were possible, I might even accept it.'

He fell asleep, abruptly, as sick men do, and I went outside, needing to be alone, for I had come to the end of hope and I found it to be a private matter. There was nothing else left to try. No more doctors, no more prayers, no more magic. And I was full of hate and fury and an overwhelming impulse to destroy. An offensive sun stood high and bright in a tawdry sky, around me a whole city was moving, healthy people going their uncaring ways, and I loathed them all, wanted each and every one of them horribly dead and their world sinking into flames around them. Reaching out I grasped a handful of roses, crushing the petals, squeezing until the thorns went into my skin and I saw my own hand, savage and distorted, stained with the bruised roses and a little blood. And then I went back into the house and smiled, because that was all there was left to give him.

The Senate adjourned for its summer recess and we took him to Campania, to the little house that had once been his father's, lying in its nest of wild flowers, where I had spent one waking night holding him in my arms, trying not to love him. But I had failed. I did love him. And now, as Lygdus and the doctor Eudemus carried him to the marble terrace built out over the sea, and he lay in his ornate golden bed, staring at the horizon with eyes that saw little and cared less, I faced despair and felt that the essential part of my own life was over.

The past year, that of his second consulship, had drained him of the will to live, and I had watched him die by inches, determined to do his duty to the end. He had gone, a walking corpse, to every function, every sitting of the law courts, every meeting of the Senate, kept on his feet by the concoctions Eudemus brewed for him and by his own iron will. And because he didn't smile, and very often couldn't speak, he had been accused of arrogance behind his back.

But now it was over, and he lay there, twice consul and newly created Protector of the People, Tiberius' heir; and because his secret had been so well kept, there was no one but me and Lygdus and the soft-footed Eudemus to watch over him. I sat beside him through the hot days and the choking heartbreak of his nights. When he coughed in his sleep I wiped the blood from his lips and the sweat from his brow, and waited. Sometimes he was calmer than I. But sometimes, waking from a fevered sleep, drenched with sweat and choking for breath, he was bitter and knew how unspeakably he had been cheated.

'I thought I was ready,' he told me. 'I had to be ready – that's why I watched the gladiators so carefully because I had to know how to die – had to learn not to care. I've always known it would come to this. I watched other men die with dignity and I thought I could do the same. But there's no dignity in it and I'm not ready, Danaë. I'm not ready. It's too soon.'

Each night was its own separate tragedy. He was shrinking under my eyes and I was terrified of falling asleep and waking to find him gone. And perhaps I survived only because something in my brain snuffed out, numbing me so that I could function usefully, even cheerfully, without going mad. Every drop of time counted and I wouldn't waste it in sleep. I sat beside him and looked at him, trying to fix his face in my mind. And when it became too much I forced myself to think of nothing at all. I emptied my head and my heart carefully, as my dancing-master had taught me to do before a performance, savage in my determination not to burden him with my grieving. And, as he became quieter, and less aware of pain, as his grip on life weakened, I went along that terrible road with him, making no attempt to revive his interest in a world whose contours were fading mercifully before his eyes. I watched him pass slowly away from pain, and when my rebel mind reeled away from so much misery, my body took over and went on smiling and talking, fetching and carrying, until his need for me was at an end.

He was determined to go back to Rome and, as the summer drew to its close, he told me, 'I think it better if I travel alone. Stay here for a few days after I'm gone and compose yourself. And then go back to all those people I don't believe in – your brothers and your sister and your strange friends – and be as you were before.'

And I nodded, for I knew that his final duty was to go home to die, and that his official death, the pomp and circumstance of it, belonged to his father, to the nation, and to his wife.

The night before he left we sat together on the terrace and I said to him, because it seemed a moment to say something, 'What will happen now?'

'To Rome? Who can say? My sons are too young. My father should adopt Nero as his heir, but he won't do it. He hates Agrippina too much for that, and he wouldn't want a son of hers to come after him. I think he'll try to live long enough for my boys to grow up. But he's tired. He doesn't really want to live that long, and he won't thank me for obliging him to make the effort.

Things won't be easy. There are too many inexperienced boys and too many ambitious men. They'll kill one another – and for what? If only they knew how little it really matters.'

'Did it never matter to you?'

'No. I would have been an efficient emperor – better than Germanicus – but I had no enthusiasm for it. But it doesn't matter. I kept well away from life, but it's life that matters: I see that now. And it doesn't help to know I was wrong. You love me, don't you? I could have had you even if I'd been a beggar? How sad that I have to die to understand that. I never believed it when I was alive.'

We sat for a while in silence, listening to the night, for we were quietly, inevitably, coming to the end of what we could bear to say to each other. He was leaving in the morning and I wouldn't see him again. Perhaps he was slipping away to a point where I, with my rude health, had begun to seem unreal. He was ready, now, to die and I knew that his apathy was a blessing.

I thought he was asleep but after a long time he opened his eyes and, in the way of old men whose memories are failing, he went on with the conversation as if it had never been interrupted.

'Agrippina will cause trouble. Augustus promised Germanicus the Empire and she'll want it for one of her sons. It's not ambition – she's no more ambitious than I am – it's just her way of proving how much she loved him. And none of his boys is like him. She'll spend the rest of her life looking for him in Nero, or Drusillus, or Caligula, and all she'll really see will be the reflection of her own face. God knows where she'll drive them. She won't mean any harm – she never did – but if she could learn to love Germanicus less then she'd serve his sons far more.'

'You don't like her?'

He smiled. 'As a matter of fact I like her very much – quite a lot more than I like Livilla. And she only hates me because she thinks it's necessary. She's perhaps the best of the lot. But she'll get on my father's nerves and he won't stand for it. He looks at her and he sees her mother, who made a laughing-stock of him with her infidelities. She looks at him and she sees what she thinks is her husband's murderer. No, no, they hate each other too well. He won't have Nero for his heir.'

'But Nero is married to your daughter. Perhaps your father will think of that?'

'I doubt it. And you shouldn't think of it either, Danaë. Don't ever risk yourself for the sake of my children. Factions are bound to form and my children can't escape involvement – my wife won't allow them to escape it. She'll use her children, just like Agrippina. But don't look for me in them. You won't find me. I've had no share in the moulding of them and I don't know how they'll grow, what sort of men they'll be. Don't fall into that kind of trap, Danaë.'

He closed his eyes again, drifting away in mid-speech, and I arranged his cushions and smoothed his brow, easing myself with these pointless women's gestures, wishing with all my heart that I was old and able to bear it – that he was old and I wouldn't have to rage for the rest of my life at the waste of him.

The next morning I was up before dawn and, looking at myself in the mirror for the first time in days, expecting to see nothing more than a reflection of decay, I was offended by the bloom in my cheeks, the futility of my own strength.

I walked beside his litter as they carried him across the garden to his coach and as we said good-bye his hands in mine were like dry leaves. I don't remember the words he spoke, nor how I answered, and it wasn't important. It was only a way of filling in the empty spaces opening around me. The sun was very high, very hot, and I remember shading my eyes with my hand as I watched the procession winding slowly down the road, slowly and forever out of my sight. Behind me the house spread its empty shadow and I wondered if I would ever be able to go inside. I waited until he had gone and then I threw myself to the ground and howled my despair into the earth like a sick animal.

12

'Oh – Danaë,' Chrysothemis said, quite blankly, as if she had some slight difficulty remembering my name and my business. 'I really wasn't expecting you today – your letters were so vague, dear. Although, of course, this is your house and one doesn't ask you to explain your movements. Danaë – welcome home.'

And, walking past her into the house that had once been the summit of my ambitions, I couldn't believe how small it was, how ridiculously proud I'd once been of these few, cluttered rooms, these gaudy colours, of these crude wall-paintings of myself dancing, done an age ago when it had all seemed so important, when I'd cared about self-advertisement and admiration; when the world had teemed with things I'd found desirable and had been ready to fight for.

'Thank you,' I said. 'If my room is ready I'll rest a while. It's been a long journey.'

And for a terrifying moment I couldn't remember which way to go.

I had been away a long time, for Rome had been impossible after Drusus died, and none of my family had known what to do with me. Paris had offered me some philosophical observations about the nature of life and death, Chrysothemis had tried to jolly me along with good food and good cheer, Marpessa had been frankly curious, and only Dion, who could neither read nor write, had proved that he could, on occasions, feel. He had simply put his arms around me, hugged me tight, carried me out of my nightmare to a ship bound for Greece; and had even travelled with me as far as Athens until an enterprising red-head caught his eye and he'd judged I could cope alone. He'd returned to Italy soon after, penniless and overweight, looking for Bassus and Erato to get him into shape again. I had lingered, giving myself time. Time had cheated me but time would heal me too, for, unlike Agrippina, who would be able to feed her grief for the rest of her life, people would soon be bored with mine, and I knew I'd have to smile when I got home.

And so I let six months pass, nine months – the gestation period for a new life, or for the hard shell I needed to hold together the old one – and here I was, embroiled again with Chrysothemis, seeing my maids take orders from her and not caring, knowing how much it had meant to her this past year, playing the mistress of my house – and of my brother, too, I shouldn't wonder. And I didn't care about that either.

'Have you got your boxes open yet?' Marpessa demanded, bursting into my room, impossibly tall and full-breasted, so eager and colourful that she hurt my eyes. 'Oh, you were sleeping. Never mind. Come on, Danaë, let's see what you've brought – oh Danaë, this red silk! You don't want it, do you? It's not your colour. And these gold sandals?' Draping herself in a crimson swirl she strutted for a moment and then plunged, rapacious as a magpie, into my neatly packed chests, decking herself in this and that, gold chains, a pair of ruby earrings, bracelets from wrist to elbow, another length of silk heavily embroidered with black and gold.

'Come on then,' she said, pouring the contents of an onyx scent bottle over her hair. 'Tell me what I can have, or I'll take the lot. You wouldn't miss it – go on, it's all for me anyway, isn't it?'

'Just give me back the rubies – they're too old for you and you'd only lose them. And you can't wear black either, your skin's darker than mine. The rubies ...'

And as I held out my hand, she tossed her head, setting the earrings dancing.

'I'm sixteen – nearly seventeen. Were you too young for rubies at sixteen?'

Managing not to tell her that at sixteen I'd been satisfied with a few painted wooden bangles, I retrieved my jewels and pushed her out of the door.

Paris did me the honour of dining at home that evening, and he too was taller than I remembered, lacking Dion's bulk but a man now, elegant and self-assured, full of the gossip of the town. And noting the fine lawn of his robe and the quality of the pearl on his hand, I wondered if there was a woman in his life I didn't know about. I had increased his allowance, it was true, but hardly enough to indulge his taste for fine jewellery and the collection of *objets d'art* I'd glimpsed in his room. Glancing at Chrysothemis for signs of strain – and finding them – I was more convinced than ever that he'd elected to follow in his father's footsteps. And I didn't like it.

'What about your epic poem?' I asked him, remembering all the education I'd paid for, and he shrugged, almost yawned; an expensive, fastidious young gentleman, a luxury item, wasted, I thought, on the likes of Cynthia or Xanthe, or whoever was paying his bills.

'Oh – coming along nicely – very nicely. I'm keeping busy. Don't fret,' he told me and, lifting his cup with a graceful flourish, he finished his wine and got to his feet.

'I have to run – sorry, since it's your first night at home. But there it is. At least you can't accuse me of being idle.' And, resting his hand for a moment on Chrysothemis' arm, a delicate gesture of possession clearly stating that their affair was now very much in his control – that he was no longer the boy who had been grateful for her favours but a man who required to be indulged and pleased – he was gone.

'Are you going to wait up for him?' I said, but Chrysothemis, who was twenty-seven now and looked older, had been through it all before and, taking the hurt out of her face, she made a perfect gesture of surprise.

'My dear, it's simply not like that. We're dear friends, as we always have been – and when he was younger he was so sweet, and quite lonely, and of course we were thrown together a great deal. There were times when I worried that he was getting too fond of me – really worried – because the last thing in the world I wanted was to hurt him, and I never forgot how sensitive he was. I told him to wait, to look around a little, and now he sees I was right. He often tells me so, and do you know, I think it's brought us even closer – in the nicest possible way.'

'Words of wisdom,' I said, remembering Erato years ago talking about Dion, filling her house with fresh-faced girls to induce him to stay. And because, for most of the time, he did stay, and because I didn't want to judge either of them, I finished my own wine rather quickly and reverted to the safe, eternal topics of the store-cupboards and the household linen.

But when the meal was over and Chrysothemis had hurried away, busy with a hundred things that seemed important to her – had they once been important to me? – I sat in the garden-court, looking at my hands, and wondering what on earth I would ever find to do. I was, by my own standards, a rich woman. I was now the owner of a pleasant house in Campania, a mile or two inland from Baiae, with an income to support it, left to me through so complicated a chain of middlemen that it would have been difficult to trace it back to Drusus. I had that magnificent parure of emeralds and an array of lesser gems, some of them personal and heartbreaking, some of them showy investment pieces intended for resale whenever the market should be most advantageous. I had money carefully invested, cash in my hand, land I had never seen in the south which yielded a useful rent. I was free from all financial cares and there had been moments, this past year, when that very freedom had been a burden. Faced with a living to earn I would have taken myself by the scruff of the neck and coped, somehow or other, but I found security, like sympathy, to be weakening, and idleness a garment I was not suited to wear.

But as the moment approached when it was becoming too much to bear, when I was about to let myself down and cry again, there was a blessed commotion at the door and a maid running to tell me, 'Madam – a gentleman – the Commander of the Guard!' – and Sejanus in full dress uniform came striding across the courtyard, the mere sound of his brisk military tread telling me that if, in the midst of my melancholy, I had whispered a prayer, it had been heard and answered.

He looked enormous, bronzed and fit and overflowing with a strength that was as basic and enduring as ploughed earth in the sun, and without speaking a word he lifted me to my feet and held me tight, releasing in me a flood of physical need I had no thought of suppressing, for if the source of my emotions had withered and run dry, my body was only just twenty-three years old, and it was a long time since a healthy man had touched me.

'I've been waiting for this,' he said, his tongue going immediately, wickedly, into my ear. 'I don't think I have to waste time, do I, darling, in making pretty speeches?' And, his mouth clamped into mine, he began taking the pins out of my hair and unfastening the shoulder of my dress.

'Bed,' he said, very decidedly. 'I've had a hard day, and I'm not a man for gardens and romance in the moonlight. Come on, Danaë – I've been promising myself this for years.'

And suddenly I was laughing, fighting him off and holding on to him at the same time, because this was the exact medicine I required, this handsome, vigorous man who had always intrigued me, and with whom I was not in the least in love.

He wasn't gentle. He was blunt and greedy and self-seeking and so, in those next few hours, was I, cramming myself with pleasure as my sister crammed herself with honied dates, submerging myself in my body's hunger and thirst; and then, when the feast was over, lying in his arms with all the mindless contentment of overeating, knowing that if he had bruised me it went no deeper than the surface of my grateful skin.

'You're beautiful,' he said, and I laughed and bit the point of his shoulder.

'I know that.'

'Well, naturally – but I thought I'd better say it. And what are you going to do with all this beauty now? We can't let it go to waste, can we?'

He got up and crossed to the wine-table someone had had the imagination to get ready, his hard, soldier's body knotted with muscle, covered with tawny hairs like a mountain lion; and I gave him a smile of pure appreciation, delighted with him because it had been every bit as satisfying as I'd expected, and I still didn't love him.

'I'm going to work,' I said, suddenly aware that I had found my salvation. 'I'm going to dance again. I was good before but I'll be better now. I don't need the money, you see, and so I can afford to be good.'

'I'm delighted to hear it.'

He raised his cup to me, drained it, filled it again. 'Couldn't be better. I'm giving a reception at my wife's house in ten days' time. Will you be ready by then?'

'Heavens – of course not. I haven't given a professional performance for nearly two years.'

'Nonsense. I'll send my freedman to you tomorrow to haggle about the fee. You'll be all right. You've got a good memory and you're fit enough – I can vouch for that.'

'Sejanus,' I said, sitting bolt upright. 'I need new material and it doesn't grow on trees. I let my musicians go when I went to Greece – and I don't even know if my old dancing-master is still alive. They keep on charging me for his rent, but that doesn't prove anything.'

But if Sejanus heard my panic it didn't interest him and, his mind already leaping ahead to the main purpose of his visit – for I knew quite well it must be more than it seemed – he stretched himself out beside me again, the wine-cup in his hand, assuming, I supposed, that if I was thirsty I would serve myself.

'You can charge my fellow what you like. I'm in a mood to cut a dash right now. You'll find changes in the city, Danaë, but not quite so many as some people would like. I can still fill my house with the rich and famous – does that surprise you?'

And perhaps it did, for at his level he had lost as much by Drusus' death as I had. There was no question now of retirement to Capri, and Tiberius, soured and sickened at having to shoulder the burden of government all over again, might well rely on him now more than ever. But everyone I had spoken to on my way home through Italy had seen the future as Nero's and Agrippina's. And, in that case, since Agrippina had always numbered Sejanus among her husband's murderers, all that was left for him was to prepare himself a place to hide.

'Yes,' he said, his eyes twinkling, 'amazing, isn't it? People are putting garlands on the statues of Germanicus again, and if you and I were to go now and take a midnight stroll around the city we'd be sure to find a little man somewhere scrawling slogans on a wall, telling us how Nero is really Germanicus come back to earth to save us from the monster Tiberius. And, of course, Tiberius will take offence – wouldn't you, if you had two grandsons of your own? Little boys, I agree, but they'll grow, if one allows them the time.'

I swallowed quite painfully, because it wasn't easy to think of Drusus' sons – he had himself warned me not to think of them – and I made some reply that sounded more like lack of interest than the concealment of pain. Yet, for the first time, I was fully aware of the change in Agrippina's position. Germanicus' death had cheated her of an empire but Drusus' death had restored it to her, for now it was Livilla and her children – Drusus' children – who must take second place, or perhaps no place at all, when Tiberius died.

'Yes,' Sejanus murmured, his mind on Agrippina too, 'I should like to hear your opinion, Danaë. Put yourself in our Emperor's place. Imagine yourself an old man, knowing how many people are waiting for you to die and praying it may be soon, before your grandsons are old enough to defend themselves. What would you do? Would you bow to the inevitable? Would you adopt Nero and his brother Drusillus as your heirs, as everyone is insisting you must, and leave your own flesh and blood to their mercy? Because however tender-hearted Nero may be, he'll have someone about him, when the time comes, to point out that so long as Tiberius' grandchildren are alive he can never really be secure. He may not want to kill them, but he's been brought up to believe that Tiberius killed his father, and he'll remember. His mother, our impeccable Agrippina, will see that he remembers. What would you do?'

'I don't know. What could I do – short of keeping myself alive, or making peace and hoping for the best.'

'Ah,' he said, 'Tiberius is an old man and set in his ways, you see, and he's hated Agrippina for so long that I wonder if he can change now? Her mother made such a fool of him when she was his wife. Can Agrippina herself ever really trust him? She believes he poisoned her husband, and there was an ugly story that he had her mother starved to death in her place of exile, in retribution for her adultery. No – there's been too much between them, and now there's too much at stake. I make no secret of the fact that if Tiberius died tonight I might as well burn myself on his funeral pyre; because not even Agrippina supposes he poured with his own hand the poison that killed her husband – and I wouldn't put it past her to entertain the notion that the pourer could have been me.'

And was it, I wondered, watching that perpetual half-smile tilting his mouth, the merry twinkling of his eyes, knowing that it could have been him, and knowing too that if I were Livilla, the mother of Tiberius' poor little grandsons, I'd make certain of keeping Sejanus on my side, whatever the cost. In her place I'd need a strong man to guard those sons of mine, someone who might care neither for me nor for them, but who had fought too hard and too long – too dirty – for his place in the sun to lose it now.

'Well, well,' he said, getting up, carefree and relaxed and as pleased with life for its own sake as he always had been, 'you could help me with this breastplate, darling – not at all the costume for visiting a lady, but a man who goes home to change can hardly call himself ardent. Don't let me depress you with all these tales of domestic murder – if one believes the half, one might approach the truth. They're nervous, the Caesars, too prone to see assassins in the dark – it comes from so much intermarriage. Agrippina may have enough to do with keeping her own brood in order. I hear that her sons are not quite the best of friends. She makes too much of Nero, they tell me, and neglects the others, and it doesn't do – really it doesn't. Creates bad feeling, even when there's just the family farm or a baker's shop to wrestle for. In this case, since there's an empire in the balance ... Brother against brother, not a pretty sight, but it happens, one can't deny it.'

I walked with him through the house, barefoot, my hair hanging loose, content with my body's exhaustion that cried out for healthy sleep; and as we lingered a final moment, Paris came in from the street and stood quite still, looking at Sejanus with the nearest thing I had ever seen to respect in his narrow, quizzical face. Not a word was spoken. Sejanus' smile deepened just a fraction, Paris made a slight bow and then turned to gaze rather reflectively at the doorway as Sejanus went through it. Suddenly the pearl on my brother's hand, the quality of his evening clothes, struck me a blow, and I said accusingly, 'You know him, don't you?'

'But of course I know him. I'd be a moron if I didn't.'

'Don't play games with me. I didn't mean it that way, and you know it. I mean, he knows you – doesn't he? Come on – doesn't he?'

'And if he does?'

'Then he shouldn't.'

'But he knows you, sister dear.'

'Oh,' I said, suddenly beside myself, 'what have you been doing? You foolish boy, you've been working for him, haven't you? Spying for him? My God, I can't go away, can I – can't rest for an hour without one of you getting into trouble? Have you any idea of the mess you've got yourself into?'

'Perfectly! Except that it's not a mess, it's a business, and a damned good one. Do stop fretting, dear. You're as bad as Chrysothemis.' And taking my hand quite coolly, he drew me into the centre of the room, well away from the columns and the hangings and the possibility of prying eyes and ears.

'Does Chrysothemis know about this?' I hissed, ready to kill her if she did, and he shrugged his complete unconcern.

'Of course she doesn't. She thinks I spend my time with other women, which makes her appreciate me all the more. But, as it happens, I'm not a particularly promiscuous man – perhaps I've seen too much of that with Dion. I find my excitement in other ways. I enjoy intrigue. I suppose I'm rather sly, really.'

'You're young,' I told him furiously, 'and you're stupid. And you've backed a loser. Sejanus can't outlast Tiberius – he's not even sure about it himself.'

'Perhaps not. But in the meantime he's an excellent paymaster, although naturally he doesn't hand me my wages himself – in fact I'm not supposed to know he's my paymaster at all and couldn't prove it even if I tried. No, there's a whole complicated network of command, with me somewhere in the middle of it, but rising, gaining ground. You see, like the rest of my family I'm cursed with expensive tastes. You should understand that – you and Dion. Is my profession more dangerous than his? I know my peril all right, make no mistake about it. And I'm good at my job, Danaë. In my own field I'm worth my weight in gold, just like Dion. The next time he calls me a parasite you'll know better, won't you, even though you won't be able to tell him so.'

'I wanted you to be a poet,' I said foolishly, and patting my cheek with a gesture that was in itself a declaration of independence, he laughed.

'But I am a poet – one of the most widely read in the city. My verses are distributed every night by little men who paint the lesser ones all over the walls of public buildings, while my masterpieces, of course, are written out on parchment and have a circulation Virgil himself would envy. You'll see, because someone's bound to toss one through your doorway during the next day or so, or slip one into your hand at the circus. You'll be impressed, and Agrippina must be in a state of bliss – even she couldn't praise her husband in more glowing terms than I do.'

'Sejanus is paying you to write poems in praise of *Germanicus*?' I said blankly and he patted my cheek again, enjoying himself hugely.

'Yes – and naturally I wouldn't ask why. Not that one needs to ask. I'm quite confident that one of my most avid readers must be Tiberius himself – which pleases my vanity no end. If he has any thoughts of getting close to Agrippina and letting bygones be bygones, well, I rather think all this passion for Germanicus will make him think again. Are you really so sure I've backed a loser?'

'I wish you hadn't told me,' I muttered, feeling the situation slipping away between my hands, knowing there was nothing I could do about it. 'You shouldn't have told me.'

And he shrugged, careless, impish, permitting himself to be amused.

'No – but then you did rather catch me out, and you do pry so, Danaë. I saw you looking at my clothes and wondering who was paying for them. I knew there'd be questions and quite honestly I just wasn't up to the effort of deceiving you. It's far better this way, and then, if I ever have to go away rather hurriedly, I won't have to hide from you as well as whoever else is looking for me. You've always been so good at shielding Dion from his creditors and his women – I know you'll do the same for me, if I ever need it. And, in any case, perhaps at the bottom of me I really wanted you to know. Perhaps I wanted you to worry about me, Danaë. If nothing else, it will make a change from worrying over Dion.'

And, dropping a brief kiss on the top of my head, reminding me how tall he was, he yawned and walked jauntily away.

13

It was Dion, in the unthinking mood where all men were his brothers, who brought Marsyas to my house on the morning of Sejanus' party – for which I wasn't ready, for which I'd never be ready – and not just Marsyas either but the usual rowdy clutter of charioteers' fans spilling into my hallway, making the street hideous with their barnyard strutting and screeching.

'Just thought we'd wish you luck,' Dion said, taking the best seat, looking around him in a rather bewildered fashion until someone handed him a cup of wine: and immediately my garden-court seemed full of women – of maids running in and out inventing errands to catch a glimpse of the charioteers; Chrysothemis, who hadn't yet managed to get to the bottom of what had happened between me and Marsyas; and Marpessa, leaning for a moment against a pillar and then stretching herself on a heap of cushions, chin on hand, moodily staring.

And as I smiled into the space above my brother's head I found Marsyas there, watching me.

'I'll drink to that,' he said, raising his cup; and recoiling, damning the sudden lurch of my stomach, the stirring inside me of things so deep-buried I had believed them to be dead, I was aware, as always, of the shock of seeing him still alive when even the most devoted of his fans could have expected him, by now, to have perished – spectacularly, horribly – and been long forgotten.

I knew what his life had been these past three years, knew about the races he'd won and the money he'd earned, the women he'd gone through, the riots he'd caused when his fans, infected by the sparks of his insanity, went on the rampage at the end of the day's racing, brawling and thieving and smashing up the wine-shops until they'd worked him out of their systems. I knew how many times the faction servants had gone running across the sand to pick up what should have been his corpse and, prising him loose from the wreckage, dragging his dying horses off him, had found him miraculously alive. I knew about his luxury and his promiscuity, how the factions hated him for his greedy haggling about his salary, and how pressure from the fans always forced them to pay his price. I knew that more than once attempts had been made to expel him from the city and had been defeated by the hysteria of his supporters. I knew, beyond question, that he was the greatest charioteer Rome had; knew, as he'd once told me, that he'd gone far beyond the threat of Bassus, beyond the threat of anything but the danger he deliberately created for himself. And here he was, in my house, a heavy gold ring on every finger, a black silk tunic tightly belted around his waist, an enormous gold snake with a ruby eye coiled on his shoulder, perfume heavy enough to keep the plague at bay marking his signature on the air around him. Here he was; and I, who sincerely loved another man, was still afraid to discover beneath all his gold glitter the lad from the Subura who had not, it seemed, relinquished his hold on the far recesses of my mind.

And it wasn't the day for it. I was harassed, suffering the worst attack of stage-fright of my life. I had enough to do without this terrible man and the fears and memories – the bitter self-knowledge – he brought me.

'You're looking good, Danaë,' he said.

'So are you.'

And in the silence that fell all around us I saw Chrysothemis' interested eyes, and Marpessa – who should have been thrilled by the presence of her hero – still lounging, chin on hand, scowling.

He was as lean as ever, his body pared down to an extension of his reins and his whip-lash, and although his hair was arranged to hide the scar on his forehead, his arms and legs were covered with bruises, the legacy – Marpessa had told me – of a crash last June when he'd been dragged half a lap before managing to cut himself free. 'He ties the reins really tight around his waist, you see,' she'd babbled excitedly. 'Not all of them do. Some of them just pretend – you can see it's all a trick and the minute anything goes wrong they can jump clear. But he really knots them so that he has to use his knife to get out, and that's what gives it all a meaning. Don't you see that? When he straps himself in that way he's giving death a slap in the eye. That's what makes him better than all the others.'

It seemed now that we had nothing more to say, for, giving me a final stare, he nodded curtly and, beckoning to the wolf-pack of his fans – a gesture that was a mere snap of the fingers calling them to heel – he walked off down the passage that led to the street, bidding good-bye to no one.

'My word,' Chrysothemis murmured, 'such manners. What a perfect barbarian.'

And, turning to agree, I was startled to see my sister glaring at me with a face of raw, sixteen-year-old hate.

But I had no time just then to dwell on Marpessa, no time to care who hated me and why, for the hour of Sejanus' party was approaching and my reputation, once again, was at stake. I had rehearsed all day and every day since the booking had been forced on me, had purchased a flute-player and a harpist at enormous cost, had shaken my old dancing-master from his twilight sleep and driven him to the rim of despair. But now that the day had dawned I felt the piece he had choreographed for me was showy and superficial, that my musicians were tone-deaf, and that the magnificent costume Chrysothemis and I had designed between us – dawn-pink, transparent, clinging to the bare skin and the girdle of real rubies beneath it – would hardly be enough to carry me through.

'Why am I exposing myself like this?' I wailed, and my anxiety was so real that even Chrysothemis was kind to me in her way.

'Don't worry,' she told me. 'You look very nice, Danaë, and that should be enough. It was always enough before.'

Sejanus' house, the official home he shared with his wife and children, was everything one expected it to be, brilliantly illuminated, over-heated, an impersonal show-piece of his success. The servants were all handsome, each piece of Corinthian bronze was known to have been coveted by some other man before finding its way into Sejanus' collection, while every possible surface seemed to be inlaid with unusual woods or encrusted with precious stones. The flowers, in stiff, professional arrangements, were all exotic and out of season, the room they had put at my disposal larger than even I thought necessary; and, sitting there in that torment of waiting, I had no doubt that much of the food he was offering to his guests had been brought great distances at enormous expense, its value lying not so much in the flavour as in the fact that it could be eaten nowhere else in the city at this time of year.

The very thought of food sickened me and a moment came

when I could remember nothing of the facile little love-story Agathon had written for me, not one step of the dance, not one movement of the mime, not a single note of music.

'I'll die,' I thought, 'it's better.' And then, 'It's time, madam,' someone murmured and the familiar miracle – the thing that always happened and that I never expected to happen again – took place. My dry throat and the earthquake in my stomach disappeared, and I was a dancer again, a professional. I had come home.

I walked into the room thinking of nothing and stood perfectly still, waiting for silence; and I waited with authority for I was no novice and it was as well to remind them of that from the start. And as the music began, it was just as it had always been – it was right. I had tormented myself needlessly, and, faced with an audience again, all my certainty returned and all my joy in doing the one thing I really understood. There was nothing here in this world of movement and make-believe to defeat or surprise me. Here I was safely on my own ground, and when it was over I took my applause with elation and gratitude, but feeling, just the same, that it was no more than I deserved.

The mist cleared and, throwing an embroidered robe around my shoulders, I went through the well-remembered, dearly-loved routine of accepting congratulations, scattering smiles, saying thank you, how kind, how very generous; and, as I tasted triumph again and found myself thirsty for more, a voice inside my head – perhaps the true essence of myself – asked me how I had ever managed to live without it.

'Superb,' Sejanus said, although I knew he didn't give a damn about my art, and probably hadn't even watched it too closely. And, as his voice produced a few standard compliments and an invitation to linger a moment and take a cup of wine – and as his eye closed in a brief wink to remind me that he hadn't always been so formal – his wife Apicata came quietly up to me, murmuring some adequate little phrase or other, and then moved away again with a careful step, not staying a moment longer than she had to.

She was very small and quiet, a little brown bird of a woman, perfectly composed and serene, with nothing in her slight body or her plain sallow face to hold a man like Sejanus. A careful housewife, Apicata, I thought, busy with her store-cupboards and her accounts, a woman who could be relied on to cope with the small crises of everyday; one who would make no difficulties – who might even be glad – when her husband squandered his excess sensuality elsewhere. Yet, as I watched her moving calmly among his glittering guests, unobtrusive, unnoticed almost, I realized she was pregnant: and I wondered.

I knew some of those guests well enough, socialites and statesmen, frivolous men who would go anywhere and serious men who, until such time as Tiberius made his intentions clear, judged it unwise to refuse Sejanus' invitations; and, here and there, men of a hungrier breed, the failures and malcontents whose expectations of life had so far gone unsatisfied and who were gambling that Sejanus would be able to put things right. There were a few society women, sensation-seekers already ogling my blue-eyed flute-player, a sprinkling of newly-married girls enjoying their first taste of freedom, and, on the less well-placed couches, two sensible ladies unworried by their grey hairs – friends, I thought, of Apicata's, who believing, no doubt as she did, that an entertainer should be asked to leave the moment the show was over, would have nothing to say to me.

And then, on a central couch, someone I didn't know, a very young man, just a boy, with narrow shoulders and a thin neck that made his head seem too heavy, a patrician face, certainly, but with weak, wild eyes and nervous hands, a lad whose unease touched me with sympathetic humour until I realized he was Drusillus, Agrippina's second son, who should not have been here, in this house, in the midst of his mother's enemies.

'*She makes too much of Nero and neglects the others,*' Sejanus had told me, '*and it doesn't do, you know. It creates bad feeling.*' And turning now, catching the wicked light in Sejanus' eyes, I had no doubt that he would find a way to exploit that bad feeling to the full.

'Yes,' he said, parting the crowd around me with his arm, 'your eyes don't deceive you – that really is Drusillus, my guest of honour. Come and smile at the lad.' And as I obeyed, the boy gulped nervously and smiled back, so tongue-tied and curious that I knew he had heard something of my relationship with his uncle Drusus and was memorizing as much of me as possible so he could tell his sisters when he got home. But even as he managed to tell me how much he had enjoyed my performance, had indeed seen nothing like it before – since his mother was not in the habit of inviting fashionable entertainers to her parties – I could almost see his anguish and his dread of discovery.

'*You won't tell anyone, will you?*' his eyes pleaded, and, because I knew Sejanus would already have instructed someone to call on Agrippina in the morning with full details of her son's treachery, I made myself as pleasant as I could, hoping to compensate in some small way for the trouble in store.

But then, with everyone else in that room, I was a witness to one of the most shocking things I had ever seen.

Knowing the value of a good exit – the art of when to leave and how to leave – I was making mine when the double doors behind me were flung open with a clatter no servant would dare to make, and a woman stood in the doorway, an angry woman betraying her upbringing, for she was a patrician and as such had been trained from childhood to conceal her emotions. And because she was a woman who had no heart – a jewelled doll who thought of nothing but her hair and her dignity – her frenzy was doubly terrible. I had seen her a hundred times before. I recognized her. But it took me a long moment to believe that this dishevelled creature was really Drusus' widow, the impeccable, ambitious, untouchable Livilla.

She walked forward in a straight line, with the blind confidence of one who knows the crowd will give way before her, and, stopping directly in front of Sejanus, she said in a toneless, well-bred voice, Drusus' voice, 'So sorry. Unavoidably detained. Is dinner over then? What a pity.' And I knew – everyone knew – that she hadn't been expected, hadn't been invited, that she had been drawn here, probably against her will, by desire for a man who, while appreciating desire, had never encouraged his women to love him.

'We are most honoured to have you here, madam – my wife and I,' Sejanus said softly, dangerously; and giving a high, nervous laugh – as if laughter, like all other forms of emotion, was so alien to her nature that it gave her pain – she turned awkwardly, stiffly, and nodded to Apicata who had come up on her quiet feet, smiling a sedate welcome.

Beside Livilla she was insignificant, plain, not even very young, but that smile just tilting the corners of her mouth held all the placid self-possession that a wife, sure of her place, can afford to lavish on a mistress. And I saw the imperial Livilla step back hastily, as one retreats from fire, and wince.

'So nice to see you,' she said, and glancing just once at the newly swelling curve of Apicata's pregnant body – the abominable proof that the man she loved still slept with his wife – she smiled her own blank, brilliant smile and walked into the crowd, her eyes passing sightlessly over the face of her young nephew who had turned pale and seemed to be looking for somewhere to hide.

They lighted me to the street after that and I set off for home to work my way through the wasteland that comes when the dance is over. I was more grateful than I cared to show when I found Paris waiting for me in the sleeping house.

'What is it?' he said. 'You look quite pale. Here I am waiting with wine to celebrate – but if it wasn't a success we can always use it to drown your sorrows.'

'No, no, it's not that. The performance was fine.' And suddenly I threw both arms around him and held him tight, knowing he didn't like to be touched but needing to feel him alive and whole.

'Well, well,' he said, freeing himself, 'what have we here – such affection! You see, I was right to let you worry about me. I should have done it sooner.'

'Silly boy,' I told him, tart with my own emotion, 'let's have the wine then, and I'll enjoy it all the more if you paid for it yourself. That opal on your shoulder – Paris, I'd wear that myself.'

'Yes,' he said easily, 'I dare say. Well, I paid for the opal anyway, and I ordered the wine, because Chrysothemis has no idea about such things, but I must confess I did charge that to you. So do have a cup.'

'Thank you,' I said, drawn closer to him by the silence, the knowledge that no one else was awake. 'Well, I may as well tell you, since you probably know more about it than I do. I saw a terrible thing tonight.'

'In Sejanus' house?' he said quickly, as alert suddenly as a cat who hears a rustling in the eaves.

'Yes. I saw a woman in love who shouldn't have been in love, and it was shattering – it was like a doll trying to come to life and just not able to cope with sensation.'

'Oh, for heaven's sake,' he laughed, slightly scornful but much relieved. 'Love – is that all it was? I thought for a moment it was something serious. I thought young Drusillus, perhaps, had misbehaved himself, or that his mother had come to fetch him home. Now that would have been something.'

'So you knew about Drusillus, did you? No, don't tell me. I don't want to know how deep you are. It was Livilla: did you know about her?'

He shrugged, uncaring. 'Oh, that's old hat, Danaë. She needs someone to protect her interests. When Tiberius dies she may have to fight it out with Agrippina and she'll need someone to command her armies – just as Agrippina will. And she'll need a husband too. Agrippina is coming to the same conclusion. The word is that Germanicus' spotless widow may marry Calpurnius Piso – wasn't he once a friend of yours? And she's on very good terms with old Gaius Silius who happens to be one of the best generals we have. So if Agrippina is making preparations for the future you can't blame Livilla for doing the same, or even going one better, because Sejanus could be her general and her husband as well. Tiberius wouldn't consent to the marriage in his lifetime because it would make Sejanus too powerful, but once he's dead Livilla can give herself and her sons to anyone she likes. And if she's in love with him, then so much the better.'

'Is that his plan, then – to marry Livilla and rule through her?'

'Oh, how you do flatter me. I'm only a humble scribe in his service, Danaë, he doesn't confide in me. But of course he wants to marry Livilla. Half of the ambitious men in Rome want to marry Livilla, just as the other half want to marry Agrippina. I'd marry either one of them myself if I had the chance. And if I did I'm not at all sure I'd be willing to step down for my wife's children when they got old enough to relieve me of command. If *I* feel like that – just a cross-bred Graeco-Roman poet – think how Sejanus, and Calpurnius Piso, and the rest of them must feel.'

'And Tiberius?'

'If you ask me he'll see to it that both those ladies stay safely unwed. But that won't worry Sejanus because he's the last man Tiberius could give Livilla to. However much the Senators may bow the knee to him, he's still their social inferior, and if he married Livilla he'd be senior to them all – senior to Nero and Drusillus. It would be the same as proclaiming him heir to the throne, and I imagine there'd be a revolution. Agrippina would have nothing more to lose, you see, and it's never good policy to push people too far. No, Sejanus can afford to wait. And in the meantime he's employed his time very sensibly by making the woman fall in love with him.'

'You don't understand,' I told him. 'It's a game to you, and to Sejanus as well. But she was in pain with it. She'd have torn the child out of Apicata's body if she could. And there's not the smallest chance that he will ever care a scrap about her.'

'I should think not,' Paris said scornfully. 'I'd have no faith in him, I can tell you, if it were otherwise. He keeps his head, and he'll see to it that she keeps hers. Now then, Danaë, while I have you to myself, there's a point I'd like to raise with you. I love you dearly, but I do think it's time I had a place of my own. I really can't devote myself to an art like mine with all the racket you create. Does it trouble you if I look out for something more convenient?'

'Do as you please,' I told him, knowing he would do just that, and when I couldn't stop myself from telling him to take care, he laughed, kissed me, and went off to bed.

But I sat for a long time thinking of Livilla – and inevitably of Drusus – and then back to Livilla again and a future torn apart by her and Agrippina. And then I thought about love. In the end what mattered most was my determination never to experience it again.

14

'*Marriages,*' Sejanus had told me, '*are tricky things. One stands to gain or lose a great deal.*' So I was astounded a day or two later when my doorkeeper, along with the flowers and messages and bookings I'd expected, brought me the news that Sejanus was to divorce his wife. The plain, efficient, pregnant Apicata was to be sent away, charged it seemed – although no one was prepared to take it seriously – with adultery. And I could see neither sense nor reason to it.

'Why?' I asked Paris. 'It's pointless. He *can't* marry Livilla, can he?'

'I'm very sure he can't. It's so completely impossible that there must be a simple explanation. I suppose the woman must have committed adultery after all.'

'No,' I said decidedly. 'Not Apicata. She was his wife when I saw her in every sense of the word, and she expected to stay his wife. It's Livilla, forcing his hand, doing illogical things because she's in love. She's stopped thinking about the Empire: she just wants him. She's made him divorce Apicata because she doesn't want him to live with another woman. And he won't like it: he hates women who fall in love with him. Yet he did it, and I wonder why? Livilla must have threatened him with something quite nasty if he couldn't talk his way out of it.'

And I knew, in spite of himself, my brother was more troubled than he would ever admit.

I gave a party that night to launch my new career in the accepted fashion, a few close friends to dinner and a general invitation afterwards for wine and cakes and gossip. My success would be measured by the number who came.

'We'll have to move house,' Chrysothemis told me, rearranging the dining-couches for the tenth time. 'It's the only answer. Since you came back this flat is nothing but a dressing-room. We should be up on the Caelian or the Quirinal, with a garden big enough to eat in and somewhere for you to work. If you keep on rehearsing on this floor, dear, you'll ruin the mosaics. We need an extra reception-room as well, because the hall is like a market-place every morning, and there's absolutely nowhere one can have a private word. Now then, I must run into the kitchen again in a minute or two, so could you have a look at what they're doing with the flowers? Those girls may be very willing but they have no taste. I told them, yellow flowers in the ivory bowls, white in the silver, red in the bronze, but if we don't watch out they'll get it all mixed up.'

And, seeing no point in telling her that they were my mosaics not hers, my bowls and my maids, I went to do her bidding.

Erato arrived first on a wave of perfume and chatter, her gold robe erupting at the hem with feathers dyed aquamarine and black, her feathered headdress anchored with sapphire pins, her eyes, as usual, on the look-out for Dion; and then Xanthe, a glorious Amazon, half-naked, her hair plaited from the crown like a horse's tail, supporting my dancing-master Agathon on one lithe brown arm.

'I found him tottering in the doorway,' she announced, 'and I just picked him up.' Putting him down again on a heap of cushions, she greeted Paris, as she greeted all men, with a hearty kiss on the mouth, earning herself a look of loathing from Chrysothemis who, on her way to the kitchen to check the progress of the sauces, thought better of it and sat down firmly by Paris' side.

Bassus, Dion's faction director, came next, suave and smooth, followed by Lygdus, who also gazed lingeringly at Paris, and was dressed, to my horror, in one of Drusus' Oriental caftans. I thought for a shocked moment that I couldn't bear it, that I'd break down and cry; but then his face above the gorgeous fabric seemed so much older, his eyes so hopeful and unsteady, that I put my arms around him and murmured, 'How are you, my dear friend?'

'As you see,' he said, waving his plump, pampered hand: 'Splendid – splendid. In the best of health and looks, if I say it myself. Now, Danaë, what have you been doing to your hair? Split ends, dear, if I'm not very much mistaken. And didn't I tell you before you went to Greece about the sun? You forgot about your parasol – oh yes, you did – and now look at your skin.'

Patting his arm I drew him towards the others and presented

him as a person of some importance, a man whose voice was listened to in high places.

My brother Dion did not appear. 'He's forgotten all about it,' Marpessa said, looking pointedly at Erato. 'You may as well start without him. I'm hungry.'

'When are you not hungry?' Chrysothemis snapped, her tongue sharpened by Paris' obvious appreciation of Xanthe, but her anxiety about the meal, and the ambitious sauces that wouldn't keep, inclined her to agree, and only my consideration for Erato decided me to wait.

'Well – do as you please. But he won't come,' Marpessa said, flopping heavily on an ivory stool not designed for rough treatment; and spinning round to tell her to take care, expecting to see a child, I realized I was looking at a woman. Her hair was caught up at the crown with gold filigree, one glossy black coil hanging to her waist, the red silk she'd begged from me clinging the whole supple length of her body. I couldn't deny she looked luscious and ripe and altogether enticing – or would have done had she been less peevish, less bored.

'He won't come,' she repeated. 'He'll be drunk, or in bed with somebody.' But then, just as Erato was making up her mind to forget Marpessa's youth and annihilate her with some deadly reply, and Lygdus was starting to tell me that over-cooked food was death to the digestion, there was the familiar disturbance in the hallway and Dion, leaving heaven knew how many fans behind him prowling around my street, strode into the room.

'Well, thank God I'm not the first,' he said. 'Can't bear to be kept waiting for my dinner,' and he headed for the dining-room, taking the couch he fancied, untroubled by such minor considerations as how I wished my guests to be placed.

'My dear, how brave,' Lygdus said. 'If your kitchen is on such a tiny scale then it takes courage to entertain –' But I had paid good money for my cook, and even Lygdus had no fault to find with the spiced sea-urchins and the stuffed dormice, and he hovered with such pleasant indecision between the fallow deer in onion sauce and the pork coated with crushed spices and baked in pastry, that he needed little persuasion to try both.

Chrysothemis had placed herself deliberately far away from Paris, hoping perhaps, that he would catch her eye across the room as he used to do in the old days. But, lounging between

Xanthe and Erato, picking daintily at his food, his opal gleaming on his shoulder, solitude was far from his mind. His couch was the gayest in the room, Erato swishing him with her fan and calling him a wicked boy, Xanthe brushing her bare foot enquiringly against his, both of them indulging themselves – taking a night off – by flirting with a man who couldn't pay their price.

'Doesn't he ever shut up?' Dion asked, eating his way solidly through the pork, far too good-humoured and self-possessed to mind that his brother was doing so well.

'Rarely,' Chrysothemis said and then turned to Bassus, asking his opinion of something or other and appearing to listen with rapt attention, while Marpessa on Bassus' other side lay sulkily against her cushions, eating almost as much as Dion and not speaking a word.

There were fried Jericho dates to follow, a soufflé of almonds and cream and rose-petals, and a mountain of fruit, but already the house was filling up with new arrivals, and as Chrysothemis slipped away to greet them, it occurred to me that Marpessa could do a little more to earn her keep these days than just sit there, moodily lounging.

My atrium was full, my garden-court was full, there were people I barely knew kissing my hands and my neck, praising my house and my looks and Drusus' glorious emeralds; people coming, as I had once gone to Erato's, in the hope of being noticed, of attracting a job or a lover or a little patronage, some of them, perhaps, because they genuinely needed a drink and a bite to eat. And then, when they had been dispersed, came the grand arrivals – Chloe wearing the pearl earrings she had once left with Drusus; an African woman with smoke-coloured skin and ebony eyes who was one of this year's new sensations; and, with something of a fanfare, red-headed Cynthia, covered, not in emeralds, since she had assumed I would be wearing mine, but in topaz and gold.

'I can't stay,' she said. 'But I thought it right just to look in for a moment – I knew you'd be expecting me and I don't like to let people down. This is my friend, Dionysus.'

And, indicating the beautiful honey-gold boy beside her, she put her hand very firmly on his arm and led him away, her gesture of perfect possession reminding me of Marsyas, long ago, wearing Cynthia's jewels and offering his scarred, half-born emotions to me. But if the memory hurt me, if I wondered where he was tonight and loathed myself for wondering, there was nothing in my smile to tell her so, nothing in her regal bearing to suggest she could be wondering too.

It went on a very long time, and although it was all for me – and I could drink flattery – standing there draped in light green silk, garlanded with those fabulous emeralds – as Dion drank his neat Falernian, eventually, when I was sure it had been a success and would be talked about tomorrow, it began to pall. And I was glad enough to shepherd most of them to the door and point them on their homeward path, creating a blaze of torchlight and laughter and an impromptu musical performance in the street that wouldn't endear me to my neighbours.

Lygdus took his leave. Paris escorted Xanthe to the door, lingering long enough to earn a mute reproach from Chrysothemis. Dion stretched himself full length on a couch and closed his eyes, Erato perching beside him, his head in her lap. Marpessa, curled up among the cushions of a deep divan, stirred restlessly, her face still peevish. The night began to turn grey with the approach of morning and, shivering slightly, feeling a sense almost of reprieve, I knew I had half-expected Marsyas and was grateful, not for the first time, that he had failed me.

'He surely won't come now, at this hour,' I thought, yawning, deciding it was time to send them all to bed; and then suddenly, like an apparition growing out of the shadows, there he was. There was no cackling of fans in the doorway, none of the raucous excitement that usually heralded his arrival. One moment he was absent, and the next he was standing among us but not with us, quite separate, the lines of his dark face deepened by fatigue and ill-temper, drained for the moment of the nervous energy that sustained him.

'And what are you looking so pissed-off about?' Dion said, opening his eyes and then closing them without waiting for a reply.

'He's searching for his lost soul,' Erato murmured. 'But we haven't seen it, darling, and we'd be sure to know it – a little black soul, all forlorn. It didn't pass this way.'

Marpessa, her face luminous as I had never seen it, sat bolt upright, her whole body drawn towards him, it seemed, as flowers are drawn to follow the passage of the sun, her excitement so obvious, and to me so alarming, that I got up too, placed myself between them, and said tartly, 'It's late. I don't know where you've come from, but you'd better have a drink, and then you can all go home.'

And since Dion had no intention of moving and Paris had turned conveniently deaf, I went with him to the corner where they had left the mixing-bowl and filled a cup.

'How did you get in?'

'Through the door, how else?'

'I didn't hear you.'

'I can't help that. I don't make a noise: other people make a noise around me. I thought they'd all have gone by now. I saw most of them leave, but then I went off walking again. I've been walking all night, in the alleys, all muffled up so nobody knew me – it's better than sleep sometimes.' And shrugging the dark cloak from his shoulders, he let it fall to the floor as he'd done once before in this house, revealing himself as he'd been at the arena that morning – his last race of the present season – his racing tunic stained with patches of sweat, his arms streaked with dust and grime.

'What a mess,' I said, aghast, and as he held out a hand for the wine his lean, ringless fingers looked oddly naked, reminding me of the first time I'd seen him.

'Yes, I dare say.'

'Aren't you well?'

'You asked me that once before. No – as it happens – I've got a disease, you see.'

'What disease?'

'God knows. I've been walking for hours thinking about it. You've heard of racing-fever? Well, it's not that. It's worse than that. The games finished today and it's the best part of a month before they start again. There'll be a few little things in October, but the class competition – which is me – won't come out again before the Plebeian Festival in November. Give me another drink – I'm always like this at the end of the season. They pay me a fortune – the factions – to take their horses round that bloody arena, and what the poor sods don't know is that I'd do it for nothing. I'd even pay them, because I can't manage without it. Well – I was going to bring you my palm-branch again, but God knows where I put it down – I don't. Don't you feel sorry for me?'

'No. You've got enough self-pity for two. And you may have lost your palm-branch but I bet you know where your prize-money is all right.' And as if he'd suddenly located that elusive source of energy, the thick, damp gloom that was oppressing him – oppressing me – lightened, and he grinned.

'You're right there. I've trained a faction servant to keep my cash away from me when I'm in this humour. Big as an ox, he is, so I couldn't take it away from him if I tried. The trouble is nowadays that when I need trouble I can't find it any more. I got into a dice game in the Subura, and in the old days it would have worked out fine. I'd have lost and when I couldn't pay, somebody would have had a go at cutting my throat. But now I win – look at this.' And tugging a leather pouch free from his belt he sent a handful of coins clattering on the table.

'Some poor bastard's life-savings, I expect. I had to knock him down to get it off him. Now why did I do that? Think about it, and tell me – Danaë.' And walking back to the centre of the garden, pausing a moment under the lamplight, he sat down beside my sister.

'Do you really think,' Chrysothemis enquired, very tight-lipped, 'that you should sit on those cushions, considering the state you're in?' But he ignored her and smiling at Marpessa, his eyes deep and glittering again, he said, 'Well, and what do you think? Your sister thinks I'm a mess, and your brother's woman thinks I'll ruin the furniture. What do you think?'

'You're not a mess, and what can a few sticks of furniture matter?'

'Not to you, at any rate,' I snapped, 'since you've never had to pay for them.' And I was aware, once again, that she was a child no longer. A child would have been overwhelmed, would have blushed and made some clumsy attempt to impress him, but my sister, her first eagerness admirably under control, looked him straight in the eye, displaying herself as he did – as I did – and gave him the long, slow smile not merely of a woman, but of a professional.

'Such a fuss,' she said, 'about a few cushions,' and grinning, he let his lean, calloused hand hover for a moment above her knee.

'I like a girl who can take a man just as he is,' he told her, and pausing a moment because he couldn't quite remember her name, he let his hand travel very deliberately from her knee to her ankle, giving me at the same time his thin, murderously sweet smile.

'Take your hand off her,' my mind whispered, everything in me rising to the facile bait he was offering, my whole body constricting in the tight anguish he had intended. But I was a professional too, and suppressing all my self-disgust and my misery, I said coldly, 'You can spare us your philosophy. And I think it's time to go now.'

'Yes,' Dion agreed pleasantly, swinging himself off his couch and coming to stand beside me. 'Much the best thing. Come on Marpessa, go and find those litter-bearers. You'll have to wake them up, I expect. Be quick about it – stir yourself, girl.' And easily, jovially, expressing the hope that Erato would have something fit for a man to eat because he couldn't remember his supper and couldn't sleep on an empty stomach, he took them all away.

But when I came back into the hallway, Marsyas, who had no litter and no torchbearers, who prowled the city alone as he'd always done, was still there.

'What's the point,' he said 'in sending me away? They'll all assume I stayed, and I wouldn't touch you tonight, even if you'd let me. But if I worked at it, you would let me, you know.'

'Shut up!' I yelled at him, 'Shut up and get out, and don't come back.'

'You don't want that.'

'Yes, I do – get out, go to hell, go strap yourself into a chariot and drive it over a cliff – just get out of my sight and stay out of my sight. You're filthy, and you make me filthy.'

'Go on.'

'I hate you,' I screamed, feeling my throat muscles tear with the violence of the sound, and taking me by the shoulders he shook me into silence, his face as naked, without its mask of mockery, as his hands without their rings.

'Yes, well that's it, isn't it? You hate me. That's real; that means something. That holds people together. You don't hate anybody else, do you? Just me. I'll take it. When I came to see you the other day you looked at me as if you'd seen a ghost. You're afraid of me too, and that's good – good for now, anyway. It would have been easier, believe me, if you'd changed – if you'd turned out to be just another Cynthia. But you're not. So be afraid of me and that'll bind you – for now.'

'No,' I said, my jaw stiff with panic. 'It won't bind me. I won't be bound. You'd better accept it and go away. I've nothing to give you.' And I believed it, although I knew I was bound already. Whatever name we gave to the feeling between us, it still existed. There was none of the devotion in it that I had felt for Drusus, none of the respect. I didn't admire Marsyas, I simply loved him as basically and instinctively – as powerfully – as I loved myself, yet I had spent these past three years growing, learning, and if I had to suffer again I'd do it with dignity, and in private. I could see no more hope for Marsyas than there had been for Drusus, and I had no intention of watching his spirit die. When he put his hands on me again, stripping those years away from me, reducing me to the girl who understood about cold and the heart's deprivation, I knew that I was fighting not merely for my dignity and my peace of mind, but for survival.

'Please,' he said, very quietly. 'Is that what you want me to say? All right then – I never said please to a woman in my life – but please, Danaë, if that's what it takes. *Please* – God damn it.'

And lifting my face as if for his kiss, knowing that it had to be done and done at once, before I lost the will to do it at all, I burst into a peal of full-throated, theatrical laughter.

'Yes, darling, that's right. Say "please" like a good boy. You can even come back and say it again tomorrow, because to tell the truth I've got a headache tonight. Cheap perfume does that to me. But do go on saying please. I love to hear it, although none of the girls will ever believe me.'

And whether or not I had convinced him, my whore's laughter punctured the uncertain storing-place of his energy, and I saw it leave him.

'Bitch!' he said, 'Bloody bitch.'

Unable to stay close to him, I walked forward and called out to my doorkeeper to bring his dogs immediately, and turned cold with horror when the man obeyed.

'The gentleman is leaving,' I said and as the burly brigand who guarded my door and his ill-tempered hounds moved closer, it was as if I had torn myself in pieces.

'I have to pay you back for this, I expect you know that,' Marsyas said, very low, very steady, ignoring the dogs and their trainer's growled command to get moving. 'And when I do, don't be surprised, don't complain.'

'I won't. Remind me to worry about it the next time we meet.'

But they were just words, the first that came into my head, a noise, no more, to cover the pain of this new, self-inflicted bereavement. And hearing the door slam shut behind him I was, for an instant, so sick and blind that I didn't see Marpessa until I stumbled against her.

'He'll pay you back all right,' she told me. 'And you deserve it.'

And when I tried to push past her she grabbed my arm and hissed straight into my ear, 'You don't understand anything, do you?'

'Yes, yes,' I muttered, shocked into speech, talking simply to make her go away. '*I* understand. You're the one who doesn't understand. You think he's splendid and fascinating and thrilling – and so he is – but that's just something to cover himself with, like a cripple would wear a gorgeous cloak. And that's what he is. He's a cripple, and I know about that, because they tried to cripple me in the same way. And I know what he'd do to me – he'd wear me out. He'd waste me, take everything I had, and then he'd blame me because it wouldn't solve anything. We'd end up hating each other, so it's better we hate each other now, while there's still a chance for one of us – for me, I don't deny it. There's no chance for him, none at all. Don't look at me like that, Marpessa – if I'd broken my arms you wouldn't expect me to carry him, would you? It's the same thing.'

But Marpessa's young face was unyielding, her lips pressed into a hard line of contempt.

'That sounds very grand,' she said scathingly, 'but the truth is you've lost your nerve.'

And leaving me standing there, my whole body throbbing with injury, she flounced away.

15

It was a year of enormous personal triumph, when everything I touched prospered and even the riskiest of my investments seemed unable to fail. I opened a perfumery in the Vicus Tuscus, and then a wig-making establishment next door to it, and to celebrate these new business ventures I set up a statue of the Goddess Minerva, patroness of traders, in my hall. I smiled at the socialite Valerius Messalla one day at the circus, with the result that I was the dancer chosen to grace his largest end-of-season party. And after that, parading myself by night in the most gorgeous costumes Rome had seen, and by day in the discreet elegance of white silk and my priceless imperial emeralds, I doubled my fees, and doubled them again, and wondered if there was a limit to what men would pay.

It was a year of triumph too for Sejanus, who, in the face of opposition and calumny and some honest panic, managed at last to secure a foothold in the imperial family by marrying his sister Aelia to the ailing Claudius, the brother of Livilla and Germanicus. His own union with Livilla might well be an impossible dream; his daughter's betrothal to Claudius' son had gone awry when the boy, like so many young Caesars, had met an early death, but his sister's marriage allied him, if only vaguely, with Agrippina, Livilla, and Tiberius himself, and was an honour no man of his rank had any right to expect.

'You may congratulate me,' he said one evening, slipping into my house at so indiscreet an hour that I knew someone – my brother Paris? – must have let him know I was alone. 'I am now the brother-in-law of Agrippina's brother-in-law, the brother-in-law of Livilla's brother and of the Emperor's nephew, and although my sister's new husband is somewhat weak in the legs and excessively weak in the head – well – he is a Caesar, this Claudius, with only five fine young nephews between him and a legitimate claim to empire. Tell me, what are my patrician friends saying about me now? That I'm getting too proud, and the higher I climb the further I'll have to fall?'

'Something like that.'

'And what do you say?'

'That you'll fall on your feet.'

But even so, the memory of Livilla haunted me, and seeking out Lygdus who was now in her service I asked him, 'What's all this I hear about your lady? You told me she was just marble and vanity, but I saw her one night last September, and the marble had melted, and she wasn't vain either. She hadn't even done her hair.'

'Oh yes,' he said, shuddering, 'I remember it well. She'd done her hair all right, and then nearly pulled it out again by the roots and thrown a mirror at her maid's head and knocked the poor girl senseless. The gentleman in question had got his wife pregnant it seems – normal enough, you'd think – except that he's her man now.'

And beckoning me to come closer, he whispered, 'There's something wrong with her. I've told you many a time, they're a queer lot, the Caesars. Claudius is wrong in his head and one of Agrippina's brothers was just the same. The next time you see Nero just look at his nails. Bitten, my dear, to the quick – turns my stomach. Young Drusillus twitches. And Livilla – I'll tell you – she's been asleep for thirty-five years, and now, with a married daughter who could make her a grandmother any day, she's a girl again – and it doesn't do. First love, my dear, that's her trouble. It may be very pretty at fifteen, but at her age it's not pretty, and it doesn't make her easy to serve either. Got him to send his wife away too, which I don't expect was any great hardship to him, but now milady, who thought she was being so clever, has gone and landed herself in another mess. What's she to do if he gets married again? He could, you know, because Tiberius likes his ministers to be married, and a man in Sejanus' position should have a wife. All Tiberius has to do is say the word. She never thought of that until a day or two back, and when she did she had a fit – I'm telling you, *a fit*. Bit her lips and threw herself about something shocking, and then just sat and stared. Not even Eudemus knew what to do, and he's been doctoring her for years. If Tiberius gets to hear about it she'll be sorry. She'll find herself on an island in solitary confinement, like her Aunt Julia – Agrippina's mother – if she's not careful.'

But that year was also the one in which Tiberius first showed his mind. He had been content, it seemed, after Drusus' death, to let things take their natural course. Sitting in lofty isolation on the Palatine, high above the schemings of Sejanus and the hopes of Agrippina, he had continued, as he'd always done, to govern without love a people who had never loved him; and although he had not singled out Agrippina's boys for preferment, he had done nothing against them. There had been, it was true, a general tightening of security, a revival of the blasphemy laws and the morality laws which made it possible for men to find themselves in court charged with vague offences they barely understood – a screen for other things the prosecutors found it inconvenient to name – but Tiberius had always believed in chastising his people from time to time, and no one seemed seriously alarmed.

Tiberius would, it was felt, bow to the inevitable, and my brother's belief in Sejanus' star was not shared by men of rank and breeding who knew that Tiberius, no matter what his personal inclinations, was an aristocrat like themselves, trained from birth to sacrifice private desires to political expediency, who would not gamble with the security of the State.

My friend Aemilius Scaurus, recently returned from his governorship of Cilicia, came to see me, full of good cheer and hope for the future, for his wife was a close friend of Agrippina and he was enthusiastic in her praises. And when I suggested that Agrippina's sons, perhaps, were giving cause for concern, that Nero was thought to be morose and nervous, and Drusillus was running wild, he immediately laid the blame at Tiberius' door.

'It is lack of employment, my dear, nothing else. They have been born to great responsibilities and I can't help feeling – in common with many others – that the Emperor should acknowledge it. He should give them something to do. Statecraft is not an easy business. It's an art, and a tortuous one, and no one doubts that Tiberius is its grand-master. He could teach them so much – he knows the necessity for it, and of course, eventually, he's bound to take them under his wing.'

And so, on the surface, helped along in some small way by an outpouring of poetry in praise of Germanicus, the magic of Agrippina's cause gained fresh potency, dazzling her supporters' eyes until they really believed Tiberius had no choice. Livilla's – and Drusus' – twin boys were simply not suitable. They were too young, too frail – one of them, indeed, was already ailing and died later that year – and for the first time since the birth of the Empire the succession seemed beyond dispute. Agrippina, fulfilling her role of the perfect Roman matron, had provided heirs in plenty and the party now growing around her was so confident of her destiny, so certain that there was only one direction for Tiberius to take, that, in their eagerness to end their lady's anxiety they dared to give him a push.

When, at the end of the year, the Pontiffs – most of them Agrippina's relatives and friends – offered the customary prayers for the safety of the Emperor and the well-being of the State, they prayed not for Tiberius alone, but for Nero and Drusillus as well, a procedure which, if allowed to pass, would be an open acknowledgement of them as his heirs. The Pontiffs, no doubt, convinced themselves that they were merely legalizing an existing situation. If Tiberius, for some sentimental or sinister reason of his own, couldn't bring himself to admit it, all he had to do was to keep silent, and the thing was done.

But Tiberius, for once in his life, chose to be less than obscure. Why, he wanted to know, had they seen fit to compare two callow youths with his august self? What had these youths done to merit their place beside him? Nothing, so far as he could see. And calling the Pontiffs to his audience chamber – a rarity in itself – he let them know that all that kept him from sending them into exile then and there was that he believed Agrippina had put them up to it.

And then the first blow fell. Gaius Silius was a military man, blunt and straightforward, and if he was arrogant it was only because he'd wielded authority for so long he'd come to take it for granted. He was charged now with complicity in a Gallic rebellion he had himself suppressed, and with extortion during his efficient administration of the province. That was the façade. The reality was his friendship with Agrippina, for if it ever came to a fight the lady's best hope of success lay with the German legions, Germanicus' own troops still loyal to his memory, and who better to command them than Gaius Silius, one of the ablest generals of his day?

Silius refused to believe that anyone could seriously question his integrity, and, knowing himself condemned in advance, he went home and killed himself during an adjournment in the proceedings. But even his dignified death, which saved the prosecution trouble and embarrassment, had no softening effect. His entire estate, less the customary percentage paid to his accuser, was confiscated, and his wife and family went into exile with barely enough to keep body and soul together. The accuser – and his name escaped nobody – was Lucius Visellius Varro, an old drinking-companion of Sejanus.

And after Gaius Silius, came Calpurnius Piso, a man of enormous charm, who had, it seemed, already asked Agrippina to be his wife and who could have held her cause together by the sheer force of his personality. The charges of treason and immorality were unworthy of him and he declined to take them seriously. Having nothing to lose he made it clear he knew why he was going to die and, after a graceful, witty speech to the Senate, he went home without any fuss and took his own life too. His accuser was Quintus Granerius, yet another associate of Sejanus.

And so, at one stroke, Tiberius had not only cut the ground from under Agrippina's feet, he had shown the whole world that she lacked the power to help her friends. But one thing puzzled me.

'Tell me,' I asked Paris, 'since you're so clever – I understand what he's done, but I don't understand why. People are saying it must have been Sejanus' idea, and certainly he's the one to profit from it. But Tiberius wouldn't have taken these drastic steps just to help Sejanus, would he?'

'My dear girl, of course not,' my tolerant, infinitely superior young brother informed me. 'I don't think we should see this as a move against Nero and Drusillus at all, but as a direct attack on Agrippina. I think Tiberius is telling her that he may well – if he feels like it – accept her boys, but that she'll have to stay well out of it herself. He's saying he won't tolerate a party forming around her, and she'd do well to listen.'

'And if Tiberius dies tomorrow?'

'Oh, anarchy, I expect, for a while. But Sejanus won't worry about that. He'll have a short way with anarchy – especially now that old Gaius Silius is no longer with us – and if he can provide stable government people will soon stop worrying about whether it's legitimate or not.'

'But can he do that? Someone said to me only this morning that even if he finds himself in a position to make a *coup*, men of integrity will not serve him.'

My brother hooted his derision. 'Yes, I dare say someone did say that. But we saw what happens to men of integrity only the other day, didn't we? A dignified speech to the Senate and then a knife in the gut. There'll be an epidemic of lost integrity pretty soon, I shouldn't wonder. By the way, darling, just who *was* it told you they wouldn't serve Sejanus?'

And although he was laughing, and didn't really want to know, cold water touched my spine, and I said hastily, 'Don't involve me. Keep me clean. You may need a pair of clean hands one day and if they're not mine, then God help you.'

I went to Campania that summer and I went fearfully, for I knew the luminous, golden season and the days of unwanted idleness would remind me of Drusus. Although I had no desire to forget him, I found it easier to preserve him as a shadow, touching but not dominating the events of every day. But perversely I rented a house in Baiae for Marpessa and Chrysothemis, and went alone – saying I needed a rest – to my own house outside the town.

It was no shrine to Drusus' memory, merely a property purchased for me through a series of agents and middlemen, which Drusus himself had never seen, a villa of moderate size with a walled garden, set in isolation among olive trees and rich cornlands. It had impersonal rooms furnished by someone who had been told to supply the best of whatever was in fashion at the time, a steward who treated me as a guest, and although solitude had seemed attractive, I soon found that these sunny, empty spaces alarmed me, and I was glad, at the end of five long days, to see Paris.

'Don't scold,' he told me, sizing up the expensive furnishings with a critical eye. 'I know you're in hiding, but this is business and you'll be as intrigued as I am when you hear it. I don't talk to Sejanus directly, as you know, but my contact came to see me yesterday, and – well – I won't trouble you with all the fancy wrapping the package came in, but the truth is Sejanus is about to pay you a visit. No, no, not to see you, love, because he can do that openly enough. He wants to meet someone else here, and I couldn't be more interested because it has to be a woman. We all know what happens to Livilla, don't we, every time he gets close to one of the daughters of the nobility, so he has to cover his tracks. And he wouldn't risk it for a passing fancy. Now don't look so put out. You may not want to get involved but there's no way you can refuse. Just keep your eyes open and make sure you get a glimpse of her face. My guess is it's one of Valerius Messalla's daughters, but it would be earth-shaking, wouldn't it, if it turned out to be Agrippina?'

Earth-shaking for him, perhaps, and Livilla, but when I had worked through my mild annoyance at being used as a screen – since even so acutely jealous a woman as Livilla would make no objection to her lover's association with a fashionable courtesan – I discovered that really I didn't give a damn. Curiosity, of course, existed, but curiosity was a poor thing to fill the growing void inside me, and I was more concerned with the pain of remembering Drusus and the necessity of not remembering Marsyas, than with the question of who was next to govern the Roman State.

It was a pale blue evening, calm and very still, and the sound of carriage wheels on the lonely little track reached me long before the vehicle itself, so that I was in time to see the horseman dismount and hand down a lady with the kind of deference that is only accorded to the nobly born. The man I knew by sight, a hard-faced, barrel-chested officer of the Guard, Macro by name, one of Sejanus' trusted captains; but the woman, wrapped from head to foot in a dark cloak, could have been anyone at all, for I could see no more than her hand holding the garment securely around her head.

'This way, madam,' Macro said, elbowing me aside with military rudeness. But once inside my hall she paused, allowed her hood to fall, and to my complete amazement revealed not the flamboyant beauty of Messalla's daughter, nor the impeccable dignity of Agrippina, but the thin, plain face of Apicata, Sejanus' divorced wife.

I gaped, I think, and perhaps I gasped too, for her pale lips moved briefly with a quiet, faintly supercilious smile.

'Good evening,' she said calmly, her hands neatly folded, her attitude as always impenetrably serene. 'My husband assures me that you are totally discreet, and I have never had cause to doubt his judgement. I assume you have dismissed your servants for the evening, as instructed?' And when I nodded, 'Good. I have brought a woman of my own to attend me – if you would be kind enough to show her where such things may be obtained I would like some rose-water for my hands and perhaps a little hot, sweet wine. I shall not be staying long.'

As I left to do her bidding, her faint smile asked me once again, *'Didn't you know there are other things besides beauty and a lithe body like yours, to hold a man?'*

Sejanus arrived soon after and, assuming I would not be needed again, I sat in the garden, swamped once more by the clinging fog that was my own lack of purpose. Three years ago I would not have believed it possible to be rich and successful, to have my health and my looks, and still be unhappy, yet now my grand achievements took the air like dust, and with nothing more to dream for I ached and was bereft.

They were together for little more than an hour, sitting in quiet consultation like any other married couple – except that they were not married – and then, as the carriage wheels crunched away, he came striding across the garden, his vitality shredding my gloom like the new sun dispersing a mist on the sea.

'What a lovely night,' he said, and even the roses, which had been wilting in the sticky heat, seemed to raise their heads, their muted evening colours taking on a fresh glow.

'Have I displeased you by making so free with your pretty house? No, surely not – I was never afraid of that. Your situation here is perfect, you see – too good to be missed, so completely off the beaten track. Yet people notice you, Danaë, as people notice me, and that struck me at once as an ideal arrangement. All Baiae – which means all Rome, or the part of it that concerns us, at any rate – will know you are here, just as they'll all know I was here too: whereas my wife is such an unobtrusive lady, I doubt if anyone watches her. Need I say more?'

'No. I understand – as much as I'm meant to understand, that is.'

'Good,' he said, and his mouth curving with his uneven smile, he held out his hand. 'Well then, since we are here, quite alone, and so many people know it and think they know why – and since I've always been a man to seize my opportunities – may I stay the night? Is that too much to ask?'

'No,' I told him. 'No. I was hoping you would,' and I gave him my hand as one stretches out cold fingers to a blaze.

'What is it?' he asked, laughing. 'Do you feel the need for some uncomplicated sex? Dear girl, you're not alone, believe me. There's nothing like it – no fuss to begin with and no tears afterwards, just two good friends together. It's the best medicine there is – and perhaps I'm ailing too, a little, in that direction. Come on then, let's get to bed. I'll talk to you later, if I can keep awake.'

But afterwards, as we lay together in companionable exhaustion, and I was longing to ask him about Livilla and if Apicata knew he had stayed with me – and if she cared, he said suddenly, 'You like me, Danaë, don't you?'

'Of course, but not enough to be a nuisance.' He laughed, leaning closer. 'Yes, I'll pay you the compliment of believing that. But what I mean is – setting aside my charm and my virility and the lovely, uncomplicated things I've just been doing to you – you actually *like me?*'

'Why ask? You know it. I always have liked you.'

'And do you know what kind of man I am?'

'Oh – I imagine so.'

'Go on – don't flatter me. Speak freely. I won't bring charges.'

'Well – you're ambitious and ruthless and quite wicked, I suppose.'

'How can you bring yourself to like such a man?'

'Because you're more fun than anybody else I know. You have something extra – don't ask me what it is – but when I stand next to you the sun feels hotter and the sky looks brighter, and I think you get hungrier than other men ... How silly that sounds. But it's what I feel about you. And it exhilarates me.'

'Quite so. Then tell me, Danaë – selfish and rough as I am, do you trust me? Consider carefully, because there are degrees of trusting and I'm not talking at the sentimental level most women are content with. Let me put it this way. If you were drowning, who would you choose to save you, me or a well-meaning, idealistic lad whose mother has only half taught him to swim? And while you're thinking it over we'll have some more exhilaration, shall we? Yes?'

And crushing his hard, tanned body against mine, he left me no breath to reply.

16

The lady Apicata came to my house twice more that August, sliding quietly through my door with the evening shadows, and when she took her sedate departure an hour or so later I was quite certain she knew that the man she still called her husband remained behind not merely to give himself an alibi but to make it a reality. So confident was she of her place in his life that I, and Livilla, and any other woman who caught his eye, appeared to have no meaning for her.

'Could there be a more perfect arrangement?' he said. 'If I could conduct all my business this way I'd be a happy man.' And just before I was ready to return to Rome, he came alone and unannounced and spent two days with me, eating enormously, making love whenever and wherever the fancy took him, leaving me purring with physical content like a cat in a pool of sunshine.

'You need a new house,' Chrysothemis told me on my return home, sorting through my correspondence, separating the offers of work from the offers of a more romantic nature, and then subdividing again into the bookings she thought I should take and the men who were paying her to put in a good word. And so, the next morning, fired with the need to make changes – to sweep my gloom away – I went out and bought one.

It was on the Caelian Hill, just beyond the gladiators' school, in a good, quiet street; a narrow entrance, like Erato's, set between two shops, opening into a pillared atrium, the rooms around it so neutral and plain that they seemed to be waiting for the imprint of my personality. There was another reception room beyond the atrium, a cosy, low-ceilinged dining-room for winter, a summer dining-room open to a garden-court full of flowering shrubs and baskets of greenery hanging from the colonnade, and, beyond that, a tiny, walled garden with roses and little trees and water splashing happily into an alabaster bowl.

I spent a month of self-indulgence, gorging myself with colours and fabrics, choosing new furniture and new servants to cope with a larger household. I had the mosaic pavement lifted from the atrium and redone in black and white, and the walls painted with groups of white-robed nymphs gracefully posing against a dawn sky. I had the summer dining-room marbled in aquamarine, the winter dining-room in the colours of ripe plums and rich, red wine, and everywhere, even among the green-veined marble fittings of the bath, I placed statuettes of myself dancing. I gave Marpessa leave to furnish a room of her own, and Chrysothemis too, and for myself I chose a retreat built off the garden-court, not really a bedroom at all, and lavished far more attention on it than was strictly decent in a woman not a registered courtesan. I had the walls painted with flowers and orchards and May-time fields, a mosaic of rose-petals beneath my feet, and although my new bed, an enormous triple couch with a silver frame, caused raised eyebrows from Chrysothemis and giggles from Marpessa, who said, too innocently, that it was a sin to sleep in such a bed alone, I was good-humoured enough, just then, to let it pass. This, at last, was my house, an extension of myself. Lying on my outrageously comfortable divan, the air from the garden-court bringing me the scent of living green and the serenade of the fountain, I was almost at peace.

Paris had spent most of the summer in Rome, working on a collection of serious poems he planned to publish later in the year, but on my return he left me in no doubt that political intrigue, not literature, had won first place in his heart.

'Come on, do tell,' he said, drawing me into the centre of the room, checking his own security as he always did these days. 'I have to know. I very nearly came down to Baiae just to find out. Who *was* the lady?'

When I told him, his disappointment was almost comic.

'Well, there's devotion for you,' he conceded. 'She allows herself to be divorced, goes off in disgrace like a tame little mouse, and still she works for his cause. She even agrees to meet him in secret so as not to upset his imperial mistress. Well, she has her children to consider. Yes, she strikes me as a sensible woman. In her place I'd probably do the same.'

'And the epic poem?'

'Yes – yes, coming along. But I need peace and quiet, you know – and an enormous amount of privacy.'

He took a flat some time later over a book-binder's shop in the

Argiletum and although he said lofty things about his desire for independence he made no objections when I furnished it for him and gave him a couple of servants to look after him. I assumed, and so did Chrysothemis, that he would ask her to go with him, and, indeed, he was well aware of the advantages in it.

'She's perfect for me – quite ideal,' he told me. 'And I know she's longing for a place she can really call her own. She'd be so busy arranging my bronzes and my ivories and planning little gourmet dinners that she'd never even notice the shady side of my nature. Yes, we could have a very pleasant, very fastidious life together. She's really too good to miss.'

But somehow the offer was never made.

He intended, half wanted, to ask. She half intended to accept. Yet he was as restless as a cat, she had a feline caution and fear of change, and their moment passed quietly away. She never told me the affair was over and neither did he. She merely grew a little paler, a little sharper, infinitely more preoccupied with my possessions and the intimate details of other people's lives, and I was sure, now, that I would have her with me forever.

I gave a great many parties that autumn and it seemed that Marpessa had decided, at last, to wake up from her adolescent sulks and enjoy herself. And since she did nothing by halves, there were times when I could have wished her still asleep. Everyone, that burnished October, was looking at Marpessa, or so she thought, and her newborn appetite for pleasure was so noisy, so insatiable, that it was more than Chrysothemis, for one, could bear.

'You'll have to do something about her, Danaë,' she told me constantly. 'She's turned seventeen. At her age you'd got up to Aemilius Scaurus. There's no time to lose now – look at her. You'd better get her settled before she does something really stupid, and runs off with a flute-player, or worse.'

But a suitable establishment for Marpessa was not the affair of a moment. It would have been a simple matter, in my position, to find her an Aemilius Scaurus of her own, to set her feet on the path I had trodden myself with such excellent results, but, knowing the insecurities and humiliations of such a life, I wanted better than that for my sister. Marriage, for her, was not an impossibility. Marpessa had never been a performer, never been a harlot – was, to the best of my knowledge and most surprisingly, still a virgin – and I knew plenty of Greek and Asiatic merchants who wouldn't refuse the dowry I could put together.

'I'll give her the rubies I bought in Greece for a wedding present,' I thought, remembering her rooting through my boxes on the day of my return. 'And if things go well this year I'll add to them.' But there was no hurry, and I was content to give my sister this time of carefree, unthinking youth, when the world belonged to her and she had no responsibility for it. I had never been so young, and although I found her vanity exasperating – having more than enough of my own – I felt that we had never been closer. We went out together to selected parties, since I had to be careful of her reputation, and it was Erato, in her ruthless pursuit of my brother Dion, who persuaded me one night, against my better judgement, to take her to a faction banquet.

It was already the middle of November, a snap of cold in the air, and because the Plebeian Games had ended that day with a resounding victory for the 'Blues', their director Bassus had spread a mighty feast at the faction club-house for his lads and their supporters, encouraging them, now that the season was over, and he wouldn't need their services again until the Festival of Cybele in April, to help themselves to as much food and wine as they could hold and as many women as they could get.

I had no idea where Bassus really lived. I knew he had a house somewhere in the suburbs, with the young wife who had once cast tender glances at Dion, and several children by his previous marriages, but this club-house of the 'Blues' was very much his creation; and as I entered it now the glare of torchlight and lamplight was painful, the odour of so many exotic foods an assault on my stomach. There were blue-clad faction servants everywhere, carting huge amphorae of wine to tables which were piled high with foreign-looking, foreign-smelling delicacies from all over the Empire, while in the place of honour stood a monstrous confection some enterprising pastry-chef had moulded into the shape and colour of a bay horse. There were horses too, cast in bronze, in niches all around the walls, the winners of a hundred races past, and portrait-busts of the men who had driven them, most of them no longer here to enjoy their fame. Demetrios, killed at twenty, after 1,000 victories; Dion the Athenian, dead at twenty-four after taking the palm-branch 1,569 times; the Judaean Simeon, who had gone back to the land of his fathers to die of his wounds at twenty-eight, and whose 3,020 victories had earned him a full-sized statue in a well-lit corner of the banqueting hall, the names of his horses and his estimated prize-money engraved on its base. But his living team-mates, dressed up in their blue silk tunics, flashing their teeth and their jewellery like military medals, seemed untroubled by these reminders of early death; and even the faction silver, engraved with dancing skeletons and the grinning jaws of the Hound of Hell, was no more than a joke, or perhaps an encouragement to drink again while there was still time.

'I was your age,' I told Marpessa, 'and younger, when I had to dance for a crowd like this.' But instead of the surprise and perhaps the glimmer of respect I'd hoped for, she said, 'Lucky old you,' and walked on ahead of me, clearing herself a pathway through groping hands and the cool stares of just about every loose woman of any standing in town.

Dion was not at first to be found, but Erato, wrapped in a feathered robe that went through every shade of blue from midnight to ice, soon had servants running here and there until someone located him and escorted us to the terrace overlooking the main dining-hall, where he had been throwing dice, squandering his prize-money, in the company of a young giant from Gaul recently recruited to the 'Blues', and Macro, the guards officer who had brought Apicata to my house. And I knew at once that our arrival gave him no pleasure, for as we came up the steps towards him he didn't even trouble to move from the double couch he was occupying alone, leaving it to Macro and the young Gaul to make room for us.

'That's right,' Erato said, taking the couch the Gaul had hastily vacated. 'Now then, if Danaë sits there, in Macro's place, and you, dear boy, get them to fetch another couch for this little girl, and a couple of stools, we shall do very well. And something fit for a lady to drink, well chilled and light – and clean goblets, please, young man ...'

And as the blond and rather beautiful boy, looking exceedingly dazed, rushed off to do her bidding, she slipped the feathered extravaganza from her shoulders, revealing a tiny brown silk body that was not dressed but simply decorated, here and there, with blue feathers and blue jewels.

'Don't put that stool there,' she said lazily, wickedly, as the young Gaul came back with an army of faction servants and an array of goblets for her to choose from. 'It might inconvenience Dion. He'd have to turn his head at least two inches to the left if he wanted to talk to me, and we can't have that, can we? I see Macro doesn't want a stool at all. He'd much rather sit on Danaë's couch, which says a lot for his good sense. So – we're all comfortable, except Dion, of course, who wishes we hadn't come. But we'll ignore him, shall we?'

'Does she always go on at him like that?' Macro asked, moving rather closer than I liked. But he was too deep in Sejanus' confidence to be offended, and I smiled.

'Yes – all the time.'

'I wouldn't like it.'

'Neither does he. But it works. They break up every few months and he vows he'll never go back. But he's lazy, and she's determined, and he always does.'

Macro was not really interested in Dion, and, his arm coming around the back of the couch, not touching me but everything in his massive, overheated body wanting to touch, he said thickly, as if he'd been wanting to say it for a long time, 'I watched you at Baiae, sitting in your garden, and if I hadn't been on duty ... Well, it passed the time, thinking about it. I'd just like to say that when he's had enough ... because I can't poach on his preserves, can I, him being my commanding officer and all? You know what I mean? You may see it as a step downhill, with a fellow like me, but I know where I'm going. When he passes on to higher things, somebody's got to step into his shoes. And he thinks the world of me.'

'I'm sure he does,' I murmured, and although the man was drunk and boastful, there was no reason to suppose he couldn't be the next Commander of the Guard when Sejanus rose to those unspecified 'higher things'. He was hard and ambitious enough, experienced enough as a soldier, and certainly, if Sejanus trusted him, he must be far from stupid. But I knew, even on that small acquaintance, that however much he tried, he could never be Sejanus. No imperial princess was ever going to risk her rank and possibly her life for him, no shrewd young man like my brother Paris was ever going to say 'He's a winner'; there was nothing in him to quicken my senses to folly, to challenge and refresh me as Sejanus always did.

'Yes, I know where I'm going,' he said, and I was spared the necessity of a reply when Marpessa, putting her hand on the shoulder of the worshipping Gaul so that she could raise herself a little and see better, called out, 'Look, here comes Marsyas. Oh Lord – do look at him – he's got his new racing tunic on. He chucked the "Greens", didn't you know, and now he's all in red. I bet Bassus won't like that.'

'He's got a bloody nerve, coming here,' Macro growled, distracted from the contemplation of his great future by his present allegiance to the 'Blues'. 'After the way he let Bassus down – yes, he's got a bloody nerve, all right.'

But Dion, who had never changed his faction, shook his head. 'To hell with that. If he lived his life by that set of rules he'd never go anywhere, because he's let everybody down.'

And, rousing himself, he went to the top of the steps and bellowed amiably, 'Come over here, you lousy bastard, because nobody else is going to talk to you.'

I saw Bassus, sitting with Xanthe in the centre of the room, raise pained eyebrows, but Marsyas gave him a companionable clap on the shoulder as he passed by, kissed the ever-obliging Xanthe on her open mouth, and running up the steps embraced Dion like a brother, whispering something in his ear that caused guffaws and back-slapping and a few friendly obscenities which they, at least, found highly amusing.

I hadn't spoken to him since the night, a year ago, when I'd turned him out of my house, a night like this one when the games had ended and he'd been struggling in the wasteland of living with himself until he could get back in the arena again. There was nothing bedraggled about him tonight. His scarlet tunic was immaculate, the swirl of black silk around it anchored at the shoulder with a massive ruby pin. His hair was oiled and curled, there was gold in his ears and around both his arms, a peacock-strutting in his step. And since he'd brought a pack of his own admirers with him – 'Red' faction supporters who, until he deserted them in their turn and went to race for 'White' or 'Green' again, would be ready to lie down and die for him – no one was in any doubt that he was looking for trouble.

'They shouldn't have let him in,' Macro grumbled, 'and Bassus ought to throw him out now – in fact I'll do it for him.' But instinctively, as he made a move forward, my hand was on his wrist, sliding up his arm, holding him back with the best weapons I had, and furious with my compulsion to use them.

'So what's all this?' Marsyas said, swaying slightly, playing drunk perhaps, although it was always difficult to tell with him. 'A family party! By God, Dion, they don't give you any peace, do they? And what's Macro doing over there? Keeping her warm for your boss, are you?'

'Piss off,' Macro said, starting to get up again, but if Marsyas wanted a fight he wasn't ready yet, and laughing, he dislodged the young Gaul from his stool, kicked it towards one of the young men who had followed him up the stairs, and with an arm around Dion's shoulder, began a rambling tale about two Egyptian girls and a donkey we had all heard before, and which was fit for no one's ears. And it was then, as I got up, intending to take Marpessa away, that the young man sitting on the stool at her feet turned his head and I saw with shock that it was Drusillus, Agrippinas second son, rocking himself to and fro in the stage of drunken helplessness where everything is funny and any mean and dirty man his friend.

'Yes,' Macro said, standing behind me, 'that's surprised you, hasn't it? He's got a natural taste for low company, that young man, so you can't blame my commanding officer if he caters for it. I introduced the lad to Marsyas myself – on instructions, of course. My commander said, "See to it that he meets a vicious man," and I couldn't think of anybody better, or should I say worse, than Marsyas. We're working for a genius, Danaë, you and I – he never leaves a stone unturned, and by God, he knows how to make use of what crawls out from under. Break Agrippina's heart, it would, if she could see her little boy now, after all she's done to make him into another Germanicus. His grandfather Tiberius wouldn't be any too pleased with him either. Young Nero, her eldest, isn't doing much better. He's not wild, like this one, but he's moody, and you and I both know somebody who'll be able to write a poem or two to make out he's queer, when the time comes. They'll neither of them look much like Germanicus when we've finished with them. I ask you, who'll risk their lives supporting lads like these?'

I sat down again, trying to tell myself I wasn't involved, that it was nothing to me that Marsyas was being paid to corrupt one young man and Paris to slander another. But when I looked up, unable to deceive myself, Macro had moved away, called to the top of the stairs by Xanthe; and a young man who had come in with Marsyas and Drusillus was standing before me, looking eager and rather foolish.

'May I?' he said, somewhat unsteady on his feet. 'May I talk to you for a moment? You don't know me.'

'No I don't, and you'd better sit down before you fall down. Not on my skirt, silly boy.'

'Oh, I wonder if you talk to my father like that,' he said, hiccupping with laughter. 'I'd just love to hear it if you ever do. I'm Lucius Aemilius Scaurus – and I've been curious about you for years. You're the most absolutely beautiful woman I've ever seen, and I can't imagine my father, with his long face – "Stand to attention when you speak to me, boy" – I just can't imagine him, puffing and panting ... I do hope you gave him a bad time. You can't like him, can you?'

'I certainly can. I like him very much, and so do you, I imagine, when you're sober.'

The grey eyes narrowed, thought about it, and then he sighed. 'Well, never mind about that. I think *you're* completely sensational – even this close. You wouldn't give me a kiss, would you? I once climbed a wall just to watch you cross the street, and fell off and cracked my ankle. It still hurts me, even now, when it rains.'

'Is that my fault?'

'Yes – I really think it is – and a kiss would go a long way to mend it.' But, as I leaned forward to give him the peck on the cheek his audacity, and his charm, deserved, a lean, jewelled hand fell on his shoulder as if it came from the sky, pinching him quite hard, and Marsyas said loudly, 'What's he after – trying to get for nothing what his old man has to pay for?'

'Oh my word, no,' young Scaurus said, blushing, hoping it was a joke, offended, I thought, by Marsyas' reference to his father; and getting up, facing him – because I was offended too – I said just as loudly, 'That's none of your business.'

And it was unfortunate that Macro chose that moment to come back and elbow Marsyas aside.

'Don't push me,' Marsyas said through his teeth, and the two men actually smiled at each other in chilling salutation, and Macro licked his lips.

'Do you want to make something of it?'

'No he doesn't,' Erato said, flitting between them in all her feathers. 'At least, I suppose he does, but not here, darlings. Go out and slaughter each other somewhere else. But don't go just yet because I've been meaning to tell you –' And standing on tiptoe, her mouth against Macro's ear, she whispered some snippet of information that contained my name, and turned his thoughts to other things.

But the spark smouldered, biding its time, waiting to force a passage through our blossom-time chatter of high prices in the Vicus Tuscus and was it true that Bassus was paying Xanthe's bills?

'That's going to cut our prize-money, boys,' Dion said and Marpessa, emerging from her watchful silence, smiled suddenly, gleefully, and glancing at Marsyas and then at Macro murmured, 'Well, never mind, you can always join the legions.'

'Not Dion,' Marsyas jeered, leaping into the gap in our defences – the gap my sister had opened for him, whether she knew it or not. 'What sort of a fool joins the legions? You won't catch Dion tramping the world with a pack on his back like a mule, and me neither. We've got more sense than that.'

'You mean you haven't got the guts,' Macro snarled, squaring up to him, and Marsyas' laugh and the gesture that went with it, was provocation enough in itself.

'Guts!' he said. 'You don't need guts to be an errand boy.'

'You mean me, do you?'

'If you say so.'

'I say so. Outside then?'

'If you think you're up to it.'

'Outside,' Macro whispered, 'in the yard at the back,' and shrugging, nodding, Marsyas unfastened his cloak pin, bent over to adjust his sandals, turned his back, and then, as Macro turned too, Marsyas spun round like a whip-lash and gave Macro a blow on the back of the head that sent him crashing down the steps, knocking over a waiter and a screeching woman and a tray of silver, so that the air was thick with flying goblets and meat pies and curses.

Macro got up, shook himself, started to mount the steps like a panther, cautious, murderous, and immediately the area was cleared, everybody flattening themselves against the wall, because this was the kind of thing one expected, and there was no sense in getting in the way. Macro was the bigger man, a solid wall of muscle and outrage, Marsyas lighter, quicker, younger; and although they both knew how to fight nasty and dirty, I thought Macro would have more staying power. Marsyas, who wanted to fight, would have to hurt Macro badly to stop him, and as they came together, blank-eyed, still smiling, I was aware of Drusillus, Agrippina's hope for the future, still giggling vaguely, peering at them through a haze of wine-fumes that obscured his own danger.

He was far beyond anything I could say to him and, slipping forward, I caught young Scaurus' arm and whispered urgently, 'Go home. This is going to be messy. Go now, at once, and take your friend with you.'

'Oh really!' He was quite horrified. 'I can't do that – it's not at all the thing, you know – one can't leave a friend when he's in trouble.'

'Marsyas? He'd leave you. And if you ask me he started this whole thing on purpose to get Drusillus talked about.' Digging my nails into his arm, I shook him slightly. 'Listen, you silly boy, if you get involved in this, the whole town will know about it tomorrow – there are people here who will see to that. You've only got your father to face, but your friend will have to answer to Tiberius. Take him away. You can still stand on your feet and he can't. Carry him, if you have to. That's friendship.'

'Yes,' he said. 'Good God, yes.' And together we got the imperial eaglet to his feet and dragged him through a side door, along a passage, until I found someone's bearers – not his, not mine – and bullied them into relieving me of the burden.

'Danaë,' young Scaurus called out. 'Danaë, thank you – really –'. But I had my sister to think about now and I ran back along the corridor into the chaos of overturned couches and spilled wine, blood and vomit and the foul heat of violence for violence's sake.

'Only men do this,' I thought. 'Animals fight for food and territory and to protect their young. Only men fight for pleasure, while other men watch and applaud and spur them on.'

They were down on the floor, locked together, biting and clawing at each other, a head smashing against the tiles every time they rolled over. Dion and the Gaul and one or two others were lounging against the wall, giving their expert opinions, taking bets, while Erato, who didn't greatly care what happened to either of them, had withdrawn to a safe distance. But the sight of Marpessa brought me to a halt. She was staring avidly, breathing hard, her fists clenched, biting her lips, and as Marsyas suddenly broke free from Macro's bear-hug and smashed his fist into the guardsman's belly, she smiled and pressed her hands against her flushed cheeks with the excitement of a child at a birthday party.

'He's winning,' she said, catching my arm. 'Macro had him down and I thought he wouldn't get up again, but he's winded him now – look, and he's bleeding. I can't tell where it's coming from, can you? Has he lost a tooth? It's nearly over.'

But it wasn't, for although Macro was spent now, blundering and stumbling like a wounded bull on a chain, the poison in Marsyas' system was still rising, still flowing free. Like so many other times, he'd picked a fight and found it too easy; and if he hadn't really been angry with Macro before, he was in a blind fury with him now for not being tough enough after all, for not staying the pace. What had been combat became butchery.

'Stop him,' I said to no one in particular, and then, seeing Bassus at the top of the steps, I pushed my way through the crowd to his side.

'Bassus, stop him. He's killing him, and he can't kill a Praetorian officer and get away with it – *Bassus!*'

But Bassus smiled and patted my arm. 'You're quite right, dear, he can't get away with it, can he? The consequences would be most serious – really – a capital offence, no less.' And, oozing with satisfaction, he beckoned to Xanthe, and walked away.

Dion, now, was my only hope, but there'd never been a faction banquet without at least one good fight, and he didn't see himself as a peace-maker.

'Not likely. If I wade in now he'll only turn on me. I've just eaten a big dinner and I don't fancy losing it. What's it to you, anyway?'

What indeed? Yet I quite simply couldn't bear to watch him, crouching now over Macro's half-conscious bulk, administering the senseless beating that could easily cost him his life. Macro alive would be bad enough, a powerful enemy who'd want his revenge. But if Marsyas killed him – a Roman of good standing, a friend of Sejanus' – not even his fans could save him. The law would chain him up in a stone cell again, strip him of his protective covering of silk and gold before they broke his neck and tipped him in the river. And perhaps I was just as bad as my sister and all the other gaping, giggling women, for I had no thought, no pity, for Macro at all.

But no fever lasts forever, and as it drained away perhaps Marsyas' split knuckles and the blood trickling from the cut beneath his eye began to bother him, for he raised his fist for another blow and, deciding it wasn't worth the damage to his own hand, got slowly to his feet and stood for a moment, panting and dizzy, by no means certain of keeping his balance.

'Get the filth out of my sight,' he said, swaying, his hand on his stomach as if his own dinner no longer felt very secure, and as the crowd shrugged its collective shoulders and melted away, disappointed because murder had not been done after all, Marpessa went up to him, kicking the debris out of her path.

'Here's your cloak,' she said. 'And your ruby pin. Your friends have gone. Can you make it on your own?'

And nodding sourly, sunk in his wasteland again, he walked past her, past me, as if he didn't see us, past Bassus and the hostile horde of 'Blues' supporters, and went away.

17

One evening in early December – the mad season of the Saturnalia, the Festival of Fools – a cancelled engagement put me at a loose end, and having ordered my bearers to carry me to Erato's, I stopped them half-way to her house, suddenly convinced that my sister's affairs could wait no longer, and that I must go home, at once, and talk to her. I must get her settled respectably. Only the shock on Chrysothemis' face as she saw me crossing the atrium brought me to a halt.

'Danaë – good heavens! What brings you back?'

'Marpessa brings me. Where is she?'

'Marpessa?' She smiled quite blankly, wiping all expression from her face like a good professional, so that I could have been talking to a statue. 'Oh yes – well – she's around somewhere – I don't know just where.'

'Oh yes, you do.'

There was something going on I didn't know about, something they'd cooked up between them behind my back. I wouldn't stand for it.

'You'd better tell me, Chrysothemis – much better.'

'She's out.'

'Out where?'

'Oh – here and there – who knows with these young girls?'

But her nerve failed her and, remembering her own uncertain position and the need to defend herself, she flew to the attack.

'You've only yourself to blame, Danaë. You're never here. You leave her to me and you give me no definite instructions about her. I don't know how much freedom she's supposed to have – sometimes it's one thing and sometimes another. And she's got a very overbearing personality. She knows I'm in a dependent position here, so she takes advantage of it. I can't order her about. She's strong-willed and she has a very violent temper, and that upsets me. I'm not always well. Don't think I haven't wanted to tell you, Danaë, because I have – often. I tried to warn you only the other day, but you wouldn't take the hint. I said if you didn't watch out she'd do something stupid.'

'She's with a man?' I said. And if that was all, then what of it? Why shouldn't she sneak out at night to meet a lover? In her place I would have been doing the same. But it had to be more than that, otherwise why that odd mixture of panic and satisfaction on Chrysothemis' face?

'What man?' I asked, and when she opened her mouth and closed it again I shouted, '*What man?*' And the threat in me must have been very real, for she backed away and then, folding her hands neatly and shrugging her thin shoulders, she said, 'You know what man, if you think about it. There's only ever been one man for her, you know it very well.'

And there it was – his revenge, her revenge? – cruel, obvious, the one thing I couldn't face; and Chrysothemis, standing there, watching me, knowing I'd have to face it, hoping perhaps to see me bleed.

'When?' I said, winded, blind. 'After that damned faction banquet?'

And she smiled. 'Oh no, quite a while longer than that, I'm afraid. It started at Baiae, in the summer, when you left us and went off to that little house of yours. Since then she's been seeing him as often as she could. Yes, dear, I'm sorry, but all the time you were making those marriage plans she was deceiving you. I prayed, night after night, that it would blow over and you'd never have to know.'

Chrysothemis had never before had the power to wound me, and so helpless was I in those first moments that I let her do it, seeing in her transparent eyes all the pain she'd suffered for Paris and her broken career; and her desire now of seeing me suffer in my turn. And I didn't disappoint her. I found myself shaking violently, my breath coming in sharp, panting sounds that scoured my ears, and mingled with the actual hurt was a feeling of pure terror at my loss of control. This, then, was hysteria, and to get rid of it I'd have to break something or beat my head against a wall, or scream until my lungs ripped apart. Only shame restored me to my senses.

'Where are they?'

'My dear – how should I know?' She made a cool gesture, telling me it had never entered her head to enquire where men like

Marsyas went to make love. I had no choice but to wait, a long, unspeakable hour in my atrium until the street door opened and I saw, between the pillars, like something happening at the end of a tunnel, Marpessa getting out of a shabby litter, casually wrapped in the black cloak Marsyas had once dropped on my floor, an age ago before Drusus died, and which I hadn't been able to find the next morning. She was barefoot, her hair tumbling down her back, and, as she swung herself out of the litter, the expensive garment parted and I saw not only that she was naked but that it gave her pleasure to come home like this, with nothing but his cloak around her. And I knew it would amuse him too. I saw them getting out of bed, laughing. I saw him wrapping her up and sending her down the stairs alone to that hired litter. And I felt I'd have to kill one of them if I was ever to be at peace again. She came strolling into the hall, swinging her sandals by their gold thongs, and so urgent was my need for murder that I daren't move, couldn't speak, and was grateful when Chrysothemis stepped between us.

I hadn't expected her to help me, but the drama of the situation appealed to her, and in any case this was an opportunity to play a starring role which she couldn't resist.

'Get dressed,' she told Marpessa coldly, and then to me, 'Go to your room, Danaë. I'll bring her to you presently.' And as Marpessa flounced away, she said rather airily, 'Naturally it's none of my business, but in your place I'd ask myself, is he worth it?'

Time passed, and eventually Marpessa came to my room, dressed and made-up, Marsyas' cloak over her arm.

'What now?' she said. 'Shall we get it over with as quickly as we can? Did you really think I was going to marry one of your worthy young men?'

'Not unless you wanted to.'

'So why all the fuss? I don't want to. And just what have I done? You wouldn't expect me to be pure and innocent, would you? Really, Danaë – brought up by you?'

'Listen,' I told her, knowing I hadn't much time, that I'd soon be screaming and raving far beyond the edge of reason. 'I came home early tonight because I was thinking about you ...'

'Now that *was* good of you.'

'I was thinking about you and it came to me that you should lead a life of your own. And I decided to offer you your dowry ...'

'Well – very handsome of you, Danaë. I'll take it now.'

'To go with him? Oh no you won't.'

'Now listen here,' she said, leaning towards me, hard and fierce and more than ready to be cruel. 'He's not your lover, is he? I haven't pinched him from you, because you hadn't got him. You may fancy him, and I'll admit he fancied you at one time. But that's old hat now, Danaë. Just give me my money and I'll be on my way.'

'If you think I'll give you one penny –' I shouted, banging my fists hard one against the other because there was nothing else to strike. 'Not a penny, and you're going nowhere, you stupid, stupid girl –'

'Just how are you going to stop me?' she said, standing very tall. 'Going to lock me up, are you, Danaë? And how long do you think that can last? Who's going to stand guard over me when you go tripping off with your fine friends? Don't hit me, Danaë, because I'll hit you back, and the difference between us is that I don't care about getting hurt. But you do.'

I took a step or two away from her and back again, struggling for control, but the venom inside me was boiling, scorching, and I had to let some of it go.

'The difference between us,' I told her, still pacing up and down so she wouldn't see how badly I was trembling, 'is that you're a slut. I've never needed a man to pimp for me, and that's all you'll be getting if you take him. You can't look after yourself, and he won't look after you. What do you know about work and responsibility? You just take and take – you just stuff your greedy face with anything you can lay your hands on, and you don't even ask where it comes from. Well, I'll tell you where it comes from – from my hard work and good management, because I sold myself sometimes to men I didn't fancy and didn't like so you'd never have to do the same – and because I kept myself clear of men like Marsyas who'd ruin me, just like he'll ruin you. I got myself out of the gutter, and you with me, and I won't let him drag you back there.'

'Oh dear –' she said, seeing I had run out of breath. 'Well, I was expecting you to say all that, and I could answer it in one word – one of Dion's favourite words – except that you don't like obscenities now that you're such a lady. You got yourself out of the gutter for your own sake, not mine, and what you've done since then has been for you – not me. I've watched you all my life, parading around, having it all your own way. Did you really think we were all content just to sit back and admire you and be grateful? You haven't the guts to take Marsyas on, any more than Chrysothemis had the guts for Paris. I've watched you with him – teasing him, leading him on. I've hidden in corners and behind pillars and spied on you. That's how I got this cloak. I pinched it out of your room the night he left it behind and I've slept with it in my bed every night since then. It held his perfume for a long time, and when it faded I found out what he used and I bought it with your money, and kept the smell of him around me all the time – that's how I feel about him. I've made love to him in my mind and in my sleep for years, and now I've really made love to him – I've drowned myself in him – and that's all I want.'

And I had no words, just a shriek of desperation and hurt and bewilderment because it was useless, now, to go on telling myself she was my little sister who needed to be protected, when overnight she'd become a woman as ruthless and beautiful as Cynthia, a rival who'd destroy me if she could. And when it came to it, I knew I'd defend myself.

'Yes,' she said, 'I'll tell you all about it – and don't cover your ears, because you'll never rest until you know, and I don't suppose we'll be speaking to each other much more after tonight. It started in the summer – five months ago, Danaë, and eight days. Nine days, now, because it's past midnight. I walked right up to him on the beach at Baiae, and when he asked me where you were I told him you were at your new house with a man. And I told him who the man was, too, although I wasn't supposed to know that. Well, he said a few nasty things about you, because it wasn't too long after you'd thrown him out, and I agreed with him; and then I told him I was bored and asked him if there wasn't anything he could do about it. And he laughed and said yes, any time. So that night I slipped out when Chrysothemis wasn't looking, and after that I'd have got out to him one way or another if I'd had to crawl.

'At first it wasn't easy because Paris was there, and he's got eyes like a hawk, but when he came back to town and left me with Chrysothemis she didn't want to be bothered with me. She just wanted to moon around all the time writing letters to Paris. When she did find out she was half scared and half pleased, because she guessed what it would do to you. I didn't know what would happen when we all got back to town. I'm not an idiot – I knew, at first, that he was doing it partly to get back at you. But it's not like that now. It hasn't been like that for a long time, and if you hadn't caught me out tonight I'd have had to tell you myself fairly soon, because it's not enough now, just seeing him in secret – having to come away before I'm ready. You think you know it all, but it's my belief you're a cold fish, even though you don't look it. Do you know what it is to devour a man and have him devour you, until you've swallowed each other like a pair of snakes, and you're still not satisfied? I could have laughed the other night at the faction club, when he was fighting and you were looking so sick – without an idea in your head that I was his mistress – thinking I was going to be a virgin bride. He rents a flat for me in the Subura, and that's where I'm going – back to the place we came from, the place you're so scared of. Well, I'm not scared. He likes the Subura, and so do I. So you see, Danaë, you wasted your time and your money. You should have left me there.'

'No,' I said. 'No. I can't.' But I wasn't sure what it was I couldn't do.

'Can't let me go? There's not a law in the world that says you can stop me. You're not my mother. My mother was a whore, wasn't she, like Marsyas' mother – like you – and that was a real whore's dream, Danaë, that scheme of yours of marrying me off and making an honest woman of me.'

And it was too much. '*Is he worth it?*' Chrysothemis had said, and I'd tried – I'd tried – because she was younger than she thought and the world harder; because she was my sister. But it was too much.

'Idiot!' I hissed, seeing her again as Cynthia, as every woman I'd ever met who'd tried to do me down. 'You've understood one thing, at any rate, and that's all you've understood. He's doing this to pay me back – that's the truth. You think you're so bloody clever, but if he wants you at all – and he won't want you for long – it's only because you look like me.' And that vicious whisper, forced by my hurt and betrayal and my instinct for self-preservation, closed that last door, that final possibility of peace between us. There was nothing more to say, and turning sharply on her heel, she strode out of the room, letting the door slam shut behind her.

'Oh dear,' Chrysothemis murmured, floating up to me. 'Poor

soul –', but I could tolerate no sympathy, no gloating.

'Leave it. Leave it. Fetch me some of those Egyptian drops, will you? I have to sleep somehow. I'm dancing at Valerius Messalla's tomorrow night.'

'Yes, dear,' she said. 'That's right. Life goes on, and you mustn't let yourself down. Get some sleep.'

But sleep was dangerous, for Marsyas, who could be locked out in the daylight, caught me in the dark, and all through those drugged, feverish hours I had to listen to his voice telling me, over and over again, *'I have to pay you back, you know that, don't you? And when I do, don't be surprised, don't complain.'*

And each time I answered him, *'How could you do this to me?'*

18

It was the beginning of a bad time. December wore itself out with ill-tempered gusts of wind and rain-storms thrown down from the sky by a peevish hand. January was grey and damp, with sullen, low-ceilinged days that merged one into another, indistinguishable, miserable. February was bitter-tasting, mean-spirited, and it was no consolation to me that I was by no means the only one who suffered.

We lived, it seemed, under constant menace of a storm, and not only from the weather, for the future which had seemed so clear had grown murky again with doubt and danger, and more than ever men watched their backs and learned to speak in whispers, or, better than that, to keep silent.

Tiberius had spoken out now against Agrippina. Two able, influential men had already died for her sake, and although the undermining of her position had caused unrest and a great murmuring against Sejanus, men who had once called themselves her devoted friends began to withdraw, remembering that they had families of their own to serve, that life was very sweet, and Germanicus had been dead a long time.

But not everyone was so faithless. There was still a solid group of aristocrats, all distinguished, wealthy, difficult to set aside, who continued to pin their faith on the destiny of Germanicus' line, and who declared quite openly that by persisting in his hostility to Agrippina, Tiberius was either deliberately endangering the State, or allowing himself to be deceived by an unscrupulous adventurer, Sejanus.

'The lady wishes only for what is right,' Aemilius Scaurus told me. 'She wishes to deprive no one, but at the same time she does not wish her own sons to be deprived – and who can blame her for that? I have not spoken to the Emperor for a long time – few people do manage to speak to him these days, since Sejanus guards him like a dog, or like a wolf – but he is looking very frail, very old.'

Yet he had looked frail before, in the days when they had all been waiting for him to die and make room for Germanicus; and now, as one of Germanicus' sons consoled himself with wine and fast company, and the other, insulted perhaps by the defection of so many false friends, grew increasingly morose, Tiberius seemed determined, if not to destroy them, at least to isolate them from the remnants of their party, and from their mother.

Nor had the marriage of Agrippina's son Nero and the lady Julia – Drusus' and Livilla's daughter – provided the male child, or any child at all, who could have drawn the opposing factions together. And in the city, as the lowering winter days went by, one heard strange tales of treachery, of fathers betrayed by their greedy sons, of wives who sold their husbands' secrets to Sejanus for money or, sometimes, for love of him; and, everywhere, of servants listening as they waited at table, spying in doorways, ears strained for any whisper against Tiberius.

Gradually, once again, as had happened before when Germanicus died, the trickle of prosecutions became a flood, and men found themselves on trial for strange reasons, for words spoken in the privacy of their own bedrooms, for opinions of their youth, long forgotten but cleverly resurrected now by experts and twisted to suit the mood of the times. Men died in bewilderment, without knowing why, or saw their sons go into exile penniless, as estates were confiscated and ancient names dragged in the dust. Patrician women, brought up to ignore the morality laws, now found themselves charged with adulteries which had been common knowledge for years, and whenever this happened it was so easy to add an extra name to the list of a woman's lovers, thus getting rid of someone without the bother of a separate hearing.

It seemed that one either declared oneself against Agrippina or one was hounded to death, and among those who refused to compromise – men of integrity and culture and immense ability – were some of my oldest patrons and friends: Aemilius Clarus and Lucius Paulinus included.

And then, a little later, there was Claudia Pulchra. She was Agrippina's cousin, a haughty but unremarkable woman, who was suddenly charged with adultery and the attempted murder of Tiberius by poison and magic. The adultery may have been true, as it would have been true of half the women in Rome, but Paris doubted, and I agreed with him, whether the murder charge was intended to be taken seriously. He thought it was there simply to tempt Agrippina into dangerous support of her own kin. They may, indeed, have found poison in the lady's house: they may even have brought it with them when they came to look.

Agrippina had not intervened for Clarus and Lucius Paulinus and the others, but Claudia Pulchra was her cousin, and Sejanus must have known she would play straight into his hands. She had not tried to see Tiberius for a long time but now she went marching into the palace without an appointment, white-faced and tight-lipped, so full of outrage that they said she barely gave the Emperor a civil greeting. There was a private interview lasting some time, and although Lygdus – who brought me the story – didn't know what had been said, voices were heard raised in anger as they seldom were in that house, and everyone knew she had made a scene in the grand manner, tears, reproaches, demands, accusations – all calculated to harden the heart of a man who had had trouble with women all his life and now, as Emperor, was no longer obliged to put up with it. Certainly she exhausted herself and had to be helped outside to her litter, but it did her no good, for Claudia Pulchra was convicted just the same.

Those who cared for Agrippina had always clung to the hope that whatever dark web Sejanus and Tiberius were weaving between them, the Emperor would never allow his own family to be touched but Claudia Pulchra was herself almost a member of the imperial family, and perhaps the whole point of her disgrace was to tell Agrippina that she was not immune, that this could happen to her too?

There was shock, disbelief, an even greater drawing-away from the family of Germanicus. 'Poor lady,' I heard, 'she's tried her best, but it's hard for a woman alone and those wild boys have been too much for her. Perhaps Tiberius knows what he's doing after all.'

'Yes, poor lady,' Lygdus agreed, accepting my invitation to dinner with the air of a man bestowing a great favour. 'They talk – these great nobles – but when it comes down to it that's about all they can do. They haven't any soldiers, you see. The days are gone when they all had their private armies of clients and dependants. Tiberius has the legions, and Sejanus has the Praetorians, and what's talk, compared to that?'

'And what about your lady?'

'Livilla? Oh, suffering, dear, I'm happy to say – suffering. And the stronger Sejanus becomes, the more her anxieties grow. She's terrified he may reach a point where he doesn't need her. Mind you, she's happier in the winter. The poor light, you know, doesn't show up her wrinkles. Have a good look at her when you get the chance – her hair's getting redder and redder, and that's my friend Eudemus with his lotions and potions. Mind you, it's getting thinner as well, but we don't tell her that. Handfuls of it, dear, on the comb, every morning.'

I worked like a demon that winter, obsessed with a great need to be first and best, to show myself to the world in a blaze of triumph, a great artiste and an eternal beauty who had no time to concern herself with the amours of any common charioteer. I dominated every one of Valerius Messalla's December dinners, rehashed old pieces and developed new ones, opened a second perfumery on Mars Field and acquired an interest in the importing of embroidered Oriental fabrics and Egyptian sandals. I lived in the centre of a crowd, smiled until my cheeks cracked, and, because I couldn't sleep, went to bed with men who were no more to me than a means of never being alone. I needed them, no longer for money, certainly not from desire, merely as a barrier between the things I could allow myself to think of and the images I must shut out at all costs, but Marsyas' face was engraved on the insides of my eyelids, and I couldn't rid myself of him. I stared at my walls and, instead of the pictures of blossom and sunlit fields, I saw him making love to my sister, saw her face, so much like mine that it became my face, gloating over him, offering the whole of herself to him as I'd been afraid to do. And I saw him take her, greedy for her because she had the recklessness I lacked, because she was younger; and I didn't know any more if it mattered to him that she looked like me. I only knew that it wounded me.

'Don't torment yourself,' Chrysothemis said. 'You did your best for her – spoiled her, in fact. But she's always been so much in your shadow. One can't blame her for wanting to grow a little, even if one doesn't altogether care for what she grows into.'

But I did blame myself, both for what she was and because I couldn't bring myself to do anything about it.

It was a long time before I saw her again. I heard, from one or two kind friends – Cynthia and Erato mainly, who each had an axe to grind – that she was living in one of the meanest streets of the Subura.

'Absolutely running wild, darling. She even looks like Marsyas. Wears his racing colours, all red and gold, with her hair tumbling down her back and barefoot when I saw her – just anklets and a big smile and not much else. After all the trouble you've taken with her, Danaë, I can't tell you how sorry I am. It must be a torment to you, dear, wondering what's going to happen to her afterwards – when he's finished.'

It was Marpessa herself, a few months later, who chose the time and place of our first meeting, for she knew where to find me. She knew the parks I walked in, the streets where I shopped, she knew my days for the circus and the theatre and where I liked to sit, and she could avoid me or harass me as she chose.

I went to the Circus Maximus on the first day of the April races because it had long been my habit to do so, and because a great many people were expecting me to stay away. And as I made my entrance at my usual hour, in my white silk and my pearls, with one of Drusus' sensational emeralds on my hand, there she was at the centre of a raucous, brash young crowd, her hair hanging loose to the back of her knees, her lithe body, as Cynthia had told me, draped in red silk in honour of Marsyas' faction, and the kind of gold ornaments he wore himself, chains and medallions, amulets and charms. She looked what I had to admit she was, a charioteer's woman, fast and flamboyant, making too much noise, calling out to people in the crowd, arguing racing technicalities with strangers. And I shuddered.

'Look at her. You'd think I'd taught her nothing.'

But Chrysothemis only murmured, 'She'll teach herself eventually. You looked just like that, years ago, at the supper-clubs – and only think how you've improved.'

Even Erato, who had been full of sympathy and indignation, scrutinized Marpessa for a moment and said, rather musingly, 'She has a lot of fire. Really – why did we never see it before? She was just a sulky little girl, and now, all of a sudden, she's like a flame. Perhaps you should make friends with her, Danaë. If she develops her style and becomes the fashion it could be awkward for the rest of us, having to ignore her on your account.'

And although her reasons were wrong, I knew in my heart that her suggestion was sound. '*Is he worth it?*' Chrysothemis had asked and, closing my eyes, shutting the splendours of the arena and the gay spring crowds away, I understood that nothing was worth this enmity, this futile wasting of that most precious of all substances, our time. But the moment passed and in the end my instinct for survival was too strong. Too many women had tried to push me aside, and I'd fought too hard for my place in the world to give ground to anyone. And although I would not have withheld my forgiveness, I knew she'd have to come and ask.

I won a little money, laughed a great deal, waiting until I could decently take my leave, but suddenly Marsyas' name began to run through the crowd like the first whispering of a forest fire, and I knew I'd have to stay until his race was run. Marpessa, on her feet now and oblivious of the man behind her who was complaining, quite obscenely, that she was blocking his view, cast a glance over her shoulder to make sure I was still there; and although the look I gave her in reply should have blistered the skin from her back, she laughed and began tossing her head about, pointing to Marsyas and telling everyone who cared to listen – or so I imagined – that he was her man. But he was not on form. He made his usual showy start, fastening the reins tight around his waist to make it that much harder for him to survive if he came to grief, careering across the track in front of his nearest opponent and terrifying the man into giving way, losing his helmet after a lap or two – something he did so often that everyone knew it was no accident but just an extra dash of bravado, of lunacy. But about the eleventh lap, when he was out in front quite alone and should have been unable to lose, he overturned by a pure error of judgement, shaving the posts directly below us, and although he cut himself free and limped away from the wreckage, shaking off the faction servants who dashed out to assist him, one of his legs was dripping blood, his horses didn't get up again, and one could see, even at that distance, that he knew he only had himself to blame and was furious.

I watched him go and then looked instinctively for Marpessa, but her place was empty. She had dashed off to interview the doctors and take him home, back to the squalor, the glamour, of their tenement rat-hole; but I had to sit it out, to prove to anyone who happened to care, or perhaps just to myself, that his injuries were no concern of mine.

My day was not over. I went back to my lovely house, my quiet, dignified little street, needing to see my own costly, tasteful things around me, needing my bath and my delicately scented oils, my fine towels, my Egyptian drops and a good night's sleep. But instead a sick and terrified man was waiting for me – someone who needed me – and it wasn't easy to realize that this stricken, ashen-faced, pathetic creature was Lygdus.

'What is it? Are you ill?'

And for a while he couldn't speak, could do nothing but prowl around the room, wringing his hands, a muscle at the corner of his mouth trembling, twitching, contorting his face with a sudden spasm of distress that set my own nerves jangling.

'Lygdus, for heaven's sake – Lygdus, calm yourself!'

But he was far beyond any hope of calm.

'No,' he said, sitting down a moment, shifting uneasily as if his own body was suddenly strange to him and he didn't know what to do with it. 'Don't talk to me about any sort of heaven. There's no such thing. There can't be. There's just sleep, isn't there, just forgetting? And then it's all right, because it doesn't matter. No one can get at you then – and no one can remember what you did – no one can hate – or suffer. Don't touch me – please.'

'But what's happened. Is it Sejanus? Is it Livilla?'

Suddenly, leaning forward, he spat out the one word, '*Livilla*'. And although I thought I had seen hate before, I knew now that I had been wrong.

'But what has she done?'

'Nothing. Nothing you'll ever know of. She's killed me, that's all, and what's that? I'm nothing. I'll live with it – live with death – that's funny, isn't it? And it should be funny, because what am I but a joke – good for a laugh?'

'Has she dismissed you? Well, you're free – Drusus freed you – you can go where you like. Darling, if it's money I can make some arrangement with you – I have a business or two you'd enjoy. And we're friends.'

And staring at me as if a ghost looked at him over my shoulder he gave an agonized shudder and jumped to his feet again.

'No,' he said, his voice breaking on a sob, and I didn't think it was my friendship he was denying. 'Don't say that to me. Don't think about me. Just – just let me stay – don't talk to me – just an hour – just let me be here.'

'For as long as you like.'

And although he would say no more and began to talk of other things after a while, he wouldn't take my hand on leaving – drawing himself away from me as if his touch, not mine, held the contamination – and would make no promise to see me again.

19

In the end my dissipations overcame me. One night at Valerius Messalla's I kicked too high, felt a muscle tear, and the following morning I awoke feeling hot and strange with a painful tightness across my chest. For ten days I coughed and struggled for breath, burning and freezing in turn, and I knew, with the panic of a healthy woman, that this was Drusus' disease and I would die. I healed, but it was the stale tag-end of the season, my leg was still painful, and feeling no inclination to start work again, I packed my bags and went to my house near Baiae.

I spent hours sitting alone in the open air, watching the sweet haze of early summer slanting across the land, weaving itself into strands of saffron and amber and gold between the blue sky and the brown of the upturned soil, and gradually, as time began to slow down, began to be governed by the rising and setting of the sun, by tender, blue-green mornings and fragrant twilights rather than the small, fevered happenings of my city life, I came to terms with myself, and knew that, quite soon, I would be strong again.

And suddenly I was longing to see Sejanus, hoping with unashamed, uncomplicated excitement that he would want to use my house this summer, as he'd done before, and that he would spend some time with me.

'Oh, I shouldn't think so,' Paris told me, walking in unannounced one evening in time for dinner. 'I think he's got to watch his step, just now. You probably haven't heard, but it seems he's over-reached himself – oh, only a shade, nothing he can't put right. He appears to have written an official letter to Tiberius proposing himself as a husband for Livilla, and my sources tell me he got a sharp reply. Well, I can't imagine he's surprised. He must have expected it. I suppose the lady needed some reassurance, and now she has it. Not much harm, is there, in promising to try something you know you can't perform. By the way, Danaë, this is really a very pleasant house – so very quiet. I could work here. If you offered to lend it to me, I could be persuaded.'

'Well, we'll see about that. But as for work, it strikes me you've got some competition. Someone threw an absolutely scandalous verse through my door just before I went away, all about Tiberius raping a little boy and his grandmother at the same time – or very nearly.'

'Yes,' my brother said, his fine, shrewd eyes quite unreadable. 'It was rather good, wasn't it.'

'I'm glad you think so. Doesn't it worry you that Agrippina is playing you at your own game?'

'Desperately,' he said, looking down at his hand, admiring the sheen of the beautiful pearl ring he wore, and then, his face alight with mischief, he clicked his tongue reproachfully.

'Danaë, I'm surprised at you. Really – a stainless lady like Agrippina – how can you suggest that she, or anyone who belongs to her, would sink to my level? She wouldn't expose Tiberius' sexual perversions even if he had any – and he probably hasn't. He's a gentleman and her kinsman, and in her world such things are simply not done. He wouldn't do it to her either, because she is a lady, and he has his code. They're really quite alike, you see. I expect that's why they don't get on.'

'What are you up to now?' I said. 'You'll drive me mad, you and Dion between you. Paris – you're not working for both sides at once? Oh, my God, you'd better go back to Athens. In fact I'll get you there if I have to pay somebody to kidnap you.'

But he was laughing now delightedly, whole-heartedly, showing off his villainy like a naughty boy.

'My goodness, I'm touched. I didn't know how much you loved me. I must remember to frighten you more often. Do you get this worked up about Dion? But there's no need: I haven't changed sides. I'm still the devoted servant of our mutual friend. Very devoted, in fact.'

'But this is madness, Paris. Why should Sejanus want to slander Tiberius?'

'Oh, for a number of reasons. Because everybody – including Tiberius – will believe Agrippina is responsible, which can only increase the bad feeling between them. And then, of course, old men embarrass easily, and it's bound to upset Tiberius when he gets up in the morning knowing the whole town is laughing about what he was supposed to be doing all through the night with those grandmothers and juveniles I've invented for him. It might even upset him so much that he'll go away. He wanted to retire to Capri and take Sejanus with him, didn't he, when Drusus was alive? Well, what's to stop him from going now? He'd have to leave Sejanus behind this time to look after things – in fact he may have been planning to do just that for some time, and only needs a little push. And that's what he's getting. A push. Now there's no need to tell me I'm wicked, because I only do as I'm told, and it can't be so very terrible to persuade someone to do what he's simply longing to do anyway. Give some thought to the house, Danaë. It would suit me down to the ground for a month or two. How about next May?'

Dion called to see me soon after, on his way to meet Erato at Puteoli, and he too saw great possibilities in my country isolation.

'Perfectly grand, Danaë. You told me it was off the beaten track, but I drove past it twice and couldn't even find anybody to ask. Well, I know where to come next time I make a friend I don't want Erato to know about. Just put your servants in the picture, will you, so there'll be no awkwardness if I happen to pop in sometime when you're not here? This walled garden is just the thing, two couches over there under those trees, and the moonlight ... it could be the end of the world.'

He stayed three days, keeping Erato waiting, well aware she'd never believe he had been with me.

'It does her good to worry. She thrives on it. Mind you, I don't fancy getting blamed for something I haven't done, so I may as well go into Baiæ for a day or two and do something she can blame me for. I've just had ten days – at least, I think it was ten days – at Misenum with some of the boys and a few girls. Nobody you know, except Marsyas and that sister of ours.'

'I don't want to know about it.'

'Oh yes you do,' he said evenly. 'So stop biting your lip and looking as if there was a bad smell somewhere. You don't have to impress *me*.'

'Well then, how was she?'

'You mean how were they? Very much as you'd expect. Tearing strips off each other the minute they arrived – snapping and snarling – him with his bad leg and her like a raging demon. She's quite a girl. If I didn't feel mildly responsible for her I'd say she was the best entertainment I've had in months.'

'You amaze me. I didn't think you felt responsible for anybody.'

'No, well, I did say mildly. If you'd seen her you'd understand. The first night they were there he gave her a slap just to keep her quiet – nothing much – and I didn't want to interfere because she'd asked for it, and after all, they are living together, which is as much as our mother and father ever did. But she didn't need me. She went for him like a tiger, fists, elbows, knees, teeth, the lot. He thought it was funny to start with, until she hit him in the gut and broke a wine jar over his head.'

'And they were like that all the time?'

He chuckled, deep in his chest. 'Most of the time, until he got himself pissed out of his mind and couldn't be bothered. I'll tell you this – if his leg doesn't heal, and he has to stop racing, that's going to be the end of him.'

We got up and walked for a moment through a silence thick enough to feel, and then he took my chin between his strong fingers and twisted my face up into the moonlight.

'Yes,' he said. 'I know it hurts – I'm not stupid, no matter what my little brother has to say – but if I don't talk about them somebody else will. Listen, I've never been sure what goes on between you and Marsyas: I just know something does. Well, he's one of my best mates, even if he is wrong in the head, and you'll have to sort yourself out with him as you think fit. But one thing I can do is to tell you that you don't have to worry about Marpessa. She's all right. She's a tough little nut, and she'll land on her feet. She doesn't expect him to go on supporting her: she knows she'll have to earn her bread sooner or later, and she knows how. In my opinion, for what it's worth, she's going to turn out very big. You and Erato started with nothing. Well – you spared Marpessa that. She's seen the way you go on, and that's the start you've given her. When he dumps her – if he does – I'll watch her and that's bound to scare off the lads who could do her harm. So you don't have to get yourself screwed up about it. Now just lend me enough to tide me over for a few days until I get to Erato, and I'll be on my way.'

And then there was Sejanus. I almost missed him. I was getting ready to move on, to join Chrysothemis who had taken it into her head to visit Pompeii – having heard, I suspected, that Paris was there – when I heard the sound of hooves on the sandy, lonely road and Macro came striding into the house as if he owned it. I'd last seen him sprawling on his back in a mess of blood and slime, but he was as fresh as the summer morning now, and, having no reason to connect me with Marsyas, gave me no trouble other than a little unpleasant groping and a wet, enthusiastic kiss before he rode away. The following evening he was back again, very correct, very much the soldier on parade, with the anonymous, carefully wrapped Apicata.

Sejanus arrived a little later and because the night was warm they sat in my walled garden under the chestnut trees Dion had selected as a perfect setting for seduction, talking, perhaps, of his proposal to Livilla. I could imagine her saying to herself as she'd waited for him, '*I must ask my husband about his new marriage.*' I watched them secretly from my bedroom overlooking the garden, this cool, plain little woman, this fascinating man, sitting a comfortable distance from each other, Apicata speaking quickly, making no gestures, not the slightest attempt to attract him, a housekeeper presenting a detailed statement of her accounts; and if those accounts were concerned with the degradation of young princes and the removal of distinguished members of the nobility, no one in the world could possibly have guessed it.

'*We should bring charges of treason against Aemilius Lepidus,*' she might have been saying, in the tone of '*There is a chipped tile in the atrium, I feel we should replace it.*' And it struck me, in a moment of wild speculation, that a day might come when Livilla, with all her tawny beauty, would be a neglected wife and mouse-brown Apicata a cherished, trusted mistress.

She left and, taking me by surprise, Sejanus bounded into my room and threw himself down on the bed.

'Well then, I'm here tonight and tomorrow, and that's the only holiday I'm likely to get. So spoil me. Come on, get your clothes off and dance that new piece of yours they tell me I'm too simple to understand. That will do to start with.'

'I don't do my new piece without clothes. That's probably why you don't understand it – you're just not looking.'

'Then do something I can look at.'

And instantly the ruthless, probably wicked man, who had hounded so many other men to death, who had set Marsyas to corrupt a son of Agrippina, and used my brother's genius for his own twisted purposes, was an impossibility. I didn't believe in him. I saw nothing beyond the merry eyes, the perpetually amused, uneven smile, the force and freshness. If he was evil to others, he was good for me.

'No, never mind the dance, and I'll take your clothes off myself presently. You're a holiday in yourself, Danaë. You're a feast. If they ever send me into exile I'll take you with me – how about it? It needn't be a bad life, exile – except that they'd never give me the chance of it. No, no, they'd fall over each other to put a knife in my gut, if they could catch me. But if it happened, we'd find ourselves an island all right, somewhere warm, and you wouldn't need any clothes at all. I'd have you pregnant within a month. Can you have children, Danaë?'

'It would appear not.'

'Have you tried?'

'Hardly – I've spent my life trying not to.'

'But that's wrong. Come with me and I'll give you fifteen fine sons and as many beautiful daughters – I'll found a nation. Does that appeal?'

'Not the fifteen sons and daughters – but the rest I'd be prepared to think about.'

'Good. And are you longing for me yet?'

'I've been longing for you all day.'

'Then approach me, madam – don't hesitate – I'm a fountain of life tonight. I'm a Hercules. I could found that nation between now and tomorrow morning, so take care.'

'I will. I don't want to wake up and find myself the mother of fifteen.'

'You won't be waking up, because you won't be sleeping.'

And it was no idle boast. We saw the dawn lighten the sky, the new sun peering between the trees, over-topping them until it came slanting across us, turning the hairs on his body and his eyelashes to gold, showing me the cleft in his chin, the warm, weathered bronze of his skin.

'Feed me,' he commanded, and I brought milk and crusty bread and dates, and served him as if he were an Eastern potentate. There were no servants in the house because of Apicata, no one to see, and so we went as we were into the garden, bathed in the fountain, splashing and shrieking like children, and dried ourselves in the sun, stretched out on the grass, his head on my stomach.

'Now then,' he said, 'how do you feel? Like a woman who's been in paradise – how many times? Tell me what a marvel I am.'

'You're a marvel.'

'Better than that.'

'Much better. You're Hercules and Apollo and all the rest. And, better than that, you're Sejanus.'

'Ah yes,' he said, 'that's right.' And turning swiftly he pressed his face quite hard against my stomach, winding me, and pulled me to my feet.

'How ridiculous, Danaë, the things that really please us. New bread and sunshine and a dip in the cold water: anyone can have those things, and if they were all I could have I'd be the most miserable man alive. But I haven't enjoyed anything for a long time as much as these last few hours. How perverse we are. Will your servants be back soon?'

I glanced at the sky, the intense blue of midday.

'Yes, quite soon.'

'Good. Then I'll just let them catch a glimpse of me, so they can feel terribly clever and think I'm the reason you gave them the night off. You can tip them too, on my behalf, quite handsomely – Marco will give you the wherewithal – and get something rather special for yourself. You don't mind getting yourself talked about for my sake – for my cause, as my wife calls it? You're very obliging, my darling. I won't be back in Campania for some time now. I'm crossing to Capri later today with the Emperor, some little building project he has there, very close to his heart. But my wife may need to avail herself of your hospitality again before the end of the season – a little matter of business she's kindly offered to handle for me. You don't mind? Don't let it inconvenience you. Go wherever you please. Macro will find you and make the necessary arrangements.'

Already his carefree holiday mood had gone. He was bland now, and affable, and mildly flirtatious, as he was with all women, a professional politician whose business it is to charm and beguile. But as I stood once again in the garden, in a cool, apple-green robe, my hair still hanging loose down my back, he put his arms around me and gave me the kind of kiss I would have expected from a soldier leaving for the front. And as I watched him go I knew that, setting aside the rights and wrongs of him, I had been happier these few hours with him – in the unreasoning, uncomplicated way children are happy – than at any other time in my life.

20

I made a little progress along the coast that year – Cumae, Puteoli, Misenum, Neapolis, a few days in bustling, busy Pompeii where I came to an arrangement with the manufacturer of an excellent fish sauce who wished to see his product on sale in Rome. I called at Ostia on my way home to inspect the results of yet another venture of mine, jars of Spanish oil and a consignment of porphyry from Arabia, neatly stacked in a warehouse by the docks. And feeling that my own little empire was growing apace, I returned to my house on the Caelian Hill to learn that I was myself still greatly in demand.

Valerius Messalla's freedman called with a list of autumn bookings, flowers were left on my doorstep in flattering profusion, and then in the flurry of homecoming Lygdus appeared, recovered, it seemed, from whatever foul thing Livilla had done to him in the spring, as sleek and pompous as ever, except that every now and again that muscle in his cheek still forced his face to perform its stressful, unco-ordinated dance. And each time it shocked me and moved me as if a painted doll, flung to the ground by a heedless child, had suddenly cried out in pain.

'Glorious weather,' he said. 'Glorious. We were at Tarracina – me and Eudemus and our lady – although Sejanus was at Capri, locked up with the Emperor. Yes, she was quiet enough because she knew he couldn't come to much harm there. Eudemus made her a new rinse for her hair, and some new concoction to stop her from having bad dreams, so she even roused herself enough to spend some time with her daughter. Poor child, two days she had to endure being questioned by Livilla about Agrippina, and then I expect she had to go back to that sickly husband of hers and be questioned by Agrippina about Livilla. I could see it was getting her down.'

'I'm glad to see you looking so well,' I told him, meaning 'I'm glad you don't hate your lady any more, glad you just despise her as you've always done.' But just as he was ready to take his leave, he said suddenly, viciously, 'She's taken it into her head now to get herself pregnant. She wants to feel Sejanus' child quickening beneath her heart – that's what the silly bitch says, anyway, and I don't suppose she's asked herself how she'll explain it to Tiberius. She's got Eudemus to brew her some foulness that's supposed to do the trick, and something else to get Sejanus into her bed a bit more often, although if he catches her slipping it into his wine he'll make her sorry. Well – I hope she manages it. Women die, don't they, in childbirth, especially at her age?'

And as he paused a terrible spasm contorted his face, every feature going separately out of control so that he covered them with shaking hands and backed away from me.

I told myself he was going through a bad time, getting older and not liking it, living in too tight a circle with a hysterical woman who couldn't face the approach of middle age either. Yet that spasm in his face haunted me, that twitch of distress, the sudden terror of a trapped animal in his eyes, if one took him unawares.

'Bedroom politics,' Paris said scornfully when I mentioned it to him. 'If he has a guilty conscience then he's probably been pinching her perfume or tampering with her letters. Or perhaps he's fallen in love with Sejanus himself. What else could it be? No one would ever be fool enough to trust him with anything that mattered – now would they, darling? What a trio, him with his twitches, and that smooth little doctor with his love-potions, and Livilla.'

And because he could be right, and because to question Lygdus only brought on his twitching and his muttering worse than ever, I tried to put it out of my mind. I had anxieties enough, Paris himself not the least among them. His apartment in the Argiletum was now a treasure-house of *objets d'art*, pieces of Corinthian bronze that seemed poised for flight from their pedestals, delicate vases of cameo-glass, frescoes of cloudscapes adorned with flowers and mythical birds painted by an artist whose reputation and whose fees I didn't despise. And when I asked myself how he paid for it, I shuddered, and began adding to the store of single gems I kept hidden beneath a loose tile under my bed, for he had nothing small enough to take with him if he had to run, and however settled the political situation seemed, I couldn't ignore the possibility of a change. Since his break with Chrysothemis there had been no particular woman in his life. I had caught a glimpse of a girl from some northern place, as white and dainty as a stem of polished ivory, and some time later a smoke-skinned African, her long, wonderfully moulded head wrapped in a piece of red silk, her liquid eyes full of adoration. But he seemed to have a collector's instinct with women too and, like his bronzes and his ivories, he cherished them for a season, displayed them to advantage, and then, when his artistic curiosity led him on to something new, consigned them tenderly to the storeroom of his emotions.

'There is a great coldness in your brother,' Chrysothemis told me. 'Something very nearly inhuman. You see how right I was to refuse him. I'm delighted to say that he means nothing to me now.'

But every time he came to dinner she sat tight-lipped, her face pinched and pale as if her head hurt her, rapping out sour little remarks that made him smile; and the next day she was sharp with the maids, tracking down specks of dust, miserable until she'd found a scratch on a piece of silver or a torn napkin, and made someone weep for it.

Marpessa moved that autumn from the Subura to a flat in the Via Nova, an old address of my own, but although she was often seen now without Marsyas and was thought to be dressing better, keeping more profitable company, I didn't believe the affair was over. There would be no tame fizzling-out for those two but a mighty clap of thunder that would deafen us all, and it seemed far more likely, as Dion had suggested, that she'd seen the necessity for earning her own living, something to which a man of Marsyas' background would make no objection. He, like Dion, like all of us, knew the difference between a business affair and a private affair, and if Marpessa had come to recognize it too I thought she could just possibly find a way to keep him and survive.

'She had a nice little set of garnets the last time I saw her,' Dion told me. 'And she didn't get them from Marsyas because he doesn't pay his women, he expects them to pay him. God knows what he does with his money. He's earning more than I am. When he gambles, he wins. He's got fans who'd give him his weight in gold if he asked for it. He didn't buy any of those rubies he tarts himself up in either. He got the lot, one at a time, from those rich old madams who follow him around. He must be loaded, and God knows why. No sense in being the richest corpse in the graveyard, that's what I say. We're getting on a bit, come to think of it, Marsyas and I. I must be twenty-eight, aren't I? You'd better start looking around for something for me to do, because I don't fancy working for Bassus as a trainer. If you got yourself a decent stud-farm, I'd consider managing it. Spanish mares, eh, and those showy little brutes from Africa? Yes, a trip to Africa wouldn't be at all bad.'

The Cybele Games began again in April with all due splendour, the supreme experience of thousands of drab lives, burning up the emotions and energies of an idle populace that could otherwise have turned to trouble. While the spectacle lasted, while a fortune in men and animals was being squandered daily for the common pleasure, men could forget the overcrowding of their tenement holes, the loss of their political rights, the aristocrats who through the generations had robbed them of their land, and the slaves who had eaten away their right to work. While the games lasted, they were all rich men, but for those of us who had lovers or brothers or friends working the arenas it was a different story.

Dion's performances had fallen off last season and the season before it, so that the fickle mob had begun to grumble that he was ageing, drinking, had lost his nerve; but the sparkling, teasing spirit of April put her loving arms around him, leading him to victory, and at the end of the six-day festival his popularity was as high as it had ever been. There was a two-day break – a breathing space to spend our winnings or make frantic applications to the money-lenders who gathered like carrion crows – and then we were off again for seven more days of riot; and all that was different about the games was their name. This time they were dedicated to the Goddess Ceres.

Nothing had been seen of Marsyas so far. He had fallen out with his faction, 'Red', in the autumn, had disappeared on a long hunting-trip when he should have been training, returning out of condition and out of humour; and then, when they complained, he'd gone off somewhere else to sulk as he often did, knowing that the fans would soon bring him back. His faction directors didn't like it, vowed that this time they'd leave him to stew, that the damage he caused to horses and chariots and everybody's nerves cost more than he was worth, but when he finally swaggered back to town and put himself up for auction, they swallowed their pride and started bidding with the rest. It looked, at first, as if he'd go back to the 'Blues' with Dion, for Bassus was too complete a businessman to bear an unprofitable grudge, but on the last day of the new games, amid popular excitement and speculation that far exceeded anything accorded to Agrippina and the imperial succession, he put on his red tunic again, and even his fans were awestruck when the size of his new salary became known.

Seeing him in the parade, expressionless and remote as charioteers always are at the start of the day, his reins fastened two or three times around his waist in tight, visible knots, his helmet strap loose to provide the familiar thrill when it fell away and left his head exposed, the crowd stirred with the beginnings of the hysteria he was hired to create. Behind me a group of girls, hanging on one another's shoulders, eyes blank and faces pale with sick excitement, began his eternal death-chant, 'Marsyas! Marsyas! Marsyas!' – just the name, over and over, like a pulse-beat that would, by the end of the day, rise to an orgasm.

And as I watched the preliminary races – lads who were making their debuts and the men near retirement who were playing as safe as they dared – the tender spring weather, the time of change and renewal, inserted itself lightly into my skin, performing some process of healing and cleansing, reminding me that my life was far from over. I had been content, so far, to acquire more of the same things, piling wealth on wealth, success on success, but what prevented me from taking a different path? What prevented me from going to Africa with Dion, from wiping the slate clean and making a fresh start? Chrysothemis would be more than glad to take care of my interests here in Rome. Marpessa was no longer my concern. Paris might even join me if I made the trip exciting enough. I'd try, I decided, and when I turned my eyes to the line-up for the next race I was almost drunk with anticipation and hope, younger than I'd felt for a long time.

There was Dion first, in his bright blue tunic, heavier than he used to be and looking bulky in the frail, two-wheeled chariot; strangers racing for 'Green' and 'White', a powerful Negro, and a boy with honey-brown hair up against class competition for the first time: and Marsyas, in the 'Red' chariot, lean and graceful, moulded into his vehicle, but having difficulty, it seemed, with a team he hadn't trained and didn't know. They were, for a few moments, like jewelled images of men, encircled by a pool of silence that set them apart. And then came the unleashing of flood waters as they thundered down the straight, raising a storm-cloud of sand in that first, vital dash for position. Dion had drawn the favoured inside lane, nearest the central Spina, and shooting away with great panache he held his place, with 'Green' and 'White' close behind, doing battle with each other, and Marsyas running last. He had established no rapport with his animals and, considering how little training he'd done and last year's leg injury which was said to be still troubling him, I doubted if he'd do great things. But lashing his horses too hard – too soon, I thought – he overtook 'White' as they rounded the turning-posts, executing one of his spectacular tight turns that sent his helmet rolling away into the dust, playing to the crowd to justify that outrageous salary. And for ten laps the positions were unchanged, 'Blue', 'Green', 'Red' bunching together now, sun and sand in their eyes, sweat in dark patches staining their backs. I wondered if Dion could keep up the pace. He was still hugging the Spina wall, maintaining a decent lead, but his horses were steaming, one of them blowing badly, and 'Green' was gaining on him, with Marsyas close behind.

They disappeared around the bend and when I saw them again 'Green' was pulling slowly, slowly alongside, so that he and Dion were neck and neck with Marsyas breathing down their backs – close, so very close, all of them, whipping and straining and snarling, axles grinding suicidally towards each other and then withdrawing, threatening and grinding back again. And then suddenly there was a line of red across the 'Green' charioteer's shoulders, oozing blood where Marsyas' lash had caught him. It could have been an accident, although no one thought so, but the man in green – and he wasn't even a man, he was a boy, seventeen years old with all his young life to lose – was startled, knocked off balance, and his horses, feeling his alarm, caught fire and surged forward in unco-ordinated panic, out of control.

He threw the full weight of his body back against his reins, but he hadn't knotted them anywhere near so tight as Marsyas, and in any case it was no more than a feather trying to hold back the wind. I don't know what happened next. No one ever really knows. He was too close to Dion, and as his horses bolted his chariot lurched sideways and his wheel and Dion's wheel seemed to touch. But he righted himself and drove off, whole, while behind him Dion's chariot began to disintegrate. I saw it, knew it, and I didn't believe it. It was so unhurried, so casual, a toy breaking up, without urgency or reality, until Marsyas, close behind – too close to stop or swerve or do anything but slice through his reins and jump – ploughed straight through the wreckage.

And into that nightmare ruin of two chariots and eight screaming horses, I saw my brother's body tossed like a rag doll.

I heard the crowd howling, the noise coming and going like waves heard through a sea-shell, but it was very far away and didn't seem to concern me. Beside me Erato bent double, as if she'd taken a blow in the gut, and then she was off, pushing through the crowd with fierce, fighting hands. And although I knew she was going to claim what was left of his body to perform the rites of her people over it, that didn't seem to concern me either. I sat down. And I don't remember how the day ended, or if anyone spoke to me as they left, but I do remember the rows of empty seats, the curious hollowness of a place I'd never before associated with emptiness. And I wondered about that.

There seemed no reason to get up. Some time ago there had been something I had meant to do, but I couldn't remember just what it was, nor why it had been important, and so I stayed where I was. Chrysothemis came and spoke to me, twittered like a bird, made a great many gestures, but it was an effort to listen, quite impossible to understand, and I didn't answer her. And then Marsyas was there, still in his racing tunic, smelling strongly of that unpleasant blending of sweat and perfume all charioteers have on them at the close of the day. He knelt down on one knee in front of me, peering at me, and I hit him hard across the face and then, when he didn't hit me back, hit him again and again and kept on hitting him until my shoulder muscles ached and my hand was numb. And, returning to reality, recoiling from the pain of it, I had no control at all over my tongue, or the venom spilling out of it.

'You filthy man!' I heard my voice tell him. 'Is it enough now? You've ruined my sister and murdered my brother. What more can you do to me? Oh, you dirty man – you poisonous man!'

And, as I flew at him again, he caught my wrists and, stooping deftly, hoisted me across his shoulder and carried me between the rows of seats and out into the colonnade where Chrysothemis was waiting. And then, setting me down, he walked off without a word, taking no notice of the people who stood aside to let him pass, or patted his shoulder, touching him for good luck.

So far as I could see there wasn't a scratch on him.

21

Dion was dead. I'd never doubted it, and so when they told me there was still a spark left in him and I could take him home or leave him to die where he lay, in the injury room behind the stables, I was astonished rather than grateful.

'Leave him,' Erato said. 'Why give him more pain?' But I could smell the horses, feel the cool indifference of these faction doctors who were paid to patch up men who could race again, and had no time to spare for the dying; and so I hired extra bearers to make the journey smoother, and had them carry him home.

His right leg was a mangled ruin, the other not much better, the rest of him a horror I wouldn't want to remember afterwards, but he survived the short journey up the Caelian Hill, past the crowd of weeping fans and sensation-seekers already milling around my door, and if he was too far gone to notice the difference between my luxurious bed and that hard faction cot, I, at least, was relieved by it.

Bassus made that unspeakable journey with me, anxious to show the world that he cared about his 'lads'. But there was no widow, no children to take care of, no prize-money owing, no noble gesture he could possibly make until the funeral when faction funds, he told me, would purchase a suitably elaborate urn; and he soon went away. Erato remained, and Paris, and we sat with him through the night, determined, whether he knew it or not, that he shouldn't die alone. And it was not until morning, when he was still alive, that I awoke to action and summoned every doctor I knew.

'Leave him in peace,' Erato moaned again, grey-lipped. 'Don't do this, Danaë – this probing and prodding – this torture. Let him die in peace, and dignity – that's what he'd want.'

But Dion was unable to speak at all, much less to reason out his chances of life or death, so I took the burden from him, and chose life.

'That's not you lying there,' I muttered. 'It's easy for you to say "let him die". He's not a dog to be put down when he's no use any more. He doesn't want to die. Nobody does. Do you?'

And since the decision was mine, and I was very strong, she turned away.

They amputated his right leg at the knee without much confidence, mainly it seemed to please me and justify their fees, and when even that atrocious butchery failed to kill him, they began to patch up the other injuries they could give a name to, warning me all the time that there was no guarantee.

'They're experimenting on him,' Erato sobbed, 'and you're allowing it. I'll never forgive you. They know he hasn't a chance and they're using him like a stray cat. I only hope you can forgive yourself.'

And Paris, gentler, with more insight, came to me as I sat sick and drowning in cold sweat after witnessing that ghastly operation, and asked me, 'Think, Danaë. If he lives, how will he live? Does he have the resources to lie on a couch for the rest of his days? He may not thank you for it. He may even hate you.'

But I stood up, fierce with certainty, and hissed at him. 'Listen to me! I knew a man who spent his life getting ready to die, who trained himself like a gladiator to meet it with dignity – and when it came to him he wasn't ready. He said there was no dignity in it, that it was life that mattered – and he'd have done anything, sick as he was, endured anything, to stay alive. I know what I'm doing. And if Dion hates me then let him hate me. You've got to be alive to hate. I can stand it.'

There were nights when I was sure he'd died, when the yellow candle-wax of his face was unreal, when I opened my eyes after a fitful doze and saw a corpse, not a man. But he continued, in spite of all their predictions, somehow to live, and when even the most pessimistic of the surgeons declared him out of immediate danger, I was the one who collapsed and had to be carried to bed. And when I got up again, after days of wandering down drugged pathways, meeting fear at the end of every one of them, he was well enough to understand his condition, and had no kind words for me.

One leg was gone, the other was crushed and useless, his ribs were broken, his chest and back scored with gashes that had not yet healed. He couldn't sit up, could do no more than raise his head to be spoon-fed by women who no longer saw him as a man;

and having lived by his strength and beauty, by the glorious physique that had clung so tenaciously to life, for many long months he wouldn't acknowledge the wreck of himself, hiding his body with my embroidered counterpane, and his face beneath a beard he refused to let me shave.

But we were the same flesh, Dion and I, the same fibre, and I knew that one day I'd make him sit up, that I'd find something to interest him, something, even, to delight him. And whatever happened, it was better than a heap of ash in Bassus' urn, or worm-eaten decay in the cold dark.

His fans stood about in the street for a day or two, poor men leaving fruit and wild flowers on my doorstep, rich ones sending wine and lobsters and hot-house bouquets. The patrician wife of the governor of Spain sent a red mullet, Cynthia a silver amulet to ward off, a little tardily, the evil eye. Warm-hearted Xanthe came herself and when he tried to turn his face to the wall told him he was as beautiful as ever, and whispered to me on leaving, with a whore's generosity, that if he ever needed to prove he was still a man – as the doctors said he was – she'd be more than ready to oblige. Marpessa sent a stiff note asking my permission to visit him at some convenient time, and interpreting this to mean when I was out, I answered she could come any time she pleased, with the result that she failed to come at all.

The young 'Green' charioteer came too, as was only right, and spent a few moments of agonizing embarrassment at Dion's bedside, for young as he was he should have been able to take that whiplash on the shoulder without losing control of his team, and he could do no other than blame Marsyas.

'The fiend was up my backside all the way,' he pleaded, desperate to be believed. 'And he knew what he was doing. He'd made a bad start and he had to smash you up, and then me, if he wanted to get placed. I've seen him do it before, except that this time I got clear and he smashed himself.'

But when he said the same thing to others, and it reached Marsyas' ears, Marsyas went looking for him at the 'Greens' club and six men were needed to separate them and hold Marsyas down while the lad got away. Hearing that, it was the first time I saw my brother smile.

Erato came to sit with him every day, finding it easier now that I had moved his couch to the colonnade of the garden-court, beneath the hanging-baskets of pink and white flowers, within sight and sound of the fountain. But conversation had played a small part in their relations, and now that he didn't flirt and tease and had no great appetites to cater for – now that no other women pursued him – he seemed quite strange to her, and she would go away sad and puzzled, worrying perhaps because already she was feeling less inclined to come again.

Paris too made valiant efforts, but matters had never been easy between them and they had nothing but an accident of birth to bind them together.

'He'll grow bitter, if you're not careful,' Paris warned me. 'As soon as he starts drinking again he'll turn as sour as an old dog chained in a kennel. I'm sorry for him – but he always knew this could happen, just as I know what could happen to me.'

But what we had all overlooked was the basic idleness of my brother's nature, the flaw in him – and in Marsyas – that made him capable of intense activity when he felt like it, but had always steered him well clear of the daily grind. And, as the pain grew less, or he merely grew accustomed to it so that it seemed less, he made the effort to sit up, accepted the services of a barber, began to complain about the food, and invented the pastime – which never failed to amuse him – of annoying Chrysothemis. And if it wasn't ideal, if it wasn't much, at least he was alive.

Yet, although my own affairs continued to prosper, I found that my ardour for profit and prestige was somehow waning, and when Erato and Xanthe came babbling about the prospects for the new season, I discovered, to my own surprise, that I didn't really care.

'Your sister was at Cumae,' Erato told me. 'Ten days ago. My dear, such a parade, and Marsyas too, of course, and that unfortunate Drusillus, quite drunk and falling all over the place with Marsyas egging him on. They were together and not together – your sister and Marsyas – if you know what I mean? She's got a gold filigree collar that looks as if it came from Cleopatra, and we know Marsyas didn't pay for it, although I can't for the life in me find out who did – nor who furnished that flat in the Via Nova. Anyway, Marsyas left without her and she kept on smiling. Well, I understand that – I've done my share of it. On dear, Danaë, you don't blame me for seeing less of Dion, do you? I still absolutely adore him and always will. It's just that I seem to irritate him so much, and I can't feel I'm doing him any good. One does have a living to earn and I don't have your advantages. I can't dance: I've got no head for business: I'm just an extremely good whore. I've only got myself to rely on, and you know how it is – every year there's a new face, and they get younger – younger and tougher.'

Watching the masterpiece of art and determination that was Erato's face, it seemed to me that there would soon be room for a new star. And I wondered if it could be Marpessa.

She had been known before as my sister, then as Marsyas' new woman, but now, returning from Cumae alone to her new flat in the Via Nova, she was like Marsyas himself come again in female form, with some extra ingredient of her own, a carelessness, a light-hearted swagger that was Dion. And she left no one in any doubt that business, not pleasure, was at the forefront of her mind. She went for a stroll on Mars Field, draped in her scarlet and gold, taller than Cynthia, younger than any of them, and the challenge she flung down was irresistible. Here, at last, was a woman with the body of Venus and the mind of a dashing, devil-may-care soldier of fortune. Here was a woman who could be a hard-riding companion all day and an imaginative lover by night, who could throw a hunting-spear and laugh at the dust and danger, who never complained when the going got rough. Diana the Huntress on one side of the coin, and on the other side Venus the Voluptuary. And when I heard that Metellus Nepos, the flamboyant governor of Syria, had returned home, I was in no doubt that Marpessa, who would need a big liaison to launch her new career properly, was in the race.

Metellus Nepos was one of those men who, without any outstanding merit or talent, are marked out as favourites of fortune. He had married two enormous dowries, inherited money from all his relatives, found favour with both Augustus and Tiberius. Now, at forty-five, he was still handsome, still looked good in a parade, and Marpessa was made for him. They met, not at all by chance, one afternoon on Mars Field. Marpessa stood in a pool of sunshine, her skin an outrageous deep amber, her mouth painted a luscious red. She looked untameable, a girl from an altogether more primitive world, and once Metellus realized she was the very latest thing, and that all his friends wanted her, there was no more to be said.

Just before the Saturnalia he moved her into a house in the

Clivus Capitolinus, and Erato was astonished and openly disapproving at the amount of jewellery and silver plate he showered on her. 'I understand he's given her the house too,' she told me. But Erato had had to work hard to buy her own home on the Aventine, and considered that Marpessa was definitely getting too much too soon.

Nor was it any part of Metellus' plan to keep Marpessa for his eyes alone. One saw her everywhere, casually draped in her red silk, looking as if she might at any moment slip it from her shoulders and run naked on the grass. One heard of her lavish parties, her habit of changing her dress ten times in an evening, starting with pale pink and pearls and working up to crimson with rubies, or, as a grand finale, appearing in nothing but her jewels. She could – it appeared – drive a four-horse chariot like a man, she was an Amazon queen one moment, and the next she was everybody's best friend, down on her knees in the dust playing Odd and Even. And no matter what the game, she played to win. She was conducting a liaison in the grand manner, the kind of thing I had been doing for years, and I suppose that had we not been enemies, I would have been proud of her.

She had not accepted my invitation to visit Dion, unwilling perhaps to face me while she was still a charioteer's woman, but shortly after her move to the Clivus Capitolinus she walked through my door one day without warning, and was almost in the garden-court before an astonished maid came running to call me.

'Well,' she said, one long, bronzed hand on her hip, 'you said I could come. Is he fit to be seen? Good old Dion. I knew he'd bounce back. Marsyas said not – said he'd be better off dead – but then, Marsyas likes the idea of going off in a blaze of glory – rather likes the idea of dying altogether. Well, I'd better see him straight away, sweetie, because time, you know, is one of the few things I haven't got plenty of. I have to call at the Via Sacra to see about the setting for a ring – I can't trust them to get it right otherwise – and I promised to run along to Mars Field because some of the boys have got up a little race. And I must have a hundred people coming tonight. You do understand.'

I left her alone with him, trying not to be irritated by the rich sound of her laughter echoing around the garden-court, and his answering chuckle, trying not to mind that, perching on the edge of his couch, swinging her long legs and telling him her ribald stories, she was doing him good. Chrysothemis came by, looking harassed, raised her eyebrows and went away. Time passed, and eventually Marpessa came strolling through his door, her wide mouth still smiling with the remains of her parting pleasantry.

'He's wonderful,' she said. 'I don't blame Erato for wasting her youth on him – not that there's much left of it.'

'Oh – Erato's not finished yet. There's no call to start writing her epitaph.'

'Metellus didn't fancy her when he saw her again.'

'I dare say. He's a fashionable man. They pass on. He may not fancy you next year.'

'I won't need him next year,' she said with the same blend of defiance and confidence Marsyas had once used to me when speaking of Bassus; and remembering him – not the Marsyas she seemed determined to thrust down my throat but the man I knew from inside myself – I hoped desperately that she wouldn't linger.

But there was still something she had to say, something to probe and uncover, something that, beneath her easy nonchalance – as professional a pose as my own – was troubling her. And taking a cluster of grapes from the garden table, she balanced their dusty purple weight on her wrist and began to eat them daintily, one by one, showing off her perfect teeth and the supple line of her throat.

'So,' she said, talking to the fast disappearing grapes. 'You're pleased with me now, are you, Danaë, now that I'm conducting my life as a woman of our sort should? I thought you might congratulate me, because I've done pretty well, you can't deny it. Naturally I can't compete with Drusus' emeralds – not yet, anyway. And while we're on the subject, what does Sejanus ever give you? Or can it be that you do it for love?'

'Professionals don't fall in love,' I said cruelly, but although there was an ache in her somewhere, she met my cool gaze without flinching.

'Oh well, not with clients, but a lasting relationship with a man of one's own class, that's something you've missed, Danaë. Dion and Erato, me and Marsyas – it works – it's a solid foundation, something real among all the froth and glitter. Erato will say the same. She forgave Dion everything, didn't she, because she knew he'd always come back? I understand that. I do the same. Marsyas makes his little excursions every once in a while. I can always tell when he's getting ready to go, and then afterwards it's like the first time all over again – all that devouring and swallowing I told you about. He rinses himself clean of whatever happens to be bothering him and then he can't wait to get back to me, and neither can I. It works, it really does. I wish you had something like it yourself, Danaë.'

'Oh – well, I shouldn't worry about it. Perhaps I could have – or have.'

'Oh?' she said, with so much pent-up aggression that I wondered, for a moment, if she thought I was seeing Marsyas secretly, deceiving her as she'd deceived me. And I didn't like the part of myself that wanted her to believe that, wanted her to suffer. '*I'm gloriously happy*,' her smile said, but she wasn't, I wasn't, and as we walked together to the door, I felt the tight, tense hurt in her and knew that our conflict was far from over.

Paris almost collided with her in the hallway. 'My God,' he said. 'What a sight – you two together. Where's the blood?' But domestic squabbles were not his line of country, and, giving her a vague peck on the cheek, he saw her hastily to her litter and, taking my arm, hurried me back to the garden-court.

'Something quite sensational, Danaë. I have it on excellent authority that Tiberius has finally made up his mind to go away – thanks, in part, I must add, to a particularly virulent flowering of my poetic genius. Anyway, he's going to make a little journey down the Campanian coast, terrify a few honest citizens of Puteoli and Misenum on the way, and when he reaches Neapolis he's going to get on a boat for Capri and never come back. Now what do you think of that? Sejanus is to be left in charge of affairs in Rome, and in charge of the imperial post, too, since the only messengers allowed on Capri are to be his Praetorians. So there's just no way for anyone to see Tiberius at all without Sejanus' permission, unless somebody cares to have a go at swimming across. What price Agrippina now, eh? Just tell me that?'

But at that moment Dion called me from the colonnade and, picking up the grape stems Marpessa had scattered on the table, dry, unhappy little things shorn of their fruit, I muttered, 'What do I think? Nothing. They can do what the hell they please.'

And Paris, tilting my chin with his fine, narrow hand, kissed me lightly on the cheek and said, 'Yes, darling – yes, I'm sorry.'

22

It happened exactly as my brother had foretold. Tiberius made his imperial journey down the coast, his passage leaving a thin shadow on the smiling land; a tired, bitter man, they said, willing to throw his people to the wolves – or a senile man coaxed into folly by a wolf's smile. Reaching Neapolis – looking frail, I heard, old bones held together by his flaking old man's skin – he boarded his boat for Capri, letting it be known that Rome, his imperial city, would be lucky, or doomed, if she ever saw him again.

Sejanus acquired a villa overlooking the bay at Neapolis, a property of outrageous splendour befitting the heir to an empire, and there, when he was in residence, Rome's elite gathered about him, some of them to beg his permission to make the crossing to Capri and see their Emperor face to face. But most of them – the sensible ones, the realists – came merely to flatter Sejanus and pledge him their loyalty, escorting him about the town like humble clients with their patron.

He had guarded Tiberius' privacy for years, turned men away, delivered messages or not delivered them as he chose, but now there was no chink in the wall, no loophole for a desperate man to slip through, no hope of attracting Tiberius' notice at the Senate House or tossing a written plea for mercy into his box at the circus. Sejanus' Praetorians policed the coast, supervised and possibly searched deliveries of anything and everything that was addressed to Capri. No one could make the crossing without their knowledge. No one could even be sure if Tiberius was sane, or still alive.

Tiberius, it was true, had not yet named his heir, and had declined to offer Sejanus an imperial bride; but the first step to ennoblement was soon to come when he – a man without ancestors – would be created consul in partnership with the Emperor, as Drusus had once been. More than ever, now, men who valued their skins began to withdraw from Agrippina, leaving her with her precious sons, her moody, difficult Nero, her weak, wild-eyed Drusillus, her younger boy, Caligula, growing to manhood among the tensions of her isolation. And although many were sorry for her, and she could still raise a cheer from the common people whenever she showed her pale, harassed face, self-preservation was found to be more appealing than self-sacrifice.

Sejanus came to me that summer like a whirlwind, sweeping into my garden and, lifting me off my feet, giving me a hearty kiss, by no means unaware of Macro's envious eyes.

'A day and a night, last year, my love – an hour, this time, if I'm lucky. Macro, go and guard the lady's gate – and, Danaë, refresh me and be quick about it. Speed, girl. I have to be in Capri by dinner-time.'

And when Macro had marched stiffly away, he held me at arm's length, his grey eyes dancing.

'What do you think of me now?'

'That you've won.'

'And did you ever doubt it?'

'No. Did you?'

'Yes – I'll say this to you and no one else – sometimes it took me by surprise. I've walked the surface of an earthquake, and still do – because I'm not out of the wood yet – but a point comes when there's no way back, and that's when some men go under. I didn't. I don't remember a specific moment in my life when I told myself, '*I'll be Emperor*', but I rather think, don't you, that that's the way it's going to be? And all I really set out to do was be a damned good commander of the Praetorian Guard. These noble Romans tried to dislodge me from my command, and the only way I could keep it was to impress Tiberius. So I impressed him too well, and aroused more envy than ever. And so it went on. They put me in a corner, Danaë, so it wasn't a question of ambition any more but of survival – because every man I've ruined would have ruined me. They should have left me alone to get on with my Praetorian command.'

Aemilius Scaurus was charged that winter with treason and allowed, as became his rank, to stab himself to death in the presence of his own ancestral statues. His considerable property was confiscated, the customary percentage divided up among his accusers, the rest disappearing into the imperial Treasury – Tiberius' purse or Sejanus' purse, one could no longer be sure. But although his wife was exiled honourably to a small Italian town where she had some hereditary connections, their son Lucius Scaurus – the young man who had once cracked his ankle trying to get a glimpse of me – did not join her, and I couldn't discover what they had done with him.

'Why?' I asked Paris, sickened and terrified and feeling truly dirty for the first time in my life. But these people were no more than pawns in the great political game to my brother, and had no faces.

'Agrippina has sons,' he said. 'Perhaps this is just a way of showing her how easily fashionable young men can disappear – a kind of rehearsal for the big event, in case it should be necessary to make Drusillus or Nero disappear too.'

And when I began to ask why he wasn't ashamed, we had a serious quarrel that ended with him striding white-lipped from the house and Chrysothemis advising me on no account to let him in again.

'Which means', Dion said easily, 'that what she really wants to do is run after him and set about saving him from himself all over again – and it won't work, dear, really it won't. Just come and settle this pillow under my back if you want something useful to do.'

Chrysothemis flounced away, and when I asked him why he didn't leave her alone, he chuckled. 'She thrives on it. She even asks for it. It beats me why she doesn't go and live with him – two cold fish together. I'll bet she's never been near a red-blooded man in her life – nor let one near her. I'll ask her, if I happen to think of it, when she comes out of her sulks. Don't look at me like that, Danaë. I've got to keep myself amused somehow or other – you're always telling me so.'

I stayed at home that night, sitting with an outraged Chrysothemis who had taken Dion's advice every bit as badly as he'd intended, and as her complaints trickled like lukewarm water on the half of my mind I gave her, there came the sound that everyone in the city had learned to dread, the arrogant intrusion of military heels, commands barked out curtly, impersonally, a house overwhelmed, in one instant, by fear, a house no longer my own. And because I had sent money to Aemilius Scaurus' wife in her place of exile, because I knew of Sejanus' meetings with Apicata and would seem dangerous now, if he thought I'd turned against him, I got up, walked forward in a cold trance, horrified but not surprised to see Praetorians in the doorway, and Lygdus standing dwarfed between them.

I froze into absolute stillness, for there was nowhere to run, and if all I had left was dignity, I wouldn't lose it by trying to resist and being dragged outside by the hair. This was the way it happened to people like me. A knock on the door late at night, soldiers like these two, without a flicker of interest in their faces, just doing their job. And the only freedom left was to walk out of the house with my head up and hope I could control my limbs long enough to get where I had to go. No one, not even Chrysothemis, knew where my jewels were hidden, and there was no time to tell her now, no time to go to Marpessa and plead with her to take care of Dion, no time to find Paris and tell him I hadn't meant any of the cutting things I'd said that morning.

The Praetorians continued to hold themselves erect but Lygdus came hurrying forward. 'It's all right, it's all right,' he muttered. 'The Lady Livilla wants you at the palace. Don't ask me why. I expect she'll have forgotten herself by the time we get there.'

And when I nodded stupidly, unable to take a step forward, he whispered quite gently, 'Come on, love. Best get it over with.' And I understood that, in his way, he was fond of me and didn't wish me to be harmed.

I thought studiously about nothing, emotion having lost its point, and it seemed just a moment before the litter – their litter, not mine – was set down and a lean, brown, soldier's hand helped me to my feet.

There were passages then, like narrow ribbons, soldiers everywhere, lining the walls, loss of direction and identity, until they opened a door and pushed me into a room that was full of sickness – a hushed darkness, an acrid blending of medicines and incantations, the smell of sweat and pain. Eudemus – Drusus' doctor – was standing beside a couch pouring something into a bowl, his whole mind on his task; and I had seen him so often like this – his careful eyes, his steady, measuring hands – that I felt my ears straining again for the sharp, dry cough that sometimes even now woke me and sent me searching for Drusus in the night.

'Ah Danaë,' he said, his lip curling his familiar dislike of all common females, and I followed the pathway of his eyes and his narrow, supple hands downwards, to the woman who lay on the couch. And although I knew she was Livilla, the future Empress of Rome and all her dominions, there was little to separate her now from any other pitiful little drab who had staked all she had on the love of a hard man, and lost.

Her face was the colour of cold ash, her lips grey and broken where she had bitten them – a ruin such as I had seen many a time fished up from the river – and it seemed that all the colour in that sombre room was concentrated in her hair, that disordered mass, gleaming red in the lamplight, lank and wet at the ends with sweat and vomit. There she was, Livilla, who had swallowed Eudemus' concoctions once too often, as Lygdus had always hoped she would, seeking a final solution; and who had discovered that it is not so very easy, after all, to die for love.

'The woman you sent for is here, madam,' Eudemus murmured and, understanding from her gesture that she still wished to see me, he snapped his fingers, bidding me come forward and kneel beside her, and then snapped them again at Lygdus, who hurriedly brought a lamp and held it over my head.

She stirred weakly, fretfully, her voice coming suddenly in a whisper, hoarse yet so penetrating that it filled my ears and my mind and the dark spaces behind me where Lygdus held his unsteady flame; for it was not at all what I had expected her to say.

'What did he say to you of me?' she croaked, her chapped lips moving with difficulty, and I sent a glance of frantic appeal to Eudemus, for I didn't know what she meant – nor whom.

But my hesitation was more than her frayed nerves could bear and, turning to Eudemus herself, as trustful as an ailing child, she whined, 'She won't obey me, Eudemus – help me –'

He thrust his hard knee into my back, pushing me against the couch and holding me there, he hissed, 'Don't frustrate her. She means her husband – your late master. Say something – and take care –'

But, in total bewilderment, I could only mutter, 'Nothing, madam – he said nothing.'

'Liar. She's lying, Eudemus – lying –'

'No, madam, no indeed. It's the truth. He wouldn't – truly he wouldn't – discuss his wife with –'

'With a whore?' She gave a high, cracked laugh, her eyes, in that ashen face, bright – as I had once seen Drusus' eyes – with fever.

'But he would. He did. He talked to you. Eudemus has told me so, and he is the only one who never lies to me. He talked to you and so he must have spoken of me. What did he tell you? Do you deny he talked to you?'

'No, madam, no – but we talked only of small things, of things people say at such times – and it is so long ago –'

'Love talk?' A great peal of harsh laughter tore itself out of her, a dreadful sound. 'Now I know you lie. He had no love talk in him, and even if he had, it doesn't interest me. I want to know of those last days, when he was delirious and cried out in his sleep. Eudemus listened as much as he could, but you were with him night and day. He had so little life in him, what could death have meant to him? Did he even care about dying? How could he care? Tell me that?'

Her face was ghastly, her eyes swelling in their sockets, flecks of foam feathering at the corners of her mouth, and even as Eudemus moved forward to soothe her, she raised herself up and, grabbing my wrists, heaved me forward so that I fell on top of her, breast again breast, and lay there, frozen with horror and disgust.

'*Tell me!*' she shrieked. 'What did he say to you about his disease, and about me and Sejanus? What did he say about that? You think he's dead, don't you? But did you see him burn? Did any of us? Who looks at the face of a burning corpse? It could have been anyone – a substitute – not him at all. When he was a boy he used to hide and listen to the things we said about him and about other people. He'd listen and use what he heard, and he was so clever we never caught him. So what if he's doing that now – hiding and listening and watching to see what we do? Don't you feel him sometimes, just beyond the edge of sight, disappearing into the wall like he did when he was a boy? Perhaps he was dead then and we didn't know it.'

Laughter came again, loaded with her sickness, laughter that would end in violence or heartbreak or some dreadful revelation that hovered between us, that was almost there, almost spoken, and then retreated, shut out blessedly by some iron door in my mind that closed, that refused to know; and the ghost went away, back to its lurking place.

And then a real door opened with a smart click, a shaft of light falling directly across that farcical, tragical display.

'What the hell?' a voice said, cutting into the murk like a draught of clean air, and immediately Livilla thrust me aside and, crossing the room with an enormous leap, nailed herself against Sejanus' chest.

'I warned you!' I heard her say. 'I said I'd kill myself, didn't I – that I couldn't tolerate – couldn't – I warned you ...' And then a guardsman had me by the scruff of the neck, pushed me into yet another room and slammed the door, leaving Eudemus standing by Livilla's bed, his hands folded into his long sleeves, his impenetrable calm closing about him. But Lygdus had fallen cowering against the wall like a rag doll, and I didn't think I would ever see him again.

An agony of time and then, at last, Sejanus came into the room, his face hard and cool, his sword at his side, my enemy, my executioner perhaps. And even then, in the midst of my terror and confusion, I had it in me to regret the passing of the man who had given me that one carefree happy day.

'Well now, you have been visiting my lady, have you?' he said, and then, the gilded veneer of his authority peeling away, instead of drawing that sword and thrusting it in my side, he reached out and pulled me against him, taking a deep breath like a man emerging from a tunnel into clean air, needing, it seemed, the feel of a healthy body, the feel of a sound mind beneath it. And, deeply moved by this first glimpse of weakness in him, by the fact that he could be in need of anything – of me – my arms went around him, cradling his humanity, guarding it, my own weakness gone.

'Thank you,' he said, and then, releasing me, 'It's good to know that you're still on my side, at any rate. So – you have seen a woman who tried to kill herself. Do you think it was done for love of me?'

'I think so.'

'And you're right – of course you are – except that it wasn't done today. Ah no – she struck a blow on my account years ago, without realizing she was striking at herself, and she's been dying of it ever since. She gave me something I didn't ask for, thinking I wanted it, thinking it would bind me to her – and so it did – so it does. And when I recovered from the shock of it – for it didn't seem at first to be at all for my good – and saw how to twist it to my advantage, I even learned to be grateful. But unfortunately I didn't learn to love her – didn't see the necessity for it. That, she says, is killing her too. She believes I want her dead, and, yes, she burdens me, and we both know it. If I was really the fiend men say I am it would be an easy matter to get Lygdus to hold a pillow to her face. He'd do it gladly, and I'd run Eudemus through myself with a good will. But I don't – somehow I don't. Can it be that I'm getting sentimental, or merely that I'm getting old?'

'Please,' I said quickly, 'please don't tell me things I shouldn't know.' And he smiled, almost sadly.

'Why not? Perhaps you know more than you think already. A man must talk to someone, and that's part of a star courtesan's price, isn't it? The ability to listen, to give an illusion of sympathy when really she couldn't give a damn. Do you give a damn for me, Danaë?'

And although I didn't want to, shouldn't want to, I found myself looking beyond him again, through the murk that now surrounded him, to the man he could have been, untouched by this evil glory, the common soldier, perhaps, with whom I could have cheerfully tramped the world. And I gave him an honest answer.

'If you were just who you are, then I think I'd care a great deal.'

'Ah yes. You mean you could tolerate my ruthlessness – in fact you could quite get to like it – so long as you never had to watch it in operation. Yes, I know, I know. You can go now, Danaë, quite freely. We have nothing to fear from each other, and that pleases me – I wouldn't have liked it to be otherwise. Kiss me before you go.'

And putting my hands on his shoulders, my cheek against his, drinking in the warm, male odour of him that, if nothing else, was still the same, I said impulsively, 'Sejanus, are you happy?'

He laughed, surprised, but pleased, I think, because few people nowadays would ask him a question like that, and perhaps the isolation of power – to which Drusus had been born – was not always pleasant to him.

'Happy – my dear girl, you are asking me something I haven't asked myself for years. One rather tends to lose sight of happiness. You set yourself a target and strive your guts out to get there, and when you do all that matters is the next one. I really don't know if I'm happy or not. But what I do know is that I'll finish this task I've set myself. I'll rule this world of ours, Danaë, and I'll do it well. I'm a professional. I know what I'm doing, and how to do it. I can maintain the order and prosperity Augustus and Tiberius created. I can keep it functioning as it should. I may have to do it through other people to start with, but I'll do it right. And I'll do it in spite of the inferior material – the rank amateurs – I have to work with. There's no one else, Danaë. There isn't going to be anyone else. Tiberius would like his grandson to be twenty years older; he'd like Drusus to be still alive: perhaps he'd like me to be a man of birth with a house full of ancestral statues so it would look better when they come to write the history books. But he's always been a realist and in his heart he's damned glad of me.'

'Don't say any more,' I pleaded, putting my hand across his mouth, and, kissing my fingers, he held me briefly against his chest.

'I regret you, Danaë. Yes, I regret you, because I don't think there'll be too much time these next few years for self-indulgence. And when I can afford such luxuries again perhaps you'll have lost your looks and I'll have lost my vigour, and we'll be no good to each other any more. And now you'd better go, my darling, for you seem to have unlocked a certain sentimentality in me that I find quite amazing – and it really won't do at all.'

Reaching behind me he pushed the door open and immediately the waiting soldiers stiffened to attention, vigorous and alert, his crack Praetorians with their own ideas of what had been happening between me and their master.

'These lads will take you home,' he told me. 'There's nothing more for you to worry about.'

And there, with the soldiers like polished statues on either side of us, and Livilla but a few doors away, drowning in her misery, he took my face between his hands and kissed me, a lover's kiss, his tongue parting my lips, lingering, exploring as if he had all the night before him; saying good-bye and, perhaps, in some tiny recess of his mind, asking for understanding and even – although I didn't know it then – for pardon.

23

The soldiers would take me home, yet I had had enough and more than enough of soldiers that night, and as we stepped out into some hidden courtyard of the palace precinct – alive when I had expected to be dead – I grew afraid again. The palace was high-walled, silent, and although I could not think that Sejanus meant to murder me, I thought suddenly of the sleek, soft-voiced Eudemus and knew that in his concern for Livilla he might have reason to fear me. And if he had offered the Praetorians gold to still my harlot's tongue, what better place than that closed official litter, a hand on my throat, a cushion rammed against my face, and a quick journey not to my house on the Caelian Hill, but to the river? And if there would be a few to mourn me, there would be none who dared complain.

Sejanus, I thought. But even if I could remember my way through those dark corridors, he would be with Livilla now, and I couldn't reach him. And so, refusing absolutely to submit to the murderous designs of a snake like Eudemus – supposing he had any – I came to an abrupt halt, inches from the litter, and said to the young guardsman at my side, 'Leave me.'

'What?'

'Leave me. I'll walk.'

'Oh no you won't, lady. I've got my orders.'

'And I'm changing them.'

But he was a man well used to difficult situations, and he said tolerantly, 'Get in – there's a good lady. Can't have you running around the streets and getting yourself molested, can we now?'

'I said leave me!'

'So you did. Just make it easy for me, will you, lady? It's been a long night and I'm off duty in an hour.'

And it was then, as I continued to stand my ground, terrified, my eyes darting rat-like for a gap in the human wall around me, that a shadow moved and a familiar voice said, 'It's all right, mate.

She's with me – or should be. And you've known me long enough.'

'You can say that again,' the guardsman muttered, grinning. 'By God, she's a glutton for punishment. The boss and then you in one night. Well, it suits me – saves me a trip up the Caelian and back in the rain.'

And, realizing they had probably not meant to harm me after all, I watched them march away, leaving me alone with Marsyas.

'Well then,' he said, a yard away from me, a heavy cloak giving his lean body additional bulk, additional menace, its dark folds broken by the insolent sparkle of the ruby on his shoulder. 'Are you all right?' And, at the end of myself, my nerves torn beyond reason, I shouted, 'Of course I'm not all right. Get me away from here.'

For what seemed a long time there were other soldiers, red-plumed helmets, ornate breastplates, suddenly appearing, officiously enquiring, as we crossed the palace precinct, but for the most part they appeared to be faction supporters too, who at the first glimpse of Marsyas' face were more concerned with an exchange of racing pleasantries than in seriously barring our way. And even when we left the Palatine, and the streets became narrow and raucous and familiar, I was still too afraid of what lay behind me – of Livilla cowering in her sick hole, of Eudemus' spider-schemings, of Sejanus who almost, but not quite, had asked me to forgive him – to question Marsyas.

But eventually, feeling the fine autumn rain on my cheeks, aware that I was wet and unkempt, with no cloak to cover me – beginning to be aware that wherever he was leading me it was not home – I came once more to an abrupt halt and demanded, 'What were you doing up there?'

'Looking for you.'

'Why?'

'Because Dion sent for me, and asked me to.'

Feeling a moisture behind my eyes that was not rain but tears of gratitude and weakness, I said petulantly, 'Well, I can't walk about like this. I'm soaked to the skin. And I can't afford to take cold – I can't afford the time.'

'Yes, you can. You can afford anything you like. You're not a working girl any more.'

And shrugging his cloak from his shoulders, revealing all the red silk and gold that told me Dion had called him away from someone's dinner-table, he wrapped the heavy woollen fabric around me, fastening it securely on my shoulder with his ruby pin.

'There – how's that? All snug and warm now?'

'I suppose so. Just take me home.'

'Yes. We're almost there.'

But, glancing around me for the first time with clear eyes, I knew we were very far from the Caelian Hill, and that I had allowed him to bring me, in the dark of my confusion, to the one place I could not bear to be. Burdened by the weight of his cloak, its perfume stinging my nostrils – stinging my memory – I felt his hand on mine and tried to pull away.

'Be still,' he said easily, tolerantly, his uncharacteristic patience scaring me almost as much as Livilla's madness. 'Be still – I want you to take a walk with me. You owe me that much.'

'Owe you? Are you mad? You came up to the Palatine tonight for the hell of it – not because you cared about me. So don't get any ideas about me being grateful. I'm not.'

And when he didn't answer, but went on looking down at me, careless of the rain and the cold, just looking at me, I couldn't meet his eyes and began muttering furiously, 'You didn't save my life. They didn't mean to harm me. And if they had there's nothing you could have done about it. So take me home – out of this damned slum – and I'll send your cloak back in the morning.'

'Keep it.'

'I'll send it back, and your cloak-pin, and you can just – Oh damnation, my sandal strap's broken.'

'Take it off,' he said, swiftly kneeling, his fingers loosely clasping my ankle. 'You've walked barefoot before – haven't you? – in this place.' And getting up, my broken sandal in his hand, he said, 'I have a room here – at the end of the street. Not far.'

'Then crawl into it. Get away from me.'

But he didn't move and standing so close beside him in the silent dark – my lungs striving to breathe in time with his, my pulse racing to catch his pulse, my whole body betraying me, dissolving with my weak, female impulse to submit – I felt the easy humour drain out of him and his harshness return.

'There's a storm coming, woman,' he said. 'And if you think I'm going to take you to the Caelian without a cloak – You can wait downstairs, if you like, in the bloody alley, while I fetch one.'

It wasn't the street I'd grown up in, this mean, merciless corner of the Subura, but it was very like it. There was a barber-shop, a fuller's, a shuttered house that could be a brothel, garbage and tight-packed, unkempt tenements that looked unsteady on their feet. And looking from one peeling housefront to another, I shuddered and nodded my head.

'I'll wait.'

But as he turned into a littered, pitch-black alleyway and kicked open a door, I followed him into the kind of narrow, stinking hallway I remembered so well, walking two paces behind him as a tenement woman should, inhaling the stale, unforgotten odour of lethargy and poverty and defeat. Glancing over his shoulder, he murmured, 'Welcome home.'

His room, predictably, was at the top of the house, wedged in beneath the roof-tiles, unpainted walls, a narrow couch, hard and impersonal, a cell in which to do penance had it not been for the stupendous black fur thrown across a stool, the heavy-lidded, silver-studded box for his silks and his fine lawns and linens, the silver jewel-casket, the array of onyx scent-bottles and oil-flasks, the embossed wine-jar.

'But it's not safe,' I told him, startled into speech by the casual display of his treasures in this perilous place.

He shrugged. 'No one steals from me. They bring me things, they don't take them away. Do you want a drink?'

'No.'

He gave me one just the same, a heavy, self-important red wine in a jewelled cup, and then went to lean against the wall, scowling, his brooding so very intense that even when the storm broke howling against the tiles above us, he barely moved. While I, my protest drugged somehow, utterly stilled, was content to sit with him, surrounded by the mortal combat of rain and thunder as the sharp-spiked lightning walked the sky, to sit in a cocoon of silence, remembering.

'Why do you live here?' I asked at last. 'You could live at the faction club – or anywhere. Why here?'

And across the dark room only his voice came to me, still rough with the accent of the Subura.

'I killed a man here once, in a street like this. And I killed my mother at the same time. Maybe that's why I can't keep out of these alleys.'

'Oh no, Marsyas. You didn't do that!'

'But I did. She was a drunk, you see. I don't think I ever saw her sober in the whole of my life. And a woman like that can't take care of herself. I'd fed her ever since I got big enough to steal. And when I smashed that bastard's head in, I knew I was killing her with the same blow. I knew I'd have to run and I knew she couldn't survive without me. What I blame myself for is for not having the guts to strangle her before I took off. I left her to rot – and that's just what she did. She starved, I heard, in an attic like this. Well, nobody could tell me just how long it was before they found her, but there are rats in all these old buildings. I still dream about it. The only time it really leaves me is when I'm on that bloody race-track. So now you know.'

But it was more than knowing. I felt it with him and for him, walked through his nightmare beside him, sharing his demons, shielding him with the part of myself that had always wanted to love him. And as my long, familiar fear of him reduced itself, evaporated by the terrors I had experienced that night, my desire for him, my buried conviction that he, alone, was the half of my true self, broke free, and I cried out most foolishly, 'Do you still see my sister?'

'Sometimes. I have to tell you about that, haven't I – tell you why?'

'No – no! Tell me nothing. I won't listen.'

'Then tell me something. Do you blame me for Dion?'

'He doesn't blame you.'

'No – well, he wouldn't. That's not what I asked you.'

'Do you blame yourself? That's more to the point.'

'I don't know,' he said, and I could feel his tension reaching towards me through the dark. 'I really don't know. I saw it coming – too fast for me to do anything about it – and I thought, "This is it. I'm a goner now. They'll all get their money's worth today." Because what else do they come for now but to see me die? I've done everything else for them but that. I don't know if I could have got round him. I think I started to swerve and if I'd stayed where I was maybe I'd have done it. I was strapped in too tight to cut myself free – but I did cut myself free. I don't remember the knife in my hand – I never do. I was expecting to die, and it didn't worry me all that much, and the next thing I was clear ... and I don't know why. But I do know this – when the doctors told you he'd had it, you should have left him alone. Or you should have put him out of his misery – like I should have done for my mother – with a knife in his gut. That's what I'd ask you to do for me, in his place. Would you do that for me?'

'Oh yes,' I said, 'oh yes, I'd do that for you all right – willingly –'

But he had heard the break in my voice and instantly he was at my side, his hands with amazing gentleness drawing me towards him, ignoring me when I went on pleading, 'Don't tell me any more.'

'I'll tell you this. No other woman has ever been here, to this room – no one. Just you, Danaë. Darling, you're shivering – let me hold you. I'll take the cold away.'

And senselessly I burst into tears.

'Oh don't,' I wailed. 'Please don't –'

'Don't what?'

'Don't be kind to me – oh don't –'

'You're crying,' he said, almost reverently, taking my face between his hands, kissing my cheeks with the tenderness a man bestows on a weeping child. Hypnotized by the strange wonder in his face – the wonder in my own heart – I made no resistance as he undid the brooch at my shoulder, watching with leisurely appraisal as the fabric of my robe fell away, and then, first tracing the contour of my breast, he bent his head and kissed it with an immense, lingering gentleness that filled my whole body, my whole mind.

There was no need to say anything more. Smiling, he slid my robe over my head and as I put my arms around him, pressing the length of my body against his in a movement of pure cherishing, he lifted me up with the same tender care, and there, on his narrow bed, we took each other as delicately and sweetly as if we had both been virgins. And when it was done he put his face against my shoulder, closed his eyes and sighed with the perfect content of a child who has come home again after a long time away.

He clasped his fingers loosely around my wrist and we lay there in a warm silence – enraptured, at peace – and then, turning towards each other at the same moment, his fingertips began to follow the line of my eyebrows and my nose and my lips with a touch that was almost innocent; and I took his face in my hands and put my mouth against his without kissing him, just to feel him and breathe him and smell him, from sheer delight in him. And so it was, until the storm was long over, and a hint of dawn was in the sky.

But the first mindless bliss couldn't last, and suddenly, sitting up, I said, 'Marsyas, I have to go home.'

'You are home.'

'Yes – but I have to go. They'll think I'm dead.'

'So you are. I saved your life, or would have if they'd given me the chance. So you belong to me.'

'I know that. But I've got to let them know I'm safe.'

'All right,' he said, still indulgent, still easy, lying on his back and smiling up at me. 'We'll go and tell them – since you'll give me no peace, I suppose, otherwise. But I want something from you first. Before we go I want you to say you love me.'

'Of course I love you.'

'Good. See that it stays that way.'

'And you?'

'What about me?'

'Aren't you going to say you love me?'

'Oh well – as to that – I'm a man and men don't have to commit themselves. Women just have to assume these things, and hope for the best.'

'Like hell they do,' I told him, twisting my fingers into his hair. 'You'd just better commit yourself here and now. This instant.' And pulling me down on top of him he fastened his mouth on to mine.

'I love you all right. I've loved you when I haven't wanted to, and hated you as well, which turned out to be the same thing. And tonight, waiting in that damned palace precinct to see if they'd killed you – well, I think that's when it struck me that I wanted to live and that there'd be no point to it – you know what I mean – without you. Oh yes, I love you. I don't know what good it's going to do us, because it won't make me docile, nor you either. And I have to tell you that if you look at another man, or let another man look at you, then you'll answer for it.'

'And if you look at another woman?'

'Maybe I won't. You can get dressed now.'

I fastened my broken sandal strap as best I could, made no attempt to do anything with my hair but leave it hanging loose and free, and as we went downstairs into the street we were children again, vagabonds in the city, kissing at every street-corner, jumping over the puddles, laughing, touching, giddy and dazzled with our delight. But gradually, as the Subura fell away behind us, and the streets grew broader, cleaner, better-tended, we began to walk more slowly, hesitantly almost, unwilling perhaps to leave the setting of our first, uncomplicated joy, unwilling to admit that this, like everything else that life had brought us, could not be easy.

'Danaë, where are we going?' he said, and I didn't know. An hour ago life had been simple and quite complete. But now my feet were taking me back to a familiar labyrinth, and I was abruptly terrified.

'Listen,' Marsyas said, and his voice was shaking. 'If you don't go home they'll think you died up at the palace. And if I'm missing nobody will be surprised. We can get out of the city now, Danaë, before sunrise – and we can get right away.'

I shook my head, not really understanding.

'Yes, yes!' he said, and there was such urgency, such pleading in his voice that I would have followed him anywhere, just for the pleasure of hearing him ask me to go. 'We have to run, Danaë. There's no other way. We can't live together in this town, with these bloody people taking bets on how long we'll last. We wouldn't last. They'd get between us, you know that. The factions would get to me, and the women. I don't know how good I am at resisting temptation: I never had to try. But I'll try now, for you. And you've got to do the same for me. We've got to start clean, and free, and there are too many things here neither of us can get away from. I'm not going to race any more, and I won't let you dance again. I know it won't be easy, wherever we are. But we have to be alone to make it work. And that's one thing this town won't do for us – leave us alone. Before we know where we are we'll be cheap and nasty like everything else has always been. And I couldn't stand that. Do it my way!'

I let him lead me on a few steps, passive, content to be taken away, to be with him. 'You'll be all right, darling,' he kept on urging me. 'And you don't have to worry about anything. I've got enough money for us both. I've spent money like water but never my own – you know that. I'm rich and it's all nicely tucked away where I can get my hands on it any time I like. I can take care of you. You've got to depend on me – belong to me.'

And although it was what I longed to do, the mist had already begun to clear, the dream to fade, and I knew it couldn't be so simple, for how could I go like that? How could I leave Paris to face his uncertain future? Or Dion, who would be my responsibility for the rest of his life? How could I allow them to think I was dead, and to mourn for me?

I started to tell him, 'Marsyas – I can't – I can't.' And when he went on dragging me with him, I fought him until he had to stop.

'Marsyas – no – it's not sense. It's not possible – my brothers –'

'You have no brothers. No one. Just me. I won't let you go now,' he said tonelessly, and because I recognized that emptiness in his voice as the prelude to a killing anger, I shouted, 'I can't let my brothers think I'm dead. I can't put that sorrow on them.'

'You'll do as I tell you,' he shouted, his hands falling on my shoulders, and as he started to shake me I cried out – because I had to make him understand, 'Don't break my heart. You know the state Dion is in and what Paris does for a living. I can't walk away from that and forget it.'

'It's not them,' he said viciously, rage and tears spilling out of his eyecorners. 'You don't care about leaving your bloody brothers. It's your money. If you disappear they'll get the lot, Paris and Dion and Marpessa. You won't come with me because you don't want Marpessa to get her hands on your gold.'

'Oh no, it's not true –' I was sobbing now, the words catching in my throat. 'Don't say it. Don't ruin everything again – not now. I couldn't bear it. I'll give everything away if you like. You're not reasonable. Let me settle my affairs, then I'll come with you – anywhere. Just let me make sure Dion is all right.'

'Do you love me?' he yelled as if he hated me, and I yelled back, 'Yes, I love you.' And, loving one another, we squared up like deadly enemies, completely beside ourselves, shaking and shouting and weeping.

'Then come with me. If you love me you'll come. It's the only way. And if you don't you'll never see me again. It's as simple as that.'

'Just let me see Paris –'

'No,' he bellowed. 'You don't know anybody called Paris. There's just me – Marsyas – I won't have anybody else. They'll take you away from me. I'm warning you – you'll never see me again unless you come now. If you love me, you'll come.'

'I love you – I do. But if you love me you'll give me an hour to ease my mind. Then I'll do anything you like. Be reasonable, for once in your life, damn you – you've got no one to leave – damn you – damn you! You left your mother once, and look what happened to her!'

Every drop of colour drained from his face and, sick with horror, I braced myself for a blow, feeling I had deserved it. But he only said quietly, 'I'll ask you just once more.'

And when I shook my head and he turned away from me into the crowd, I did what Cynthia and probably Marpessa and every other foolish woman in his life had done. I screamed out at his retreating back, 'Don't leave me!'

He stopped, and without turning round, looked back over his shoulder. He had been crying but his face was hard and set now, and my feet seemed to have taken root in the ground. He wouldn't come back. I couldn't go forward. And so we stood there, staring at each other, until the early morning crowd flowed between us. And when it thinned out again, he was gone.

24

It was the start of a dreadful time. I staggered back to my house that unspeakable morning with no word for any of the anxious faces assembled in my hall, and going to my room, bolting myself in like a sick beast in its lair, I lay for a long time on the cold floor-tiles, misery dragging me to the ground as it had done long ago when I had mourned for Drusus. And I grieved once again with the pain of bereavement, for I knew that Marsyas was just as dead to me now. I had made my final, bitter decision and I could feel nothing inside me but the chill of utter hopelessness. And when I learned that Marsyas had left Rome after a mighty flare-up at his faction club and had taken a woman with him, a seedy drab from the Subura, the chill overcame me, so that I was altogether cold and dry and bare.

Metellus Nepos, Marpessa's lover, married his third big dowry soon afterwards, the wedding being celebrated with great pomp in the presence of both Sejanus and Livilla, her face – according to Lygdus – a masterpiece of the cosmetic art, her hair a deeper orange than the bridal veil. The bride was a daughter of the Sulpicii, a woman of vast expectations, and on the wedding-night Marpessa gave a party of her own – financed by Metellus – to which everyone of note in our *demi-monde* except myself was invited. Erato was there in all her feathers, Cynthia in her emeralds, Chloe in white with pearl flowers in her hair, Marpessa herself in Metellus' parting-present of rubies, a fine company of actors and artists, sportsmen of every faction and every calling, my brother Paris, my brother Dion – conveyed in a litter I'd had specially designed for him – and even Chrysothemis who, unwilling to be accused of taking sides, nobly offered to decline.

'No,' I told her, 'go and enjoy it and let me know. You can wear my sapphires.' And, having no engagement that night, I waited up for her, spending the hours with my account books and the problems of a venture in Judaean turquoise that was not paying quite what it should – waiting as she had waited a thousand times for me.

'Well, it was all quite splendid,' she said, gratefully unfastening her sandals on her return. 'Very fast and furious and likely to go on for the next day or so by the look of it. The house is every bit as luxurious as we heard, no expense spared, except that I can't help feeling it's not quite tidy – you know, it's hard to tell in such a crowd, but little things, you can't miss them. She revels in it, but I don't think she takes much care of what she has – she never did – and I could see she's the kind who'd throw her silver away when it gets scratched and buy new – or get someone to buy it for her – instead of making sure the maids keep it polished. Silver statues all over the place, dear, the great big Diana in the hall with a rope of pearls twice round its neck and hanging to its knees. Ostentatious, I thought. And cartloads of flowers, thrown into vases just anyhow – and there's no excuse for that when you consider the hours I've spent showing her how to make arrangements.

'Well, I didn't expect to be well placed at dinner and of course I wasn't – absolutely squashed against the wall – not that it mattered, because people started helping themselves and eating all over the house, taking things from trays before they'd even got into the dining-room, and leaving their fish bones and their chicken bones wherever they happened to be – you'd never have allowed it. Her dogs were everywhere too, and not very nice dogs either. I saw one of them lift its leg against a brand-new damask divan-cover. And she had some sort of a monkey on her shoulder most of the time, and birds, dear, not in cages but just flying loose and screeching – and that's simply not clean. But people seemed to find it all very exciting. There was plenty of money being frittered away all right, flasks of perfume rolled up in every napkin – not from *your* shops either ... Anyway, after dinner other people started to arrive – my dear, it was like a circus crowd, hardly room to breathe, and I had to speak quite sharply once or twice because I will not be stepped on and pushed without an apology. And the servants kept on delivering messages and flowers. Most of them were from nonentities and I expect she sent some of them herself to create the right impression, but they were saying she's had an offer from the consul Satrius Saturninus, and from that man who's just come back from commanding the armies of the Rhine. Certainly one of those bouquets had a gold bracelet fastened around the stems – she made sure we all saw it, although she wouldn't name names.

'Erato, of course, got very drunk, and cried all over Dion and told everybody how his accident had ended the best part of her life. And then he got very vulgar and asked her, among other things, what she thought it had done to him. But Xanthe came over and smoothed things out, although she could have saved herself the trouble because I could have managed perfectly well. Naturally, I didn't expect Paris to pay much attention to me, and he didn't, but never mind about that. Marsyas was expected, but he hadn't arrived when I came away, which doesn't signify a great deal since he could very well turn up tomorrow morning and still get his dinner. She was very busy making out she knew exactly where he was and that it was all right by her, but if she convinced herself, she didn't convince me. It's my belief she hasn't seen him for ages.'

Dion and Paris arrived soon afterwards, Dion heavy-eyed but considerably mellowed by wine, looking like some gigantic jewelled Bacchus as they carried him into the hall, his maimed limbs richly covered by a robe of Milesian wool, his face older than it should have been, but firm enough around the jaw, his cheeks beginning to fill out again. And as Chrysothemis began to bustle around him, organizing the weary bearers to take him to his room, and his masseur to attend him there, I asked Paris, 'Did he enjoy it? Was he all right?'

'Yes – I'm sure he did. He had the women cooing over him, which he thought would never happen again, and, do you know, it occurs to me that when he wasn't racing he never did move about much anyway. You may have been right after all.'

'It was all very grand then?'

'Yes, and quite predictable. I was watching Chrysothemis tonight, sitting among all those over-paid beauties, and really – since she's just as lovely as any one of them, and far more cool and graceful, and better-behaved than most – why is it that no one notices her? What does she lack?'

'Does it worry you?'

'Well, yes, as a matter of fact it does, because sometimes I think I'd rather like to have her back.'

'I think she'd come if you asked her.'

'Yes, that's what I think – and perhaps I will. But what I really wanted to tell you – and keep it to yourself – is that it seems Sejanus has written to Tiberius *again*, asking permission to marry Livilla. So now we know the point of that fake suicide, dear – he couldn't afford to lose her, could he? But once a woman starts drinking poison every time something upsets her, there's no telling how it could end.'

'Do keep your voice down,' I pleaded, terrified as always by these revelations which proved the depth of his involvement, the extent of his danger. But it only pleased him to see me worry on his account, and he smiled.

'All right then, I'll whisper, and this next part needs whispering about. They tell me Tiberius refused, as was expected, made some sarcastic comment about feeling sure Livilla would wish to dedicate her life to the memory of her husband, in the manner of her cousin Agrippina. But then, instead of being formal and offended as he was the last time, he started saying very encouraging things about Sejanus' future. And then – and listen carefully to this – he told Sejanus to be patient a while longer, because his Emperor was already planning to give him all the official recognition he could require, and a marriage alliance beyond his wildest dreams. Yes, you may well look blank. It knocked me off balance too when I first heard it. I haven't felt so excited in years.'

'But who, Paris? Who? If he won't let him marry Livilla, who else is there?'

My brother's face was a mask of mischief. 'It has to be a member of the imperial family, and we know it couldn't be any of Agrippina's girls, so there's only one other person possible. It has to be Livilla's daughter, the Lady Julia.'

And, as he spoke, Livilla's wasted face floated sickeningly out of the shadows of my memory, her hoarse, despairing whispers filled my ears, and I said, 'That's horrible. That's one of the most horrible things I've ever heard.'

'Oh, I don't know,' he said airily, taken aback just the same by the repulsion I couldn't conceal.

'It's cruel, Paris.'

'Cruel to Livilla? Possibly. But if Tiberius wants to honour Sejanus, Julia is a much better bet. She's much closer to him than Livilla. She's his own granddaughter – Drusus' daughter. She's young. One imagines she could bear children if she had someone better than that sickly Nero to father them for her. Sejanus must be cock-a-hoop, and I expect Livilla's at the poison bottle again, unless they've managed to keep the news from her.'

'And Nero? He *is* Julia's husband.'

'So what of it? He'll hardly be in a position to do anything about it if Tiberius asks for her back. Danaë, you've actually got tears in your eyes. What is the matter with you? Livilla only has herself to blame. She used to be quite suitable at one time, but look at her now. She's a nervous wreck, and no man likes that. And by the way, while we're on the subject of nervous wrecks, your friend Marsyas turned up at Marpessa's after all, and I don't know where he's been but it certainly hasn't done him any good. Gaunt would be the polite description. To tell the truth he looked like a skeleton walking about. His faction is going to give him hell. I reckon Marpessa was just as surprised to see him as anybody else. He hadn't any flowers for her, and no gold bracelets either, but she as good as asked me to tell you he'd turned up again. You'd be friends again now if it wasn't for him. Leave him to her, Danaë – he's not your kind, and he may well be hers.'

Then, catching the frozen agony of my face, he quickly remembered another appointment and hurried away.

Marpessa made her choice some time after, and left for a holiday in Toscana with the former commander of the Rhine army, returning bronzed and fit from hunting and riding, and possibly marching, in the noonday sun. She looked magnificent when I saw her one day strolling along the Via Sacra as if it belonged to her, an almost transparent linen robe revealing every supple inch of her amber shape; but as she replied to my greeting her face was hard and sarcastic, bristling with a hostility that communicated itself to the dogs on either side of her, causing them to snarl and bare their teeth so that I was glad to walk away.

Although Marpessa troubled me, it was Livilla who haunted me most – Livilla the broken doll soon to be tossed aside to make room on the puppet-shelf for her own daughter – and her sick fantasy that Drusus had not really died got into my dreams, so that every restless night I believed he was somewhere in the house, stiff and cold, but alive, and that I couldn't find him.

A bad time then, a bad, bare time, so that when the disaster which had been stalking the city finally overtook it, I only said 'How terrible,' because everybody else was saying the same, and it was easier to swim with the tide.

The Empress Livia, Tiberius' ancient mother – Drusus' grandmother, Agrippina's grandmother – died that year, and no sooner was the breath from her body than a letter arrived from Tiberius, addressed to the Senate, denouncing Agrippina and her eldest son Nero as traitors. The wording was obscure, as Tiberius had always tended to be obscure in weighty matters, but the Senate knew what was expected of them, and trembled. They had believed – had wanted to believe – that the loss of her supporters and the now almost complete isolation of herself and her family would be enough. They had told themselves, and each other, that she was harmless now, and had chosen to ignore the common people who, having no estates to lose, went on obstinately cheering her and putting sentimental garlands on Germanicus' statues whenever they felt inclined. Perhaps that popular devotion to a poor widow signed her death-warrant.

The shame-faced senators were given no explicit instructions. Tiberius simply informed them that Agrippina and Nero were a danger to the state and to his own safety. And although a few of them – Sejanus' men – were clearly determined to push the matter through at all costs, the majority were moderate and compassionate in their hearts – or liked to think that they were – and it was a little too much for them. They were Roman senators whose fathers had been the elite of a free republic, standing shoulder to shoulder in equality before the law, not Oriental despots for whom these palace massacres were a matter of course. And they didn't like it. While they hesitated, the news leaked out and the common people came surging around the Senate House, carrying statues of their dead hero and his children, crying out loud the things the senators dared not say.

'It's Sejanus' doing,' they howled. 'The letter is a forgery. He may be a filthy old man, Tiberius – but he wouldn't kill his own brother's girl.'

And, in fear of their lives, the senators adjourned, getting home as best they could to pass a tormented night.

'So,' Paris said, dropping in to see me at dinner-time, 'I may be out of work tomorrow, but I don't think so. If he can pull this off there's nothing else to stand in his way. And don't ask me why Tiberius is playing along with him. He's an old man. He may be senile – or perhaps he just doesn't care. If this works out, Sejanus can safely look forward to his Empire, and if it doesn't, they'll tear him to pieces. I wonder if he'll sleep tonight? I have a strange feeling that he will.'

But the next morning the chanting, parading crowds were out again, and the Senate hesitated so long that for a while it seemed they had won the day. But it wouldn't do. Tiberius wrote again, deeply offended, threatening no one directly, but letting it be known, just the same, how foolish it would be – how very unwise – to defy him. And, torn between the menace of the mob and Sejanus' highly organized Praetorians, and having no leaders left who could weld them into a unit capable of withstanding the sinister, inscrutable will of Tiberius himself, the Senate collapsed.

It was over. It had seemed a monstrous impossibility, yet it had taken no more than a letter, a word of command, the determination of two men working together for different reasons – and it was done. The mob dispersed, the senators went home, avoiding each other's eyes, Agrippina was exiled to the bleak little island of Pandataria, where her mother Julia, Tiberius' unfaithful second wife, had also been an exile: and Nero went to Ponza. They died quite soon, and although there were rumours that they had been starved or suffocated by their guards, it made little difference since they would have had to die anyway. Exiles can always be rescued, taken to the legions and used as a rallying point for fresh revolution, and neither Tiberius nor Sejanus would be likely to risk that. Indeed, we heard through Xanthe, who had friends among the Praetorians, that Agrippina had actually met her death here, in Rome, as a precaution against just such a rescue, and that the closed litter which took her into captivity had nothing in it but a corpse.

It was over. Or perhaps not quite, for there was still Drusillus – the wild-eyed young man who had once wept on Marsyas' shoulder because his mother didn't love him – and although for a season, and then another, one saw him occasionally, paler, older, fading visibly, a moment came when he was whisked away – charged with immorality and the inevitable nameless treasons – and he was never seen again.

A bad time. Marsyas disappeared again, and again returned, raced for every faction in turn and quarrelled viciously with them all, greedier for money than he'd ever been, although it was difficult to say why, since he would only emerge from his kennel in the Subura in his splendour of rubies and gold when somebody else was paying the bill. I saw him, often enough, surrounded by hysterical fans, letting them kiss his hands and stroke his arms, kicking them out of his way when he'd had enough, but – in spite of his age and his temper and all the fresh-faced, handsome newcomers who were filling the factions – his popularity was undimmed. He had only to appear, his reins strapped around him in those complex knots, bareheaded by the second lap, his helmet rolling away under somebody else's wheels, for the arena to be in an uproar. He had only to stretch out his rapacious hand and somebody would fill it with gold; only to snap his fingers and some woman would fall rapturously at his feet. But he never looked my way, nor Marpessa's way either, it seemed. And when I met her now in the street she always smiled with frozen brilliance – hating me – and passed me by.

I expanded my interest in turquoise from the Sinai Desert, planned little journeys that never got under way, danced occasionally for a few favoured patrons, becoming something of a collector's item, an artiste who could afford to condescend. I became difficult, obsessed with profit – since that, at least, was straightforward enough – and tried not to notice that every day seemed identical to the last.

A bad time.

25

I didn't want to see Sejanus again. The time had finally come when I could no longer separate the cold, ambitious killer from the man with whom I could undoubtedly have been happy, and since I couldn't risk being happy with him again, it was better not to see him at all. I couldn't judge him. Like any other great leader, he was a hero if he happened to be on my side, a murderer if he was against me. Yet the thought of him made me uneasy, the world outside my door – and my own place in it – made me uneasy too, and like so many others, because I couldn't change what I saw, I turned away from it, to my account books and my own still-beautiful reflection in my mirror.

No, I wouldn't see Sejanus again. He was too high now, too covered over by layers of glory for me to recognize the man I knew. His success made him terrible. I encountered him sometimes, making his progress through the city streets, surrounded by fawning senators, applauded by that part of the crowd his agents – Paris among them – paid to applaud, and by the part that would applaud anybody. I passed his villa, once or twice, at Neapolis, bristling with soldiers like a royal residence, caught fleeting glimpses of his yacht making the crossing to Capri, and I couldn't think he would have any further use for me.

Livilla was sometimes seen with him, when he presided over the games or journeyed from one rich Campanian villa to another, but Nero's death had set Livilla's daughter free, and Paris was convinced Sejanus would eventually marry her.

'Yes, yes, Tiberius must have had her in mind when he promised Sejanus an imperial bride. Livilla may want to be his wife, but now she'll have to settle for being his mother-in-law. I don't see what she can do about it, short of murdering him, or Julia.'

Lygdus, when I mentioned the matter to him, and when he had recovered from his emotions, thought murder a highly acceptable solution.

'That is, if Sejanus kills *her* first,' he muttered, hate tightening the muscles of his face into an illusion of raw youth. 'Yes, that's what he ought to do – kill her first. I'd help him. Eudemus watches her, but I'd get past him one way or another – who better than me? Lygdus the clown? Wouldn't harm a fly, Lygdus. Faints at the sight of blood. But I'd do for her all right – and I expect she knows it. Well, I just hope he knows it too, because I'll be ready – any time he likes.'

'Oh Lygdus,' I said, half laughing, half touched by his comic determination, 'you're a many-sided man, but I can't see you as a murderer.' And because he cried easily these days, and mumbled a great many wild things, I paid little heed to the tears in his eyes, the grotesque twitching of his lips.

The bad time, I thought, was passing. Life might be far from ideal but it could be comfortable. It had its satisfactions. Yet I was not by nature one of life's spectators and when Macro appeared one hot, August morning at my lonely little villa near Baiae and told me my discretion was again required, it was a relief to have something to do.

'I don't know if the great man is coming himself or not,' Macro told me, standing too close, his insolent eyes fixed on the outline of my breasts. 'But I'm to escort his lady wife to your address – and another person after her. It may be he'll call in later, to see how the meeting went, and pay his respects to you. I know I would – in his place.'

And so, as I'd done many times before, I supervised the cleaning and the flowers and the cooling of the wine, dismissed the servants with money in their hands to the village until morning, and then, as the shadows began to lengthen, sat in the garden, oppressed by time and silence, hoping he wouldn't come, hoping I wouldn't want him if he did. It wasn't the first time Apicata had made use of my house on her husband's business without his presence, but the fact that I had been asked to stay, not simply to hand over my keys, indicated either that he was expected, or that I was needed as an alibi for the person – presumably a man – Apicata was coming to see.

Several times before my name had been linked with men who had needed to make arrangements with Sejanus in private, and although I didn't much care which elder statesman, which foreign potentate, Macro would bring to my door, I did wonder what

Apicata thought about her husband's proposed marriage to Julia. Julia, so different from her flamboyant mother, would be clay – surely? – in Apicata's capable, workmanlike hands, a little shadow in Sejanus' imperial bed, disturbing neither of them. And the barrenness of her future life struck out at me like a nervous little wind coming from the cold night, tingling my spine and filling my mind with so acute a memory of Drusus – her father – that I clenched my fists and pressed them against my eyes. And when I recovered I was no longer alone.

The garden was completely silent, as it had been before, the night coming on now. There had been no footstep, nothing had stirred, yet someone stood there, a shadow among the shadows, someone just beyond the edge of my vision, someone perhaps, or something, that raised the hairs on the nape of my neck. For I was alone until Macro came – unless indeed it was Macro come early for purposes of his own? But Macro had bulk and heat and, straining my eyes through the treacherous twilight, this form was tall and lean, delicately put together, a long narrow head, something about the moulding of it that I knew so well. Too well for sanity. And suddenly, calling out and receiving no answer, nothing but the silence that stood around him, whispering to me *'You vowed to mourn me forever. How is it you don't even know me now?'* – suddenly it seemed that Livilla's sick fantasies had infected me, that I was part of them, hearing her say all over again, *'He's not dead. He's hiding somewhere, spying, waiting to catch us out.'*

And with a movement of pure joy, pure fear, I called out, 'For God's sake, who are you?'

'How strange that you don't know me,' a voice said, a cool, clipped voice, speaking the purest Greek I'd ever heard – Drusus' Greek, although surely I'd called out in Latin? Then, as breath left me, as life froze, crystallized, he stepped forward – Drusus' long mouth curved in that faint, sardonic smile, Drusus' hooded eyes, Drusus himself, for one crazy instant, in those cheating shadows. But, in the lamplight of reality, not Drusus but a boy still in his teens, his smile deepening now with a reckless gaiety that had nothing of Drusus in it at all.

'My dear lady,' he said, 'have I absolutely scared you to death? Please don't die, they'd never forgive me for it. May I assume you mistook me for my uncle Drusus? They say I am very like him. No, no, please don't be alarmed. I'm no one of any great importance, just the youngest son of Agrippina – her only son, in fact, as matters have turned out. I'm Gaius, the one they call Caligula. Surely, you have heard of me?'

'Yes,' I said, teetering on the edge of a terrible gulf and then withdrawing from it almost reluctantly, realizing for the first time how tempting fantasy can be, how easy to cling to. 'Yes, of course I've heard of you.'

'And you were expecting me?'

'Surely not. I was expecting –?'

'Yes,' he said quietly. 'You were expecting me. Naturally, they didn't tell you, and perhaps you were not intended to see me, but don't worry about that because I shall go away again presently. I am to meet the good Macro, an hour from now at a secret spot a little way along the road, and he is to bring me here to speak with a lady. Well, I shall not keep him waiting, and if you happen to see me later on you may be as surprised as you please – in fact I think you *should* be surprised, for when people wish to keep secrets I find it usually pays to let them. I live with my grandfather Tiberius now on Capri, and I'm playing truant. Well, the soldiers would wink at it, you know, even if Macro hadn't ordered them to, because they've been boys themselves and they know how dull it is on Capri, whatever the graffiti have to say to the contrary. It was a clever move to think of bringing me here. If my grandfather catches me, what could be more natural – a beautiful, rather famous woman, my youthful curiosity? Yes, very clever. As to the lady Apicata, who would notice her when you are here?'

He walked forward a little, looked around him quickly, nervously, as Paris often did, checking the possibility of unseen eyes and ears, the nearness of the trees that could conceal an enemy with a knife or a pair of strangling hands, or the taut little rope that crushes the windpipe; making sure there was a clear way out. And, having done that, he turned to me again and flashed a dazzling, well-rehearsed smile, ready to play the hare-brained, disarming youth which, already, I knew he was not.

'I climbed your wall,' he said, 'oh, ever such a long time ago – and I hid in your lovely, shady tree. I watched you bustling around, doing housewifely things, and then I watched you send your servants away, as I'd been told you would. After that I almost spoke to you, because you looked quite sad and very lovely, sitting so quietly, but I thought it best to wait. You see, you might have been expecting someone else – someone they hadn't told me about – and when in doubt, I find patience to be the greatest virtue. My mother, poor soul, had every virtue in the world but patience – and look what happened to her. But when you're the youngest of a large family, waiting seems natural – certainly it's inevitable. So I waited, and I'm almost certain, now, that no one was lying to me – not tonight, at any rate.'

I sat down, feeling weak and cold. 'You thought they meant to lure you here and kill you?'

'Why yes, of course I did.' He smiled again, that flash of brilliance, that flamboyant parting of the lips that was an actor's mask of gaiety, totally unreal. 'In my place, wouldn't you have thought the same? Of course you would. After all, they killed my mother and my brothers, and possibly my father, so why not me? I'm growing up, you see, and I perfectly understand what a nuisance that must be to them. But, with the very best will in the world, there's not much I can do about it. Of course, I'm very young for my age – I make sure of that – but however one looks at it, time is hardly on my side. My grandfather Tiberius and I are both getting older. You do see that, don't you?'

I saw it, understood very clearly that he was here to negotiate with Apicata for his life. And since he was the only person left alive who could possibly succeed Tiberius, who could possibly marry the Lady Julia – since he was a son of Germanicus – who could blame him? Yet, as he sat down beside me, moving his face into the light, I turned to him with compassion and then, abruptly, backed away, for although he was quite beautiful – Drusus in his early years, Drusus as he should have been without his melancholy and his bitter reserve – there was something wrong with his eyes. They were long and dark, deep set, extremely bright, but beyond that brilliant surface there seemed to be nothing at all. I seemed to be looking not into human eyes, but at jewels set in the face of a living statue. And it was uncomfortable, disconcerting – it was wrong.

'Oh,' he said, aware of my recoil and not in the least worried by it, 'you're afraid of me – how absolutely marvellous. And really very flattering, unless, of course, it's just my resemblance to my uncle. Do tell me it's more than that. I'd hate to be just a shadow of dear Drusus senior, especially when he died so young, as most of my family seem to do. Do tell me that I disturb you for myself alone.'

And although it was all said so charmingly, so carelessly – although it was just a boy, like Lucius Scaurus, telling me he'd climbed a wall to watch me and cracked his ankle – it did disturb me, and I was relieved when he kissed my hand briefly – a gallant little salute – and got to his feet.

'Ah well. I must go and meet the trusty Macro. If I'm not there, trembling with eagerness, when he arrives he'll want to know where I've been and I do so hate to tell lies. You won't give me away, will you?'

'No. I won't do that.'

Once again that dazzling, almost painful smile flashed out and he made a movement of pleasure and gratitude, a piece of expert theatre.

'Oh, how sweet you are. Do you think I could see you again? I'd ask Macro to arrange it, except that I don't want him to think I'm *quite* so mature as all that – so I'll have to arrange it myself. They'll whisk me back to Capri tonight double-quick, but I'm quite good, sometimes, at just slipping away. Shall you mind?'

And that too was theatre, a boy old before his time playing young in case I betrayed him, deliberately leaving me with the memory of a charming scatterbrain, just a lad who'd sign away his birthright, forget about his murdered mother and brothers, so long as they'd let him have a little fun.

'Oh no, I shan't mind,' I said automatically, and as I watched him go back over the wall lightly, easily, showing off since he could just as well have used the gate, I made up my mind to leave for Rome the next morning. I didn't really think he'd risk his grandfather's displeasure for any woman – although with those empty, jewelled eyes one could never tell – but I wanted no involvement with this youngest child of Agrippina – young enough to have escaped his family's massacre, old enough to remember it – for I knew, even on such short acquaintance, that, like Marsyas, he was a diseased bud which, if it flowered at all, would flower venomously.

'Good-bye,' he called, straddling the top of the wall. 'Wish me luck,' and as the tricks of twilight and distance turned him into Drusus again, I sat down and wept as unrestrainedly as a child, and for a long time.

'Yes,' Paris said excitedly when I told him the news, 'that ties up the loose ends very nicely. I was wondering what plans they had for Caligula. Well, if he's willing to see things Sejanus' way, I suppose they can let him live – because if Agrippina's son says it's all right to be friends with Agrippina's murderer then nobody else need feel ashamed about it. Yes, if the lad has any sense that's exactly what he'll do – although from what I've heard of him, sense doesn't seem to be what he's best at. Quite the little dandy, they tell me, thinks about nothing but his hair and his nails and playing pat-and-tickle with the maids. But however frivolous he is, what happened to his brothers can hardly have escaped his notice. I expect he's got sense enough to know that in his case honour and revenge are just not going to pay.

'Well, it looks as if the excitement's over for a while, so I think I may take a little trip – Athens again, I thought, and then I may like to have a look at Asia Minor. What do you think? It occurs to me that I could take Chrysothemis along. It can be tedious travelling alone – one can't always be sure of decent company, and then one gets bogged down by so many pointless details, arranging accommodation and transport and making sure of acceptable food, and Chrysothemis would enjoy doing all that. Shall I ask her?'

'If you want to take her then you'll take her, whatever I say. But what about when you come back?'

'Oh, as to that – we'll see how it works out on the trip. If it works well I could even marry her, I suppose. Why not? Nobody else in our family has ever been married before, and I like originality.'

'And babies?'

He looked, for a moment, quite stunned. 'Oh my goodness no. Not that. Even I wouldn't take originality to those lengths. Surely she's too old – isn't she?'

'I doubt it. She's not much older than me, and I'm not thirty yet – nowhere near. I could have babies.'

'Danaë – please don't,' he said. 'I think I'd be jealous – and Dion too. No, Chrysothemis wouldn't do a thing like that. I'll have a word with her today.'

But, although he hung around for a while, and Chrysothemis, sensing something was afoot, kept glancing at him enquiringly, he didn't speak, and in the end the moment passed. He began to talk with great enthusiasm about his latest finds in the antique markets while Chrysothemis – who had probably heard the tale before – went off to supervise the preparation of Dion's special dinner, and interview his new doctor whose ideas on diet seemed strange to us all.

26

Dion had vowed, with a fine flair of obscenity, that he would never endure the humiliation of crutches. He would allow himself to be carried to parties, magnificent in the long, linen robes I'd designed for him, embroidered with blue and gold thread and heavily fringed at the hem for the extra weight he needed to cover the absence of one leg and the mutilation of the other. He would have his hair curled once, or even twice a day, would decorate his broad chest with gold chains, his arms with wide, gold bracelets, and, installed on the best couch in the centre of somebody's reception room, would be a jolly good fellow, a hero, and increasingly an idol. He would let himself be promenaded about the streets in his splendid litter, stopping every yard or so to greet acquaintances, and his old faction-supporters. He would wink at the girls and, when the lamps were out and his room in pitch darkness, would allow the chosen few into his bed. He would submit, some days more willingly than others, to the ministrations of his doctors, to the constant, often painful, massage they prescribed, and would occasionally astonish them by a sudden mood of co-operation. But he would not, he declared, humiliate himself by dragging his broken body about on crutches like an old man.

But I had been told that, although naturally he could never walk again, this permanent immobility was bad for him, could damage his spine and result in a dangerous increase in weight. And so I ordered not one but dozens of pairs of the most elaborate crutches that could be devised, had their tops embroidered in rich fabrics to match his various gowns, and told him to get on with it. And although he resisted me for a long time – swore at me and threw the painted, shameful sticks at my head, even struck me across the back with one of them when he found his aim to be less than deadly – he knew I'd give him no peace until I had my way.

Shuffling across a room, stumbling, fighting to regain his balance, he reduced both of us to tears more than once, but his torso was still immensely strong, the living half of his body superbly nourished, and when one morning he stood in my hall, his gown tightly belted and flowing richly to the ground, his back and his head erect and beautiful, Erato, seeing him, swooned clean away – or gave a very good impersonation of it – and Dion was far too delighted not to do it again. Afterwards, even on his days of pain when he lay in his room and bellowed for attention, or, worse than than, turned his face to the wall and refused to speak a word, his crutches, the remnants of his freedom, always lay to hand.

'He hasn't enough to do,' Chrysothemis insisted. 'I've offered to teach him to read, but he says he can't see the necessity for it – and that amazes me, since people do keep on writing to him. And really – I've got better things to do than write out his replies.'

But Dion's correspondence, like mine, became one of the main preoccupations of Chrysothemis' life, and I would often see her, perching with her fluid grace on the edge of his couch, her silvery hair in its immaculate coils, her face sharp with disapproval as she read out those warm-hearted offers of temporary devotion, while he, lounging among his embroidered cushions, his blue eyes shimmering with glee, dictated replies that should have made the pen burst into flame.

'No, no,' she would say. 'That's enough about her breasts and thighs – there are other aspects, you know –' And leaning forward to whisper in her ear and try to bite it, he would receive nothing for his trouble but a severe 'Dion – do try to behave.'

In the spring of the next year I danced for Sejanus, an honour, a royal command nowadays, and when he addressed a few words to me afterwards, I knew I was speaking to a stranger, the future Emperor of Rome, and was grateful for the attention. I remember that he was quite plainly dressed, a white synthesis, just one gold ring on his hand, elegant and almost austere as Drusus had always been in public, as if his authority had no need of rich fabrics to endorse it. He had as yet no hostess. Apicata, who had used my house twice more after her meeting with Caligula, had returned discreetly to her suburban retirement. Livilla, they said, was suffering from some obscure affliction of the nerves, for which rest and seclusion were the only cure. Her daughter, the sad-eyed Julia, was living quietly in the country, recovering from the massacre of her husband's kin. But watching Sejanus as he moved among his guests that night with the total self-assurance of an experienced adult in a schoolroom of timid children, I felt sure that her widowhood was being relieved by visits from a lover far more ardent than any she had known before.

Perhaps the idea of marrying him – if her grandfather had troubled to inform her of it – had revolted her to begin with, but I knew Sejanus wouldn't be content with an unwilling bride. Her great name and her body would be his for the taking, but he would want her to want him too, and I didn't expect him to fail.

I had invited Lygdus to supper and, finding him waiting for me on my return, I was delighted by the change in him. He had been moody and morose for so long that these little suppers of ours had become an ordeal, an act of charity which I couldn't set aside; but tonight, in a Persian robe that glimmered like a peacock's tail, flashing a handful of rings, he was the Lygdus I knew of old, his eye taking in every detail, telling me before I had taken off my palla that my hair-dresser needed a good talking to, and that he couldn't help wondering why I still insisted on wearing so much white.

'It's death to anyone over twenty-five, dear. I've told you many a time. It's not fair to your skin to ask it to cope with all the glare. Apricot, now –'

He ate and drank a great deal, criticizing imaginatively as he went along, calling for more sauce, making a great display with his hands as he ate, so that his rings caught the light. And knowing his immense pride in them, I said, 'How beautiful. You carry a fortune on your fingers.'

'Ah yes. Everyone says so, and of course, there's a lot of envy – a nasty thing, envy. Not everyone can wear stones of this value, even if they can get them. People say "Hasn't he been lucky", and that makes me laugh, because it's hard work, dear, and years of putting up with other people's tantrums and clearing up other people's mess, that's earned me these. They've all got faces, every one of them – just like friends, and they'll never stab my back as soon as it's turned. I can rely on them. Look, this ruby cost more than I wanted to pay, I don't mind admitting it, but they tell me it compares very well with the one your sister had from Metellus Nepos. What do you think?'

'I'd say yours is much more tastefully set.'

He smiled, utterly delighted, almost childlike, more himself than he'd been for years, and spreading his hand flat on the table he separated the fingers the better to display his treasures.

'This topaz is a little love, but then, everybody has a topaz or two; and this little emerald – not quite like yours, I admit – and then this one, this one's my favourite. This one has a meaning.'

He raised his right hand, dipping it into the lamplight so I could see the pearl on his little finger, a large, round, perfect pearl placed delicately and lovingly in a setting of gold filigree that wound around it like a nest. 'Look at it. You can lose yourself in it. I could talk to it, sometimes, if I'd let myself.'

He turned his hand into the light again, smiling at the pearl with affection and knowledge; and, lost in admiration, communicating in some deep, inner way with the beauty he loved, he was not immediately aware of the sound of heavy footsteps coming directly towards us, telling me that there were soldiers in the house. And if they were in my house, they had come – once again – for me.

Chrysothemis was a step ahead of them, her face chalk-white, but they swept her aside and quietly, without any fuss, the room was full of them. Four guardsmen, enormous and beautiful in their crested helmets, all of them tanned and fit and hard as iron, men with a job to do and all the pity disciplined out of them; and, out in front, bigger than them all, Macro, trusted lieutenant of Sejanus and Apicata, the very man they'd choose to tidy up the loose ends, to sweep their path clear of the small-fry – the actresses and writers of obscene verses – who knew too much.

He looked me up and down leisurely, the corners of his mouth tilting into brief amusement, and then he shook his head.

'Not you, darling,' he said, and his gaze moved slowly, tantalizingly, away from me, and behind me, and stopped.

'The old man wants you,' he said and, spinning round, I saw Lygdus turn grey, not just his face but the whole of him, as if he was being transformed into some terrible grey vapour. His mouth opened and made the convulsive, gasping movements of a fish floundering on dry land, but there was no sound, and I saw the effort he was making to force his lips together, to keep them still, so that in this dreadful moment, he would not be ugly and ridiculous.

The Praetorians never moved a muscle but Macro took a step forward, looking at Lygdus keenly through narrowed eyes.

'Try and make it on your own two feet, lad,' he said with the mild irritation of a man who has seen it all before. 'You're no lightweight, and you won't look pretty if we have to cart you out like a sack of flour.'

Again Lygdus' mouth opened, tried to say something, but he was crumbling, cracking; and knowing he couldn't move, I went up to him and put my hand on his arm, gripping him tight so that at least he would know someone was there.

'Lygdus – darling. I don't know what it is, but you have to face it. Think about making a good exit – you'll be glad, later –'

And the eyes he turned on me were a silent scream.

'You don't know,' he said. 'I hope you never know. Remember I said that. Whatever they tell you, I didn't want you to know. You're the reason I made the effort – kept myself sane – so you wouldn't find out. And I didn't even like you to begin with.'

Macro stirred impatiently, stifled a yawn. 'Well then, we're ready, are we? If you want to kiss her good-bye get it over with. Not that I ever thought kissing women was much in your line.'

And that crude, unimaginative remark stirred something in Lygdus, for he took a step forward and then, with a clumsiness totally out of character, tugged the pearl ring from his hand and pressed it into mine. 'Take it,' he said hoarsely. 'I've never given a woman anything in my life before. Look after it.' And so I knew that whatever it was he had done, he expected to die for it.

I went to Paris the next morning, but he'd heard no rumours, no ripples. The city was quieter than it had been for years. Tiberius was in Capri. Sejanus was in Rome. The frontiers were peaceful. Paris was not inclined to take Lygdus seriously.

'Bedroom politics,' he said, and the only thing that interested him was Macro's statement, '*The old man wants you*'. Macro was a Praetorian captain – Sejanus' man – and he'd never heard Sejanus referred to as 'the old man' before.

'Don't worry,' he said carelessly. 'Livilla has probably poisoned herself again – or someone else has done it for her. Really, darling, it couldn't matter less. She won't be missed.'

'But that's just it,' I said, almost in tears. 'He wasn't himself last night – he was better than he's been for years, as if some terrible load had been lifted from his shoulders. I thought he was happy, but now I wonder if it was some kind of euphoria?'

'You mean you think he'd killed Livilla and was basking in the afterglow?'

'It's possible, isn't it? He talked about killing her, not so long ago. He was hoping Sejanus wanted her out of the way because of Julia, and he said he'd be delighted to help him – that he was the only one who could get past Eudemus. Supposing he'd done it – whether Sejanus asked him to or not – or supposing Sejanus has just used him as a scapegoat. I'll never forgive Sejanus, never, if he's done that.'

Paris looked at me for a moment, reflectively, and then he shrugged.

'It's possible. The woman could be a nuisance, and Sejanus would use a man like Lygdus and then throw him away. But there's nothing you can do about it, Danaë. Absolutely nothing. If it's happened, it's happened. Go home and put it out of your mind. I didn't know Lygdus meant so much to you.'

'You don't know half as much as you damn well think,' I growled, and although he was still smiling, he could see my distress was real and he took me home himself and handed me over to Chrysothemis as if I'd been a child.

27

Five days crawled by, six days, and then, knowing I was a fool, that I should stay well away from it, I sent a message to Eudemus – Livilla's doctor, Lygdus' closest associate – and, receiving no reply, enquired a second time. Two more days, three, and then a message in a neutral hand, telling me Eudemus was out of town and was not expected to return. And the news turned me sick, for the three of them – Lygdus, Eudemus, Livilla – were bound together in my mind, and if two of them were missing, what had happened to the third? What had happened to them all?

'*The old man wants you,*' Macro had said to Lygdus, and if it indicated, as Paris thought it must, that they were taking him to Tiberius, what could it mean? Did Sejanus even know it? But Macro knew – Macro, who was Sejanus' man and would like to be Sejanus if he could. At the end of the tenth tortured night I could no longer rid myself of the suspicion that there was some conspiracy, some nastiness, hatched by Macro for his own advantage.

'*I've no complaints to make of him,*' Sejanus had once said, speaking of Macro. '*He's ambitious enough to want to be me, but clever enough to know he'd never make it.*' But had ambition finally over-ridden common sense? Had Macro seen an opportunity of discrediting Sejanus and decided to use it? And was he using Lygdus as a sacrifice to that ambition? Once again, Livilla's tormented face entered my mind, Livilla eaten away by jealousy, who must hate Sejanus now. Could it be that rather than lose him to her own daughter she was willing to destroy him? And if so, surely she would know something against him which she and Macro could use together? If there was treachery, then whatever Sejanus had done to Scaurus and all those others, he was a better man than Macro, and I knew where my loyalties lay.

I kept my suspicions tight inside me for two more days, until I could bear it no longer, and then I ordered my litter to take me to the Pincian Hill, to Apicata's sheltered, shuttered house, for although there was no way for me to approach Sejanus, nothing but convention prevented me from speaking to his divorced, devoted wife.

Leaving my servants well behind me, I walked fearfully, in acute embarrassment, down the quiet street. It was an area of large walled gardens and tall trees, almost a country setting, more disturbing to me than any teeming alleyway, its loneliness following behind me, cutting me off from my bearers like a crowd of invisible assailants. I had no speech prepared, no certainty of even getting beyond the threshold, for my coming here was an impertinence and I might well encounter some officious servant who – lacking Apicata's calm good sense – would turn me away. But at least I would have tried, and, hesitating outside the house, my throat tense and dry, my feet more than ready to carry me back to safety, the space on either side of me was suddenly filled by two men who despite their plain tunics and bare heads I knew to be soldiers.

'Not a word, little lady,' one of them said. 'And not a backward glance.' And surrounding me with their authority, they took me into Apicata's dimly lit hall and held a lamp to my face.

'Very nice,' one of them murmured; and the other, nodding, grinning, 'We'd best let the boss have a look at her then?'

And walking with them through the too-silent house I felt an enormous sense of relief, for the 'boss' they spoke of could only be Sejanus, and he wouldn't punish me for my concern. He would be pleased, touched even, as he'd been on that sorry night at the palace when I'd asked him if he was happy. Thinking of him, I was taken completely off guard when, emerging from the shadowy colonnade into a garden full of moonlight and slanting, silver-flecked, water, I saw that the man standing beside Apicata was not Sejanus, her adored husband, but Macro, the very man I had come to accuse. And I saw too, by the flash of anger in his face and the tightening of her pale lips, that the soldiers had blundered.

Had she said coolly, 'How dare you bring this common woman into my house?' perhaps then it could have been explained away, for there was no reason in the world why Macro should not be here on her husband's business. Had she calmly gestured them all aside and said, 'Now then, girl, you must have some good reason for coming here. Out with it quickly,' then, no doubt, I would have gone away satisfied. And perhaps, if she had had a moment to reflect, that is exactly what she would have done. But there was no moment to ponder, no time to cover that strange excitement in her face, and, looking from her to Macro who was choking with rage and fear behind her – fear of his own fat, greedy life that would make him careless of mine – I knew that there was a conspiracy, that Macro was a traitor, and that the devoted, efficient, self-effacing Apicata was a traitor too.

Fear, then, more than I had ever known, for I had walked into a trap and I didn't suppose they would let me out again. Fear, betraying me as Apicata's excited eyes had betrayed her, so that, staring at me for a moment, her plain, unremarkable face made memorable at last by hate and cruelty, she said to Macro, 'How much can she know?'

'Not much.'

'That's not an answer.'

'Well,' he swallowed, looked away, amazing me by his fear of this little brown sparrow, 'she was asking after Eudemus – and I picked Lygdus up at her house.'

'Idiot,' she said. 'I told you – did I not? – to be careful?'

'You told me to be quick,' he blustered. 'You said pick him up wherever he was, anywhere except the street, or the palace; and a whorehouse seemed as good a place as any. How was I to know she'd come looking for him? And what difference does it make? Who's going to ask any questions if she doesn't show up tomorrow?'

She stared at him, the same pale, cold gaze she'd turned on me, her head and neck snakelike, darting venom towards him, and then she shrugged and folded her competent, housekeeping hands.

'Very well. Get rid of her. But not here. Take off her jewels, bruise her a little, then take her to the river and drown her. And tomorrow arrange for those rings of hers to be found in the possession of some cut-throat or other – preferably a dead one. You understand? And do it well, Macro. It may seem a small matter to you, and perhaps she represents no real danger. But the word *perhaps* is one I rarely choose to employ. I repeat – do it.'

'Yes,' he said, moving towards me. 'Very good, madam,' and as my hands clenched into fists that intended to strike and go on striking, however hopelessly, she nodded her head with calm satisfaction.

'Yes, my dear, do fight him. No doubt he'll enjoy it, and that way when they find you your nails will be broken and your knuckles split. That will exactly suit our purposes.' And, her hands still neatly folded, her lips parted in a smile that nauseated me more than anything else in my life.

But there was still one small, crazy hope. If Macro turned me over to the soldiers then I was lost, but if he chose to handle the matter himself then perhaps there was something I could do. He was a greedy man, a proud man, and since Apicata had shamed him and he had always wanted me, perhaps I could buy an hour or two, could live a little longer. With my whole mind focused on him, willing him to remember the afternoons he'd guarded my gate while Sejanus had made love to me, it seemed at first that the new voice, speaking out of the shadows, was no more than a trick of my own, cringing senses.

'Such an excess of zeal,' the voice said. 'My dear lady, quite admirable, absolutely first-rate. But I ask myself, is it necessary?'

And as Macro and the soldiers stiffened to attention, a graceful, beautiful figure walked forward into the moonlight, and Caligula, the youngest son of Agrippina, bowed easily, with the utmost politeness, over Apicata's hand.

'Really,' she said, the severe little housewife again, the good manager whose store-cupboards and linen-closets can always accommodate an extra guest. 'There is nothing here that need alarm you, sir. You can safely leave the woman to us.'

Looking down at her, still holding her hand, his brilliant smile flashed over her and through her and then rested in turn on every one of us, making absolutely certain, like any good professional, that he was playing to the centre of the stage.

'But I am not alarmed, madam – not in the slightest. I have the most perfect confidence in you, you know that. If I thought you doubted it I should be quite upset. I know your experience of life – and Macro's too – reduces mine to the merest whisper, but, in this case – and, of course, if I'm wrong then do tell me so, because I'm anxious to learn – I have a funny feeling that all that's really required is to detain the lady until our business is over – the day after tomorrow, isn't it? The whole world will know then what you think she knows tonight. Do agree with me, Apicata. I'm sure you don't *really* want to kill her – such a sweet lady like yourself –

and I'd be delighted to think I'd found a way to spare you distress.'

He released her hand and I saw it fall to her side, nervously flexing, her face sharp again with venom, the tame sparrow growing talons and an eagle's beak that could take pleasure in pecking out the eyes of a woman like me.

'No,' she said tonelessly, speaking to the heir of the Caesars as if he meant no more than the meanest of her slaves. 'Kill her. And do it now. Not you, Macro. Give her to the soldiers. She'll not charm them into disobedience.'

'I wonder,' Caligula said. 'Dear lady, forgive me, but ask yourself this – if she knew the truth of the matter, what reason would she have to go running to your husband to warn him of his danger? Since that can be the only reason for her death – well – I for one see no reason at all.'

And, quite impudently cupping her chin with his young, cruel hand, he bathed her once again in his luminous smile. 'Apicata – if you really wish to wound her, as I can see you do, then tell her the truth as you understand it – as you have told it to me and my grandfather. Tell her the whole, horrifying, somewhat unlikely truth – and let her live with it.'

She dashed his hand away furiously – for how dare he touch her? how dare he defy her? But she was a woman of immense control, of formidable composure, who had waited a long time, it seemed, for whatever vengeance she had planned, and, meeting his jewelled eyes for a moment, her nervous fire extinguished itself and her shoulders moved in a brief gesture of assent.

'As you wish – naturally. Send the soldiers away.'

And as they marched off, glad, I thought, to make their escape, she took a step or two towards me, her hands clasped tight together now, her lips parted again in that wolf's smile – Apicata, so calm, so sensible, Sejanus' plain, passionless wife, trembling now from head to foot, her frail body a battleground of poisoned emotions.

'Yes, I will tell you the truth. I will, and who knows, afterwards we may have a new recruit to our cause. And in the end, although I ordered your death just now, you will have me to thank for saving your worthless life. If I had not used your house to meet with this gallant young gentleman he would never have seen you and it would never have entered his head to convince his grandfather – the Emperor – that you knew of our business and were a willing partner to our conspiracy. You would have been arrested, my girl, ten days ago – arrested and disposed of. Well then, listen Danaë – Danaë, such a lovely name, such a lovely face, such sparkling wit – "She refreshes me," my husband used to say, "she's a feast in herself". Oh yes, he talked of you, and others, talked of everything to me, his honest, loyal wife. All that we did, we did for each other, and for our own children.

'Unfortunately it is no longer so. The man who was my husband is going to die, and I am responsible for it. You suspected Macro, didn't you – when the oaf took Lygdus from your house and you discovered Eudemus was missing? Yes, and you're clever enough to know he wouldn't be working alone. So you came to warn me – about what? About Macro and Livilla? Yes, Livilla had every reason to betray my husband. She'd put her life in his hands, her youth, ruined her reputation and her health for his sake – and then to be thrown aside for her own daughter, to be forced to see him, every day of her life, with Julia on one side of him and me on the other. How could she bear it? She couldn't – and I, who loved Sejanus more than any of you, have saved her the trouble, because I have destroyed them both. My husband is going to die, Danaë, because he is a murderer. You always knew that, of course, and it made no more difference to you than it made to me. But perhaps your loyalty – or whatever it is you feel for him – may be shaken a little when you know that his first victim was your lover, your precious Drusus. He needn't have died, Danaë – he could be with you now, coughing and spitting of course, and shrivelling up more like his disgusting old father every day – but with you. Except that he'd have paid you off and forgotten about you long ago.'

Silence. Death, I thought, because life could never be so still. An emptiness, an absence of feeling, of functioning, nothing inside me, nothing left of me. Space and silence. And then a great aching and roaring in my ears, the feeling of blood flowing again through crushed limbs, and I was in pain.

'She's mad,' I said to Caligula. 'She's mad – isn't she? – please?' And, standing close to me, one hand quite gently on my arm, his face, that could have been Drusus' face had it not been for those odd, jewelled eyes, the only thing I could distinguish clearly, he said, 'Mad? Oh, as to that, who knows? Which one of us can be entirely sure of his own sanity? But I think you must believe her.

Certainly I have every intention of believing her – and my grandfather seems to find it quite convenient to do so as well. Danaë, darling, are you going to swoon? Please don't, we really can't spare the time.'

'How touching,' Apicata said, a long way behind me, her voice fading into the distance and then coming back to strike me between the eyes. 'How terrible for her, one of her lovers has killed the other, and she doesn't know which one to weep for first. And how pretty she looks while she's about it.'

'Hush,' Caligula told her. 'You have no sense of theatre, Apicata, as I have.'

And then Macro's voice, gruff, easier to understand. 'She's going, sir. Here, let me take her.'

And then silence again, blessed silence and darkness, an awareness of movement about me, but no sense of belonging, no involvement. Nothing in the world but a vast, empty sky, a motionless cloudscape, myself without words or knowledge, nothing to hurt because I was nothing again. But as the sky lightened, an intruder, an alien, evil thing came sniffing around my consciousness, a dreadful beast called memory waking me to sickness; and a strange serving-woman helped me to my feet and then let me slide to the floor again and watched as I curled up my woman's body with the panic and despair of a child, and sobbed.

I was in a small bedroom, nothing but a bedcover around me, and when the unknown woman judged me calm enough she got up, a neatly folded garment in her hands, and held it out to me.

'You vomited,' she said cheerfully. 'I washed you and looked after you, and now you'd better put this on.' And she slipped over my head a linen robe, fastened a belt around my waist, threw a palla around my shoulders, turned me this way and that as she pleased.

'That's better,' she said comfortably. 'Yes, that's decent – if you didn't look so yellow. Oh dear, you're not going to be sick again, are you, because you're bigger than the mistress and I've nothing else to fit you. This belonged to the mistress' sister – a fine young woman – and even so it's tight across your chest. But you can't go home in a bedspread, dear. I'll do what I can with your own clothes – lovely fabric – and I expect you'll let me know where to send them?'

'Keep them,' I said, amazed that I could speak, that enough of me remained sufficiently intact to function even at this superficial level of a serving-woman's constant hunting after a good tip. 'Keep them, or sell them.'

And as she began to thank me, Apicata came into the room and sent her away.

She was completely calm, the woman who had sat quietly in the garden at Baiae, talking to her husband, the small brown bird in the shadows of his life, the mother of his children, content with her place. What had he done to her now, in the moment of his triumph, to turn her against him? And why was it that, loving Drusus, I still didn't hate him?

'Good,' she said, seeing me on my feet, as if nothing more serious had happened than a cup of wine too many. 'They're ready now, and if you're well enough, you can be off.'

'Off?'

'Yes. They're taking you with them. Oh – not far and not for long. Is there anything you require for the journey?'

'Nothing.'

'Well then, here are your rings. You may not have noticed, but I removed them when you were unwell. Naturally I like to feel I can trust my staff, but it is unwise to put temptation in their way.'

And when she saw that I couldn't take the jewels from her outstretched hand, couldn't bear any physical contact with her at all, she smiled, put them down carefully on the bedside table, and waited as I slipped them on my fingers.

There was a carriage waiting a mile or so from the city, and as Macro lifted me from the litter to the carriage, I closed my eyes, straining to achieve again that state of non-being where there was no need to question myself, no need for suffering. But the weather continued to worsen and quite soon Caligula, who, having survived the massacre of his family, had no intention now of succumbing to the cold, dismounted and came to sit beside me.

'Well,' he said, spreading a blanket over his knees, another around his shoulders, 'isn't this cosy? And didn't I do well by you just now? Oh dear, I see you're wishing I'd just let them kill you because you can't bear the pain, but you'll feel differently later on – which is why I insisted on bringing you with me, in case Apicata had a little accident in mind for you, as I'm sure she had. Because of course she is mad, there's no doubt about it, just like a little spider patiently spinning a web to strangle people with. Don't shiver, Danaë, you're quite safe from her. Evil, I suppose, takes a little getting used to, and I have more acquaintance with it than you have. I was determined to save you because I do so love beautiful things. When I have the means, which should be fairly soon, I shall make such marvellous collections. I'll have the most beautiful possessions in the world and the most beautiful people around me. I'll send my legions out looking for exquisite *objets d'art* instead of battles. I'm going to be the next Emperor, you see. Sejanus felt quite safe because he thought there was no one else, and when he's dead – the day after tomorrow – there *will* be no one else. My poor little cousin, Gemellus, my Aunt Livilla's boy, doesn't count. He's just a bag of nerves, moodier and twitchier than my brothers, and he'll give me no trouble. Do you believe me? Or don't you care?'

'I don't care. But I believe you. Did he – what she said – is it true?' He smiled and put his long, elegant, completely cold hand over mine. 'You are quite unable to speak their names, aren't you? How interesting to see such true emotions. Did Sejanus kill my uncle Drusus? Well, you know, I certainly hope so, because he's going to die for it and just think how badly he'll feel if he's innocent. I'll tell you about it, if you like. It will pass the journey and I can see you won't talk about anything else. It all came about because of my grandfather's odd inclination for solitude. It seems, some years ago, that he wanted to retire to Capri and take Sejanus with him, leaving my Uncle Drusus in charge of affairs in Rome. You may remember the incident? Of course Sejanus didn't want to go, and my Aunt Livilla, who was madly in love with him by then, didn't want to part with him. And so, according to Apicata, she persuaded her faithful doctor Eudemus to brew her a clever little poison which, when given to him in small doses, made him quite ill; and since he was ill anyway, which wasn't quite such a secret as he supposed, nobody was too surprised when he died. Don't cry, Danaë, just hold my hand and be glad that when we tortured Lygdus and Eudemus, and they made their confessions, they both said you'd had nothing to do with it. Which was a great relief to me, since I'd been telling my grandfather the same thing and he positively delights in proving me wrong. Are you going to be sick again? Shall I ask them to stop?'

But somehow nausea retreated, defeated by the total emptiness of my body, and marvelling again that I could speak at all, I said,

'Not Lygdus. No – not him. Is he dead?'

'Oh yes, and quite glad of it, I imagine.'

'And Livilla?'

'My grandfather has her in his keeping, which is the same as being dead. Naturally he can't risk the indignity of a public trial, so he'll be her judge, jury and executioner too, I shouldn't wonder. Poor Aunt Livilla, I don't think she's too sorry about dying either – one can hardly say she's been enjoying life these last few years. Naturally, we must call them criminals, all three of them, but, do you know, listening to them these past ten days, it struck me very forcefully that they weren't very good criminals – not wicked enough by half. I wonder if you know what I mean? Take my grandfather, for instance. When he murdered my father I'm quite sure he never gave it another thought. You wouldn't catch him mooning around feeling guilty. I wonder how many sleepless nights my mother cost him? Not one – I'd put money on it. I don't sleep well myself – I dream quite abominably, and I have this positively foolish fear of being murdered in my bed, I can't think why – so I'd know, wouldn't I, if he was awake too? But Livilla was absolutely eaten away by her crime, and that poor Lygdus was the same. He insisted they'd used him and that he'd only found out about it later by overhearing Livilla raving in her sleep. I was quite ready to believe him – not that it made any difference, since he was the one who used to measure out my uncle's medicine and give him the glass, wasn't he? And so he had to go. Eudemus was the only one who had any dignity. He said he'd done it, told us how he'd done it, and closed his eyes. Quite an impressive performance. He created rather a moving moment, artistically speaking. I had to force myself not to applaud.'

'And Sejanus.'

'Oh good, you managed to say his name. Well, he doesn't know he's been caught yet, does he? And what we're not sure of – although once again it doesn't make any difference – is whether Livilla actually told him she was murdering her husband, or whether she just kept it as a lovely surprise, rather like one's pet cat bringing one a dead mouse and hoping to be praised. Possibly Sejanus thought it a rather extreme measure – a little more than he'd bargained for. And of course, to work his way out of the dilemma he then had to set about killing my mother and brothers and all their friends – although I don't suppose he minded about that. He was going to kill me too, until Apicata persuaded him it would be useful to keep me around a little longer if I renounced my claim to marry Julia, and promised him my support in other ways. I promised like mad, I can tell you. Oh, he has to be guilty. It's much neater – and if he didn't actually tell her to do it, as Apicata insists he did, he was quick enough to reap the benefits. Of course, my poor Aunt Livilla wasn't at all a good accomplice, and I can quite see what a shock it was to her when he fell in love with my cousin Julia.'

I had not expected anything, ever again, to surprise me, but now I heard the sharp gasp of my breath, and saw, by the glee in Caligula's face, that he had achieved his aim.

'Oh yes, Julia – my thin, sad little cousin – she has caused all this trouble. Imagine it. Nobody ever wanted her before. My brother Nero only married her because my mother told him to. Nobody ever looked at Julia, even though she's got lots of money and rather nice manners. Except Sejanus. All my grandfather had to do was drop a little hint and Sejanus was there, looking her over, letting her look at him, relying on his famous charm to win the day. And of course it did. I can just see the two of them, Julia being bashful and Sejanus playing the gentleman for the first time in his life, because that was the only way of going about things where Julia was concerned. Can't you feel the poetry of it – the hard, cynical politician, and the shy, innocent young widow? And when I think of my brother Nero, she might even be a virgin, which would be even more poetic. Can't you just see it? And, of course, the trouble was that Apicata saw it too. She didn't mind him marrying Julia any more than she minded him marrying Livilla, or sleeping with you. None of you could ever succeed in taking him away from Apicata – or so she thought. But falling in love was another thing altogether. Even then, if Julia had stayed aloof and gone on disliking him, I think Apicata would have got over it. But, naturally, my poor, plain little cousin started loving him back just as hard as ever she could, and that signed his death-warrant. The moment Apicata realized that he could be happy with Julia, have children perhaps, start a whole new life that had no place in it for her, she decided to kill him. After all, she'd given him her life, so she felt she had every right to take his. She got in touch with me through Macro, who had access to Capri. The three of us hatched our plot – in your sweet little house – and when the time was ripe I informed my grandfather, who didn't believe a word of it, until we put Eudemus before him and he spent a few hours alone with Livilla.

'Yes. I understand Apicata very well, Danaë. There's something wrong with her, because she won't feel remorse for what she's done. And when I'm feeling very lucid, as I am tonight, I know there's something wrong with me too. I can't name it, and it doesn't trouble me, but I know I'm not exactly the same as other people. I don't feel things as other people seem to do. Perhaps I'm like my Uncle Drusus; they say he didn't feel things either. Tell me. I am like him, aren't I?'

And although it wasn't true, I knew I was more afraid of this boy than of anyone I had met before, and I would do well to agree.

'Yes, you're like him.'

'And you loved him – how encouraging. But, of course, he didn't survive. I shall take good care that no one murders me. One thing I must bear in mind, thinking of Drusus and Livilla: when my grandfather dies it would pay me to start a rumour that her affair with Sejanus began much sooner than it did, some time before my cousin Gemellus was born, so that people will begin to wonder just who his father was. I must get someone to write a few verses about it. Sejanus employed a very clever fellow for that kind of thing. I wonder if Macro has his name?'

And leaning his head against the carriage door, he sighed contentedly and closed his eyes.

The miles wore on, fifteen, twenty, I didn't know, didn't care; but at last there was a halt, a house, a blind blank wall, unlit and unwelcoming. Instantly awake, Caligula handed me down and, followed by Macro and a dozen soldiers, led me through dim corridors, shrouded rooms, lined by more soldiers who froze to attention as we passed.

'Not a particularly inviting house,' Caligula said, pausing by an open bedroom door. 'Nothing to please the eye except these magnificent guardsmen posted in every corner, and I don't suppose you're in the mood for that sort of thing. So I can only offer you good food, and when you've had your cry, your appetite may return. And if you can't sleep, and you get to hating Apicata, just remember one thing – the only thing she appears to have overlooked herself. If Sejanus was involved in my Uncle Drusus' murder – and she's positively adamant that he was – then she must have been involved in it herself, since she also insists that he did nothing without consulting her. I really don't think my grandfather has any intention of letting her get away with that, do you?'

And, taking my hand, he examined it as I had seen Paris examine a piece of rare ivory, kissed it very gently, and calling to Macro, walked away, everything in his carefully graceful posture telling me he expected to be watched, with admiration and respect, until he had disappeared from view.

28

I went into the bare, undecorated room and lay down fully dressed on the bed, my eyes wide open and burning inside their sockets, my body aching. It seemed I had lost, or forgotten, the art of sleep.

Drusus need not have died, and if he had lived Agrippina and all those others would have been alive too. So, because his death had not been a blind act of chance, I had to mourn him all over again, and it is of no interest to anyone but myself how I did it.

Images came into my mind that night – Sejanus standing beside me in the garden at Laurentum, watching Drusus walk back to the house, his voice urging me, '*If he's not well you must tell me*'. And although he had killed the best man in the world, and a great part of myself with him, when I tried to hate him I was appalled at my failure. '*Murderer*', I accused him, and he replied, '*Yes – but all I really set out to do was be a damned good Commander of the Guard*'. And although I couldn't forgive him, I believed him. Then Lygdus came to me, a shadow in my mind, formless now that they had taken away his rings and his embroideries, and I came near to loving him from sheer pity. '*I didn't want you to know*', he twittered feebly, and I discovered that he had loved me too.

I got up at daybreak because there was no reason to stay in bed, no one to detain me. An unthinking sun shone brightly and as I went through the colonnade and out into the garden Macro came striding towards me, smiling with a huge delight.

'Congratulations,' he said breezily.

'On what?'

'On staying alive. That crazy bitch gave you a bad time and I'm sorry about that but you've got to understand there wasn't much I could do, not with her looking on at any rate. Anyway, that's over now. You're coming back to Rome with me tomorrow.'

'Am I? What happens tomorrow?'

He grinned. 'Tomorrow we get rid of Sejanus, darling, that's what we do.' And his eyes blazed out their eagerness, he licked his lips, savouring it, most obscenely desiring it.

'Will it be so easy?'

'Easy? Just about as easy as falling off a log. You haven't met the old man or you wouldn't ask. There's never been such a cunning old devil. He may look senile, he may even want to look senile, but he's as sharp as a needle. He's known about this business of Drusus for months, and anybody else would have waded straight in screaming for blood. But not the old man. He writes Sejanus friendly letters by every post. He makes him consul, keeps on promising him an imperial bride. And Sejanus believes it because it's what he's been working for for years, and he thinks he's pulled it off. He's never been happier. He's having such a good time lately, flirting with that scrawny Julia, that when Apicata told him she was spending a few weeks in the country it never crossed his mind she was going to Capri. And it never crossed his mind that I escorted her there. So tomorrow, when I arrive in town with a letter from the old man – who's supposed to be still in Capri – he'll let me read it to the Senate, because, after all, that's what I am, an imperial letter-carrier. All I have to do is drop a hint that it's about his marriage and his glorious future and that it wouldn't be seemly for him to read it himself. And that's the way it starts off – praises and promises. He'll lap it up, and when I get to the part about him being a traitor, he'll still have a smile on his face when they go for his throat. Believe me, they'll tear him limb from limb. It's what they've been waiting for for years. And tomorrow I'll be the Commander of the Guard.'

'Aren't you telling me a little too much?' I asked quietly, and he smiled again, the same smile of fat content, and let his hand brush against my cheek.

'I'll see you later, darling,' he said, and I felt quite sure of it.

A young soldier brought me bread and cheese and an indifferent wine at noon, his eyes wide with curiosity. And when I had eaten, I went out into the garden again, feeling strange in the simple linen robe that had belonged to Apicata's sister, my hair hanging loose down my back like a young girl's because I had no mirror, no pins, nothing of myself at all but the rings on my fingers, one of them Lygdus' lovely, tender pearl. I walked for a while aware of comings and goings in the house behind me, of fresh detachments of soldiers arriving, horsemen riding off into the distance, carriage-wheels; but no one had anything to say to me and, sitting at last on a stone seat by a pool of drooping lilies, I may even have dozed a little when suddenly the young soldier was there again, in a considerable state of agitation, urging me to get to my feet. And startled, jumping up, I saw an old man standing there looking at me, tall and painfully thin, stooping a little and wearing his garments tightly around him as if he felt the cold. An old, old man, the oldest, I think, I have ever seen because, surely, he had never been young. Yet there, somewhere behind the sour lines of his face, drowning in age and bitterness and weary disillusion, I saw Drusus – a truer image of him than I had seen in Caligula – looking at me out of his father's eyes.

'The Emperor, madam,' the young soldier said unnecessarily, and with the briefest, most complete gesture of authority I had ever seen, Tiberius waved the lad away to join the dozen or so others who were stationed at a discreet distance behind him.

'I see you recognize me,' he said in a dry voice which could have been Drusus' voice had it been a shade lighter – the same precise, clipped tones speaking the same flawless Greek.

I nodded, and then, realizing it was not enough, whispered, 'Yes, sir.'

'Good,' he said, and lowering himself carefully on to the stone bench as if his body was a precious, intricate mechanism which required to be handled with care, his eyes passed over me, assessing, judging, nailing me to the earth; and his mouth spoke one word, 'Sit'.

And taking good care that not one fold of my garment touched one fold of his, I moved forward, the slowest, most painful steps I had ever taken, and sat down beside him.

'I realize, madam, that you are afraid of me, and that is quite natural. But unfortunately, in this case, it is also a nuisance. I have very little time available and it would irritate me profoundly if you were to remain tongue-tied. Do you understand?'

'Yes, sir.'

'Well then – when my grandson informed me of your presence in this house I had no intention of granting you an interview – nor can I imagine that you would have wished for one. But I saw you, just now, from the terrace, and it occurred to me that you might have information?'

And then, seeing my terror as Lygdus' broken shadow passed once again through my mind, he shook his head and smiled, a movement of the lips alone.

'No – no. It is not of my son's death that I wish to question you – I have all the information I require on that score. There has been a great deal of dying – a surfeit of it – and my mind is turning now to other things. My son spoke to me once of you, an impertinence on his part, naturally, to introduce his mistress' name into a conversation with his father and his Emperor. But he was rarely impertinent, and since he was very near death at the time, I chose not to be offended. I sat with him during his last days – it was the only time we had ever spent really alone together – and when we had spoken of the things which concerned us both, he told me you had been of great service to him. He also told me you were the only honest woman he had ever met, although he was still lucid enough to qualify his statement by adding that you were only honest in your dealings with him and could be excessively dishonest with others. I wonder if you will be honest with me? No, no, I do not require an answer. You could do no other than say "Yes, sir", and that is no answer at all. My son believed – perhaps in his delirium – that you loved him, and since it appeared to give him comfort, I made no attempt to dispute it. Did you love him, madam?'

'Yes sir – yes, I loved him very much. I love him now.'

'Indeed? One can only regret that he is not here to take advantage of it. Tell me, did he love you?'

Although love was the last thing I had expected this sombre man to speak of, I knew he required the truth, and, recognizing his absolute authority, his total absence of the illusions which nourish the rest of us, I said quickly, 'No. He didn't love me.' And glancing down at me briefly, he nodded and smiled.

'So – that is one honest answer. Now I wonder if we may have another? *Why* did he not love you? Apart from your common origins you have much to recommend you. He spoke highly of your gifts of sympathy and humanity, and I am sure you did everything in your power to fix his affections. Why did you fail? Was it a flaw in you? Or a flaw in him?'

And as his dry voice halted, the words of his mind came clearly into mine, and I knew, at this solitary, bitter ending of his days, he was not only grieving for his son – and finding no one in the whole of his vast dominions but one lowborn woman to grieve with him – but he was asking, '*Was it a flaw in me? Was he unable to love you or anyone else because of the loneliness that I bred in him?*' And I knew there was no answer I dared to make.

'Yes,' he said, his lips moving again in that painful smile, 'I recognize your dilemma. If you lie to me I will know it – yet how can one poor woman fling an unpleasant truth in the face of majesty? Then let me put it another way. You have met the young man who chooses to call himself my grandson, although he is only so by adoption and because it suits his convenience. Caligula believes his resemblance to my son is his passport to my favour, and puts his fine profile into the lamplight at dinner-time to remind me, thinking me prone to an old man's sentimentality, as others have done to their cost. Was Drusus like him?'

'No. Not at all. Absolutely *not at all*.'

'You speak with feeling. May I take it then that my grandson has not gained your favour? You must never tell him so, for he has a vast appetite for praise. No, he is not like Drusus, but I wonder sometimes if he is like me. That may be why we hate each other so much, and smile at each other so brightly. But hatred, which I have always found to be the most reliable of emotions, is fading now. I thought hate, at least, would last me to the end, but it's going, and I shall miss it. It has sustained me, in its way, and without it I wonder if I shall care enough to do what must still be done to ensure the succession for my own son's child – my poor Gemellus. If hate deserts me, then I may well be content to let things take their course. I have been deeply shocked, madam, by these revelations about my son's death. Of course I will go through the motions. I will take what will be seen as vengeance on my son's murderer, and perhaps I may even manage a smile at the uproar. But Sejanus' death will mean little to me in itself, since it has always been my intention that he should not outlive me.'

'*Don't*,' I thought, '*don't tell me things I shouldn't know*,' and remembering how many times I had said those words before, to Sejanus, to Paris, I looked up straight into his eyes and recoiled from their unbearable shrewdness, knowing myself in the presence of total cynicism, recognizing his grand mastery of the art of survival at which others – compared with him, Sejanus among them – were mere novices. And I wondered why so bitter and separate a man should have troubled to survive at all.

'I did not know my son Drusus very well, madam,' he said. 'Children die so easily – imperial children in particular – and I was busy about the affairs of empire – Augustus' empire then – very much abroad. It seemed wiser, safer, to keep my distance. And, in any event, the keeping of distance has always been a habit with me. But he was my son. He would have succeeded me admirably, and when he died, leaving that poor scrap of a Gemellus behind him, I saw no reason to allow Agrippina to profit from it. I am not fond of my grandson Gemellus. He has nothing of Drusus in him that I can see – more of his criminal mother – but he *is* my own flesh and blood; and so I looked about me for a tool. Tools have always come quickly to my hand. Sejanus and I knew each other very well, madam. I allowed him to destroy better men than himself, my own brother's grandchildren among them, to clear the way for Gemellus. And he must have known I meant to kill him before I died, for how long would Gemellus have survived in his hands?

'I imagine his next move would have been to dispose of Gemellus and Caligula – in his place it would certainly have been mine: unless he had finally realized that the simplest solution of all would be to poison me, or get one of his Praetorians to hold a pillow to my face as I slept. No one would have wondered at my death, for I am an old man, and certainly no one would have mourned. It must have crossed his mind. But I grew senile, you see, frail and forgetful – or so I let him think – and he saw the advantages of playing along with me for a while longer, of allowing me to live out my remaining years, because a man who is senile is persuadable. Yes, I understood his reasoning very well. If I could be persuaded to marry him to my granddaughter and adopt him as my son, then there would be no need to kill anyone else. Apart from the obvious advantages to that, he had had rather enough of killing. It had begun to worry him. That was his weakness. He should have killed me, or tried to, as soon as Agrippina and her brood were out of the way. He would have had his difficulties – somebody would have opposed him, as somebody always does when the profits are high – but he would have prevailed, married my granddaughter and rid himself of her brother and her troublesome mother, I am sure of it. But he hesitated. He was like a whore, you see, who, having made her money by any means available, wishes to be a respectable woman at the end. He gave me time to make my final move and win the game.

'So what do you think of that, madam? I have scattered my

enemies once again, and I am left to grapple with the enemy inside myself that prevents me from caring, that forces me to look at Gemellus and acknowledge him as a weakling, a neurotic little scrap with his mother's face. And it occurs to me that I have wasted my energies on his behalf – occurs to me that Drusus himself would not have thought too highly of this son of his if he had seen him grow. Now I find that my interest is running out – failing – and the temptation to wait and see, to let matters arrange themselves, is growing. I hardly recognize myself. Caligula, of course, is marked for death too, for he is a snake who will swallow my mouse Gemellus as soon as ever he can. But sometimes it hardly seems worth the trouble. Someone must succeed me and I wonder, now, if there is anything to choose between Agrippina's son and Livilla's son? They are both – annoying – in their different ways. And Drusus is dead. Perhaps it would have been better if I had lost interest then – when he left me – and saved myself all this trouble. But I am glad, at least, to know that you agree with me about Caligula. It would have saddened me to think that Drusus had been like him. Yes, I'm glad of that.'

And, his eyes hooded again, lizard-like, by their scaly lids, his hand descended briefly on mine, the touch of his dead, dry fingers bestowing on me one of the most profound shocks of my life.

'You look quite ill, madam,' he said, peering into my face.

'Yes. I am ill.'

'Indeed. Is that what love does for you? You would do well to go about your business and cease to think of my son, for I doubt if there is anything left of him anywhere in this empty universe to think of you. Why torment the nothing that is you for the nothing that is him?'

And at last I found my tongue.

'Because it exists in me, sir. Because he had integrity and courage that shouldn't be forgotten. And even though I'm not very much, I can't accept that I'm nothing at all. He didn't think so, and I trusted him. He told me to live, and I won't fail him, because he never really allowed himself to be alive, and he knew, at the end, that he'd been wrong. Time must be the most precious substance in the world, and I shall use mine now, as he couldn't. I shall try to use it well.'

'Ah,' he said, getting to his feet, gathering his limbs together carefully. 'I see you have had some kind of a spiritual revelation.

Since such things are not greatly to my taste, I will leave you to enjoy it. You are quite impertinent, child, when you find your tongue, and you will do well with Caligula, should he survive me. He will be an impertinent Emperor, a popular Emperor – for a while at least. Rome will be excessively gay with Caligula – unless, of course, I decide otherwise.'

And, wrapping his garments tightly around him again, he turned and walked slowly away from me, withered and stooping, an old man who found no warmth in the sun, whose aching bones could snap as easily as parched twigs, yet who, even now, had more power in one gnarled hand than any of the rosy young soldiers at his side.

29

I slept at last and when they woke me an afternoon and a night had gone by and dawn was breaking. Although everything was ready for a journey and Macro assured me I was going home, I kept glancing behind me on my way to the carriage, waiting for the flash of a knife-blade or the bite of the thin, taut cord around my neck; and I knew I wouldn't really believe myself alive until I was in my own house again.

'Dear Danaë,' Caligula said, appearing from the shadows of the courtyard. 'You will remember me, won't you, how I saved your life. And you'll believe in my great future?' And bending his elegant head he kissed my throat and bit the lobe of my ear quite hard, laughing delightedly at my gasp of pain.

'Overbred young fool,' Macro muttered, watching as Caligula strolled nonchalantly away, making his exit to imagined roars of applause. 'He'll wake up tomorrow morning in Capri with his grandfather – that's his future, and he's welcome to it. I wouldn't change it for mine. I'm Praetorian Commander now, darling. I'm Sejanus. Well, it's going to be a busy day. There's my old boss to see to first, and then all his so-called supporters to flush out of their rat-holes. There won't be a man alive in Rome tomorrow who ever worked for the bastard, unless I'm more than certain I can trust him to work for me. And while I'm about it, I'll pay off a few old scores of my own. I won't have an enemy in the world by morning, because they'll all be dead. So we'll make a start, shall we?'

And as he lifted me into the carriage I remembered Marsyas and the beating he had once given Macro; remembered Paris; and my body, clasped in Macro's greedy arms, turned cold.

I didn't see what happened inside the Senate House. I only knew that it would happen exactly as Macro had told me, because Tiberius willed it so. They had released me at the city gates and when, after an hour of frantic searching, I couldn't find Paris, I joined the crowd in the Forum – Macro's crowd with Macro's gold in their purses, knowing what was expected of them. I saw Sejanus arrive in the midst of his splendid entourage, some of whom would have taken Macro's gold too, and I saw him smile, raise a regal hand to that false gathering which, as instructed, cheered him to put him even more at his ease, to convince him still further that the private note he had received from Tiberius that morning, hinting at immediate confirmation of his marriage to Julia, was no less than the truth. And I didn't know, have never known, whether or not I wanted to warn him. Macro was with him, Tiberius' official messenger, with that fateful, lethal letter in his hands; and he held it aloft as they approached the doorway, and then stood deferentially aside to let Sejanus pass. '*This is it, sir,*' he was saying. '*This is what you've been waiting for.*'

And so, in fact, it seemed, for I heard later that the opening sentences were so rich with Sejanus' praises that when the promise of certain glory became a savage denunciation of himself as a traitor, he went on smiling, blanched for just a moment, and then smiled again, knowing, I think, that he was dead and that, for him, death would not be clean. And even as he raised his arms to show that there was no sword at his side, the wolf-pack, those senators who had been warned in advance and knew that the Senate House was ringed by Macro's men, those fastidious gentlemen who had licked his boots for so many years, fell murderously on him.

I heard the tumult, heard the crowd around me take up the wolf-cry. I froze, and then, as that bleeding figure was pushed out into the sunshine, jostled by Macro's soldiers – *his* soldiers, yesterday – I saw the effort he was making to keep his balance, not to be trampled underfoot. And for one moment of pure horror the crowd was sucked away, and I was alone with him. Although his eyes were too full of blood to see, I thought he saw me. I reached out my hand, and it was Baiae, bread and cheese and laughter, and his voice, '*I'm a fountain of life. I'm a Hercules. I could found a nation between now and tomorrow morning.*' And I was sick, wretchedly, achingly sick over the ground and the feet of the man next to me, who cursed and struck out at me hard, although I couldn't feel. 'He killed Drusus', I thought, 'and now they're killing him. Be glad.' But hate had deserted me as it had deserted Tiberius, and I only knew the killing was wrong, that men who destroy each other achieve nothing but their own destruction. And it no longer seemed strange to me that I could love them both; and Marsyas with them; and Marpessa who once would have killed me, if she could, for love of him.

It was only a little way from the Senate to the prison, but they marched him slowly, slowly, loosely grouped around him so that everybody could see, everybody could touch, anyone who chose could pelt him with filth and stones and abuse. I don't know how much of him got there alive. But they strangled him – as I knelt retching at the gates of that dreadful place – to make sure, and threw his tattered body on the Weeping Stair for the mob to play with. And before my sickness was over, before I'd dragged myself to my feet and begun to totter away, a man with calm eyes, standing near to me, suddenly threw up his arms in false hysteria and began to scream, 'He murdered Tiberius' son. He has sons of his own, hasn't he? Can we let them live?' And I sank back to the ground again, remembering Apicata – who was one of Drusus' murderers too – and Caligula telling me, '*I really don't think my grandfather has any intention of letting her get away with that, do you?*'

I went home then, needing a hole to crawl into, and I think I was surprised to find the house still standing just as it had always been, instead of a smoking ruin and everyone who had ever lived there ancient dust. But the frightened faces in my hallway asking me what to do, where to run, brought me back to earth, and knowing I had no time for them I clapped my hands, sending the servants running for cover, and snapped out at Chrysothemis the one word, '*Paris?*'

'Oh, I don't know. I don't know. I sent a servant to his flat but he wasn't there, Macro's men are all over the place. They've been into all the houses, dragging people out, taking them away. They must have taken him too.' Pulling Apicata's linen robe over my head, I got into my own clothes and set out again, a bag of single rubies and emeralds clasped in my hands, another tucked away in the folds of my palla, for the only hope I had of my brother's life was to buy it. Macro would know his name and face, would class him among the vermin he intended to exterminate to make room for his own. But although Macro was vindictive and couldn't be bribed now that he had the power simply to take what he wanted, he wouldn't soil his own hands on Paris. He'd send a soldier to do the job for him and if I could get there first with my jewels and my expensive, experienced body, there was a chance.

I went again to his flat but it was empty. The door was open, hanging on its hinges, his precious collections of bronze and ivory scattered about the floor, his vases smashed or missing, and there was no one at all but a young lad who bolted when he saw me, clutching a bundle of my brother's lawn tunics in his arms.

Down in the streets detachments of Praetorians coldly paraded, steel-eyed, steel-hearted. And leaning against the wall, trembling, I knew my brother was dead, or dying, began to mourn him, and then shook myself hard, picked up my jewels and began again. No one would talk to me. I went to the Subura where help and information could usually be bought, but nobody was taking a chance and doors that had stood open for years were closed now. The faction barracks, 'Red' and 'Blue', were deserted. No one had seen Marsyas, no one had heard of Paris, no one wanted to hear of me. The city had been turned over to Macro for chastisement, and if Paris had been picked up I knew they wouldn't waste time on him. There'd be no trial, no formalities. They'd strangle him, tip his body in the river, and for the rest of my life I'd never really be sure, never entirely lose that painful hope. And Marsyas? Macro wouldn't forgive him for that beating. But Marsyas had been on the run before: perhaps he'd have a chance. If he was still in the city, and in trouble, would he come to me? Or would he go to Marpessa? So long as he was safe, I didn't care.

Night came and its dangers, and because I was achieving nothing I went home to find a message – thrown through my door by a stranger – telling me Paris was in hiding at the flat of my old dancing-master Agathon, so unlikely a choice that even I had not thought to find him there. And knowing there was nothing more I could do until morning, I was on my way to bed – thinking I must sleep and worrying that I wouldn't be able to – when there was a noise at the door, the confused gasping, the almost visible thread of fear snaking its way towards me that spoke of intruders, soldiers coming to search and take me away again.

Calling out to Chrysothemis to close Dion's door, not to let anyone in to him, I ran forward, determined to shield one brother at least, wishing desperately that I didn't know where Paris was, for how could I ever live with myself if I told them? But the hallway seemed empty and, in my blessed relief it was a moment before I saw the mess on the floor.

A bundle of bleeding rags had fallen through the doorway and lay there quivering and oozing red slime on the marble, a heap of garbage the dogs had rooted out and finished with, and there was an instant of disgust before I fell on my knees and heard myself moaning, 'Don't die. Marsyas, don't die.' And I found myself stupidly gathering as much of him as I could into my arms, rocking him and hurting him, for this was how I had always expected to see him at the end – this was how Dion had looked when the chariots and the crazy horses had been over him – and the despair took my sense away, reducing me to a voice that could do nothing but wail, skin without bones or resolution, nothing but grief and shock.

One of his eyes was half open, the other was an obscenity of blood and pus, blood everywhere, old blood clogging his nostrils, new blood still trickling from his mouth, his chin, his nose – I couldn't be sure which – a red, bubbling gash on one shoulder, a knife wound with something white and gristly at the bottom of it, and so much else, so much grit and raw patches, so many strips of peeling skin, so much destruction, that he could only have crawled here to die, or been flung through my door by someone who knew that this would destroy me, and who wanted me to be destroyed.

My brain reeled, for an instant, wondering who, and then I knew it didn't matter. He was here. And if anyone had wished to harm me, they had succeeded. They had done it well. Both earlobes were torn through, the earrings ripped from them either from greed or because it was convenient to offer a motive – robbery – for his death. There were no rings on his fingers either, no chains and medallions around his neck, just bruises on his knuckles where his jewels had been pulled away, a raw weal across his throat where they'd tried to strangle him with his own gold, blood under his nails. And putting my face against his, into the muck and the slime, a window opened suddenly in my brain, my head cleared, and I knew what had to be done. I heard Chrysothemis' light step beside me and I said curtly, 'A doctor – think of a doctor – not Dion's doctor. A discreet one. Somebody who needs the money.'

'No,' she said. 'It's horrible.'

'Calm down,' I snapped. 'You know all sorts of doctors. Get one here!' And she hurried away.

I called my bearers and we carried him painstakingly to my room. As we lowered him on to the bed, blood came spurting from his nose and mouth and I thought it was death, but the dreadful flow seemed to awaken him just a little, and he groaned, made a cackling sound in his throat, lived, and then seemed almost to die again. But I couldn't save him by sitting and crying over him.

I assembled my entire household in the atrium, every man and woman, and counted them over to make sure they were all there. 'Listen carefully,' I told them. 'And remember. A man came here a little while ago. One of you has surely recognized him by now and so you all know who he is. If you know what's good for you, you'll forget it. If any information about him gets outside this house I'll sell the lot of you, the men into the mines and the women into poor families where they'll work you to death. So if anybody thinks there's a profit to be made out of this, they're mistaken. You can't spend money down the mines.'

And I stalked off, hoping there was no one among them with the sense to know that if Macro discovered what I was doing, I would be the one to choke my life away in those underground tunnels.

The doctor was the suave, crumpled little man I'd expected, the kind one goes to for love-potions, cheap abortions, and poisons. But he was not drunk and appeared to understand exactly what was required of him. I stood over him while he made his examination, noticing with relief that his hands were clean and steady, and he looked up and smiled at me companionably, a friendly little man, accustomed to dealing with hysterical women in unusual circumstances, quite willing to be insulted and abused or whatever else I had in mind, so long as I paid for it.

'My goodness me,' he said soothingly. 'What a dreadful sight – is no one safe these days? Robbery, madam, without a doubt, as the gentleman was returning home. I see they took his earrings. What a pity. Well, there is a tooth missing – here at the back – and a great deal of blood naturally comes from that, and from his nose, and he has a slit in his tongue too. He must have bitten it, I suppose, when they kicked him in the face – military boots of some sort, I should think. The tongue bleeds quite atrociously, you know – makes a terrible mess. The poor gentleman has been struck quite heavily across the back of the head – ah yes, some of this hair will have to come off – there's a nasty gash just here, if you care to look – quite unpleasant. There'll be scars, of course, dear lady – a bad one here on the shoulder, and I'll make no promises about his left eye – foolish to raise false hopes, I always think. Some of his ribs are broken, needless to say – one expects that in these cases – but perhaps he's had broken ribs before and they heal themselves, you know, quite nicely, although it's a painful process and he'll find breathing something of a nightmare. Ah – good gracious me – I think his leg is broken. I'll set the bone, and it may heal cleanly – but then – however, one may hope for the best.'

He worked quickly, a plump little partridge of a man with something of the air of a good seamstress about him, and when he had finished he washed his hands fussily, rinsing out all the creases, and turned to me with a beaming smile.

'Well now, dear, that's as much as I can do. I've taken care of everything that shows on the surface, but a man sometimes bleeds inside himself and when that happens – well – some live and some don't. I can't say fairer than that. And of course there's the danger of infection.'

I paid him what he asked, an exorbitant sum, and as I handed him the money he said, 'That's a very pretty ring you're wearing,' so I gave him that too, and slipping it on his fat finger, he beamed at me again.

'If he lives you won't need me again,' he said pleasantly. 'But if he dies and you have a body to dispose of, then I may be able to help you. A few days ago you'd just have tipped him in the river and that would have been the end of it, but it's not safe any more. They're keeping a sharp look-out at the moment. And, of course, he'd be recognized. He's not precisely anonymous, is he? By the way, there's blood on your doorstep and quite a lot of it in the street – I'd get someone to wash it away.'

I stayed beside Marsyas all night, dozing a little. By daybreak my eyelids were burning, I was sticky and unclean, aching from head to foot, and I had solved no problems, made no decisions. He was alive, and so far as I knew Paris was alive, and if they were both alive tonight I could only count it as progress. I scrambled into clean clothes, dragged a comb through my hair, made a tour of my sullen household, checking that everyone was present and suitably cowed. And then, as I went on into the hall to make sure they had cleaned up the mess, my doorkeeper, who should surely have known better, threw open the door, his eyes popping with curiosity as Marpessa came sauntering to meet me.

30

'Well, well,' she said, swaying towards me, 'we've come to join the party – my friend and I. There is a party, isn't there? You do have guests?'

And with a lovely sweep of her bare arm she indicated the man behind her, a young guards officer, a glorious giant with an athlete's broad shoulders and narrow hips, and the gloating, eager eyes of a man to whom promises have been made.

'This is Larcius,' she said. 'Larcius Macedo – one of Macro's very promising young men – and now he's my young man, or will be, as soon as I get him home. Say hello to my sister, darling.'

But although he bowed to me courteously enough, his eyes were fastened with greed and something approaching awe on Marpessa, and, seeing it, she stretched out a languorous hand and tickled him under the chin as she did with her dogs.

'I have no guests,' I told her coldly, chilled with protest and hurt, for I hadn't wanted it to be her, hadn't wanted her to be driven so far. But she merely shrugged and advanced further into the room, her eyes everywhere, her perfume and the vibrant red and gold of her filling the air between us, warning me that I would have to take care.

She was – I couldn't deny it – magnificent, her hair falling in a lustrous cascade to the backs of her knees, her long brown limbs nonchalantly draped in some Eastern fabric that had the sheen of antique gold, her whole body garlanded with Metellus' rubies; and the challenge of her wide, red mouth, the amber glow of her skin, the hard brilliance of her eyes, overwhelmed me, made me feel tired and pale and old.

'Yes,' she said, still pacing the room. 'You've redecorated since I was last here. You must show me around. I love exploring other people's houses – one simply never knows what one might find. By the way, darling, before it slips my mind – have you heard what happened to Marsyas last night?'

I shrugged. 'No. But why should I? Things are always

happening to Marsyas.'

'Mmmm –' she ran her hand appreciatively over a cedar-wood table, moved the silver rose-bowl on its polished surface a fraction to one side, and then, looking me full in the face, gave me her luscious, professional smile.

'Oh yes, things are always happening to him, except that this time it must have been painful, and rather fatal. Macro's men got him. They cornered him in an alley, which, you must admit, does seem appropriate, and beat him to death. Messy – and I understand it took six of them to do it. Then they pinched his jewellery to make it look like robbery because Macro doesn't want to upset the racing-fans. Can't have them complaining that he's butchered one of their idols, can he? Anyway, when Larcius told me about it, I said, "Come on, darling, they want the body to be discovered, don't they? Otherwise why go to all that trouble? I'll be the one to discover it." But do you know, when we got there the body had disappeared. Somebody must have got there before me, and whoever it was had a sense of humour, because the alley was quite clean – not a drop of blood anywhere. I've never seen an alley so tidy.'

She paused, the nerves beneath her amber skin taut, ready to snap, her whole face a mask of icy brilliance, and seeing me shiver, she stretched herself, pushed the vigorously curling hair back from her forehead, and laughed.

'I'm sorry,' I said and she nodded. 'Yes, you're sorry. That much I will believe.'

The young man behind her stirred restlessly, his mind full of the delights in store, and turning swiftly, so fiercely that I thought she meant to strike him, she snaked an arm around his neck and brushed the tips of her breasts against him. 'Darling. You don't mind waiting outside do you? – for just a little while? No, of course you don't. I have one or two things to say to my sister that would bore you to death. When I've finished we'll spend the whole day in bed. I won't be long.'

And as the blood rushed to his face and he turned to go, comic in his quite unmanageable desire, she watched him, her face hard and sardonic, and, when he was out of sight, she turned to me and said with cold accusation, 'He's here, isn't he?'

'Marsyas?'

'Of course – Marsyas. Who else? They caught him just around

the corner from here, and why else would he be this side of the Caelian if he wasn't coming to see you? He was a fool to stay in town, a bloody fool, because he knew Macro was after him. But he always was a fool where you were concerned.'

'You seem to know a lot about it.'

'Oh yes, I know a lot about it, and a lot about him. We haven't been very good friends lately – Marsyas and I – but I'll tell you this, I got Larcius to take me to the place where they'd left him because I knew there was a chance he'd be alive, and I'm a good girl to have around when there's trouble. They think they're clever, this new lot, but it's all going to Macro's head and now that he's got rid of the real professionals who were too hard for him to handle he's left with nothing but a lot of youngsters to do his dirty work for him. And they're not thorough. I knew Marsyas could fool them, and I knew I could fool Larcius, so – if I'd found him – I could have got him out of the way. But he wasn't there. And I'm telling you, Danaë, he's here, and either you admit it or I'll call Larcius and get him to look.'

I opened my mouth to tell her to go to hell, but I knew that wasn't the way, and speaking slowly, flinging each word at her like stones, sharp-edged, intended to hurt, I said, 'All right. He's here. He crawled here last night, a lot more than half dead, with a trail of blood behind him like a snail. I thought he was an old carcase, at first, that they'd thrown out of a butcher's shop. Well, he was alive a few minutes ago – just – but I couldn't really say if he's alive now. Shall we go and look?'

'No,' she said, her arms making an awkward gesture, palms outwards, as if she was fighting her way through seaweed, her face contorted for a moment by a spasm that could have been distress, or hate, or love, or a perilous blending of them all. And facing her, aiming once again those accurate verbal stones, I said, 'What are you going to do about it? Are you going to turn him in? I can't stop you. And he wouldn't give them any trouble. They'd only have to tip him out of bed and kick him around the floor a time or two. That should do it. You and your friend Larcius could manage it between you.'

'Bitch,' she said, pacing abruptly away from me, her hands clenching and unclenching, the long red nails biting into her palms. 'I don't know what I'm going to do. I don't know.'

'Then be still, and think about it.'

'Still? I'm never still. I've never been still since the day I met him – don't you know that? He burns me and hurts me, and I'd be glad to be rid of him – except that I love him. I just looked at him when I was a kid – he didn't even notice me – and I loved him. I knew his nature as easily as I knew the colour of his eyes. And I knew something else too. I knew he wanted you all right, but I knew I was the one he *should* be wanting – I was the one he needed. I thought he'd mistaken you for me, and so I ran after him. I wasn't ashamed because I thought he'd soon see his mistake. I was sure of it.'

She sat down suddenly, heavily, for a moment and then leaped to her feet, pacing around me again, stalking me, twisting her hair around her fingers and tugging it viciously, inflicting upon herself the kind of punishment she could handle, to lessen the pain she couldn't escape.

'It was the best time of my life,' she said, 'those first few months with him. I was on fire all the time. I could get an orgasm sometimes just looking at him. He exhausted me body and soul, stretched me to my limits – but it was good – it was right. We could have made it together, Danaë, that first time, if it hadn't been for you. I was determined to root you out of his mind, determined to make him see I was the one – that I was like him, that we matched. And we did, we did. He admitted it. But what betrayed me was my own face. Oh yes, I've got a style of my own now. I'm wild and exciting – not like my elegant sister at all. I'm Marpessa, and there's only one of me. But that's in the daylight, in the sunshine. When the make-up comes off and the gold dresses get put away, I'm left with a face like yours – so I wasn't making him forget you, was I? Not at night, anyway, when we were alone together and it mattered. He was looking at my face on the pillow and seeing you, just like you said he would. By God, Danaë, I used to wish you dead.'

'Don't,' I said, reaching out into thin air, and she brushed my gesture of concern savagely aside.

'It's funny really – because nobody else does that to me. I grew up knowing I was just "Danaë's sister", but I changed that, and now, darling, believe it or not, in some circles, they only know you because they know me, and they don't think you're so special. But not Marsyas. Well, you warned me, and I should have listened, because you're always right – you've told me that often enough.

Do you know how it ended that last time? I'll tell you because we've had a variety of endings, and that last one was a real gem. It was the night Metellus Nepos got married, the night I gave a big party and invited everybody but you. He'd been away wallowing in his misery – because he'd seen you somewhere and you'd said something to upset him. Well, I didn't know if he was coming back, although I wasn't going to say so. But he did, looking like hell. He'd lost weight and he was grey in the face, coughing, haggard, but he was beautiful and he was home. And when everybody else had gone he put his arms round me and snuggled into my shoulders and said all the things I'd always wanted him to say – asked me not to leave him, asked me to love him and understand him, said he'd try not to go away again. He was mine for an hour or two, and then, just as he was falling asleep, he sighed like a little boy and said, "I promise we'll make it this time, Danaë." Oh, I knew it was only a slip of the tongue. He knew I was Marpessa all right, knew he was talking to *me* – but I almost killed him. I couldn't stop myself. And afterwards he just shrugged and laughed and told me I knew where to find him when I'd got over it. And I did get over it. But it was never the same again. Never.'

She bit off the last word, gritted her teeth on the bitterness still remaining, and silence spread between us like a pool of poisoned water, swamping us both, until, sitting down again on a low stool, she hissed at me, 'Don't you dare pity me.'

'No. And I won't hate you either, whatever you do.'

'Good heavens,' she said. 'Why ever not?' And wiping her eyes with the flat of her hands, giving herself time to breathe, she muttered, 'By God, that needed to come out. Danaë – go tell that oaf waiting outside to go away, will you? Tell him I died. I feel as if I have.'

And, smiling, I sat down as close to her as I dared, for it was a time now for common sense and trust.

'There's Paris too, Marpessa.'

'I should say so. All those comic verses – Macro won't stand for that. Where is he?'

'Hiding at Agathon's – but he can't stay there. And Marsyas can't stay here.'

'No. We've got to get them out of Rome. Have you any ideas?'

'Not one.'

'Neither have I. We need a miracle.'

And suddenly, as we sat together in the miracle that was our newly won friendship, there came the familiar tap and shuffle on the marble floor, and the miracle that was our brother Dion dragged himself into the room, his forehead beaded slightly with sweat, but his mouth curved into a grin of satisfaction and superiority.

'You need a good man,' he said. 'That's all you need, and half of me is a damn sight better than a dozen others.' And as we flew to help him to a couch he shook his head, still grinning.

'That's right. Make a fuss, and be quick about it, before Chrysothemis locks me up again, because she thinks the excitement does me no good. Well, she's wrong for once, because it's exactly what I need. I've worked it all out. I lay awake and planned it as soon as I knew Marsyas was here – so listen.' And putting his arms around us, he drew our heads together, an indulgent elder brother outlining a scheme which could well end in death and destruction, but which, he said, was too obvious for a clever bastard like Macro to think of, and had as much chance of succeeding as anything else.

31

We should have acted at once, in those first few days of confusion and gloating, before Macro had time to get organized, but Marsyas wasn't fit to move and, as Dion put it, there was no point in risking our lives to find we'd nothing but a corpse at the end of the road.

'Of course he could die anyway,' Dion said cheerfully, 'and save you the trouble. Then you'd only have Paris to worry about.'

But Marsyas' body clung as tenaciously to life as Dion's had once done in similar circumstances. He lived. And I knew that even if he looked beyond me to Marpessa, his life in itself was enough.

She sat with him too, bringing him the gossip of the town, her salacious tongue embroidering the meagrest of incidents to make him laugh, but it seemed that for the moment love and jealousy had been set aside, to be taken out again, perhaps, later, and shared among the survivors. Marpessa and I were partners now in a desperate undertaking and, for as long as it lasted we could rely on each other. She was, as she'd said, a good girl to have around when there was trouble, and afterwards, who could tell?

I saw Paris every day, for I alone could produce a reasonable explanation for so many visits to my dancing-master's flat, but he was better equipped than anyone else I knew for solitude, and hadn't realized he was lonely until I told him so. Installed in a small room at the back of the apartment, surrounded by every comfort I could provide, he was spending his time writing poems in praise of Agrippina, Tiberius, and Caligula, slanders against Macro, and had started a life of Sejanus and Germanicus, not from any sense of loyalty or remorse but simply to have something to sell whichever way the wind blew. And since he was only in danger so long as Macro lasted – for Tiberius couldn't possibly know his name and he had high hopes of Caligula – he was cheerful about the future, and not too depressed about the loss of his possessions.

'Macro won't last the year out,' he told me. 'He tries too hard, and he has no flair.'

But as an immediate problem Macro was dangerous enough and it was Marpessa who pointed out to me what I already knew.

'You'll have to see him, darling,' she said. 'I'd do it for you if I could because he's quite a pet in his better moments, and one can see the advantages of his acquaintance just now. But he has this thing about you, I'm afraid – he wants everything Sejanus had and you'll have to give it to him if you want him to leave you alone; just enough so he can enjoy telling everybody about it, but not so much that he can't get along without you. Otherwise he'll come looking for you, when he can spare the time, and we're planning to take Marsyas to your house in Campania, and Macro knows the address. It would help to know if he thinks Marsyas is dead.'

And so I danced for Macro one night as I had danced for Sejanus, and endured his kisses afterwards, and his hot, urgent embraces, listened to his crude boasting, murmuring and cooing to him, 'How clever you are. How shrewd.' And I learned eventually that Marsyas was dead, beaten to a pulp in an alleyway, which was just what the bastard deserved.

'Yes, my lads did a good job,' he said comfortably. 'And he must have been unrecognizable afterwards because his body got picked up with the rest of the garbage, and nobody the wiser.'

And winding my arms around his thick neck, I kissed him with a good will.

But concealment was becoming increasingly hazardous, and the day came when Dion dragged himself into Marsyas' room, installed himself luxuriously on the couch by the bed, and said jovially, 'Get up, old man.'

'He can't,' I said instinctively, and immediately Marsyas was struggling and groaning, cursing Dion for thinking he could and me for thinking he couldn't, and when he finally got to his feet he was drenched with sweat, shaking as if he had a fever.

'You're getting old,' Dion said with enjoyment. 'Here's a stick. Try hobbling about a bit. You won't look pretty, but if I can do it with one leg you can surely do it with two. You're going out in a cart but I can't guarantee you won't have to totter a few steps somewhere along the way. Well, come on, let's see what you're made of – because I'll tell you this, you were a bloody awful charioteer – not a scrap of technique. And by the way, you're going out tonight.'

'No,' I said, 'he's not ready.' And Marsyas, crucifying himself to stay on his feet, biting his lips until they bled, shot me a murderous glare and fell back on the bed, swearing horribly.

'Your sister's worth two of you, damn you,' he snarled, and, snarling back, 'And that makes her worth two hundred of you,' I swept his table clear of its contents with a furious hand, and ran.

We were to take them out separately, differently, so that one, at least, would have a chance. That night a covered cart was driven to my door and we loaded it with bales of linen and furnishings – the kind of paraphernalia a rich woman might be expected to take to the coast with her – and with Marsyas. I had begged Dion not to be further involved, to leave it to us, and even at the last moment, as my sweating bearers hoisted him into place and he leaned back against the specially constructed rest, I couldn't bear the idea of him going into danger.

'This is madness,' Chrysothemis muttered. 'Absolute lunacy, risking his life for a creature like that. I've been surprised at you before, Danaë, but this time I'm shocked. This time I really don't think I could forgive you if anything went wrong.'

But Marpessa, bare-headed, her robe slipping off her shoulders, pushed between us, brushing us aside like a pair of clucking hens.

'Just leave Dion alone,' she said. 'Let him enjoy himself. He doesn't give a damn for Marsyas one way or the other. He just wants a little fun, and he hasn't had such a good time in years.'

And jumping up beside him, taking the reins from his hands, she gave us a dashing, military salute and drove the cart down the empty street with all the delicacy and style of a four-horse chariot in a parade.

As Dion said, it had as much chance of success as anything else. The night-time streets were full of carts creaking in from the country with the fruit and vegetables for tomorrow's markets, clogging the narrow alleyways with their bulk and their weary, obstinate draught-animals. The soldiers couldn't search them all. And there was no reason in the world why Marpessa shouldn't take her belongings and her brother to the coast. They would be stopped at the gate, we knew that, but Dion had always had a following among the Praetorians and the men on duty might well remember his exploits in the arena, might pat him on the shoulder and wish him luck as I'd seen them do often enough. In any case, who would suspect a cripple of such a risky enterprise? And if anyone did, Marpessa would be there, swinging her long legs, displaying her bare shoulders, making sure that no one – no man that is – looked too closely at anything but her.

Yes, there was a chance – if Marsyas didn't groan too loudly, if the over-loaded cart didn't founder, – and because there were a hundred reasons, and the road was long and hard, and treacherous for a woman with two injured men, I went inside and, changing into my white robe and black palla, I fixed a smile on my face and set out, for what must surely be the last time, to dance for strangers.

The next morning I went to Agathon's, taking four tall, brown-haired maids with me. When I came out there were five. I kept Paris in my house for two days, prevented from setting out by another invitation from Macro, who by the end of the evening showed blessed signs of boredom with my company. I knew then that there need be no more delay.

Paris, in a somewhat casual, obscure fashion, asked Chrysothemis to be his wife the night before we left, and, looking at him blankly, her mind clearly on something else, she murmured, 'Silly boy – what an idea. Now please don't tease because I have a hundred things to do. A house like this doesn't run itself, you know. I don't know when you intend coming back, Danaë, but I thought I'd take the opportunity to get things really sorted out, Dion's room especially – because he'll hardly let me in there when he's at home. I'd like to put his boxes in order, and give his mattress a good airing. I expect he'll come back weak and fretful and he'll need a few days in bed. I'd appreciate it, Danaë, if you'd keep a watch on his drinking – I really don't approve of his seeing Marsyas again.' And very obviously checking the contents of the linen cupboards in her mind, she smiled vaguely at Paris and moved away.

'And that is the woman who used to love me,' he said, his face amused and rather relieved.

'Yes – well, you didn't deserve it.'

'Quite so. But do I read the signs aright? Could there possibly be something between her and Dion? *Dion?* My God, after all the women he's had, it's incredible. And she was terrified of him.'

'But he's no longer so terrifying now, is he? And he's still beautiful.'

'Then you approve?'

'I think so.'

'And do you approve of me?'

'No. But I love you – that makes it easier.'

'Good,' he said, embarrassed as always by emotion. 'Then you'd better set about saving my life, as you've been longing to do for years. And Danaë – if it looks bad at the gates, if I get the feeling it's not going to work, then I'll just disappear into the crowd – all right? – and you'll go on alone. Which means, I suppose, that I love you too.'

I had in my possession a gorgeous extravaganza of a litter, a tremendous confection of silk and silver with a towering crown of black and white feathers, and dressing myself to match in a black tunic encrusted with amethysts and pearls, and a white palla stiff with pearl embroideries, I set out – a well-known woman going about her business, attended by her five tall maids, identical in their auburn wigs and simple white gowns. I had no way of knowing if Dion and Marpessa had got through, nor if Marsyas had survived the journey, no way of knowing if I would get through myself or be dragged back to town – and Macro – in chains. Yet perhaps because I had no choice, fear seemed pointless, and I was calmer than I would have believed.

'You look as if you were going out to dinner and looking forward to it,' Chrysothemis said roughly, unwilling to let me see she cared; and patting her arm, promising to supervise Dion's diet, I installed myself among my cushions and had them carry me away.

I chose early evening, a romantic time of day when the streets are full of party-goers and ladies hurrying to meet their lovers, and we got through the gate and past a detachment of soldiers just outside it without any trouble. But a mile or two further along the Appian Way we met up with a second detachment and this time the officer in charge was young and enthusiastic and he signalled us to stop.

'May I ask where you're off to, madam?' he enquired, and seeing his men behind him grinning and winking, and feeling that he was aware of it too, I fluttered my eyelids at him and smiled.

'I do *wish* you hadn't asked me that. He most particularly asked me not to tell.'

'Who might that be, madam?'

And, winding an arm around his neck, copying Marpessa's snake-like movement, I put my mouth against his ear and whispered the name of Marpessa's illustrious general, smiling as the young man came smartly to attention within my embrace.

We had no more trouble after that. A few miles from town a carriage was waiting and Paris jumped into it, chuckling, charmed now with the whole affair. But, as the day passed and the physical discomfort of the road wore his spirits away, he became quieter and held my hand, remembering that this could well be the last journey we'd take together.

And then, after a long silence, he said, 'Listen, Danaë. I'd better tell you this. I don't like the fellow and it's against my nature to tell you anything to his credit, but – well – the night you disappeared Chrysothemis came to fetch me, and when I'd done everything I could think of Dion told me to go to Marsyas. He said he'd help – and he did. He was ready to risk anything. If he'd known you were with Tiberius I imagine he was mad enough to have come looking for you himself. Anyway, when Sejanus fell and we realized what was going on, I scuttled into Agathon's as if the Hound of Hell was after me, but Marsyas went on looking for you. He could have got away – but he didn't. I thought you ought to know.'

'Yes,' I said, 'I know.' And Paris shook his head quite sadly.

No one pursued us. We reached Campania, the smiling cornlands, the olive-groves, and my quiet little house enclosed by its ivy-covered walls. And as I ran through the empty rooms and out into the garden – praying they would be there, praying they'd be alive – the only thing I could see was Marsyas in the colonnade and Marpessa beside him, her head thrown back, laughing straight into the autumn sunshine.

32

We had not been all together under one roof for years, and it couldn't last for long. Marsyas was safe now, if he kept out of sight, but for Paris there had to be another journey, a ship, and at the end of it a new life or a time of waiting until he could return to the old one.

'You can come with me, if you like, Danaë,' he offered, but I shook my head, and he smiled.

'Yes – well – I didn't think you'd want to. But it's an alternative. You don't have to rush into the – the other thing – because you think there's nothing else to do.'

He left for the coast two days later and I walked with him to the carriage, the soreness of tears in my throat.

'You have talent,' I told him. 'But so far you've turned it to mischief. I have to tell you this, because I may never see you again. I don't think you'll improve much. You'll just go on, I expect, like a butterfly – but that's what you are, and I still love you. I thought I could smother it with disapproval, but it gets through.'

And as he drove away it was the first time I had ever seen him cry.

The next morning Marpessa's carriage stood at the door, for she had her engagements to fulfil, important men waiting for her who couldn't be relied on to wait too long; and she came out of her room early, her hair done, her make-up on, with the air of someone going back to work after a holiday.

'I won't say it hasn't been fun,' she told us, stretching herself in the sunshine, a last breath of air before getting on the road. Then, turning to Marsyas, one hip slightly forward, pulling the fabric of her robe tight across her supple thighs, she tossed her head and said, 'Perhaps I won't go back to Rome. Perhaps I'll just go where the horses take me – right out into the sea and out the other side, anywhere the wind blows. How about it, Marsyas? Shall we go and see what we can find? There's a lovely, crazy world out there. Why confine ourselves to one little corner of it? You can make it to the carriage, can't you?'

And, her eyes fixed on his face, she opened her arms wide in a peacock gesture of display.

'I'll give you a bad time,' she promised him. 'I'll give you as much trouble as a team of wild horses – but you like wild horses, don't you? And everything that goes with them?'

And beneath her words she was saying, '*I'm as strong as you and as tough, and there's the same madness in me. I'm the mate you should have.*' And the tone of her voice was so thrilling that Dion gave a low whistle of appreciation and I knew he didn't expect Marsyas to turn her down.

'Well?' she said, and Marsyas leaned forward, his total concentration on her, shutting the rest of us away, and there was something in his face I had never seen before – an immense, warm kindness which sat oddly on him and which I forced myself to recognize as a look of love and perfect understanding. And then he said the simple word, 'No'. And his voice too was warm and loving.

She laughed. 'Well, at least you can never say I didn't ask.' And, kissing Dion on the mouth, she went down the steps and swung herself jauntily across the courtyard, her head high.

I followed her, catching her up as she reached her carriage, and we stood for a moment side by side.

'Let's not get sentimental, Danaë,' she said. 'I know you think I'm a hell of a girl right now, but we could soon be at each other's throats again. I don't suppose you'll be back in Rome for a while, will you?'

'I suppose not.'

'That's what I thought. Well, you've finally decided which one of us is your baby, have you? First it was Dion, then Paris, then Dion again after that – and now it's finally Marsyas. Yes, he needs you all right, but that won't make him any easier. You'll have your hands full. They may have smashed him up a bit and damaged his eyesight, but that won't keep him down for long. It's only going to make him worse, because his racing days are over, and he'll make somebody pay for that.'

'Yes – and I suppose it has to be me.'

She smiled, not looking at me, looking straight into the sunshine, and perhaps there were tears in her eyes.

'Well then, I'll be off. No point in hanging around. I knew he wouldn't come with me. I just asked him because, in a way, he does love me, and I wanted you to see that.'

'I saw it. It's something I'll have to live with.'

'Yes – you do that. Well, I'd like to say I'll miss you, but seeing how smitten with you Macro was, I think it suits me better to have you out of town for a while. I'll keep Macro's mind on other things – me, for instance – because he's certainly the man of the moment, at the moment, and that makes him very much my kind of man. There's not really very much competition right now. Erato and Cynthia are finished, whether they know it or not. Xanthe is getting commonplace, and the rest of them don't worry me. There's a villa across the Tiber I've got my eye on, and I expect Macro could get it for me without too much trouble.

'I suppose we'll meet again one of these days, Danaë. You'll be back in Rome as soon as Macro gets what's bound to be coming to him, because Marsyas won't stay out of the city any longer than he has to, whatever he likes to think. He'll talk about settling down, he may even want to, but just you watch his face when that messenger comes to tell you that Macro has got his comeuppance, and you'll know different. And when you do come back, if he needs a change and I can see my way to providing it – well – I might not be able to resist. Is that understood? Because I'd hate to be accused of doing anything behind your back.'

'Yes. It's understood.'

'Good.' She smiled and took a step forward and although my heart was bursting to say something more – to offer affection, a new beginning, some explanation of the past – I knew it wasn't possible, and all I could do was to murmur inadequately, 'Take care.'

'Oh yes, I'll take care all right,' she said, and leaping into her carriage she rattled away – Marpessa, brave soldier of fortune, who'd hold back her hot tears until she was well out of my sight, or who perhaps wouldn't permit herself to cry at all.

Marsyas was not there when I went back into the house, but Dion was waiting, a little strained around the eyes, but smiling, lounging at ease among his cushions, with wine and honey-cakes and fruit comfortably to hand. Kneeling down beside him I said, 'Dion darling – I was right, wasn't I? – to make the doctors do all those things to you? Right not to let you die? It's better, isn't it?'

'Oh yes,' he said casually, 'much better – in fact at times it's bloody good. I amaze myself, really. Chrysothemis is teaching me to read, did you know that? Well, it gives her pleasure and I enjoy that. I actually enjoy watching her enjoy herself. So don't worry about me. Just let me rest a day or two and then send me back to her, because she thinks I'd fall apart if she's not there to hold me together. Of course I wouldn't – not a bit of it – but she likes to think so, and she's never had much, has she? So she may as well have me. We suit each other now, and between the two of us we'll keep your affairs in order. Think about yourself for a change, and think what you're going to do about him. He's gone into the garden to wait for you. He's not the man I'd have chosen for you, but you never would listen to me, and if he's what you want ... Well, I wish you luck – you'll need it.'

Marsyas was standing by the chestnut trees, keeping his balance somehow or other, his hand clenched around a stick, the knuckles showing white, his face drawn and pale and distinctly unfriendly. If I had expected him to be tender, or kind, or grateful, I would have been disappointed. But I didn't expect it, and it wasn't necessary. There was no need to say very much at all, for we had gone far beyond that, to a point where we could finally admit that our minds were linked together, that we needed each other. There would be storms and difficulties, but we would face them together. The world was false and dirty, that much we both knew, but we would be true to each other – if to no one else – and that was more than either of us had been raised to expect from life.

'Well,' he said sourly, 'that was a very pretty offer I turned down just now. What have you got to offer me in its place?'

And going gently into his arms, so as not to knock him over again, I kissed him and told him, 'Peace.'